Around the World
on Five Sous

Around the World
on Five Sous

by
Henri Chabrillat and Paul d'Ivoi

translated, annotated and introduced by
Brian Stableford

A Black Coat Press Book

Visit our website at www.blackcoatpress.com

ISBN 978-1-61227-369-3. First Printing. April 2015. Published by Black Coat Press, an imprint of Hollywood Comics.com, LLC, P.O. Box 17270, Encino, CA 91416. All rights reserved. Except for review purposes, no part of this book may be reproduced or transmitted in any form or by any means, electronic or mechanical, including photocopying, recording, or by any information storage and retrieval system, without permission in writing from the publisher. The stories and characters depicted in this novel are entirely fictional. Printed in the United States of America.

TABLE OF CONTENTS

Introduction

Les Cinq sous de Lavarède, here translated as *Around the World on Five Sous*, was first published in book form in 1894 by Librairie Furne, Jouvet et Cie., with the by-line "H. Chabrillat and Paul d'Ivoi." Its first publication, however, was in *Le Petit Journal*, from 24 August to 27 December 1893.

The two authors responsible for it were Henri Chabrillat (c1842-1893) and Paul Deleutre (1856-1915); the latter signed all his published works Paul d'Ivoi. Of the two, Chabrillat was by far the best-known at the time of publication, the novel in question being his last and d'Ivoi's first, at least under that name. "Paul d'Ivoi" went on to become enormously popular, however, writing no less than twenty more novels in a similar vein to *Les Cinq sous de Lavarède*, comprising a series of 21 volumes collectively entitled "Les Voyages Excentriques," most of which were published as feuilleton serials before book publication.[1]

Whether the present novel was planned from the beginning as a collaboration or whether d'Ivoi took over a work begun by Chabrillat—who died some time before its publication and probably before the completion of the text—is unclear, but its subsequent absorption into the long series resulted in Chabrillat's name being dropped from many of the later editions, somewhat unfairly given the initial boost with which he helped to provide it. It is impossible to tell whether the story's frequent changes of tone and pace mark points where one writer took over the text from the other, or whether they simply result from the general circumstances of the writing, but there is no reason to doubt that the text is an authentic collaboration blending two sources of complementary inspiration.

Both writers began their careers as reporters for *Le Figaro*, although their debuts were separated by a considerable interval of time. Chabrillat achieved early fame of a sort when he was one of two war correspondents who got a little too close to the action during the Prussian invasion of 1870 and were captured by the enemy—which, of course gave him ample fodder for his subsequent reportage. In 1878, however he was appointed director of the Théâtre Ambigu-Comique, which became his principal occupation thereafter, although he continued to write for *Le Figaro*. Chabrillat published several novels in various genres, including *Les Amours d'un millionaire* [The Loves of a Millionaire] (1883), *La Fille de Monsieur Lecoq* (1886, with William Busnach; tr. as *Lecoq the Detective's Daughter*) and *L'Amour en quinze leçons* [Love in Fifteen Lessons] (1887). He was credited with a hand in the published versions of various dramatic works; most of those he wrote or co-wrote were light operas, although he

---

[1] A bibliography of all 21 volumes of *Les Voyages Excentriques* is iincluded at the end of this book.

also staged several notable adaptations of Émile Zola's dramas at the Ambigu-Comique, mostly scripted by his most frequent collaborator, William Busnach.

Paul d'Ivoi's name was attached to several dramatic works produced in the late 1880s, and the two writers were probably acquainted for at least a decade before they undertook the present collaboration, via the theater as well as *Le Figaro*. The name "Paul d'Ivoi" does crop up even earlier than that—among other places, on the preface of a work published in 1860 by Antoine Gandon, *Récits du Brigadier Flageolet* [Tales of Brigadier Flageolet]—when the pseudonym was probably being used by Paul Deleutre's father, Charles Deleutre, who also published two books under his own name; it might also have been used by Charles' brother, Édouard. The overlap in usage causes some confusion in the catalogue of the Bibliothèque Nationale and elsewhere.

It is also possible that Paul Deleutre wrote a number of feuilletons under other names before he adopted the Paul d'Ivoi pseudonym for himself, although none have been identified. In effect, however, his career as a novelist began in earnest in 1894 with the present text, and it went from strength to strength thereafter. In his heyday his feuilletons were published in *Le Matin*, but some also appeared in the rival daily newspaper *Petit Journal*, and others were serialized in the weekly *Journal des Voyages*. He wrote a number of other novels outside the Voyages Excentriques series, some of them in collaboration with a writer who signed himself "Colonel Royet," who went on to write numerous novels after Paul Deleutre's death, but about whom nothing seems to be known.

Les Cinq sous de Lavarède was a tremendous success, not only as a book—it has been more or less constantly in print since publication, latterly in paperback versions, some of which split the text in two, titling the second half *Les Compagnons du Lotus Blanc*—but also in adaptations in other media. *Le Figaro* reported that d'Ivoi had submitted a dramatic version to Émile Rochard, the director of the Théâtre de la Porte-Saint-Martin in 1894, but it was not produced until 1902, although it then had a successful run; it was filmed in 1927. It became the most successful of all "Vernian novels," and the series of Voyages Excentriques with which d'Ivoi followed it up, producing one a year until his death, was the most successful series in that subgenre after Verne's model series of Voyages Extraordinaires.

Les Cinq sous de Lavarède is, of course, one of several novels operating various transformation of the theme of Verne's enormously popular *Le Tour du monde en quatre-vingts jours* (1872; tr. as *Around the World in Eighty Days*), which had always been a prime target for writers deliberately following in Verne's footsteps. Alphonse Brown's first novel featured a world tour by airplane, similarly couched as a race against time to win a bet, *La Conquête de l'air: 40 jours de navigation aérienne* (1875; tr. as *The Conquest of the Air*)[2] and Louis Boussenard's greatest success was *Le Tour du monde d'un gamin de Paris*

---

[2] Black Coat Press, ISBN 978-1-61227-143-9.

[The World Tour of a Parisian Street-Urchin] (1879-80 in the Vernian *Journal des Voyages*), which also became the basis of a successful series. More than any of the novels by earnest Vernian acolytes however, *Les Cinq sous de Lavarède* owes a debt to the affectionately parodic homage paid to the great man by Albert Robida in the bumptious *Voyages très extraordinaires de Saturnin Farandoul* (1879; tr. as *The Adventures of Saturnin Farandoul*),[3] one of several previous works echoed in the present text.

The theme of the round the world race against the clock was amenable to continual updating because the voyage featured in Verne's novel had been on the very edge of contemporary practicality; the challenged it posed was soon met and outdone, by the American journalist "Nellie Bly" (Elizabeth Cochrane) among others, but that only served to illustrate how rapidly the edge of practicality was making progress, continually offering world tourists new means of progress and new potential obstacles to overcome. In addition, knowledge of about distant parts of the world was increasing rapidly, driven by intense curiosity about geographical science, providing a context in which further works of the type had the kind of best-selling potential that Chabrillat and d'Ivoi exploited so successfully. The perpetual movement and dramatic scene-shifting of such narratives also lends itself exceptionally well to the feuilleton format which was still enormously important in the French literary marketplace in the 1890s, although it went into a marked and terminal decline thereafter.

In some ways, *Les Cinq sous de Lavarède* exhibits all the worst features of popular fiction of its period; it is derivative, slapdash, uneven, full of outrageous coincidences and, if the pattern of its events is considered with a clinical eye, monumentally silly, but none of that mattered much to the readers who loved it, and there is no surprise in the fact that it made no difference to the book's enormous and enduring popularity, whereas the novel's positive features—the balance struck between comedy and melodrama, the introduction of the additional complications of the miserly spending-limit imposed on the hero, and the extraordinary stubbornness of the villain intent on stopping him—made a very considerable difference to it.

The novel is pure entertainment, written according to a pattern that makes for easy and relaxing reading, long on story and short on plot. It has an engaging hero and a moderately engaging heroine—although she seems to lose her initial spirit and gumption before the end, perhaps when Chabrillat's contribution to the writing petered out—and the awkward politics of their love affair is handled with a certain winning charm. The authors cannot match Verne for ingenuity, verve or panache, but very few of his imitators could—Robida is perhaps the only one—and Chabrillat and d'Ivoi did contrive to reproduce the essence of Vernian appeal as well as anyone, compensating by means of their determined

---

[3] Black Coat Press, ISBN 978-1-934543-61-0.

9

contemporaneity for the fact that, by 1894, Verne's landmark account of Phileas Fogg's journey around the world had already begun to seem quaint.

Nowadays, of course, *Les Cinq sous de Lavarède* is bound to seem exceedingly quaint itself, and it is certainly not easy for modern readers to relocate themselves imaginatively in a time when the pneumatic bicycle tire was the acme of modern technological achievement, but quaintness has its own attractions, with which the present novel is replete. It is, in its unassuming fashion, a classic.

This translation was made from the version of the Jouvet text reproduced on the Bibliothèque Nationale's *gallica* website.

Brian Stableford

AROUND THE WORLD ON FIVE SOUS

I. Cousin Richard's Will

"Your answer, then?"

"I've already told you, Monsieur Bouvreuil—never!"

"Thank about it, Monsieur Lavarède."

"I've thought about it. Never, never!"

"You don't understand, then, that you're in my hands—that if you push me to the end, I'll sell your furniture tomorrow, and you'll be homeless, with nowhere to go."

"You might as well add: with no money."

"Whereas if you agree, it's a good marriage, a fortune, independence..."

"And you think I could look myself in the face if I became the son-in-law of Monsieur Bouvreuil, former crooked businessman and police informer?"

"A poor devil of a journalist like you ought to be very honored to become the son-in-law of a prosperous landlord, and rich financier...not to mention that my daughter Pénélope loves you, and that I'm giving her a dowry of two hundred thousand francs, plus very good expectations..."

"Your daughter has nothing to do with it, Monsieur; it's not the prospect of marriage that I find repulsive, nor the young lady I'm refusing—it's the father-in-law."

"You're not very polite, you know, Monsieur Lavarède."

"I absolutely don't give a damn, you know, Monsieur Bouvreuil."

The landlord had one last argument in reserve. Slowly, he displayed a number of legal documents, some white and some blue, originals and copies, which he began to list.

"Here are your three demands for rent arrears, and here are various obligations that I took over in order to have leverage on you. All your debts are paid."

"You're truly very kind," said the young man, ironically.

"Yes, but I'm now your only creditor. If you marry Pénélope, I'll hand you the file. If you refuse, I pursue you relentlessly."

"Pursue away, as you please."

"The total is twenty thousand francs. With the expenses I'll land you with, it won't take long for the sum to be doubled."

"I can see that you understand legal matters marvelously."

"It's absolutely necessary that you make a decision immediately, because I have to leave for Panama. A syndicate of shareholders is sending me to make enquiries on location."[4]

"The syndicate in question is placing its trust in a singular manner, then. As for my decision, I believe that I've already made it sufficiently clear to you not to have to return to the matter. Let's leave it there, my dear Monsieur; we have nothing more to say to one another. Go see your bailiff—go see all your bailiffs, solicitors and advocates. Go browse your legal documents, if that nourishment suits you; it's indigestible to me. *Bonjour*."

Monsieur Bouvreuil collected his papers, put on his hat, went out and slammed the door. He was not happy.

From the comments exchanged above, Monsieur Bouvreuil's character is sufficiently clear: he was one of those individuals who have enriched themselves unscrupulously, for whom money is insufficient, and who is also ambitious for worldly esteem.

However, Lavarède, our hero, requires a few lines of biography.

Armand Lavarède, born in Paris of a father from the Midi and a Breton mother, participated in two races, borrowing from one his impetuous spontaneity and from the other his reflective calm. Parisian to boot, he received the gift typical of the children of Lutece: an unconfused and satirical mind, as difficult to astonish as to frighten. Orphaned at an early age, he had been brought up by his Uncle Richard, who, although he had paid for all the necessary lessons and tutors, had paid scarcely any attention to the simultaneous education of his nephew's character. He had had too much to do, the poor fellow, with his own son, Jean Richard, who was, in consequence, Armand Lavarède's cousin, but was completely different in temperament. Whereas Armand was healthy, joyful and prodigal, Jean was sickly, sad and economical.

Jean was a little older than Armand. In 1891 the former was nearly forty, the latter thirty-five. Jean had taken over his father's business, had taken a generous commission, and had quickly become rich in consequence. Frail in health and sour in character, he had ended up taking against Paris, France, his friends and his relatives and had gone to reside in Devonshire, in England. A commercial hazard, an unpaid bill for consignment of American cotton, had brought him, as reimbursement, a beautiful country house. Having become a misan-

_____

[4] Work on the Panama Canal had begun in 1881 under the direction of Ferdinand de Lesseps, the celebrated architect of the Suez Canal, but it ran into dire difficulties because of the climatic conditions; the initial company went bankrupt in 1889 with colossal losses, ruining many shareholders and causing an enormous scandal, replete with accusations of fraud and mismanagement. A new company took over the project in 1894, but the novel is set in 1891; the shareholders represented by Bouvreuil are presumably those in the original company, still hoping that the disaster might be redeemable.

thrope, he was glad to go and live in a country where he did not know anyone, and nobody knew him.

In the meantime, Lavarède, audacious and enterprising, but a lover of chance, had "rolled around," as the saying had it. While still a boy, in 1870, he had volunteered for the army, seen action in the army of the Loire under the orders of General Chanzy,[5] and thus begun his apprenticeship in courage. Afterwards, he had resumed the course of his studies, tried out medicine and had not taken long to become disgusted with human miseries dissected at too close a range. He had begun working as a naval engineer, had done some sailing and some shipbuilding, and when he knew enough practical mechanics for what remained unknown no longer to interest him, he changed tack again.

He returned to Paris, departed as a war correspondent for the Turko-Russian war, traveled around, lived in Plowna, headed into Asia, and on his return, thought he had found his Road to Damascus. He was an excellent reporter, the Sire de Vapartout[6] encountered him in Tunisia, Egypt, Serbia, Russia Spain and so on—in all the countries to which the Parisian press sent its representatives. Having a keen intelligence and prompt in decision, and his solid health and complete education having left him a superficial acquaintance with all of modern knowledge, Lavarède became a journalist.

And it is in that situation that we found him at the beginning of this chapter, in rather bitter conference with Monsieur Bouvreuil, his landlord.

We have silhouetted him sufficiently for it to be easily understandable that, spending his money without keeping count, careless of the morrow and retaining in his heart an immoderate love of his independence, Lavarède was not rich. He earned a good deal of money, but he did not accumulate it and lived handsomely, from day to day.

---

[5] Antoine Chanzy (1823-1883), having been suspected of collaboration with the press, was initially refused command of a brigade when the Prussians invaded, but when the going got tough he was hastily recalled from Algeria and put in command on the XVIth Corps of the Army of the Loire, participating with distinction in the only significant French victories of the entire war, most notably at Coulmiers. Although Lavarède is the same age as Paul Deleutre was in 1891, this part of his biography surely reflects Henri Chabrillat's experiences.

[6] I have reproduced this name as it is given in the text, although the reference is obviously to *Le Sieur de Va-Partout* [roughly, "Sir Go-Anywhere"] (1880), a novel by Pierre Giffard (1853-1922) which was the first to feature a globetrotting reporter as a hero. Giffard worked with Chabrillat and d'Ivoi at *Le Figaro* and with the latter at *Le Petit Journal*; they both knew him well and his influence is manifest in the present novel, especially in the final chapters. In 1908 Giffard wrote a long future war novel, *La Guerre infernale*, published as a part-work illustrated by Albert Robida

His conversation with Monsieur Bouvreuil, however, had caused him to re-flect.

That animal, he thought, not without reason, *is going to put a claim on my salary from the paper. He's going to seize and sell my furniture. It's certain that I'll be greatly annoyed twenty-four hours from now—so, let's make the most of today. There'll always be another day's work to be done.*

And in fact, he went to sleep that evening as peacefully as a judge in court, and was only woken up the following morning by his concierge, who had a good deal of amity for him.

"There's a letter for you, Monsieur Armand. It was a notary's clerk who brought it; he didn't know your exact address, and must have gone to look for your yesterday at the newspaper, the restaurant and I don't know where else. Finally, he arrived here late last night and asked me to hand you this first thing in the morning."

"Thank you, my good Madame Dubois—but are you sure that it was a no-tary's clerk?"

"Well, he said he was."

"Hmm! I'm rather afraid that he might have been a bailiff's clerk. It's Bouvreuil commencing hostilities."

Lavarède was endowed with such insouciance that he did not open his let-ter immediately. He read the morning papers, got dressed and went out to get something to eat. It was not until he was in the street that he decided to unseal it.

It really was a letter from a notary: a summons. Maître Panabert simply asked him to call in at his office in the Rue de Châteaudun urgently "on a matter of concern to him"—a banal formula that did not say very much.

Having nothing better to do for the moment, Armand went to the notary's office after lunch; the meeting was at two o'clock.

On the way, he noticed an English family on the sidewalk, going the same way.

There was no mistaking it, they were definitely English. The man, about fifty years old, had the classic stiffness, the well-known side-whiskers and the check suit, with the ulster by means which everyone recognizes traveling com-panions. An old lady, mother or governess, with a wretched round hat and green veil, and a long shapeless mackintosh, accompanied a young woman. The latter, of course, was fresh and pretty, white and pink, as Anglo-Saxon women are when they are neither withered not ill-tempered.

Lavarède had looked at her mechanically.

A hundred paces further on, at the crossroads of the Rue de Châteaudun and the Faubourg Montmartre, three carriages were passing by, coming from different directions. The young Englishwoman avoided two of them, but did not see the third, and might have been about to be run over when Armand leapt for-ward and, with a solid hand over the nostrils, stopped the horse dead in its tracks.

14

The coachman swore, the horse whinnied, the passers-by cried out, but the young woman got away with a fright.

Although slightly pale, she remained quite calm. Extending her hand to Armand, she thanked him with a vigorous handshake, in the English manner.

"It was nothing, Mademoiselle; there's really no need."

The father and the governess also approached, and Lavarède's hand was forcefully shaken three times in succession.

"No, really," he said, with an entirely sincere modesty. "It might seem that I saved your life, but you would have had time to get past—our cab-horses are very slow, I assure you."

"You've rendered me a service, even so—isn't that right, Father? Isn't it, Mrs. Griff?"

"Certainly," opined the two witnesses.

"So I have the right to be grateful to you. It's just that I'm not used to walking in our Parisian streets, and I'm always a little frightened, especially when I'm trying to find my way."

"May I be of assistance?" Lavarède asked, politely.

It was the father who spoke, taking a letter from his portfolio. "We're going to see a notary."

"Why, so am I."

"A notary that we don't know."

"Just like me."

"Who lives in the Rue de Châteaudun."

"Mine too."

"Maître Panabert."

"That's his name."

"A curious coincidence."

"But providential, Allow me, then, to guide you."

They all arrived, handed over the letters summoning them, and were introduced into the notary's study—except for the governess, who waited in the outer office.

It's for the same business, then, thought Lavarède and the Englishman.

The coincidence was bizarre, between people who did not know one another and found themselves summoned thus by a ministerial officer whose name had been unknown to them the day before.

A greeting, an introduction, no preliminaries; Maître Panabert is a notary with no time to waste. He begins immediately

"Monsieur Lavarède, Mr. Murlyton, Miss Aurett, I have the honor and the regret of informing you of the decease of one of my best clients, the proprietor of the Château de Marsannay on the Côte-d'Or, two houses in Paris situated in the Rue Auber and the Boulevard Malesherbes, and the estate of Baslett Castle in Devonshire. I am referring to the late lamented Monsieur Jean Richard."

"My cousin!" exclaimed Lavarède.

"My neighbor!" said the Englishman.

The two men looked at one another, utterly nonplussed but without suspicion, with nothing but evident amazement.

The notary went on, impassively: "In conformity with the intentions of the deceased I have summoned you to hear the reading of his will, handwritten, duly signed and registered."

He read the legal formulae rapidly, and slowed down slightly in order to articulate:

"'Including the houses and properties designated above, the income bonds, shares and obligations, as well as the liquid assets deposited with my notary, my fortune amounts to approximately four million. As I have no brother, wife, child, or direct ascendant or descendant, my sole heir is my cousin, Armand Lavarède...'"

"What did you say?" Armand interrupted.

"Wait," replied the notary. "...'But I only institute him as my universal legatee on one express condition. The fellow does not know the value of money; he would squander my fortune, would throw it to the four winds, as occurred on a pleasure trip we once took together to Boulogne-sur-Mer, which cost him two thousand francs, whereas I only spent a hundred and sixty-four francs eighty-five centimes.

"'Thus, Lavarède must leave Paris with five sous in his pocket, like the Wandering Jew, and, like the celebrated Semite, he must go around the world with no other sum at his disposal. He will thus be constrained to be economical. I give him a year, to the day, to carry out this clause.

"'Obviously, he must be monitored, and I designate to accompany him a man who will have a personal and considerable interest in fulfilling his mission: my neighbor at Baslett Castle, Mr. Murlyton, whom I institute as my universal legatee instead of Armand Lavarède, if the latter does not accomplish the prescribed condition rigorously...'"

"What, me?" said the Englishman. "But I scarcely know that eccentric, and we were constantly involved in lawsuits."

"'Mr. Murlyton,'" the notary went on, imperturbably, "'is a stickler for his rights. Every time I got bored, I had a conflict with him, either with regard to a boundary wall, a stream separating our parks, or the trees bordering our estates. That cheered me up, and relieved the tedium of my life. In consequence, Mr. Murlyton, for whom I have created a conditional right to my fortune, will know how to make the most of it. It is understood that he will lose any right to my fortune if he commits any act of treason toward poor Lavarède. He must monitor him simply and honestly. But I confess that it is not without a malign pleasure that I see in advance my handsome spendthrift cousin so inescapably disinherited.'"

Even the irony of the final sentence did not succeed in brightening up the man who pronounced it—but the reading produced various effects on his listeners.

Lavarède smiled. Perhaps the smile was jaundiced, but its color was undistinguishable. Mr. Murlyton remained as calm as he would have been in the presence of a slice of roast beef. Only Miss Aurett was visibly agitated. First she blushed, and then went pale. Her gaze played over the two men who were about to start a fine hunt, whose prey was worth four million.

She was the one who spoke first. "Father," she said, "you can't despoil this young man, who isn't your enemy and who has just saved my life."

"Business is business, my daughter," he replied. "It's not practical to lose this fortune, because it is impossible, not only to go around the world, but even to go from Paris to London, with twenty-five farthings, a fifth of a shilling.[7] Good business!"

"Then you won't renounce it?"

The notary intervened in the conversation. "Mademoiselle," he said, "even if your father refused to accept the conditional clause, Monsieur Lavarède would not then enter into possession of the inheritance. He only has a right to it on certain conditions, expressly indicated. And unless he renounces it himself..."

"You're joking!" said Lavarède. "Millions are falling from the sky, and you think I won't do anything to get my hands on them? First of all, what my cousin demands isn't so difficult. When one has been from the Bastille to the Madeleine without a single sou, one can go to America, China and the Devil with five."

"You want to try," said the Englishman. "So be it! I'm rich, my checkbook is always to hand; I won't leave you alone for an instant, and we'll see whether I haven't won the game within two days."

"Well, I accept the duel," riposted Lavarède, coldly. Addressing the notary, he said: "Do you have a railway timetable in your offices, Monsieur?"

"Here's one, my dear Monsieur."

Lavarède consulted it. "Tomorrow, the twenty-sixth of March 1891, at nine o'clock in the morning, there's a train to Bordeaux, connecting at Pauillac with a transatlantic liner bound for America." He concluded, with devastating aplomb: "I'll see you at the Gare d'Orléans tomorrow morning, Mr. Murlyton."

The two rivals bowed to one another courteously while the notary arranged the Richard file methodically, and Miss Aurett smiled on seeing the young man so confidant.

---

[7] Twenty-four farthings used to be six pre-decimalization pence, which was half a shilling. Twenty-five centimes (five sous) is, of course, a quarter of a franc, so it is not at all obvious where Murlyton's arithmetic comes from, even if he is using "farthings" in some strange figurative sense.

The latter addressed Maître Panabert again. "I must return to your office on the twenty-fifth of March 1892, before it closes for the day."

"At the latest, Monsieur."

"Perfect. I'll be here."

And he went out, tranquilly.

II. Hide-and-Seek

On leaving the notary's office, Lavarède lit a cigar and walked for half an hour, thinking about what he was going to do. He found his initial idea excellent: that departure in quest of an exceedingly golden fleece appealed to his spirit of adventure.

He had no doubt that he would succeed. On reflection, however, he took account of the innumerable difficulties that he would encounter.

Suddenly—he had arrived at the Madeleine—a smile illuminated his darkened face. He had thought of something. But what? He retraced his steps and went to his newspaper, a boulevardian periodical, the *Échos Parisiens*. There, he wrote a piece for the following morning's edition in which, without identifying the individuals other than by semi-transparent pseudonyms, he recounted the story of the will.

Then he went to the cashier's office, where an initial tribulation awaited him, without surprising him overmuch. A bailiff commissioned by Bouvreuil had put in a claim on his salary.

"Well," he said, "it's starting."

He went home. In the same way, Madame Dubois told him that another bailiff had come, on behalf of the landlord Bouvreuil, to seize his furniture.

"What does it matter to me?" he said cheerfully. "I'm leaving for the other world tomorrow."

"Oh my God" said the worthy Madame Dubois. "You're not going to kill yourself, my dear Monsieur Armand! A wound in the pocket isn't mortal."

"Don't worry," he said, laughing. "The other world I'm going to is America. I'm going to collect the inheritance of a relative who was a millionaire four times over."

"You gave me quite a fright."

Lavarède knew enough. He took a cab and had himself taken to the shipping office at the Gare d'Orléans at top speed. He knew one of the clerks there, to whom he gave theater tickets from time to time. He spent a few minutes with him, and then went to inspect a loading platform, where he found all sorts of bales, crates and baskets piled up.

Doubtless satisfied with his visit, he returned to the office, wrote a letter of dispatch that astonished the clerk and made the supervisor who had accompanied him smile.

"It's really for Panama?" asked the supervisor.

"Yes, for Panama," said Lavarède, "at top speed. The parcel has to leave tomorrow morning on the express connecting with the steamer of the *Chargeurs Réunis*.

For greater surety, he went back to the platform, asked a crewman for a brush and a bucket of black paint, and wrote in large capital letters on an enormous wooden create the word *PANAMA*. The crate had the form of a grand piano. Vast and oblong, it already bore other inscriptions, which he erased, and other dispatch and reception labels, which he removed. Then he gave a tip to the employees who had helped him, and a cordial handshake to the clerk, who had not ceased to manifest a genuine amusement.

"As a joke," the latter said, "it's good enough—but at least you can assure me that the Company won't be defrauded?"

"I'll answer for everything. And when I've won my bet, I promise you a good dinner, and a box at the Opéra afterwards."

He got back into the cab and went back toward the boulevard. He had not wasted his afternoon. He interrogated his purse and saw that he had a few louis left. It was necessary to spend them that evening, or during the night. That would not be difficult. A few invited companions, a lavish dinner washed down with good wine, a pleasant and joyful evening, a fine supper with champagne, would soon put an end to it. He arranged matters so that by morning, he would have nothing left in his pocket but a two-franc piece.

"That's exactly what I need. Thirty-five sous for a cab, and five sous to go around the world!"

Lavarède was, therefore, carrying the twenty-five centimes ordered by the testator when he disembarked at eight o'clock in the morning at the Gare d'Orléans.

He had not slept all night, to be sure. But *I'll have plenty of time to sleep on the way*, he thought.

Immediately, he disappeared in the direction of the shipping office.

Shortly afterwards, among the travelers preparing to take the express, several whose acquaintance we have already made were to be seen.

First of all there was the excellent Monsieur Bouvreuil, whom his daughter Pénélope had come to see off at the station, accompanied by a maid.

We shall cast a glance over Mademoiselle Pénélope. Frankly, one could not blame Lavarède for not wanting to unite his destiny with that of the young woman in question. Too tall to be elegant, bony rather than thin, of bilious complexion and a haughty and smug expression—what vulgar people call, in their vigorous mode of expression, "looking down her nose"—that was what the daughter of the good Monsieur Bouvreuil looked like. She knew that she was rich, and took a rather stupid vanity therein; her pride had been wounded by Lavarède's refusal. She was the one who had advised her father to starve the young man out.

The old fox was attentively reading a newspaper, the *Échos Parisiens*, which had just appeared, and, in that paper, Lavarède's article. As he found himself indicated therein under the name of "Monsieur Chardonneret, landlord, of the race of undomesticated vultures,"[8] he read the rest of the article, and read between the lines. Then he passed the paper to his daughter, and made her party to his reflections.

"What!" she said, after having read it. "The fellow who doesn't want me is going to inherit four millions, if he succeeds in making such a voyage with no money?"

"You can see that he's mad, even to attempt it."

"I hope he won't succeed, then."

"Don't worry—he'll be back in Paris before long, crestfallen and repentant. And he'll find himself trussed up so tightly in my web of legal paper that he'll be happy to accept release, along with your hand."

Pénélope sighed. Already not very beautiful at rest, she was quite ugly when she sighed.

"It's just that he's charming, the monster," she said, rolling her eyes, like those of a swooning carp, toward the heavens.

At that moment, crewmen transporting a crate of unusual size and shape into the baggage-car attracted all gazes.

"Look," said Bouvreuil. "There's a parcel making the same journey as me."

"It's going to Panama?" asked Pénélope.

"Yes—it's written on top."

"It must be a piano," the demoiselle guessed.

"Doubtless some engineer out there who wants to charm his leisure hours."

"Be careful of fevers, Father."

"Don't worry—with money, one can purchase perfect hygiene. Anyway, I won't have to stay there very long. Time to inspect the yards, to verify the utility of the expenditures and the progress of the work. I'll take a few notes and draft my report for the syndicate on the boat coming back. A fortnight should be amply sufficient."

With the outward and return journeys, and the stay you anticipate, that adds up to an absence of about six weeks."

"At the most. I'll telegraph you via the cable to let you know the date of my arrival and that of my departure."

So saying, Bouvreuil installed himself a first class compartment, where he was not long delayed in being joined by two other people.

Mr. Murlyton, escorted by his daughter, Aurett, and her governess, Mrs. Griff, had arrived at the station at the appointed time, with the precision and exactitude of the islanders of Great Britain. Looking around in all directions,

---

[8] Chardonneret is the common name in French of the finch family of birds, of which the bouvreuil [bullfinch] is a member—hence various avian puns, such as the reference to Bouvreuil as a vulture.

they had not seen Lavarède. The latter, as we know, was not on the passengers' platform.

"Has he already given up on the adventure?" the Englishman wondered.

"It's not probable," Aurett replied.

Time passed, however; the moment of departure drew near, and Lavarède still had not appeared.

"Ach!" said Mr. Murlyton, discontented.

"You have to accompany him."

"For that, it's necessary for him to be here."

"Perhaps he thought it prudent to leave Paris for Bordeaux alone, before you."

"That's right—in order that I can't check his ticket, which cost more than twenty-five centimes," he said, laughing.

They carried out a rapid inspection of the carriages that were already packed with passengers. Lavarède was not among them. Suddenly, Aurett had an idea.

"In Paris, Father, in the bustle of the station, you run the risk of losing sight of him, but by going to wait for him at Bordeaux, you'll be sure of not missing him there. To board the steamer there's only one route—the gangplank. He said that the train connects with the steamship line at Pauillac—you ought to go that far, anyway."

"Oh, we Englishmen are great travelers—that can't bother us much. A mere stroll, after all."

"Yes, and if you're good, I'll go with you, to give you a kiss before you leave on your world tour."

"But what if the gentleman arrives late, after the express leaves? How will I know?"

"Mrs. Griff saw him yesterday, in the street and at the notary's. She has only to stay here and wait. She'll recognize him and send us a telegram at Bordeaux-Pauillac station, or the office of the Maritime Mail,"

"That's true."

They explained to the governess the role that she was to play, and they bought two tickets. Miss Aurett, with the gaiety of her twenty years, was delighted with that brief excursion, which resembled a schoolgirl escapade.

Mrs. Griff kissed her, gravely. "Until the day after tomorrow, then, Miss?"

"Perhaps tomorrow. The ship leaves this evening; it won't be necessary to stay overnight in Bordeaux. I'll take the night train, and it's not improbable that I'll be back tomorrow, not the day after."

"I'll come back here to meet you, then."

"I'll let you know by telegram."

The father intervened. "One last instruction, Mrs. Griff. As soon as my daughter returns, you'll leave Paris and return home to Devonshire. I don't know whether my absence will be long or short, or even if I'll be embarking; it doesn't depend on me but the other. In any case, I'd prefer to know that you were at home in England."

Mrs. Griff bowed respectfully. Murlyton and Aurett climbed into the only compartment that was still partly free. They sat down opposite Monsieur Bouvreuil, whom they did not know.

The latter had taken an enormous portfolio from his pocket—the portfolio of a businessman—and was making a few notes, while waiting for the train to depart, while Mademoiselle Pénélope searched with her eyes for her maid, who had disappeared.

On a blank sheet of paper, Bouvreuil wrote:

1. Choose English hotels for preference, they're more comfortable.

2. Avoid the society of the French, except for the Company's engineers.

3. Don't discuss politics with anyone.

4. In case of difficulties, first go to see the French consul.

He had reached that point in his wise previsions when his daughter ran toward the compartment. Her face seemed distressed, but radiant.

"Papa!" she said. "Papa! I've got some news."

"What is it?"

"Monsieur Lavarède must be on the same train as you."

"On the train? I haven't seen him."

"Nor has anyone else. He's in the crate."

"What crate?"

"You know—the big crate bound for Panama."

"The one we thought had a piano in it?"

Murlyton and his daughter could not help exchanging glances and a brief word.

"Ah! Monsieur Lavarède..."

"I knew it!"

Bouvreuil looked at them, astonished to hear Lavarède's name pronounced by the two strangers. He did not have time to interrogate them about it, however, because the conductors were already closing the doors of the compartments and he was about to be separated from Pénélope. Leaning out of the window, while his daughter stood on the footstep, he said: "But how do you know that?"

"The maid told me."

"Bah!"

"One of the crewmen is from her native town, Santenay on the Côte-d'Or. They recognized one another, and the man told her, laughing, that he'd seen someone climbing into the crate at the shipping depot. The description is Monsieur Lavarède's, there's no doubt about it. A clerk from the office came, very cheerfully, to close the planks forming the door, and told the crewman to keep quiet..."

"An instruction that he hastened to disobey."

23

"Oh, with his compatriot, it didn't seem important—but no one in the station knows that."

"Very good—I've got him! I'll have him arrested at Bordeaux, and his four millions will go up in smoke!"

"Thank you, Papa—and tell him that he only has to come to the house, that I authorize him to pay court to me and that we can be married in five weeks, when you return."

"Understood."

Aurett and her father had not missed a word of that conversation, conducted in loud voices.

A blast of the whistle gave the signal for departure. The train pulled away. Bouvreuil, still leaning out of the window, waved goodbye. And everyone was on their way to Bordeaux-Pauillac, Lavarède in his crate, Murlyton, Aurett and Bouvreuil in their compartment.

The discretion of the English, who never speak first to people they do not know, is well-known. It was, therefore, Bouvreuil who began.

"I beg your pardon," he said to his neighbors, "but just now, you appeared to know this Monsieur Lavarède, about whom my daughter was speaking."

"We do indeed know him," said Mr. Murlyton. "But to whom do I have the honor…?"

"Bouvreuil, landlord, financier, President of the Syndicate of the Shareholders of Panama," he replied, presenting his card.

"Very good, honorable sir. For myself, I am Mr. Murlyton, and this is my daughter Aurett."

"Ah! Are you the Englishman designated in the article in the *Échos* under the name of Mirliton, esquire?"[9]

"I don't know the article in question."

"Here—read it."

After a rapid examination, the Englishman said: "Yes, that must be me. And you're the bird of the vulture species?"

"Exactly—the blackguard!"

"You're not one of his friends, I can see."

"Oh, no!"

With a polite smile, Aurett put in: "However, your daughter, just now… is there not a question of a marriage between the two of them?"

"My daughter would like that, but he, the rascal, won't hear of it."

"Oh, forgive me…" And a bizarre, enigmatic smile played over her lips, in place of the courteous and amiable smile that had previously been sketched there. Aurett had seen the face and the disagreeable personality of Mademoiselle Pénélope, and privately sided with Monsieur Lavarède. In her thinking, the poor

---

[9] A mirliton is a toy trumpet, once very popular in France at carnival time.

fellow who had saved her life—she had not let go of that idea—deserved better than that unbecoming spouse.

But the two men continued chatting.

"Yes," said Bouvreuil, "I'm going to make him lose his inheritance. He'll be arrested this evening; that ought to satisfy you, since you're his competitor, and you'll be glad to help me."

"Oh, I don't have anything against him. It's a question of honor, foreseen by the will. I must only verify, without creating any obstacle myself."

"It makes no difference. I'll do it myself, and he won't get past Bordeaux."

After a four-hour journey, the baggage was taken down on to the quay for loading the ships. Bouvreuil did not lose sight of the crate that contained his enemy. Rubbing his hands, he headed for the customs office.

At the same moment, a knocking was heard on the side of the crate, and a soft voice called: "Monsieur Lavarède! Monsieur Lavarède!"

It was Aurett who, instinctively and without reflection, was taking Lavarède's side against Bouvreuil. In so doing, she was also setting herself against her father, but she did not even think about that. Her first impulse—the best, according to Talleyrand—pushed her to defend the young against the old, the handsome against the ugly, the poor against the rich. Let us not reproach her for that natural generosity—it is so rare in life, although it is common enough at Aurett's age. Is not the twentieth year one of illusions?

It is certain that if the young Englishwoman had been a person of common sense, if she had been taught to count at school and if she had been informed of the value of money, she would have said to herself: *There's a fellow who seems to me to be quite determined. If no one stops him, he's capable of earning neighbor Richard's millions. Now, those millions might be mine one day, or perhaps serve as my dowry. Whereas, if that vile bird named Bouvreuil is allowed to have his way, the young traveler will be arrested, put in prison, condemned at the least to a fine that he'll have to pay. At any rate, he'll be obliged to lose time, to go back, to explain, to go to court, to earn money by working; in the meantime, the days will go by, perhaps months. And the fine millions will go their own way, without him, soon to revert to Papa Murlyton.*

That reasoning, so logical and sensible, never entered her virginal head. Her honest mind refused even the mute and tacit complicity of letting matters take their course. And quite naturally, as if it were her duty, she went to tap on the crate with her dainty fingers and repeated: "Monsieur Lavarède."

No sound; no response.

Still in a soft voice, she went on: "Don't be suspicious, I beg you. A danger is threatening you, and I've come to warn you."

Then, from inside, came a muffled voice. "One might think that was your voice, Miss Aurett."

"Yes!" she said, joyfully. "Get out of there, quickly."

"No, Mademoiselle, I shan't come out until my bedroom is embarked aboard the steamer and the movement indicates that the ship is en route for Colon."

"But they won't even load your...the shocking thing that you've just said."

"Why not, Mademoiselle?" he asked, struck by the young Englishwoman's desperate tone.

"Because Monsieur...I don't know his name—the bird of the vulture race..."

"Monsieur Bouvreuil?"

"Exactly...has just gone to fetch the customs officers and the employees to have you *pinched in the box*."

"Pinched! Damn it!"

So saying, he opened the door. Miss Aurett was blushing.

"Oh!" she said, confused. "Perhaps *pinched* isn't a very nice word. It's what he said a little while ago. He also said *the box* when he was talking to my father."

"But what the devil is he doing here?"

"My father? He's escorting you, as he has to do."

"No, not your father—the other one."

"He told us that he's going to Panama."

"Good, good—thank you, Miss...so Monsieur Murlyton's in on the plot?"

"Oh no! Papa's very correct. He's promised not to do anything, so he's gone away."

"To let the other have his way?"

"He can't stop him, Monsieur...but I..."

"You!" exclaimed Lavarède, jumping down on to the quay. "You're Providence. It's perhaps to fulfill that role that the good God made you so pretty..."

"No compliments, Monsieur my savior. And hide, quickly—here they come!"

"Thank you, my good angel."

And, blowing her a kiss from his fingertips, Armand hid himself behind the bales and barrels that formed an enormous heap not far away. Aurett, slightly troubled deep down, but calm in her facial expression, saw Bouvreuil coming with a customs officer and a railway employee. She had taken the precaution of reclosing the crate.

"He's in there," said Bouvreuil, with a gesture that was not without analogy with the one made by Napoleon at Marengo.

"You're saying that there's a man in there?" said the bewildered railway employee.

"Perhaps a malefactor in hiding," Bouvreuil added.

"In any case, live meat, human flesh, undeclared merchandise, legally speaking," pronounced the customs officer.

The two men did not know how to open the crate in order to verify the contents. Nor did Bouvreuil. All three tried in vain, watched by Aurett, who had difficulty keeping a straight face. Their attempts had only one result, which was to shift and shake the crate. It was immediately recognized by the men, accustomed to handling parcels, as being very light, and hence empty.

"You're crazy, my man," said the railway employee to Bouvreuil. "There can't be a man inside."

"Yes there is!" he affirmed.

"No," the other insisted. "Look—I can lift it up one-handed, without difficulty."

"That's true," opined the customs officer.

"But I can attest that I was told, in Paris…"

"In Paris, my colleagues were making fun of you."

"At any rate, it's only necessary to open it, and we'll see."

"But we don't have any tools here, and I wouldn't dare take the nails out, anyway, except in the presence of my superiors. I'll go fetch some comrades to take the suspect package to the office."

"And I," said the customs man, "will go to fetch my brigadier. We'll observe the autopsy."

"That's right!" said Bouvreuil, raising his arms to the heavens, with a distressed expression. "And in the meantime, the brigand who's in there will escape from his cavern!"

"Well then, remain here on sentry duty on and you'll see him if he comes out," said the other two, going away.

Bouvreuil was left alone, pacing up and down in a small empty space between the piles of crates, barrels, bales, baskets and merchandise of all origins and all kinds that were coming from or going to America.

We say that he was alone because Aurett, a little while before, had gone to Lavarède's hiding place, where he was showing signs of distress.

"I beg you, Miss," he said, "don't stay here. It's necessary that there shouldn't be a single witness to what's about to happen."

Without replying, she bowed to Bouvreuil and went away in order to catch up with her father, who was making his way toward the steamer.

"Well, my daughter?" he asked.

"Well, nothing definitive."

"Ah! And Monsieur Lavarède?"

"I believe he's going to embark."

"Then I'll go and pay for my passage."

"Our passage, Father."

Without showing any sign of emotion, Murlyton said: "You want to come with me?"

Just as coldly, like a true Englishwoman, she replied: "Yes Father. This little excursion to Panama might be instructive. I haven't been to Central America as yet."

"Travel forms youth. But what luggage do you have?"

"My traveling valise and my handbag."

"Do you think that will be sufficient?"

"No, but I can make the indispensable purchases rapidly."

"All right—but what about Mrs. Griff?"

"I'll take advantage of my travels to send her a telegram telling her to go back to our cottage in Devonshire alone, right away."

"Everything's in order, then. That's good."

They exchanged a handshake and separated, she to go out into the environs of the maritime station of Pauillac, he to go aboard the ship and reserve two cabins. Neither of them had departed for an instant from the classic British phlegm. They were going to America as they would have gone to Asnières, still with the same calm.

While that little scene was occurring in front of the *Lorraine*, the transatlantic liner commanded by Captain Kassler, this is what was happening in front of the culpable crate.

Abruptly, the smiling Lavarède appeared in front of the angry Bouvreuil.

"Ah! I knew it!" said the latter, triumphantly

"You knew what?" enquired the young man, graciously."

"That you were in there." He pointed to the crate.

"You were mistaken, my dear Monsieur. I was somewhere else."

"I know what I'm talking about."

"Not as well as I do, believe me. I'm taking a stroll before making a little tour of America, like you. Except that I'm running away from your bailiffs, your amiable bailiffs."

Bouvreuil assumed an expression of ironic pity. "Yes, as you say, you want to run away to America, but by traveling in a fraudulent manner, with the aid of a shady ploy."

"The fact is," said Armand, sardonically, "that one can't see very clearly inside those planks. Shady is the right word."

"Whereas I, Monsieur," continued the financier, in a smug tone, "am traveling in broad daylight, paying for my passage, Monsieur, having reserved cabin number ten, not burying myself in the depths of an unspeakable parcel, Monsieur!"

Every time he emphasized the word *Monsieur* his voice swelled, taking on a majestic, pompous and melodramatic inflection.

Timidly, Lavarède riposted: "I do what I can, Monsieur."

And, with a rapid movement, he opened the door of the crate, shoved the unfortunate landlord inside, and swiftly replaced the planks—but he released the catch with such a violent effort that Monsieur Bouvreuil was no longer able to get out of the infernal box.

The latter began by crying out, appealing for help, but his voice soon faded away. A shadow came over it. Was it anger that had stifled him, or was it the rarefaction of the breathable air?

Lavarède did not even ask himself that question. Briskly, he made off as fast as he could, and ran all the way to the gangplank where the passengers of the Lorraine were embarking.

He was just in time. Two minutes later, four crewmen or stevedores arrived on the cargo quay, preceded by the customs officer.

"Why," he said, astonished, "the old fellow's no longer here!"

"He must have got impatient," said the employee. "He'll have gone. It's just as well."

The stevedores started to lift the crate.

"Uh oh!" said one of them. "It's heavy!"

"That's true. It weighs more than it did just now."

"So there really is something inside?"

"Yes—it's moving."

"Look—when you lift one side, it goes the other way."

Indeed, a dull thud could be heard

"It's rolling."

The customs officer put his ear to the crate.

"And one might think that it's groaning."

"Aha! We've caught the prey."

"It's the contraband."

"For sure?"

"Let's take the parcel away. First, I'm going to put it under lead seals. Nobody will touch it until the brigadier's had lunch. He's given orders that it should be taken to the lieutenant's office. It'll only be opened in the officer's presence."

That was immediately done—and the poor president of the Shareholders' Syndicate, who had presumably lost consciousness, had time to come round. But we shall not occupy ourselves with him any longer, for the time being, and return on board the Lorraine.

Everything is ready for the departure. The ship is under steam. The engine is heating up, with the dull purr of a tame beast. The plume of smoke is thick and black. The sailors are attending to the rigging or occupying themselves with the luggage that has been brought aboard. Everyone is on deck. Relatives and friends have left the ship after the final adieux. The gangplank is about to be withdrawn. The mate summons the passengers.

"Let's see—no one missing? We have cabins eight and nine, which have just been reserved."

"Eight and nine are for me and my daughter," Murlyton replies.

"Good! You're aboard. But there's still ten, who hasn't responded. Let's see who he is. Booked in Paris at the Agence Maritime..."

A man races over the gangplank, just as the sailor is about to remove it. "Number ten—that's me. Here I am!" he shouts, urgently

"What name?"

"Bouvreuil, Paris."

"That's right. Let's go!"

A whistle-blast, a clanging bell. The *Lorraine* pulls away majestically. It is under way.

Two passengers encountered one another face to face, beneath the poop deck.

"Ah!" said one. "Monsieur Lavarède."

"Indeed, Mr. Murlyton. Has Mademoiselle your daughter returned to Paris?"

"No, Monsieur; she's here."

"On board! Truly delighted to be commencing our voyage in such gracious company."

"Pardon me, Sir, but how do you come to be here? I know the price of a passage; I've just bought two of them—and it surpasses the sum that you ought to have in your pocket."

"To be sure...so I haven't paid, and here are my twenty-five centimes, still intact. You can check them, my strict accountant."

"All right—but that doesn't answer my question."

"It's quite simple. I have cabin number ten, whose reservation was made and paid in advance by the excellent Monsieur Bouvreuil, first class service and nourishment included."

"He reserved it...for you?"

"No, for himself."

"Oh! I don't understand."

"What's complicated about it? I'm in his cabin."

"And where's he?"

"Him? He's in my crate, of course."

"The crate's aboard?"

"No, it stayed behind."

"With him inside?"

"Certainly...with him inside."

Murlyton thought for a few seconds, and then smiled at his daughter, who had heard the last words as she approached. "Not at all correct," he said, with gravity, "but very ingenious." Then he turned on his heel and went to lean on the bulwark.

The two young people exchanged a few words.

"You've succeeded, Monsieur. I congratulate you."

"If I've avoided the first danger, Miss, it's to you that I owe it. I won't forget it."

"Oh, Monsieur, we're not quits yet."

"You still think, then," he said, smiling, "that you owe me your life?"

"I'm intent, above all, on not damaging your interests."

"Even at the expense of your own?"

Miss Aurett made no reply, and went to join her father. It was quite natural for Armand to follow the young woman, so devoid of avarice. In any case, his new friend authorized him to do so with a glance.

When the group was reunited, she said: "You're going to think me very curious, Monsieur Lavarède, but when, by chance"—she blushed vividly as she pronounced those words—"the door of your little apartment opened a little while ago, I seemed to perceive something like a padded armchair. Was I mistaken?"

"Not at all, Miss."

"Ah! How and why was it padded?" asked Murlyton.

"Because it had been prepared expressly to make a long voyage, from the Pyrenees to Paris, by a fantasist, the story of whose adventure I reported in my newspaper. I remembered it. I was sure that the crate, about which all Paris was talking, was still at the Gare d'Orléans…so I made use of it. That's the whole story."

"As I said," observed the Englishman, "you're a very ingenious gentleman."

A smile from the young woman confirmed her father's opinion.

Leaning on the bulwark, Murlyton paraded his marine binoculars over the strip of land that was beginning to disappear in the distant mists. Something caught his eye.

"Look, Monsieur Lavarède," he said, passing the binoculars to him. "Can't you see something agitating at the end of the jetty?"

Armand looked. "Yes—a short man making broad gestures. But he's being pursued. One can't quite make out the nature of the uniforms of those giving chase to him—gendarmes, no doubt."

"What do you think is happening?"

"Oh, without hesitation, I imagine that it's Bouvreuil. He didn't die of apoplexy on the spot. So much the better, so much the better."

In the meantime, they had emerged from the estuary, and no signal recalled the *Lorraine*. Lavarède therefore thought that he would be safe for the duration of the voyage.

III. Ports of Call

The first two days of the voyage were very agreeable for Lavarède. Each morning found him on deck in the company of the other passengers, and there were very pleasant conversations with the young woman, which revealed the delightful and innocent soul of the young Englishwoman.

Although they talked a little about everything, and Armand's and her father's numerous travels furnished ample material for interesting conversation, there was one subject that Aurett was very careful to avoid. The name of Mademoiselle Pénélope was never pronounced. Never was the slightest allusion made to the projected marriage to which Bouvreuil had referred in the carriage on departure from Paris. That idea seemed to be repugnant to the young Englishwoman. Was that not one of the little secrets that the mysterious hearts of young women conceal?

Lavarède could not think about that, for two reasons. The first is that he was completely unaware that Aurett was informed of the ideas conceived by Mademoiselle Pénélope Bouvreuil; the second is that the latter did not come to mind at all; entirely given over, as he was, to the gentle charm to which he was unconsciously and involuntarily subject, he never spared a thought for that lanky and disagreeable individual.

One morning, after exchanging the quotidian *bonjours* he said: "How is it, Mademoiselle, that you, who are foreign by birth, speak our language so purely?"

"There's nothing astonishing about it, my dear Monsieur. Like the majority of well-educated young women in my country, once my studies in London were complete, I was sent to the continent to improve my fluency in French. My father placed me in an institution in Choisy-le-Roi—Madame Laville's—where I encountered a dozen of my compatriots, boarders like me, but rather free, in view of their age and English education, and we came to Paris in a group almost every day."

"With the result that you're almost a little Parisienne?"

"With the *coquetterie*, at least—the word has no literal translation in English."[10]

"But with, in addition, the aplomb and the calm that initiative and liberty provide: a special aspect of the manner in which young women of your nationality are brought up."

"That's true. Besides which, Paris is a city very well known to us. My father lived there for a long time. He was at the branch that our London company has in the Rue de Paix, and I spent several long sojourns in your capital."

---

[10] Except, of course, "coquetry."

"Well, I confess to you, Miss, that you're even more sympathetic to me now that I can almost consider you a compatriot."

The expression that he used—"sympathetic"—had no implication that was not perfectly polite and thoroughly decent, but Aurett blushed and seemed embarrassed. She made no reply—and perhaps the two young people would have been slightly inhibited, with regard to continuing the conversation, if her father, Mr. Murlyton, had not arrived conveniently to tell them that the dinner bell had rung.

It is well-known that the table of first-class passengers is lavishly served aboard our great transatlantic liners. The luxury is, so to speak, princely. And it is marvelous to find far out at sea, where one could believe oneself to be a long way from abundant and delicate culinary resources, a menu and service worthy of the best Parisian restaurants. That comfort is appreciated and admired by travelers from all lands.

The table is presided over by the captain. The ship's officers are in daily contact with the passengers of both sexes, and nothing is more agreeable than those rapid and worldly relations with our courteous mariners.

Lavarède was addressed as Bouvreuil whenever they spoke to him. For everyone aboard, he was Monsieur Bouvreuil, the authorized occupant of cabin ten. He had made that name an excellent reputation. Full of wit, his repartee always lively, his ripostes swift and pointed, and his memory stuffed with amusing facts and interesting anecdotes, he pleased everyone. It was with amiable smiles that the captain and the first mate greeted Lavarède's appearance at the communal table twice a day.

"What a pleasant companion you are!" the *Lorraine*'s second-in-command said to him. "When I think that you nearly missed the departure in Bordeaux!"

"The fact is that if I'd arrived five minutes later, the ship would have left without me. But who could have foreseen that?"

"Would it be indiscreet to ask, Monsieur Bouvreuil, the cause of that delay?"

"Not in the least; I'll tell you."

And, with his marvelous aplomb, which made Aurett and her grave father smile. Lavarède improvised a little story and a big lie.

"Can you imagine that I was pursued from Paris, and for a long time beforehand, by a kind of madman, a journalist—or at least he claimed to be—by the name of Lavarède, I believe, whose mania was to pass himself off as me."

"Mania?"

"Yes—to the point that he's succeeded in convincing himself that his madness has become reality. He's convinced that he is Bouvreuil. It's a particular form of mental alienation. In the meantime, so far as others are concerned, his folly is mild and there's no point in locking him up. After all, it only inconveniences me mildly, and I take it in good part."

"But it must case you many annoyances."

"Oh, not so many this far, and now I'm rid of them for the duration of the voyage. Except that when he sees me, when I maintain that I'm really Bouvreuil and he's Lavarède, he sometimes flies into terrible fits of rage. A simple cold shower and a few days rest easily put an end to those violent fits, though. Confronted by those mad rages, in any case, I never lose my calmness."

"It's the only sane conduct a man can adopt in the presence of an unfortunate whose ideas are disequilibrated."

"Isn't it? Such is certainly my opinion. My fellow had followed me all the way to Bordeaux, and I had great difficulty shaking him off. But for a few customs officers and employees of the shipping line, I wouldn't have succeeded in getting rid of him in time to embark. But that's enough talk of such things, which are sad in spite of their amusing appearance. Is the *Lorraine* headed toward Lisbon at present?"

"No, Lisbon's the port of call for the mail-boats; our first stop is at Santander."

"And will we take on passengers there?"

"Oh, no—there are no more cabins. There's only one free, and that has been reserved telegraphically by a passenger who's waiting for us in the Azores, where we'll call in before reaching Portugal."

"Is that passenger French? Is he a compatriot?"

"I don't think so…not judging by his name, at least, or names: Don José de Courramazas y Miraflor."

"Oh! That does, indeed, sound like a hidalgo."

The crossing continued without a hitch; two days after the departure they were in sight of the Spanish coat; they put in at Santander, where they were to stay for one day, and our friends disembarked.

The beautiful flowers of the region, and the limpid azure sky, were not what astonished them most. That was visiting the cathedral of Santander, where they found the most curious impression of the voyage.

For the price of one franc twenty-five, Murlyton bought an indulgence from the beadle, granting absolution for the crime of murder. He had the right to kill someone and go to heaven anyway, on condition that he did not leave Santander; outside the diocese, the indulgence was no longer valid.

Lavarède amused himself greatly as he returned from visiting the city to re-embark with the two English people. As the *Lorraine* was about to set out to sea again, however, an incident occurred that could not fail to disturb him, and caused him to forget the picturesque scenery.

A local carriage, low-slung on large wheels arrived at top speed. It contained a traveler with haggard eyes and a wild expression, with unkempt hair, to whom three or four days growth of beard gave a singular appearance. One might have thought him a madman or a malefactor.

It was Bouvreuil.

He leapt from the carriage, launched himself over the gangplank and appeared n the deck of the steamer, shouting: "The captain! Where's the commandant!"

"The commandant is still ashore," said a sailor. "He has papers to sign at the harbormaster's. We'll be casting off as soon as he's back aboard."

"But I want to speak to someone in authority."

"Well, here comes the first mate. Address yourself to him."

Lavarède was chatting to the officer in question. "It's my madman," he said to him, in a low voice.

"What? He's come all this way?"

Approaching the second-in-command, without having yet seen Lavarède, Bouvreuil cried: "Monsieur, I'm Bouvreuil!"

The other laughed in his face. "But my poor man, Monsieur Bouvreuil has been aboard since Bordeaux."

"In cabin number ten, no doubt?"

"Naturally, since it's his."

"Oh, this is too much! But the cabin's mine—I'm Bouvreuil, of Paris."

"In that case," said the mate, with an ironic expression, "who's our passenger?"

"How do I know?"

"Lavarède, perhaps?"

Bouvreuil started. He truly looked like a lunatic. "Lavarède!" he cried. "The brigand—it's him! Ah, I've found him. Thief!"

It was necessary to calm him down. Two sailors took hold of him firmly.

"But I have my papers!" he howled.

The officer turned to Lavarède and the other passengers attracted by the noise, Murlyton and his daughter among them.

"He's having a fit," said the officer. "He needs a cold shower."

"No," Lavarède interceded. "Let me talk to him."

"As you please—but the cold shower would be better."

While these words were being exchanged, Bouvreuil spotted the Englishman. "Ah!" He's someone, at least, who knows me and can affirm that I'm not an impostor."

But Aurett leaned toward her father and said, rapidly, in a low voice: "You can't say anything, Papa. You mustn't take sides against Monsieur Lavarède; it's a question of honor."

"But..."

"Remember that you'll lose your rights to the four million."

"That's true."

Bouvreuil addressed himself to Murlyton. "Come on, Monsieur—tell them who I am."

"But I don't know you."

A cry of rage replied to him, uttered by Bouvreuil. "It's enough to make one go mad!" he cried.

"Alas, that happened some time ago, old chap," riposted the first mate.

At that moment, Lavarède's angel, his Providence, as he had called Aurett, had a precious idea.

Lavarède was standing beside the officer. Turning to the young man, she said to him: "Monsieur Bouvreuil, try to find out how this poor man got to Santander." She added, significantly: "It might be interesting."

"In fact, you're right, Miss."

That intervention on the young woman's part had the initial result of impressing more deeply than ever in the officers' mind the idea that the false Bouvreuil was the true one; but it was also useful to Lavarède with a view to his future defense. The danger that he had thought he had escaped seemed stronger than ever.

During the time that these scenes had lasted, however, Commandant Kassler had returned, and had given the order to depart. The *Lorraine* was already under way, taking the two Bouvreuils away when their conversation began, in the presence of the two Murlytons and the first mate, who stopped whenever his duties permitted.

The unfortunate Bouvreuil—the true one—had had all the difficulties in the world in Bordeaux. First of all, it had been necessary to pay for the transport of the crate, and the latter's return to Paris, and then the price of his own voyage—because, in the confusion, he had lost his first class ticket and no one had wanted to believe in his "invention." Finally, he had settled everything, grumbling and cursing Lavarède.

He thought it was settled, and had only one thought—to get aboard the ship—when the customs officers intervened. The railway company had no further demands to make, so be it—but what about the customs? And the special commissioner? There was a fine legal tangle. It could not be sorted out just like that.

Bouvreuil told them all to go to the devil, and started running.

That was when the gendarmes joined the party. There was a hue and cry. They ran after him. He knocked over a customs officer and shoved a gendarme out of the way. Finally, he was apprehended, put in prison and charged with resisting arrest by the agents of the public force. The day went by like that—and God knows that Bouvreuil was foaming at the mouth, at the thought that Lavarède was getting away.

Finally, a Commissaire de Police arrived, who, after interrogating him, allowed himself to be persuaded to telegraph Paris for information about the accused.

Rich landlord, important financier, was the reply.

On the assurances of the Panama shareholders, Bouvreuil was finally released, not without having to pay a heavy fine. He was only able to avoid an appearance before a judge and sentencing—which is to say, a considerable loss of time—by pouring a considerable sum into the coffers of the town. After which, having sought information, he took the train to the Midi in order to catch up with the *Lorraine* at her port of call in Santander.

In sum, the transportation fees, fines, legal fees, bribes, rail tickets, etc. cost him more than three thousand francs.

That was stiff.

And the more Lavarède laughed as he listened to that tale of woe, the more Bouvreuil got carried away. The more he got carried away, the more plausibility he gave to his enemy's lugubrious deception: the more he looked like a madman. He even ended up be delivering such imprecations that Murlyton threw a punch at him—one of those English punches that can knock a man out cold.

"He can't use such indecent terms in front of my daughter. It's too shocking."

Bouvreuil had collapsed under the shock, and did not get up again. Sitting on his backside, he said: "Oh! He's against me too! I thought he was my ally! This Lavarède is the very devil!"

"A benevolent devil, at any rate," replied Aurett, "since he's talking about you to one of the ship's officers."

"About me! Great God! What is he going to do?" And he stood up briskly.

Indeed, Lavarède and the first mate had presented a request to the Commandant."

The *Lorraine* was under way, and the poor fellow really could not be thrown into the water. They asked that he be kept on board. He would be put to bed in the infirmary, as a measure of prudence, in case of a crisis, and he would be allowed to eat with the sailors. In order to make himself useful he could lend a hand to the stokers; there was always a spare shovel in the coal-bunker.

On learning, from the coldly mocking Lavarède, the fate reserved for him, Bouvreuil flew into an extreme rage.

"Here we go!" sad the first mate. "He's off again."

"But I don't want to be treated as an indigent passenger!" cried the unfortunate man. "I'm Bouvreuil! I have money!"

So saying, he brandished a wallet.

"Your wallet, undoubtedly?" said a sailor to Lavarède. "We'll get it back from him."

Armand stopped him. "No," he said. "Let him keep it for a while, since he's so determined. It would only bring on another fit. Just make sure that my ticket is in it."

Aurett and Murlyton made a gesture of satisfaction. Lavarède had tricked his adversary, but he was not stealing from him.

It took seven days to go from Santander to the Azores. Poor Bouvreuil did not have the strength to spend seven days doing the work of a stoker. At first he had tried to protest—nothing doing. He was obliged bear his misfortune patiently. Before the third day, however, he was exhausted, and did not even have the strength to complain. He no longer uttered anything except faint groans when he was in the presence of an officer.

Thanks to a generous tip given to the mariners in the in the engine room, he was not given any work to do. He remained lying down on the coal heap. The overheated atmosphere in that part of the ship, however, to which he was unaccustomed, put pressure on his lungs, and he asked not to be taken down there again. It was Lavarède, at whom he still launched furious glares when he saw him, who interceded with the first mate in order that his unfortunate landlord could remain in the infirmary, and even obtained permission for him to take a little air on deck.

"On deck, all right," said the officer, "but never aft with the passengers; let him keep to the fore with the crew. There, our men can keep an eye on him."

That was too much satisfaction for Lavarède, so he made use of a topical argument in order that his victim should not be sent down to be roasted alive in proximity with the steamer's engine. He argued that a man subject to fits of madness was a danger to the safety of the passengers; he would only have to throw a switch to cause an accident to the machines.

The reasoning was sound. The officer took account of it—but, also thinking of his responsibility, he had a better idea.

"I'll put him in irons until the next port of call, and we'll put him ashore in the Azores. There, the Portuguese gendarmes can take him to the French consul at Ponto Delgado on San Miguel. He'll take charge of repatriating him."

The second part of the plan was too useful to our friend for him not to be content with it, but he insisted that Bouvreuil be left at liberty, although still mingled with the crew and not allowed to leave the bow of the ship.

"So be it," said the mate. "We won't put him in irons right away, but I'll have him watched by one of my best seamen—and if he puts a foot wrong, he'll be locked up."

Bouvreuil was informed of all that—and as the reasoning of the strong is always the best, and he knew that he was by far the weaker, he knuckled under, chewing at his bit. One can imagine how much hatred was heaped up in his heart, however, on seeing Lavarède stretched out idly, fanned by the *punkah* of an Indian servant, one of the servant of the first class cabins, treated like a passenger of note, while he, who had paid for the other's passage, was reduced to the treatment of a stowaway or a crewman.

Conversely, however, Lavarède enjoyed his comfort with all the more pleasure. The voyage was commencing well. He was already in mid-Atlantic, and had not yet stumbled, in spite of all the difficulties that had cropped up.

Murlyton was glad to recognize that, but, being as tenacious as all of his countrymen, and knowing the force of money very well—and thus appreciating the weakness of those who have none—he waited patiently for the first breach of the conditions of the will, in order to observe it immediately and then take advantage of his right to the four millions.

On the fourth of April, the *Lorraine* came within sight of Flora, the first of the islands where the French mail-boats of the Compagnie Générale Transatlantique make landfall. She only stopped there as an exception, however, because of the traveler that had to be taken before the district governor: a senior functionary of a Central American state. That was what the first mate explained to Armand, who asked him how long they would be stopping there.

"These marvelous corners of the Earth," the Frenchman said to Aurett, are among the most beautiful in the world—the most beautiful and the best. By an exceptional privilege, the archipelago of *Autours*, or *Açor* in Portuguese, has no poisonous animals. A local legend even holds that they can't be acclimatized here—but as the geographer Vivien de Saint-Martin[11] says, it might not be prudent to make the experiment.

By saying that, Lavarède made the young Englishwoman smile.

"Go on, please," she said.

"Continue my lecture? So be it, but let's try to make it amusing and instructive. You'll notice, Mademoiselle, that the population, which surpasses two hundred thousand for the nine islands—San Miguel, Terceira, Pico, Fayal, San Jorge, Graciosa, Florès, Santa Maria and Corvo—is almost white: paler, at any rate, than those of the province of the Algarve in the south of Portugal, with superb black hair.

"The Azoreans, for the most part handsome and well-built, their women renowned for their fecundity, experience the three elements that have concurred in the population of so-called 'African' islands, such as Madeira, the Canaries and the Cape Verde Islands, even though they are closer to the European continent than the African.

Those three elements, fused for centuries, are the cultivators, Moorish in origin, the conquering Portuguese, who arrived in the middle of the fifteenth century, and—less well-known—the Flemish colonists sent shortly thereafter by the mother of Charles the Bold, the Duchesse Isabeau de Bourgogne, to whom her brother Édouard had made a gift of the islands, then newly acquired from the Portuguese crown.

"Because of that, they even bore the name of the Flemish Islands during the time when they were governed by a gentleman of Bruges, Jacques Hurter, but it soon came to an end and the Azores followed the destiny of Portugal, their

---

[11] Louis Vivien de Saint-Martin (1802-1897) was the editor of and a principal contributor to the *Nouveau dictionnaire de géographie universelle* (1876-95), a standard reference text used as a source by numerous Vernian writers for their didactic interludes.

first possessor—but not their first explorer, for the archipelago is described in Italian maps of the fourteenth century, notably that of the Medician Portulan."[12]

Aurett took pleasure in listening to these things recounted by Lavarède, whose memory was admirably furnished. That occupied the last moments before the Lorraine stopped. A numerous crowd of curiosity-seekers was waiting for the ship, because our boats do not make regular ports of call in the Azores. The services go via Madeira, or follow the direction from Dakar in Senegal via the Cape Verde Islands. This time, however, it was necessary, as we have said, to take aboard an important individual, and the exception was justified.

The arrival of Don José de Courramazas y Miraflor was an event on the island. Short and stiff, with dark olive skin, Don José was a cousin in the Extremaduran manner of a female relative of the governor of San Miguel. Was she really a relative? The Lorraine did not remain in the archipelago long enough for us to be able to resolve that problem—in any case, a beautiful woman who ran the household, the governor included.

Her cousin might have been Colombian by birth, but in consequence of certain voyages of adventure he had felt a vocation to become a citizen of Venezuela, and from time to time of Costa Rica. In his new fatherland, he had thrown in his lot with a general whose name escapes us, the competitor of a physician whose name is unimportant. In the wake of the annual revolution, motivated by the weekly pronunciamento, which succeeded fifty per cent of the time, the friends of the general having been beaten, Don José had been obliged to embark for Europe.

Like every good flashy foreigner, he had come to Paris first. What he did there we shall find out in due course, and perhaps soon. Then he remembered that he had family—an ambitious female cousin. He had searched for her and found that she was the "relative" of the governor of the Azores. It was with her that he came to rest and wait for better days. Those days arrived. The chronic pronunciamento came around in time. The partisans of the physician took steamers for Europe or North America in their turn, and the general's friends replaced them in the well-paid positions. Everyone has his turn in the republics of Central and South America.

Don José de Courramazas y Miraflor received, for his part, the equivalent of a prefecture; he was appointed governor of Cambo, and telegraphed a representative of his nation in Paris to book his passage aboard the first departing transatlantic steamer, in order to take up his position.

That representative in Paris never changes, whatever the outcome is of the annual revolution. That was thought preferable, in order that he could be more up to date. That is sound reasoning, for, by virtue of seeing governors, deputy governors and other civilian and military functionaries shuttling back and forth,

---

[12] The Medician Portulan, also known as the Laurentian Portulan, is ancient map allegedly dating from 1351.

arriving and departing, only to leave again and come back again, the American in question learns the itineraries by heart and becomes expert in the art of travel. Thus, if he had not booked a passage on the first transatlantic ship leaving Bordeaux on the twenty-sixth, immediately after receiving Don José's dispatch, the future Gobernador of Cambo would have been obliged to go from the Azores to Madeira first, on a wretched merchant vessel.

There he would have seen the French mail-boat going from Senegal to Brazil, but he would only have seen it, for it is in Maderia, by virtue of a treaty, that parcels and passengers are routinely transferred to ships of the Florida and Liberia Circular Steamship Company, based in Tallahassee in Florida. Don José would not even have traveled for an hour on the French ship; on quitting some wretched coaster he would have boarded an American vessel, on which people have no respect or regard for functionaries of petty Hispano-American republics. They are seen to change too frequently to be considered well-established.

By choosing a cabin on the ship departing on the twenty-sixth, by contrast, it was ensured that Don José would be treated very appropriately and would enjoy the elegant comfort of our French services. And as the *Lorraine* was stopping expressly for him, what prestige that gave him in the eyes of the Azorean people! That prestige would even rebound on to his demi-relative the governor, since his relative also had her share of it.

Everything, therefore, worked out for the best—and such was the new passenger that we see embarking to join the company of our old acquaintances.

A guard of honor, escorting the Gobernador and forming a cortege for Don José, accompanied him to the gangplank extended from the boat to the quay. Miraflor came over first, presented his homages to the Commandant, sketched a reverence addressed to the other passengers, and then, with a rounded gesture, he saluted the crowd, his cousin and his host.

After these ceremonies, the question of Bouvreuil was raised. It was learned on board that there was no consul; they were in an interregnum, between a resignation and an appointment—but the indigenous merchant charged with French interest until a new consul arrived had escorted the governor.

"Would you care to relieve us of a kind of madman embarked accidentally?" one of the ship's officers asked him.

That fashion of recommendation caused the Azorean to grimace. "But what do you want me to do with him?" he asked.

"Look after him and repatriate him at the first opportunity.

The brave businessman had an excellent inspiration for avoiding that chore. "First of all," he objected, "I have no funds for that. Secondly, as services for France aren't regular here, I don't know when he can be re-embarked. It would be necessary to feed him; who would pay? I don't have any prison in which to lock him up. Wouldn't it be better, since he's on your ship, for you to keep him until your destination? At least you're certain of returning to Bordeaux, after reaching America. You'll be able to get him home much sooner than I would if you leave him in my care."

The officer understood very well, but he continued to resist. "I assure you," he said, "that I'd rather confide him to those gendarmes over there."

At this point Don José intervened, magnanimously and generously. "No, Monsieur," he said. "The agents of the Portuguese authority will not have to intervene." With a superb movement, he gave them a signal to withdraw. "I shall take the unfortunate fellow under my protection," he added. "I shall keep him with me throughout the crossing."

"Pardon me," said the Commandant, "but in what capacity?"

"As my servant."

"Then you'll take responsibility for his nourishment on board?"

"Yes, Commandant."

"And you don't fear his crises, his fits?"

"I hope he won't have any—and if he does, I shall treat him gently."

"Do you know him, then?"

"Yes; I met him in Paris. He rendered me a service, and I shall repay him."

"So be it, Monsieur—but you'll be responsible for his actions, whatever might happen. I hope that you won't regret this benevolent impulse."

Then the gangplank was withdrawn. Last signs of adieux were exchanged, and the *Lorraine* continued her route through the islands of the gracious archipelago, soon regaining the open sea.

Lavarède had watched that entire scene mutely. Bouvreuil and he had only exchanged significant glances. The journalist remained silently on deck, wondering what was happening between the two men.

Once again, it was his young Providence, Aurett, who informed him. With the finesse particular to women, she had noticed a gesture of astonishment that had escaped Don José when he came on deck. Bouvreuil had immediately put his inner over his lips, evidently recommending the foreigner to silence. That had intrigued her. Slipping rapidly behind the mizzen mast, she had hidden briefly, just long enough to overhear the brief dialogue that she reported to Armand.

"What!" Bouvreuil said. "The expected person of quality is you?"

"Me," Don José relied. "Not a word, I beg you—my position and future depend on it."

"I won't betray you—I have several reasons for that with which you're familiar, and one more of which you're unaware. You need me and I need you—things are working out marvelously."

"What do you want of me?"

"They want to out me off the ship. I have a great interest in staying aboard. Keep me with you—even as a servant—and that will be sufficient."

"That's easy."

"One important point: here, no one wants to call me by my real name."
With an ugly grimace, he added: "They call me Lavarède."

"That's perfect."

And Don José had immediately kept his promise.

From the young Englishwoman's confidence, Lavarède was only able to conclude that a mysterious bond linked the two men. But what was it? How could he discover it?

One thing was certain, though: the *Lorraine* was now carrying two enemies instead of one, and that complicated his situation.

IV. Baptism on the Line

Even if Lavarède had known Señor José's biography, he would not have been greatly assured. The individual was, as we have said, one of those adventurers devoid of a fatherland, who does not recoil before any indelicacy.

In Paris, it had been necessary for him to make a living. Once he had eaten through the sack of piastres he had brought from America and exhausted the small credit that foreigners always obtain so easily in France, the series of dubious means had commenced.

At first, José had exploited the hearts and the pity of the numerous refugees in Paris speaking the Castilian language, but they were not rich and that seam soon ran out. The relative glimpsed in the Azores, however, brought her contingent of material support for a while. Soon, however, she was obliged to think of herself in order not to sink into the Parisian mud.

Don José then joined forces with certain exotics whose dossiers are not well-enough known and penetrated into the gambling dens inappropriately known as "clubs," where he exercised various industries, each as shady as the next: a little deception, a great deal of mendicity, passionate borrowings, and no probity at all. That program is a slippery slope; our individual slid, and soon descended into criminality.

The victim was a money-lender—or, to put it more accurately, a usurer— but he was only a man of straw, the representative of another "speculator" who exploited passionate gamblers and the sons of good families down on their luck. That entrepreneur of loans at usurious rates of interest was none other than Monsieur Bouvreuil, one of those archers whose bow has many strings. Bouvreuil did not easily tolerate anyone putting one over on him.

In those days, Don José had simply been known as Miraflor; perhaps it was his name, perhaps that of his village; history was not yet clear on that matter. At any rate, one day, integrated by a compatriot as to what had become of the adventurer, Bouvreuil replied: "Your friend, if he carries on, is heading for the Mazas."

And, in fact, he went there, for Bouvreuil had him condemned to prison. At the same time, however, Miraflor had found the *nom de guerre* under which we find him today.[13] His Iberian ears, seduced by the consonance, adopted the sonorities of the phrase. That was how Don José had become Miraflor y Courramazas, gentleman of one of the South American republics.

---

[13] In French, what Bouvreuil says of Don José is that "*il court à Mazas*" [he's heading for the Mazas]. I have retained the variant forms of the improvised name given in the text rather than unifying them.

Such was the existing relationship. As one can imagine, they put the crook at Bouvreuil's mercy—but on the Lorraine, Bouvreuil needed Don José, and their common interest so united those two honest men. While the ship sailed from the thirtieth degree of north latitude to the Tropic of Cancer, heading for the fictitious line of the equator, Bouvreuil brought his new associate up to date with his difficult situation. Examining it attentively, Don José made an accurate remark.

"Aboard the ship," he said, "There's nothing better to do than this. I've taken you on as my so-called servant, so you can be tranquil for the remainder of the voyage. As soon as we disembark on American soil, however, I'll become an important person and you can count on me."

"Ah! I'll be very grateful to you."

"But I remember that, during our little difference before, in Paris, the court official observed to me that the condemnation to a few months' rest, for what your French law calls a crime, still left me your debtor."

"Oh, let's not talk about that," said Bouvreuil, negligently.

"On the contrary, let's," said the other, emphatically. "I remained so much your debtor that your bailiff reminded me of it, and that was one of the causes that made me quit such an inhospitable city. Don't you think that it would be a nice gesture to liquidate those petty arrears?"

Bouvreuil was caught.

"I'd like nothing better…but you must remember that I don't have the necessary papers to hand…the file is in Paris."

"A simple receipt would suffice," said José, coldly. "Think about it."

"Agreed—when we disembark."

"It will be dearer then."

"Really?"

"Undoubtedly—because it will be necessary to get rid of your enemy, and that will be a surplus expense."

"A surplus?"

"Even in the equatorial countries, my dear Monsieur, revolver shots cost money."

Bouvreuil went pale. "But I'm not asking you to kill him!" he exclaimed.

"Bah! Half-measures are never any good. I can assure you that you're making a false economy."

Don José was beginning to show himself in his veritable aspect. To tell the truth, he frightened the vulture Bouvreuil, a civilized rogue whom the Code had made, whose schemes did not exceed legal limits—although they went quite far enough, and French law sanctions actions that are not always very pleasant, equity and the possession of stamped papers being quite different matters.

The *Lorraine* drew closer to the equator. The crossing of that imaginary zone is the occasion of a celebration for sailors, which is familiar to all those who have done a little sailing. Lavarède and the Murlyton family talked about it in full knowledge of the circumstance. Already the crew could be seen preparing covertly, with enigmatic smiles, the accessories of the famous baptism, whose grotesque features have been popularized by cartoonists.

"A strange custom, all the same," said Miss Aurett.

"Oh, Mademoiselle, if antiquity is an excuse, it's very pardonable, for it goes back a long way. No one knows whether it's the corruption of a pagan ceremony, a few shreds of whose rites have been allowed to persist by Catholicism, but some people think that it's the memory of a profane ritual in the vague religion of navigator peoples attached to the worship of the sun."

"But I've read in my books," observed the young woman, "that the custom doesn't seem to have been practiced by the companions of Christopher Columbus, which doesn't give it such an ancient origin."

"However, Mademoiselle, our most ancient mariners have made mention of it. Jean de Léry, who left Honfleur for Brazil in 1557 talks about it as custom already followed by the first explorers who left Le Havre and Honfleur long before him.[14] Another, Souchu de Rennefort, who wrote a history of the Indies in 1688, describes the tropical baptism as it is practiced in our day aboard all ships of war and commerce."[15]

Murlyton also put in a word. "Monsieur Armand is right, my child, and I believe that the ceremony as bequeathed to us by the Normans—not our present neighbors or those who came to England with William the Conqueror, but the true 'men of the North' who came down as pirates to the regions bordering 'our channel,' as the French call the English Channel."

"On what do you base your opinion, my dear Monsieur?"

"On a Swedish tradition of the eleventh century. In the time of King Valdemar the Victorious, who reigned from 1170 to 1241, the mountain of the Kullaberg in Scandinavia was inhabited by a sorcerer known as the Man of Kulla, who only allowed the navigators of the period to double Cape Kullen after having played the role of douser with him, since fulfilled by Father Tropic on the equatorial line."[16]

---

[14] Jean de Léry published a book in 1578, *Historia Navigationis in Brasiliam, quae et America dicitur* {History of a Voyage to Brazil, also known as America], about an unsuccessful attempt to found a colony, France Antarctique.

[15] Urbain Souchu de Rennefort's *Histoire des Indes orientales* [History of the East Indies] (1688) was the work of a colonial administrator who undertook at least one exploratory voyage to the region in question in 1667 but seems to have been based in Madagascar.

[16] These data appear to come from a volume published in 1891 entitled *L'Intermédiare des chercheurs et curieux* by Benjamin Duprat. Murlyton, as an Englishman, would be far more likely to have been familiar with the markedly different account of the naval line-crossing ceremony and its origins given by Captain Robert FitzRoy of *H.M.S. Beagle*.

"All that is very curious," said Aurett, "but I've never seen the baptism—although I wouldn't like to be its heroine."

"Oh, have no fear; your father will pay the sailors the little tribute they demand that serves as a ransom for that chore. Besides which, the patient has already been selected. A passenger who has never crossed the line before is usually chosen. We have one aboard."

"Who's that?"

"The excellent Monsieur Bouvreuil; I only have to say a word to the bosun and we'll see him plunged into the tub tomorrow, to receive the traditional bath."

Aurett smiled; the smile was an acquiescence, and Lavarède promised himself that little vengeance.

As soon as he mentioned in, in fact, the bosun replied: "The madman—of course! A good cold shower can't do him any harm!"

The next day, therefore, in spite of his cries of protest, Bouvreuil was led forward by four men dressed as Neptune's attendants.

The ship's officers closed their eyes as custom required. Don José also let it happen; deep down, he was not sorry—Bouvreuil had given him too much trouble in the past for him to consider the debt settled.

The passengers had taken their places aft; the band struck up a triumphant march, and the party was started, which everyone enjoyed except the unfortunate Bouvreuil.

The ceremony commenced. Musket fire was heard, and the cortege of the god of the Line appeared while sailors perched on the mast threw handfuls of beans on to the deck. The god, giving his arm to his spouse—a cabin-boy whose face was framed with tufts of woodchips representing hair—took his place on a throne installed at the foot of the main mast. Around that group the dignitaries of the tropical court were ranged—the astronomer, Cupid, etc. They were all wearing fantastic costumes and long oakum beards.

Then the Tropic god stood up and, in a classic speech, announced that, in his paternal solicitude, he had resolved to cut off their heads on order to cure their migraines and saw of their legs to prevent rheumatism—after which the procession of patients began. Each of them, seized by two guards, as led to a vat covered with a plank and decorated with drapes. He slipped a coin into the hands of his guardians, the sacred ferule was applied to his lips, eau-de-Cologne was poured into his sleeve and collar, and the farce was played.

That first part of the enjoyment was somewhat skimpy; the crewmen were in haste to see Bouvreuil's turn arrive. The madman had been abandoned to them, and they awaited him impatiently. Unsuspecting, the landlord watched his companions pass the vat, and, when his name was called, he surrendered himself complacently to the guards charged with bringing him before "Père Trois-Piques."[17] A joyous hurrah vibrated in the air.

Bouvreuil looked around, astonished. He saw all the delighted faces; the sailors and passengers were all radiant Lavarède was in the front row, beside Aurett, who was laughing enough to draw tears. In spite of his British phlegm, even Murlyton, lending his arm to his daughter, appeared to be on the brink of yielding to the general hilarity. The worthy gentleman certainly resisted, but the struggle between laughter and gravity resulted in the most comical contraction of the facial muscles.

Bouvreuil had a presentiment of disaster. An enemy's joy is always a bad omen. He tried to escape his guards, but they held on to him and sat him down, perhaps a trifle rudely, on the plank covered the large vat. He tried to struggle, but the heavy hands of the sailors nailed him to his seat. Two others representing the tropical sea-road took hold of him by the head and feet, in such a way that he was reduced to complete immobility.

One of the executors approached him and, holding an enormous nail perpendicularly above his head, put on a show of driving it in with mighty blows of a hammer. In any other circumstances, Bouvreuil would have understood that it was merely a joke, but, having been harassed, ill-treated ad manhandled by everyone since he had set foot on the accursed boat, he had lost his sense of proportion. At the sight of the hammer and nail he believed that he was doomed and uttered a cry of terror—to which a loud burst of laughter replied.

The nail was made of colored bread. The terror was ridiculous. The usurer sensed that, and his rage increased. He darted a glance at Lavarède that would have made the latter shudder had he not been occupied in telling the English-woman a story, to which the young woman was listening with half-closed eyes, with a rosy tint in her cheeks and her lips parted in a smile.

The victim was not at the end of his troubles, though. A second executor advanced, armed with enormous pincers. He announced that he was going to rip out the patient's nails. And he took off his shoes.

A third arrived carrying a saw, with which he threatened the unfortunate victim's neck.

Bouvreuil was no longer flinching. He allowed another executor to paint his face black and white, with the aid of a rod covered in sheepskin.

After that operation, the guards released him. He thought that his ordeal was over, and made as if to stand up. As if they had only been waiting for him to move, his tormentors tipped over the plank on which he had been sitting, and the usurer, with a very pleasing pirouette, disappeared up to the neck into the vat filed with old sauce, ivory black, salt, pepper, wax and, in sum, all the ingredients that the ship could furnish.

---

[17] The pun connects the word tropic to the three prongs of Neptune's trident.

Bouvreuil made a heroic effort. Clinging to the edge, he tried to climb out. Immediately, however, the nozzle of a hose was introduced into the vat and liquid sprang forth, falling in yellow-tinted floods on to the head of the unfortunate victim, and all around him. At the same time, the contents of several buckets of water poured down from the height of the mast, where the sailors had kept them in reserve in order to complete the singular baptism.

Blinded and half-asphyxiated, Bouvreuil struggled desperately beneath that interminable downpour, howling and gesticulating.

Hectic laughter shook the entire audience. Even Murlyton let himself go now. The shower continued falling.

The ship's doctor encouraged the sailors. "Go on, lads! It's a service you're rendering the poor fellow. Cold showers are the usual treatment for the illness from which he's suffering."

The mariners did not lend a deaf ear to him, but human strength has its limits, and they were laughing too hard to do much work. The dousers put down their buckets; the guards ceased holding on to the patient. As rapid as thought, Bouvreuil took advantage of the opportunity. With one bound of which his numerous clients would not have thought him capable, he leapt out of the vat and fled—but in what a state!

Dripping, trembling and bewildered, his face and hands an indescribable color, water streaming from his hair and his garments stuck to his body—and drunk with anger to boot, threatening all those people delighted with his discomfiture with his fist—he ran to shut himself up between decks, where Lavarède sent him a change of clothes taken from his luggage, which had been transported to the cabin before departure.

That attention did not calm the usurer down, for, an hour later, cleaned up and dressed in dry clothes he met José and drew him aside.

"You said, my dear Monsieur, that it's easy to get rid of a man in America?"

"Everything depends on the price," replied the foreigner, smiling. "There's no lack of bravos there."

"Well then, perhaps we'll talk about it again."

V. The Antilles Sea

The last few days of the crossing were calmer. Only one incident occurred in the approaches to the Antilles Sea. In the distance, at sunset, a waterspout appeared on the horizon. The water, lifted up in a Pelasgian column, met up with a thick black cloud, seemingly engulfed therein.

Although by no means common, the phenomenon did not astonish the navigators unduly. The spectacle is very curious, however, when it occurs at a sufficient distance not to be disturbing.

That same evening, when night fell, the sea became phosphorescent. Silvery waves unfurled against the *Lorraine*'s hull, causing millions of sparks with vivid scintillations. The anterior presence of the waterspout and the dense clouds was sufficient evidence that the atmosphere was charged with electricity.

That led to the eternal discussion regarding oceanic phosphorescence. Lavarède attributed it to an electrical cause, while Murlyton held the traditional opinion that attributes the phenomenon to myriads of animalcules of a special kind. Miss Aurett was unconcerned with the cause and contented herself with admiring the slightly magical effect, which spoke to her soul.

While they were raising their spirits in response to the spectacles of nature however, others were lowering themselves to the vilest of human schemes. A kind of pact had been concluded between Bouvreuil and José. The old fraudster had taken advantage of the days of the crossing, spent in observation. He had perceived the young Englishwoman's nascent sympathy for Lavarède very clearly.

"That fellow," he said to the Venezuelan, "Is capable of having several strings to his bow. If his cousin's fortune escapes him, as is more than probable, by the regular route of inheritance, he'll find a plank of salvation. The four millions will revert to the Englishman, and then to his daughter. And by taking advantage of her, he'll recover by marriage the money he lost along the way."

"The girl is going to be very rich, then? asked José, already stimulated by such gilded perspectives.

"Yes. Murlyton has a considerable personal fortune. "You know the English; for them to stop work it's necessary for them to be more than well-to-do. Aurett is his only child. Yes, if her father's millions are joined by those of Cousin Richard, it'll be a princely sum."

"It would be a great pity to let it fall into your enemy's hands."

So saying, José had his malevolent smile—the smile of the days when he had been "heading for the Mazas." And Bouvreuil replied by a circumflex twitch of his lips, which did not embellish them. Neither of them said anything more.

Privately, Bouvreuil was thinking: *What about Pénélope? What will my Pénélope do if I don't bring back her infidel, as I promised her?*

For his part, Don José was glimpsing a horizon of rest after the storms of his adventurous life, with the Englishwoman's millions to cushion his old age, and her pretty bright smile to dissipate bitterness.

The mute dialogue ceased abruptly. The two men had reached an understanding.

"Fair exchange is no robbery...as always," said the American. "I'll help you prevent this Lavarède from succeeding in his enterprise, but in return, you'll help me to obtain Miss Aurett's hand."

"Understood...and the treaty has no need of being signed."

"No, not between honest men."

"And our interests are the same."

"Perfectly exact."

Fundamentally—deep down inside, in a hidden corner of the back of his head, Don José did not really care about the blonde child's hand; it was the fortune alone that tempted him. To be the governor of Cambo, Bambo or Tambo, various prefectures that had been offered to him, was certainly very nice, even flattering, and productive up to a point, but was it not a precarious lot? The immovability of functionaries is not written into the laws of Hispano-American republics, much less that of their salaries. And the chronic revolution, which was as yet only twice yearly, might easily become thrice yearly. Defeated parties had thought about that several times. Then again, the Treasury was dry; salaries were paid with noticeable delays. One day, the political seesaw would only have to tip before the financial disbursement.

Having weighed up all that, a good marriage seemed more solid. Don José was still young; his title in the country to which he was going was of a nature to flatter the self-esteem of a young woman; there was no lack of honorable means of seduction. Nothing would be easier than compromising Miss Aurett and rendering the union necessary.

The most urgent thing was to link himself gradually, during the last days of the crossing, to Murlyton, and that was the direction in which Señor Miraflor extended his efforts.

Bouvreuil did his best to aid him. His gaze even became less ferocious when it encountered Lavarède, to the extent that the latter was able to think that the antipathy of his landlord and creditor had dried out along with his clothing.

He was mistaken. Bouvreuil was planning a coup in his own style.

"My dear friend," he said to Don José, "here, aboard the *Lorraine*, a rogue has taken my name. He is Bouvreuil, a respectable man, and I am Lavarède, an individual devoid of importance, half-mad, the butt of the crew's jokes. So be it...let's be patient for a few more hours. We'll soon be disembarking in Colon, and there, I'll take advantage of the situation created for Lavarède and Bouvreuil on board."

"What do you mean?"

"Simply this: Monsieur Bouvreuil is an important person. Well, once ashore, I become myself again, I become Bouvreuil, which is easy enough for me, since I have all my papers, and we'll find regular authorities there."

"Certainly…and then?"

"Then Lavarède is only a sort of parcel to be repatriated out of charity—or by force, as he chooses. All the officers of the *Lorraine*, and the sailors too, will testify to that. Nothing will be easier that to obtain an order of repatriation from the French consul, as was already planned for me in the Azores."

"I understand. I'll act as intermediary with the Commandant to ask for the document, and once it's signed, it will be the veritable Lavarède who is seized and boarded."

"That's right—his world tour won't have been long."

The plan was, indeed, excellent. By virtue of its very simplicity, it had every chance of success. Unfortunately, Lavarède was not a simpleton, and as they drew nearer to the American shore, he sensed that his paradise was about to end and his inferno to begin. Quite sincerely, he opened himself up to Aurett, who asked him, laughing, how he was going to tackle the next stage of his journey.

"As you'll understand, Mademoiselle, I'm going to quit the identity that I've donned for the crossing. I'd no sooner have set food on land at Colon than serious obstacles would arise."

"What are you going to do, then?"

"I don't know yet; but I've decided not to wait for that before disembarking."

When the Lorraine called in at Guadeloupe, nothing had yet changed; our characters were observing one another.

Lavarède, in order to maintain his role, contented himself with recounting a few details about the coral reefs that were growing every year, especially along the shore of the large island. He had a memory of Marie Galante, an anecdote about La Désirade. All the islands went by: Saint Barthélemy, which the Swedes returned to us in 1878; Saint Martin, which we share with Holland. He called attention to the Grandes Mornes, from which La Soufrère looms up, with its plume of smoke; he pointed out the valley of the river Goyaves, and recalled the incident of the earthquake of 1843 that destroyed Point-à-Pitre in a minute—or seventy seconds, as accurate writers say.

In brief, nothing in his appearance or his conversation revealed his preoccupation. He did not set foot on land.

It was only in Martinique, where the boat dropped anchor for more almost a day that he did as most of the passengers did and descended at Fort-de-France. As for Bouvreuil, he was still detained.

"Is it necessary to bid you adieu?" Aurett asked.

"No, Mademoiselle…must I not, in any case, allow your father to carry out his mission?"

"The difficulties haven't discouraged you, then?"

"On the contrary, they're exciting me. We're in French territory here and, in truth, I'm going to search for a means of continuing my world tour without violating the clauses that have been imposed on me."

That was simple enough to say, but less simple to carry out. He knew the colony, having stayed there during one of his voyages. He headed for the Place de la Savane, giving himself a goal for his mechanical stride in order to let his thoughts wander.

And he thought.

Let's see...what can I do? If I continue the crossing on the Lorraine, *we'll call in at ports in Venezuela and Columbia before reaching the isthmus. On those coasts, the roads are so nearly non-existent that postal deliveries are made on muleback. I'd lose precious time going that way...and how would I live? If, without quitting the island, I go as far as Saint Pierre, I can find a ship there for North America. At Saint Thomas I'd find one of those maintaining the service between the Antilles and Mexico...that would get me further forward, but how could I pay for my passage? That's truly not very comfortable. The Lorraine will be putting to sea again in a few hours; it's necessary to be there...*

As he went around the statue raised to the Empress Josephine, he saw someone looking at him.

"Lavarède? Is that really you?"

"The same." Armand looked at the newcomer, whom he recognized almost immediately. It was an old school friend. "What the devil are you doing here?" he demanded.

"I'll tell you, but first I'll ask you the same question. I've been on the governor's staff for a while."

"So you've become a creole?"

"No, an immigrant, since I'm not a native of the colony. Your turn, now."

"I'm just passing through, and I've come to breathe the urban air while our transatlantic vessel has dropped anchor.

An absinthe and coconut milk was quickly offered, and conversation engaged. Armand asked for news of a few childhood friends, and others he had known in the Lesser Antilles.

"Georget?"

"Dead, bitten by a fer-de-lance viper on the bank of the Lamentin."

"Dramane?"

"Caught yellow fever in Pointe-au-Diable on the Caravelle peninsula."

"Subit?"

"Visiting the ravine of Pitons, the source of the Absalon, where he's taking the waters to cure his old wounds."

"Jordan?"

"Emigrated to one of the eighteen Hispano-American Republics. The last I heard was that our friend Jordan, ruined as a result of youthful follies, had set off for Caracas, having realized his last ten thousand francs."

A district commissioner, one of the local functionaries, also knew Jordan. It was only a short distance away, so they went to see him. He was a character: a creole, a correspondent member of various scientific societies, and a pretentious bore. That was obvious as soon as he spoke.

"I'd like to know what has become of our friend Jordan, who used to live in Martinique," Lavarède said, very politely.

"You mean," the erudite individual objected, "that he used to live in Madinine?"

"The creole name, no doubt?"

"No, Monsieur, the true name of the island, the one that the original inhabitants gave it."

"Oh, very well…but I don't know Caraibe, myself."

"You mean Carib—the other word in the French corruption. The English, more obedient to the oral tradition, write *caribbee*, which is correct."

Lavarède had no wish to argue with that found of local knowledge, and returned to the subject of Jordan.

"Monsieur Jordan is resident in Caracas, where he has founded the French Bazaar."

"A bazaar—everything going cheap."

"Monsieur is doubtless Parisian," said the commissioner gravely. "In the Venezuelan state, the Bazaar is something like the Louvre, or the Bon Marché, crossed with the Temple and Les Halles. Everything is sold there; everything can be found there."

"Even pianos?"

"Yes, Monsieur, and potatoes, if required. We're the ones who furnish the sugar."

"Sugar and coffee?"

"Alas, no. At present, the island no longer produces either coffee or cotton, but we remain in the first rank for sugar-case and tafia rum."

"I'm delighted for Marti…pardon me, for Madinine. But I'm even more delighted for our Captain Jordan."

"You certainly can be. His capital has multiplied tenfold. He goes to France every two years to make his purchases and avoid anemia, which afflicts Europeans who never leave these regions. He has even founded several branches in Bolivar, Sabanilla and Bogota, in the great centers of New Grenada, or, to put in more modern terms, in the capitals of the United States of Grenadine Colombia. He has, I believe, extended as far as the republics of Ecuador and Bolivia, but his principal establishment—the mother-house, as he calls it in jest—has remained in Caracas.

"Do you see him sometimes?"

"Yes, but never in the winter—which is to say, from July to October. He returns to France, during the cool season, where there are never any hurricanes."

After a few thanks and polite farewells they took their leave. Time had passed. The governor's secretary escorted Lavarède as far as the ship. There, everything was in turmoil, in complete chaos. There had been a tidal wave.

The bizarre phenomenon in question is common enough in the regions, but is no better explained for that. In a dead calm, without the waves out to see even being agitated, long swells are produced, becoming more accentuated as they approach the shore, to the extent that along the coastal shelf the sea becomes furious, as if unleashed over the land.

Fortunately, the port of Port-de-France is secure, the best-sheltered in the Antilles, so the effects of the tidal wave had not been deadly for the *Lorraine*.

"It's still lucky that we haven't seen a cyclone," said one of the sailors. "That would have smashed all the houses and boats."

"Are these cyclones very terrible, then?" asked Aurett.

"Certainly," Murlyton replied, "and they're particular to the Caribbean Sea—that's the name that the English give to the Antilles Sea."

While the ship raised anchor, an officer recalled a few that Martinique had suffered: that of 10 October 1780, still known as "the great hurricane," that of 26 August 1825 and that of 4 September 1883, when the town of Saint Pierre had been half-obliterated and twenty ships lost in the harbor. There was silence. The evocation of those disasters was not calculated to make anyone laugh.

A few moments later, Lavarède, alone on deck, was watching the nearby coast pensively.

He asked the first mate: "Our next port of call is La Guayra?"

"Yes, then Porto Cabello, also in Venezuela; then Savanilla in Colombia, but we'll only stop there to drop off and pick up mail. We'll stay there longer on the return journey to take on cargo bound for Europe."

The *Lorraine* continued on her route. Lavarède had gone back to his cabin. He said that he was feeling ill, and did not appear at table.

The next day, Murlyton asked for news of him. Bouvreuil and Don José were looking for him everywhere too. They did not find him.

Lavarède had disappeared.

Everyone was anxious, except for Aurett, the only one who appeared to be conserving her British phlegm.

VI. On American Land

As can easily be imagined, the disappearance of Lavarède was a major event aboard the Lorraine. For a while it was thought that he had fallen into the sea, but Murlyton went to speak to the Commandant after the halt at Sabanilla and reassured him. He had found a note in his cabin from the traveler, conceived as follows:

Wait for me in eight or ten days in Colon, at the Isthmus Hotel, where I shall doubtless rejoin you. I see nothing inconvenient in the unfortunate Bouvreuil recovering his real name and his cabin, now that I'm no longer sailing with him, but I would be grateful if you would wait until the Lorraine *next drops anchor to reveal the truth.*
My homages to your daughter.
Ever yours,

Armand Lavarède,
future millionaire.

The Englishman complied with these instructions. It seemed probable that Armand had left the ship at Guayra, the Venezuelan port of Caracas, from which it is only five leagues distant.

Bouvreuil's identity, attested by his papers, was confirmed by Murlyton and by the illustrious passenger Don José Miraflores y Courramazas. Everyone was lavish with their apologies, but those regrets were only superficial. The ship's officers had a weakness for the cheerful adventurer who had disappeared in South America, and involuntarily showed themselves cold and reserved with the individual to whom they had given so much difficulty during the voyage. He resumed his rank as a first class passenger nevertheless, and the voyage finished far better than it had started for him.

However, a singular doubt and a strange mystery subsisted during the final days, and people still talk aboard the transatlantic liners about that strange substitution, which has never been completely explained.

Those events had necessarily brought the four passengers who knew Lavarède closer together. Don José took advantage of that to execute a few preliminary approaches, in order to begin the siege of the young millionaires.

It was a waste of time. The young pearl of Great Britain remained untouchable, like the English formations at Waterloo.

Bouvreuil, for his part, tried to discredit the absentee in the mind of Mr. Murlyton. "He's a Bohemian, devoid of consistency, status and fortune," he said.

"Unless," the impassive rival objected, "he inherits Cousin Richard's millions in a year's time."

A shrug of the shoulders was the sole response of the irritated landlord. That was, indeed, very improbable.

The *Lorraine* reached Colon without a hitch, and, once ashore, everyone resumed their personal occupations.

Coldly and mathematically, Murlyton and Aurett booked rooms at the Isthmus Hotel, an English establishment maintained with the comfort dear to the islanders—all the dearer because it costs an arm and a leg.

Bouvreuil followed them there. That was, in any case, in conformity with article 3 of the program he had drawn up on departure: "Stay in English hotels for preference." Moreover, he did not forget what he had come to do in the isthmus: as the representative of an important group of shareholders, he wanted to see the real state of the works and to take account for himself of the possibility or impossibility of arriving at a definitive result within a given time.

He had a report to make, and to begin with, he took to the railway, traveling by train all the way from Colon to Panama and back again, hoping that he would see something interesting. It was, in any case, a short journey, since the distance is inferior to that between Paris and Montereau. It would have required other eyes than his to obtain any result, and specialist knowledge that he did not have. He thought it advisable to make contact with Frenchmen, whom he supposed would be happy to encounter a compatriot in these distant lands, but he did not find any naïve enough, or talkative enough, to open up to him, sly and crafty as he was. He waited for an opportunity that his lucky star might send him.

In the meantime, he wrote to his daughter, Pénélope, to tell her that Lavarède was invisible and undiscoverable.

Wandering in some republic in South America, separated from all regular communication by the double chain of the Cordilleras of the Andes, it will take him several months to arrive in a land where communications are easy and the road civilized, so to speak. You can be tranquil. The eccentric of your dreams will not succeed in his stupid enterprise. I only have one wish for him, which is that he doesn't sink into the lagoon of Maracaibo or get lost in the marshes of Magdalena, or fall from the 5.400 meter height of Tolima, if he tries to get close to Panama. (Don't be surprised that your father has become so well-informed about geography; it's an engineer of the isthmus who gave me the information.)

He has to return in this direction, necessarily, because it's only from here that ships depart in all the directions of the world. He's mad enough to try to continue his route, but before he does that I'll raise a few obstacles that will join forces against him with the most dangerous of all, time. In fact, the weeks are passing, becoming months, and your handsome Armand will be very happy, once the appointed date arrives, to come back to Papa Bouvreuil's daughter.

As for Don José, it was noticeable that once disembarked, he had extinguished his Castilian arrogance and seemed to want to make himself unobtrusive, in order to go unnoticed. That was because in Colon he was in the state of Panama, one of those forming the United States of Colombia, and the adventurer did not want to attract the attention of the Colombian authorities. He even disappeared completely for two days, without his companions being able to explain the eclipse.

Nothing, however, prevents us, who know everything, from revealing the truth. Don José, in reality the son of a Guaymie, the issue of some miserable Indian peon, had gone as far as Miraflores, a small town on the slope of the mountainous massif overlooking the Pacific Ocean. There, he had embraced his mother, a good woman working in a lowly job in an agricultural plantation, a *cafetale*, or coffee farm. A good son, at least he had left her a few piastres, while promising her more once he had taken up his post as prefect of Cambo.

That specifies, therefore, the hitherto indecisive nationality of the flashy foreigner in question. Miraflores was the name of his native village. Originally, he was thus Colombian, but his adventures, which had made him successively a Venezuelan and a Guatemalan, had definitively established him as a Costa Rican. There alone had he pledged himself to one of the claimants for the presidency, to whom he had attached his fortune. We have seen that, for the moment, José had done well.

When he reappeared in Colon it was to announce his immediate departure.

By way of land, that did not seem either safe or rapid. Merchant ships departed continually for Limon, the port of Costa Rica on the Atlantic, as Puntarenas is that on the Pacific. Furthermore, an isthmic railway had linked them to one another a few years before.

José recovered his habitual emphasis to say farewell to the Murlyton family

"It is not *adieu*, Miss, that I say to you but *au revoir*. I shall take possession of the government that the nation has confided to me—a hundred and eighty-five thousand inhabitants, counting the Indians—and I hope to see you again there and welcome you. When the sun has seen the English rose, it is to her that he sends his rays henceforth. He has no more to do than fade away before that blonde and pure beauty."

The compliment that left the "English rose" cold enthused Bouvreuil. As he accompanied his accomplice to the port he said: "Whatever happens, I'll persuade Murlyton to take the overland route."

"One could tell him that Lavarède is in Costa Rica, in a town I'll specify."

"Yes, that means might perhaps..."

"I'll send relays of mules to the frontier, and once past the Sierra, I'll take care of the rest!"

Bouvreuil, still fearful of an offensive return on Lavarède's part, was not sorry to retain Jose's aid. It would at least assure him that the exceedingly gilded rose's personal millions would not go to him as compensation for his cousin's inheritance. That was even better than having his future son-in-law murdered.

Meanwhile the weeks went by. The deadline fixed by Lavarède drew closer, and no word from him had been heard as yet. Bouvreuil was manifestly delighted; he had ended up making the acquaintance of a certain Gérolans, a director of works, who indicated to him a great many little-known features of the land, and who called him "Monsieur l'Ingénieur," laying on the flattery thickly.

Murlyton and Aurett remained calm and tranquil. They spent their time taking walks in the direction opposite to the marshes, and avoided going out during the torrid midday hours—for the climate of Colon is unhealthy, precisely because of the humid heat that reigns there and the marshes surrounding the town. Once they had made the tour of the statue of Christopher Columbus three times, however, they knew the tiny city very well. Colon had only been built in 1840, when there had been talk of the interoceanic railway that had preceded the canal, and a criminal arsonist had destroyed part of it in 1883.

"In the beginning," Gérolans explained, "the city was called Aspinwall, the denomination that the North Americans preferred—the name of their compatriot, one of the United States financiers who contributed to the building of the railway.[18] Aspinwall chose for the site of the town, the head of the line, the little island of Manzanilla, thus called because of the *manzanillas*—manchineel trees—that used to grow here.[19]

To begin with, Stephens, Baldwin, Hugues and Totten preferred a more westerly point in the bay of Limon, but Trautwine's advice prevailed; the depth of the water is more considerable off the shore of the island and that settled the matter. Except that it was necessary to construct a causeway to link Manzanilla to the mainland and consolidate the road that traverse the miry marsh of Mindi. Finally, in 1855, the railway was functional from coast to coast."

Our friends were obtaining their local instruction in that fashion when Lavarède reappeared, to Bouvreuil's great despair and the joy of Aurett, shared to a lesser degree by the impassive Murlyton.

"Tell me," said the latter, "how you've been living in recent days."

"First come with me as far as the port and come aboard the *Maria de la Sierra Blanca*, the ship that has just brought me here. I'll tell you the story of my odyssey—which is quite simple—before witnesses."

A few minutes later, Lavarède began

---

[18] The shipping magnate William Henry Aspinwall (1807-1875).

[19] *Manzanilla* means "little apple," the plants in question being given that name because of a superficial resemblance of their fruit. Nowadays they are known as *manzanilla de la muerte*, because the fruits turned out to be extremely toxic.

"When we called in at La Guayra, night had already fallen. I took advantage of that to go ashore with the lifeboat, whose men assumed that I was a deserter from the ship's crew. As there's a shortage of inhabitants in all the South American republics, especially of specialists, they give a good welcome to Europeans, supplying them with weapons and luggage. If that doesn't happen as much in Venezuela, I'm not teaching you anything by reminding you that Paraguay, Argentina, etc. attract migrants from the old world by any means possible, admissible and inadmissible. So, I was welcomed in La Guayra, and even nourished. That evening, I sought information about the road of Caracas, scarcely twenty kilometers away. I set out, and arrived in the city the next morning."

"Why the devil did you go there?"

"I had an idea. I asked for directions to the French Bazaar and introduced myself to my old friend Jordan, who has become one of the most important businessmen in the region. I explained my situation to him; he laughed a great deal and promised to help me—which was easy for him to do, as you'll see."

"The French Bazaar? But that's a market of all sorts of European products: textiles, manufactured goods and comestibles."

"Exactly. A good idea, eh?"

"Yes, but like all good ideas, it was an Englishman who had it first. In Bayswater, in London, you can find an establishment of that sort: Whiteleys."[20]

Lavarède was not about to argue that point of mercantile chauvinism with Murlyton. He continued his story.

"My friend Jordan has already founded several branches of his company, but he's dreaming of others. He offered to commission me, first of all to go and inspect the one that has been begun in Sabanilla, and then to inspect the American coast and go as far as Vera Cruz, stopping wherever it seemed useful to do so. For that purpose he put at my disposal the *Maria de la Sierra Blanca*, where we are at present, commanded by Captain Delgado, to whom I have the honor of introducing you and who rapidly brought me here, the only place that it seemed 'useful' to me to stop, in accordance with my instructions, since it was here that I had arranged to meet you."

"Very good, but where did you get the money?"

The trap was too obvious. Lavarède did not fall into it.

"But my dear Monsieur, there was no need of money for any of that. Jordan has fed me; I've worked for him; we're quits. Señor Delgado can confirm that for a week, I've been an employee such as he has never seen."

---

[20] Whiteleys was London's first department store, created in the 1860s by the rapid and massive expansion of a drapery shop owned by William Whiteley. It was devastated in 1887 by an enormous fire, so one would not have been able to find it in 1891, although a lavish new building was constructed and opened in 1911.

The mariner nodded his head. "Never," he opined, "have I seen anyone as disinterested as this Frenchman."

"Thank you for the certification," he said. "It will be your adieu, because I'm leaving you."

"What? Aren't we continuing coasting in the Antilles Sea? But we're supposed to go as far as the Gulf of Mexico. What will Mr. Jordan say?"

"Have no fear; he's fully informed and only wanted to help me through a difficult stage. So, let's part, and may God protect you."

"I invite you to dinner," said Murlyton, laughing. "That remains, I think within the conditions of the contest. In addition to the fact that it would be agreeable to my daughter, I confess that I find you infinitely amusing."

"Truly delighted," said Lavarède—who was not lying, for he was glad to meet up with the young miss again.

Over dinner, the conversation resumed.

"You'll need to tell me," the Englishman said, "where and how we're going to continue our world tour, now that you no longer have Captain Delgado's steamer."

"Where? Via Central America...then Mexico, then San Francisco, then..."

"Good, good...but how?"

"How? Oh, on foot, of course."

"My God!"

"And without losing any time, for I only have twelve months. If you're too tired, stop...personally, I shall continue tomorrow, the fourteenth of May."

"But this evening, since we're not leaving right away, where are you going to sleep?"

"Don't worry about that. I found, on arriving at the Isthmus Hotel, an old teacher at the School of Maritime Engineering, Monsieur Gérolans, whom I knew in Brest, and he's putting me up for the night. So, until tomorrow morning...goodnight, Mademoiselle."

Left alone with his daughter, Murlyton murmured: "A devil of a man! What determination! He's worthy of being my compatriot."

"Yes," said Aurett, "but what good humor too! He's definitely a Frenchman."

The next morning, Bouvreuil had arrived first at the house of his "friend" Gérolans. He had written to Don José beforehand to tell him about Lavarède's reappearance and his desire to continue his route overland, for want of any other gratuitous means. He had learned those things from Gérolans, who had not thought he was doing any harm by revealing them.

The Englishman and his daughter soon joined them.

"I don't know whether you know the country," Gérolans said to Lavarède, "but I believe you'll have difficulty finding a beaten track. Less than a day from here you'll run into impenetrable forests, lairs of snakes and predatory animals, which are only inhabited by half-breeds, black Zambos and adventurer of all colors, searchers for rubber and tagua. The best you can hope for is to encounter an Indian tribe with gentle mores, if there are any—but there are others, the *Valientes*, proud, independent and sometimes ferocious."

"That picture isn't encouraging," Lavarède replied, "but it won't stop me. For want of roads traced by humans, Nature has made one, since beaches follow both sides of the isthmus to take us through the neighboring republics. Isn't the Cordillera itself a route? It's parallel to the two seas and the numerous villages, whether Indian or immigrant, must have links between them. Anyway, if there are carnivorous animals in the forests, logically, there must be those whose mission is to be eaten, comestibles like the guinea-pig. Finally, if need be, we can open a route with machetes."

"I'll give you two of them—there's no shortage of them here. I'll do better than that. We—I mean the agents of the canal—have certain facilities for circulation on the railway. I'll take you as far as the middle of the isthmus, to the pass of Culebra in the middle of the Sierra. In the personnel under my orders I've noticed an Indian from Putriganti—Espiritu-Santo to the Spanish—who knows the west of the *Estado de Istmo* as far as Chiriqui. He has a great affection for whites since a French doctor saved his wife, who was threatened by death. If he agrees to accompany you, he'll be very useful."

"It's my star that sent you," said Armand, laughing. "Am I not something of a doctor?"

And the little caravan set off, including Bouvreuil, under Gérolans' guidance. If Lavarède had studied medicine, he had also studied engineering, and the works that he would have before his eyes interested him greatly. For his part, Bouvreuil was too determined to know the truth for the conversation not to come around to the spectacle that was beginning to strike them.

"The canal," said Gérolans, "first crosses a low plain extending between Colon and Monkey Hill and Lion Hill, where the excavation has been very easy. It's thereafter, between Gatum and Tabernilla, at the bottom of the Gamboa massif, that a lot of problems crop up."

"Gatum is that large township on the right?"

"Yes, it has the biggest banana warehouse in Central America, I believe. Export to New York began as soon as boats were designed capable of taking aboard and conserving large quantities of the fruit."

"Aren't we on the right bank of a river? Is that the famous Chagres, about which so many engineers talk?"

"Yes, we'll pass over to the left bank via the iron bridge at Barbacoas. Here, the Chagres has benevolent air, but further on it's terrible. For a start, look around, now, at those marshes, where it has been necessary to dig thirty-meter trenches. The subsoil is impermeable, and we lost thousands of human lives here."

Indeed, as far as the eye could see, the plain was strewn with pools of water with leaden reflections. A perpetual fog gloated over the muddy side-branches of the river. The travelers felt themselves enveloped by a heavy, sickening, salty atmosphere that provoked nausea.

"Hereabouts," said Gérolans, "abundant sweating exhausts a man. An inextinguishable thirst grips him. And, like a new Tantalus, he can't drink the water that surrounds him—that would be drinking death. Not to mention the mosquitoes, the chigoes, whose venomous suckers dig into the skins of travelers."

Eventually, they emerged from that Hell.

"Wouldn't it be possible to avoid that region?" Bouvreuil asked.

"It's the shortest route to reach the lowest pass through the Cordillera."

"In that case," said Lavarède, who had become very serious, "it would have been a better use of time, lives and money to commence work by draining the marshes. Our engineers have already accomplished that prodigy in France, and the Italians are imitating them in the Roman campagna."

They had left the railways some time before, and Gérolans was guiding his friends beyond Tabernilla. From there, they could look down on new trenches, and everything was topsy-turvy. After the marshes, the trail encountered the Chagres, a torrential river of which the promoters of the enterprise did not seem to have taken any account.

"It is, however, a peculiar watercourse," said Gérolans, "since, although one can pass over it at times almost dry-footed, it can happen that in two hours, after a rainstorm, its level rises by six or seven meters. Then the waters, flowing impetuously down the slopes, drag enormous blocks of stone with them. Not long ago, the trench was filled in and the works lost several weeks. They began again, and the Chagres began again too. It would have been comical if it hadn't had lugubrious consequences."

"But simple common sense would indicate to anyone the danger of establishing a worksite in such an inconvenient, unstable neighborhood!"

"That's exactly what the State councilor sent by the French government observed, in my presence."

"Well," said Lavarède, gravely, turning to his friends, "I was speaking too lightly just now. It's certain that one couldn't think of draining a marsh of this extent, maintained by torrents that come to empty out here. Before anything else, it's necessary to excavate another bed for the Chagres and deflect it away from the path of the canal. Then it would be mere child's play to sanitize the marsh."

Bouvreuil, amazed, was all ears. He was seized by a doubt, though. He interrogated Murlyton.

"Do these things seem possible to you?"

"I think," said the Englishman, "that it's the voice of reason itself."

"Is it really possible," said Bouvreuil to Gérolans, "to deflect a watercourse?"

"Of course. Sometimes a simple barrage is sufficient. There are ten or twelve well-known examples in France. It would be feasible here too. From

Tabrilla onwards, the escarpment begins. From that town to Obrasco, passing through Manuel and Gorgona—the mid-line of the waters is a little to the west of the latter locality—the Cordillera raises hillocks, imprisoning Lake Gambon with its undulations, from which the Chagres appears to emerges, although it's also alimented by another torrent coming from the East. Well, a barrage of a good size and sufficient thickness could send the river along another grove in the Sierra."

"Then Lavarède might have found the key to the continuation of the interrupted works?"

"Perhaps—for the remainder won't be any more difficult to excavate than the commencement was in the plain of Monkey Hill. Beyond the massif, toward the Pacific, through the valley of the Rio Grande, the track rejoins the vast bay of Panama, following an almost straight line."

"Oh! A straight line…that's dangerous, with natural accidents."

"No; after the depression of the rocky central ridge, one only has to traverse a fecund wooded region, in which, amid the richest vegetation in the world, the picturesque villages of Emperador, Paraiso, Miraflores, Corosel and La Boca are situated, ending up opposite the islands of Perico and Flamenco."

"But of course!" Bouvreuil exclaimed. "That's my report, which Lavarède has jus dictated to me. What a man! If only he were my son-in-law, he would soon have multiplied my fortune tenfold."

The instinctive egotism reappeared. The Vulture saw nothing but the exploitation, to his profit, of strength and intelligence. Lavarède gained from it, however, that the idea of ferocious reprisals—reprisals after the fashion of Don José—were no longer haunting his adversary's mind.

Meanwhile, Gérolans had sent someone to look for his Indian, who lived in San Pablo, to the south of the track, on the road to Bahia Soldado.

Tall and lithe, with a coppery complexion and an exceedingly soft gaze, the India as pure bred—which is now exceptional in the State of Panama. By virtue of his regularity and his polite obedience he had become the foreman of a crew; he was one of the rare natives remaining in the service of the Company. In the beginning they had been numerous, as had the blacks, but the marshes had soon caused them to disappear. And it is well-known that in order to recruit replacements it had been necessary to go as far as African negroes, Annamites and Chinamen. The region of the marshes had absorbed them all.

"Ramon," Gérolans said to him, "this is one of my compatriots, my friend, an engineer and a doctor, who has to go to Costa Rica. Will you guide him?"

Superb and dignified, the Indian looked at him. Gravely, without speaking, he reached out his hand. Armand misunderstood the gesture.

"Add," he said, smiling, "that I'm traveling without money."

Ramon's hand remained extended. Instinctively, Lavarède placed his own in it. A flash of joyful pride appeared in the Indian's visage. He had been treated as an equal, not a servant.

"You friend is mine, Caporal," he said to Gérolans.

"Why *Caporal?*" Armand asked.

"It's as if he were saying *cacique*, or *chief.*"

"But the white men say 'Captain' for *cacique.*"

"Ah, that's amplification, an exaggeration carried over from the Castilian language."

"So you really want to leave this place?" said Lavarède.

"Oh," said the Indian, in a melancholy tone, "I only stayed here out of gratitude to the Company doctor who cured my Hoé. All those of my race who didn't die in the 'hell-hole' have gone back to cultivate their tribal lands. I'll gladly leave, never to return. The road you need to follow is the one that leads to my mountain. We'll take it together, with your companion and mine."

He had indicated Aurett, who blushed.

"Shocking," murmured Murlyton.

"The young lady isn't my companion."

"Good…Hoé will salute your sister this evening, in my house in San Pablo."

There seemed to be no point explaining to the Indian that Aurett was not a relative. Gérolans made a sign no leave it at that.

"But I'm not alone," said Lavarède. "I have my tribe," he added, cheerfully, indicating Murlyton, who was slightly alarmed.

"They will march in your path. You are French, and a doctor; for that I love you and respect you. You are an engineer; I ought to obey you. But first, since you are French, come; I will take you to a place where you will have pride and contentment."

The others followed. As they went through Gorgone, Gérolans understood and smiled. The little troop took a mountain path, and climbed for a long time. When they reached the Cerro Grande, the Indian marched straight to a tall tree, made a sign to Lavarède indicating that he should climb it, and simply said: "Here it is."

"Oh!" said the Frenchman. "How beautiful it is!"

In the blink of an eye, all the others had similarly climbed into the branches of nearby trees, in order to see what was so beautiful. Only the Indian waited, placidly.

From that point, one could perceive both slopes of the Cordillera and the two immense oceans whose extend ended there, the valley of the Rio Grande leading to the Pacific and that of the Chagres to the Atlantic. The track of the canal, interrupted by the mountain, seemed an infinitesimally tiny human effort in the face of imposing Nature.

"A superb viewpoint!"

"And rare," added Gérolans. "With the tropical vegetation of the isthmus, there's almost nowhere else from which you can see the whole."

"Thank you, Ramon, for having brought me here," said Lavarède, coming back down to the ground.

"It's the French tree," said the Indian, simply.

"Which signifies...?"

It was Gérolans who had to explain, while they resumed the route to San Pablo.

"In 1890, a ship's lieutenant, Bonaparte-Wyse, who was the most ardent apostle of the work of the canal,[21] with another naval officer, Armand Reclus, ended up after long research discovering the place in the Sierra from which one had before the eyes the demonstration of the project's objective."

Murlyton seemed as satisfied as Lavarède. "You're content," he said. "Me too..."

"Not as much as me," replied Lavarède, "since it's a matter of a discovery made by one of my compatriots."

"And I say," the Englishman riposted, "that I'm more content than you, for, if it was a French officer who was the first to see the place where the two seas are so close together, it was an officer in the English navy whose was the first to foresee the place to which your compatriot had to come."

That was true, and British pride had reason. In 1831 Captain George Peacock determined summarily, but with a sure eye, the line that a communication between the two oceans ought to follow; the railway, and then the canal, had justified his anticipations. In the same way, the Scotsman William Paterson was one of the first to divine the importance of the American isthmus, which he called "the key to the world," and wanted to conquer for his fatherland. He was beaten and expelled in 1700 by the Spanish general Thomas Herero, who has a statue in Panama to commemorate that feat.

"It's well-known, in any case," Lavarède said, having become serious, "that it's not just in our day that there's been a question of piercing the American isthmus. The first person who thought of it was none other than Charles the Fifth, on the advice of Alvaro de Saavedra Cerón, who, in 1523, charged Cortés with seeking *el secreto del estrecho*—the secret of the strait. In 1528, the Portuguese Galvão boldly proposed the execution of the project to the Emperor, and Gomara, that author of a history of the Indies, which appeared a few years later, even indicated three different routes."

"But in that case," said Murlyton, "Why has it taken three centuries for studies to be resumed on the basis of Humboldt's indications?"

"Because Charles the Fifth's successor, the devout Philippe the Second, didn't want to modify nature, for fear of changing what God had wrought...and humanity had to wait until a French adventurer, Baron Thierry, who later be-

---

[21] Lucian Bonaparte-Wyse (1845-1909), the grandson of Napoléon Bonaparte's brother Lucien and the son of the Irish politician Sir Thomas Wyse, was the naval officer who obtained the concession from the Colombian government to permit the building of the canal. His associate Armand Reclus (1843-1927) was the elder brother of the famous geographer Élisée Reclus.

came king of New Zealand, obtained a concession in 1825, of which he was unable to profit, and for which President Bolivar had studies carried out for the route in 1829. Since then, there have been no less than sixteen projects proposed by engineers of all nations."

"You know a great many things about the past," said the Indian suddenly, to Lavarède, "but perhaps you don't know certain things about the present that I have seen with my own eyes, and which will explain to you why the work has been so difficult and troublesome."

"What do you mean?"

"That the situation created for the workers was atrocious. The water of the marshes was deadly, the heat crushing and debilitating. Where could the men— he whites especially—recover their exhausted strength? In the unsupervised canteens where the tariffs regulated by the Company were not observed. Thus, certain 'businessmen' sold French water at half a piastre a bottle. If you bear in mind that the marshland has no drinkable water, you'll see that the workers were condemned to die of thirst or dysentery."

"That's not possible!"

"Yes," Gérolans put in. "Unfortunately, Ramon isn't exaggerating. What he calls French water is Saint-Galmier water,[22] which the vendors dared to sell for two francs fifty a bottle. So, frequent riots took place. Several supply depots were pillaged and burned, but the trade was so profitable that after two or three disasters of that sort, the estimable businessmen left the isthmus with considerable savings."

"Alas, how many poor devils did that lack of supervision condemn to death!"

"There too," Ramon put in, "your companions have paid a considerable tribute. After the annihilation of the French crews, they were formed of men of all countries and all colors, men with white, bronze or black skin. But you will understand why my brothers, the Indians of the Chiriqui, and also the black Zambos of the isthmus, have obstinately refused to participate in the works."

Bouvreuil took notes. These were as many elements that the enquiry was furnishing his report. But where would he write it? When would he send it? He no longer had any idea.

When the Indian had rejoined his carriage, a "fly," and had installed Lavarède, Aurett and Murlyton therein, the usurer dared not request a place there. To be frank, Lavarède had been very naïve to bring him along.

With Gérolans, Bouvreuil returned to the railway and went back to Colon to await Don José's reply. First he cabled a telegram to Pénélope, saying to hr:

Not returning yet. Departing for God knows where following Lavarède. Astonishing man. Go rest at Sens, in our country house. Await news.

---

[22] Nowadays known as Badoit mineral water.

In the meantime, the little caravan had arrived at Ramon's habitation. The Englishwoman received the most fraternal hospitality from the Indian woman Hoé. Lavarède, Murlyton and the Indian bivouacked as best they could, and it was agreed that they would set out *en route* the next morning.

Did not Lavarède have reason to be proud of his lucky star? Had not chance, mingled with a little initiative, served him every time he found himself at grips with any embarrassment, by bringing him unexpected help?

Such were the reflections that our hero made the next morning, as he made his way along the road from San Pablo, heading toward Chorrero, leaving Arrayan to his left. The word "road" would appear a trifle pretentious to a European, accustomed to our broad and well-maintained roads. In all the countries of the isthmus, including Mexico, there are roads, sometimes traced and at other times divined, along which carts hold jolting competitions, and which only mules can follow. Often, they are not even paths.

"All the same," he said, aloud, "what splendid vegetation!"

"So fine," murmured the Indian, "that it will soon cover the workings of the canal if they're interrupted for long." So saying, he indicated the region that our voyagers were leaving behind.

The three men, Armand, Ramon and Murlyton, marched together. Hoé and Aurett were in the fly with the luggage, hauled by a picturesquely harnessed mule, which guided itself without needing any *arrieva* to direct it. By eye, the animal followed its master.

The two young women had immediately become good friends. The Indian's naïve simplicity had charmed the honest purity of the Englishwoman, and vice versa.

"So," said Hoé, "the young man is neither your husband or your brother, as we thought…but you follow him everywhere!"

"In company with my father," said Aurett, blushing.

"But you're very interested in him. Is he your fiancé, then?"

"No, no…"

"But you have affection for him?"

"Me!"

"Yes, that's evident, obvious in your disturbance and emotion when you talk about the dangers he has run, and those he has yet to run."

"He has a noble heart, and he's my friend, that's all."

"Ah!" the Indian relied, simply, darting a glance at her companion that visibly embarrassed her.

Then the two women fell silent. Indians do not talk much. Aurett was thoughtful, wondering whether the naïve Hoé might not have guessed correctly. In any case, if she was attached to her traveling companion, it was still in an entirely unconscious fashion. She was revolted by the idea that her affection might appear so tender as to motivate such a suspicion.

At that moment, Ramon leaned toward a plant, a few sprigs of which he picked. He handed them to his wife, who put them away carefully. Lavarède asked for an explanation.

"It's guao," the Indian replied. "The plant that cures the bite of the coral snake."

"Ah! The pretty little snake that resembles a woman's bracelet?"

"Pretty, indeed, with its red color and its golden velvet rings; small too, as it does not surpass twenty or twenty-five centimeters—but terrible; its bite causes instantaneous death."

"Brr!" said Armand. "And you can preserve us from it?"

"Yes, with the aid of that plant. Does the Creator Spirit not always place the remedy near the evil?"

"That's true."

Murlyton, who had been listening without speaking, began walking prudently, looking at the ground carefully.

"What are you doing?" the Indian asked, smiling.

"I'm looking out for little snakes."

"Really? Then don't look at your feet. It's higher up that it's necessary to keep watch."

"Why is that?" asked the two men.

"Yes—the coral snake winds itself around the ends of branches that overhang the road. You can easily mistake it for a flower."

At an indicated spot the experiment could be made. A clump of trees encroached upon the road. There was *conacaste*, a kind of mahogany of inferior quality, *madera negra*, also known as the *madre de cacao* because cacao grows in its shade, and *chapulastapa*, producer of a brown wood, reputed to be the most beautiful tree of those climes. At the tip of one branch, under which the carriage was about to pass, a red dot began to agitate. Ramon took a flexible twig and brought down the coral snake with a sharp blow, cutting it in two. A strong odor of bitter almonds immediately emerged from it.

"Prussic acid," said Armand.

The animal had fallen on to a verdant tuft. Murlyton at his daughter's request, wanted to pick it up, in order to keep it as a souvenir, but he withdrew his hand swiftly, uttering a cry of pain.

"Is the coral snake still alive?" Lavarède asked.

"No," said the Indian, "But that bush on which its cadaver is resting is a *chichicaste*,[23] and your friend has been stung. Here's your snake; give it to the young lady."

"But you haven't been stung?"

"It's sufficient to hold one's breath to be able to touch the nettle-bush with impunity."

---

[23] *Urera baccifera.*

Armand certainly knew many things, but he had not known that.

"One learns while traveling," he said, smiling at Murlyton, who obtained some relief by pressing his wound with a *quita-calzones* leaf that Ramon gave him.[24]

There were few incidents thereafter; the landscape changed. There was no longer the forceful tropical vegetation, brightly-colored flowers and strangely-formed fruits, but the thick dry grass known as *para*, which constitutes a special forage, marvelous and nourishing. That modification indicated the proximity of haciendas—ranches and agricultural plantations, whose owners are always called "Spaniards" no matter what their nationality might be. For the Indians and the poor, every bourgeois is a Spaniard and has the right to a humble salute, almost a genuflection, accompanied by the words: "You Grace." That opening of conversation goes back a long way, two centuries, to the conquest.

Lavarède's astonishment was considerable on perceiving, not far from the road, a red deer stag absolutely identical to its fellows in the forest of Fontainebleau. The animal had emerged from the high grass of the savannah to browse the *para*—worse luck for him. Ramon felled the deer with a single bullet, and thus, with few tortillas prepared by Hoé, assured the subsistence of the little caravan.

Another astonishment awaited our friend an hour later. He saw a peon who as gravely placing large pebbles on top of one another.

"What are you doing there, José?" he asked. All Indians answer to the name José, as all Indian women do to the name Maria; from Mexico to South America the tradition still persists.

"As Your Grace can see. I'm building a safety column."

Lavarède opened his eyes and ears, but it was necessary for Ramon to explain that unclear explanation.

"An Indian who is leaving his home for a time heaps up twenty-two stones, not one more or less. He piles them up, and, on his return, if the column is intact, it's because his wife has not ceased thinking about him."

In spite of his native gravity, Murlyton could not help smiling. "But might not the wind, or the rain, not to mention a storm, break the fragile edifice?"

The other Indian looked at the Europeans. "Undoubtedly," he said, "but it's still necessary for the saint of Esquipulas to permit it."

Another request for explanation.

"That miraculous saint," said Ramon, "is a great negro Christ who lived far from here in Guatemala. He suffered all the evils on earth, plus the hatred of his wife, and as he was a poor Jesus who loved Indians, his fellows, he worked this miracle for his friends of the savannah."

---

[24] The reference is probably to *Digitalis purpurea*, although the designation does not seem to be common.

That legend was recounted without any intention of joking, but also without exaltation, as a natural thing, in such god faith that Lavarède did not dare show manifest any doubt, lest he cause his friend chagrin.

Toward evening, they came back to the savannah again. Armand had not wanted to stop in Chorerra or in any village of *ladinos*—which is to say, descendants of the conquerors of old, Spanish/Indian half-breeds. There, he would have needed money to pay for his shelter.

With blankets and branches, Ramon had soon improvised a shelter. Hoé cooked a haunch of venison. Murlyton passed round some old brandy from his reserves, and the night passed almost tranquilly.

We say "almost" because the chigoes and mosquitoes tormented the English violently. Nevertheless, Aurett endured it bravely. Fundamentally, the child found adventures amusing.

As for Lavarède, following the advice and example of Ramon, he had gone to sleep in the highest branches of an *almendro*, which overlapped at a height of fifteen meters with those of its neighbor, a cedar. He established himself astride a branch, well braced to the left and right, and, wrapped in a mule-blanket, slept like a judge. The flight of mosquitoes is heavy and low; there was nothing to fear up there but the tropical bats known as vampires, but Ramon kept them away by smoking a certain aromatic plant.

At daybreak, our friends looked at one another. Poor Aurett had a horribly inflamed shoulder, because while she slept she had disturbed the thick coverlet in which Hoé had wrapped her, and the malevolent nocturnal insects had been able to assault her pale flesh. The unfortunate Murlyton no longer had a human face; his nose was inflamed, his eyelids swollen and his cheeks were dotted with enormous lumps, making him a mask that even pity could not prevent the others from finding comical. From his portable pharmacy he took alkali and phenol, which almost cured his wounds.

Another peril is always to be feared in such journeys: fever. Murlyton had his remedy—quinine—but Ramon had indicated another, simpler and more practical.

"You can avoid fever be drinking rum grog," he told Lavarède. "I have some in my luggage—it's Antilles rum. Afterwards, you eat little and take a cold bath every day."

"Eating little is easy," our friend replied, laughing. "As for the cold bath, we encounter enough *rios* along the way to facilitate that hygienic operation."

VII. In Costa Rica

For a week, Lavarède had the leisure to understand the inanity of scorn for wealth, because he was the only one going on foot.

Murlyton, weary of walking, had simply bought a mule from a passing Indian and, having mounted it without a saddle, escorted the carriage in which Aurett and Ramon's wife were ensconced.

Although a trifle crestfallen, Armand put on a brave face at this ill-fortune, and doubtless the god who was protecting him was pleased by his good humor, because he came to his aid on the ninth day.

They had all slept in a *tule* pueblo. *Tule* is the true name of the people the Spaniards incorrectly named Indians. They were crossing the great savannah, heading for Chiriqui, one of the numerous volcanoes in the region, always in eruption, when the journalist spotted a muleteers' camp near a fast-flowing stream, the Papalayito.

There were only two mules; they were browsing. The brasses of their harness were gleaming in the sunlight, and their appearance contrasted with the wretched allure of the two men who were guarding them, lying in the shade of a tree.

"Are they arrieros?" Lavarède asked.

"No," said Ramon. "They don't have the costume. One of the two is a Zambo and the other a Do Indian; his tribe is a long way behind us, south off the workings of the isthmus."

"From which you conclude?"

"That they're thieves. We'll soon see."

Abruptly approaching the, he said: "Thank you, Comrades, for having come to meet us with our mounts. These mules were to wait for us near Chiriqui—but I don't see our *mozos* with them." Then without saying another word, he mounted one of the mules. Lavarède imitated him.

The Zambo and the Do looked at them in surprise. Ramon went on: "His Grace will give a piastre to each of you to thank you for the trouble you've taken."

The two men immediately put out their hands. Lavarède, who did not have a single cuartilla, understood and reacted with aplomb.

"Rogues!" he cried, raising his stick. "You were trying to steal my mules."

"No, no, Your Grace! It's Hyeronimo, the Costa Rican muleteer, who sent us, promising us a good price..."

"That's all right...go and look for him at the house of the Alcalde of Galdera."

And, with the impudence of an honest man, he moved off, followed by Ramon. For once, the Indian's gravity gave way to merriment. Laughing, he drew the moral of the incident.

"It's a double pleasure to rob a thief."

At least they knew one thing: that the mules belonged to a Costa Rican muleteer named Hyeronimo. And to judge by the splendor of the harness, that arriero must be in the service of some high-ranking individual.

A few days later, Ramon let it be known that they had arrived where he wanted to go.

"This is the region inhabited by my tribe. Your road is ahead of you. To-day, you'll leave Colombian territory for that of the Costa Rican Republic. Keep the two mules that God has given us; they will service you and your companion. Your friend the Englishman has one too; you will thus be sure to make good progress. Hoé and I will go to find our parents and our brothers. I have been glad to guide you and be useful to you; do me the honor of shaking my hand."

That speech did not lack grandeur in its simplicity, and it was not without a certain emotion that Lavarède separated from that friend of a few days, who had rendered him such great service.

"Perhaps we'll never see one another again, Ramon..."

"*Quien sabe?*" murmured the Indian: *Who can tell?*

"But neither I nor my companions will forget you. Wherever I am, if you have need of me, you have only to call to me—even if I'm on the other side of the world."

"And me, likewise," said Ramon, resolutely.

Then they parted.

The route was not too difficult, all three of our friends being mounted on excellent mules.

Only one incident distinguished that last day: subterranean rumblings were audible—but that was not surprising in that volcanic region, where earthquakes occur sixty times a year.

Dusk fell. As far as the eye could see, enormous rocky massifs were piled up in all directions, in the gathering mist. Our voyagers nibbled a maize tortilla, from the provision that Hoé had left them. It was necessary to sustain themselves, at least, since they did not know where they might find shelter.

On the frontier there was a little hut, but it was only a shelter for soldiers. Without stopping, the caravan saluted the three somewhat ragged warriors who represented the army of the United States of Colombia, and he mules moved on to Costa Rican soil. A hundred meters further on there was a right-angled bend in the road. Suddenly, Armand, who was in the lead, perceived a kind of encampment behind a rock; there were arrieros and muleteers, but also a few soldiers. He stopped and signaled to the English duo to approach prudently.

At the same moment, shouts rang out. The muleteers, all on their feet, were all trying to shout louder than one another.

"There they are!"

"Those are our mules!"

"I recognize the harness."

"The thieves have the cheek to come here!"

"Hyeronimo! Where are you?"

"Look for him! Tell him to come right away."

"In the meantime, let's take this lot to Captain Morales."

"Oh, their goose is cooked!"

In the blink of an eye, Lavarède, Murlyton and Miss Aurett were surrounded, pulled off their mules by twenty-four vigorous hands, jostled somewhat excessively, and finally taken to the Captain, who was lounging on a tree trunk, smoking a cigarette. They had not had time to explain.

A man was sitting beside the officer, enveloped in a cape whose high collar hid is face. He leaned toward his neighbor and spoke a few rapid words to him in a low voice. The officer immediately stood up.

"Silence!" he said, authoritatively. "Leave that young woman and her honorable father alone, and another time, try to recognize people more accurately."

The arrieros went away.

"Señorita," the Captain continued, "and you, Señor, we are here by order of our new governor, Don José Miraflor y Courramazas, to serve as your escort and do you honor. Those mules were intended specifically for Your Graces. But we were only expecting two visitors and there are three of you. Who are you, the third?"

"Armand Lavarède, free citizen of the French Republic, traveling...for his pleasure."

Hyeronimo arrived at that moment. "The French Señor," he said, was mounted on one of my mules, which disappeared three days ago. I accuse him of having stolen it."

"Error, estimable but naïve arriero. Three days ago, I was not here. As for your mule—or, rather, mules—far from having stolen them, we have recovered them from the thieves. I have witnesses, in any case; Mademoiselle and Monsieur can testify that I'm telling the truth."

While he recounted the incident on the road thanks to which Ramon had taken custody of the animals, the man in the cape spoke to the officer again.

"All that is very well," concluded Captain Morales, but I'm not an Alcalde or a Judge, and don't have the authority to decide. I am the head of the escort, and we shall conduct the guests of the Señor Gobernador to him with all the honors due to them. As for you, Señor Frenchman, I arrest you on a charge of the theft of the two mules. You can explain yourself to a court as soon as we arrive in Cambo."

There was no argument. Appearances were against Armand; he understood that, and placed himself, meekly and fatalistically, between the designated soldiers. Then the escort and the travelers set off, our poor friend on foot, the others mounted. His good genius, Aurett, was alert, however.

"My father had a mule of his own," she said to the officer. "I see that no one is making use of it, and I would be obliged if you were to give it to the young man, whom we know, and who is the victim of an error."

"Oh, that can be done," replied Morales, gallantly. "I have orders to comply with all your desires."

And Lavarède at least had the consolation of going on muleback too.

"In any case," said the leader of the escort, "We have a long way to travel this evening. At the moment we're skirting the Cerro del Brenon; after crossing the Rio Coto and the Rio Colorado we'll stop at the foot of the Cordillera de Las Cruces. There is a rancho there where rooms and supper are being prepared for your lordships."

The young Englishwoman reflected. This surprise awaiting her on Costa Rican soil did not suggest anything good to her, and Don José's name did nothing to reassure her on that score. After all, though, her father was there, and Armand too, if needed. It therefore seemed that she had nothing to fear.

Meanwhile, the mysterious man in the concealing cape had let Captain Morales go on ahead, and, having sowed his mule down, fell into step beside Lavarède. At first he did not say anything, but only uttered a little muffled giggle, which intrigued Armand greatly.

After a few more strides, however, he spoke, and said to his neighbor in excellent French: "Well, my dear Monsieur, I believe I shall have my revenge for the *Lorraine*."

Lavarède could not suppress an exclamation of amazement. "Bouvreuil!"

"The same."

"What good luck, my dear landlord, to encounter you in this remote land!"

"Mock, Monsieur, mock. He who laughs last laughs longest, and you'll see tomorrow how good your luck has been."

"So you've cooked up some new rascality with your pal, the flashy foreigner?"

"First of all, my dear Monsieur, my pal, as you call him, is the master here. He represents the government, and as he won't refuse me anything, you're somewhat in my power. To him, the demoiselle; to me, the handsome Parisian."

"Really," said Armand, shivering in spite of himself at the thought of that division.

"And since, this time, you're well and truly beaten, I can't refuse myself the satisfaction of telling you in advance what your fate will be."

"Let's see the future, then, my dear magician."

"It's quite simple. Tomorrow, you'll be sentenced to a year in prison for the theft of Hyeronimo's mules. In these parts, a twelve-month holiday isn't too painful, and you won't get old. But you'll have lost your wager and your cousin's millions. I can even predict that after that period of meditation, you'll marry Pénélope."

"Brrr!" said Armand, trembling ironically.

"Exactly: you'll have the joy of becoming my son-in-law."

"But Monsieur Bouvreuil, that's an increased penalty not foreseen by Costa Rican law…and I promise you, for my part, to make efforts worthy of Latude and the Baron von der Trenck to escape the destiny with which you're threatening me."[25]

"Do whatever you like; you won't escape. Oh, perhaps you were wrong to pass this way, where my friend Don José is in autocratic command, as prefect and governor…in brief, as dictator!"

"As befits any functionary of a free nation," added Lavarède.

He had to confess, however, that Bouvreuil was right. Yes, it had been a poor inspiration to come and place himself in the claws of his adversaries in this way. But what could he do now? Resign himself, for this evening, sleep on it, and wait until tomorrow to make a decision.

That was what he did, when they arrived at the Rancho del Golfito.

Bouvreuil, benevolently, had not condemned him to die of hunger; his victory achieved, the vulture as tamed, and Lavarède ate supper at the same table as Aurett, Murlyton, Morales and his "future father-in-law." By virtue of a special favor, the soldiers guarding him remained outside and it was the muleteer Hyeronimo who served the Frenchman more particularly. He did not spare the exceedingly strong Spanish wine that is commonly drunk in Central America.

The ranchero had distinguished himself as a host; he sensed that he was dealing with important people, and Concha, his wife, had prepared excellent dishes of all kinds. The menu ought to be conserved; it was the first of that kind that our friends had eaten, and the Englishwoman inscribed in hr notebook:

Soup of black haricot beans and crushed sea-biscuits.

Chaplet of iguana eggs.

Roast young parrot.

Cucumbers in sauce.

Preserves of guava, pineapple, etc.

All washed down with Alicante, Val-de-peñas and aguardiente.

It is necessary to confess all in this narration; the supper was joyful. Murlyton was very drunk, and Lavarède even more so. At least, it is necessary to suppose so, for he fell asleep at the table and the mozos were obliged to carry him to the room set aside for him. One would be wrong to think that it was a

---

[25] Jean-Henri Latude (1725-1805) escaped from Vincennes after being imprisoned for offending Madame de Pompadour, and then embarked on a long career of escapes and recaptures, which made him famous. Friedrich von der Trenck (1726-1794) escaped from the fortress of Glatz in 1746 after being imprisoned by Frederick the Great

ruse on our friend's part. No, he really was asleep, and he slept as only a poor devil could who had been dosed with a narcotic on the instructions of that Mephistopheles Bouvreuil. He slept so deeply that he did not hear a thing, and did not even perceive the dirty trick played on him by the man who wanted him for a son-in-law.

Stealthily, in the middle of the night, Bouvreuil went into Armand's room. The arrieros had undressed him and put him to bed. He was snoring like a set of bagpipes and a piledriver. The digestion of iguana eggs and young parrots tends to be noisy.

"Whatever you say," the satanic landlord murmured, "you won't be continuing your journey."

Slowly and methodically he picked up the journalist's clothes and made a parcel of them, only leaving him his shirt, underpants and boots. Then he went out, threw the packet of clothes into a ravine in the sierra some distance away, and went to bed, his soul tranquil—which permitted him to enjoy an agreeable repose.

It was, in fact, quite simple. In order to travel, if Armand succeeded in escaping Costa Rican justice, he would need clothing that he could only procure by paying for it; that is obligatory in every country in the world. Now, as he only had five sous, he had every chance of remaining in the lost Rancho de Golfito for a very long time. Even if he found the opportunity to get away, he would violate the clause of the testament. Lavarède was caught this time, and well trapped.

When everyone woke up in the morning, and Murlyton and Aurett were in the saddle and the escort in position, Captain Morales observed the absence of his prisoner.

"He's still asleep," Bouvreuil whispered to him. "It will suffice to leave a muleteer and a few soldiers, who can bring him before the Alcalde of Cambo later. Don't waste any time completing your mission, which is to take the young Englishwoman to Don José at the Château de la Cruz."

A military man only knows his orders. Morales carried them out. Furthermore, the French señor was not in the official program; it was by chance, of which Bouvreuil was able to take advantage, that he had been found in the expected caravan, under a hypothetical accusation of theft. It was quite natural that he should resume his march without him.

But as soon as they set out, Aurett, who had recognized Bouvreuil the previous evening, and who knew about the conversation exchanged between the two enemies on the road, asked in a detached fashion where Monsieur Armand was.

"Sleeping off his wine," replied the hateful individual. "He's staying at the ranchero, under the guard of the muleteer Hyeronimo and two soldiers."

"But I thought that we weren't to leave him, or at least not to lose sight of him."

77

"Oh! That's true," said Murlyton.

"Have no fear," Bouvreuil riposted. "He'll catch up with us during the day. His guard has received the necessary orders. As for us, we ought to recognize the politeness of Monsieur the Governor and respond to his amiable invitation without delay."

That same evening, Captain Morales received the congratulations of the Señor Gobernador for having brought the illustrious persons confided to his care to the "château."

What Don José pompously called the Château de la Cruz was a hacienda surrounded by coffee plantations and enclosed by thick cactus hedges. It was situated on the road leading to the gold and quartz mines, and then to the port of Cambo, his official residence on the Golfo Dulce.

He began by showing his guests around, with the manners of a caballero, but his true nature, of a somewhat savage adventurer, soon showed itself. The civilized man disappeared behind the despot who sensed that everything was permissible. Squarely and brutally, he asked Murlyton for Aurett's hand.

"The padre is here, in the chapel that I've had set up, and the ceremony can take place immediately."

"My daughter is a protestant," Murlyton objected, at least wanting to gain time. "The marriage wouldn't be valid."

"Nothing prevents it from being validated later, before your consul."

"But I refuse to get married!" exclaimed the young woman. "And you wouldn't dare constrain the will of an English citizen!"

"I would dare," said José, with an evil snigger.

In response to a curt order, four soldiers surrounded Murlyton and tied him up.

"Imprison him and talk sense to him," said José, "until he decides to give his consent." He had pronounced the last words in a perfidious tone, while gazing at poor Aurett.

"Monsieur," she said, resolutely "I may die, but I'll never marry you." And, searching with her eyes for a weapon, she prepared to defend her honor. But there was no weapon to hand.

Don José approached her, honeyed and obsequious. "No, Miss," he sniggered, with hypocritical softness, "but you'll cause the death of your father, if, in an hour's time, you haven't made the gesture and pronounced the word that I expect: to give me your pretty hand and say yes!"

And, leaving her devastated, the Spaniard went out with Bouvreuil, who murmured in a low voice: "Lavarède won't have the little Englishwoman's millions, but it seems to me that my terrible friend José is pushing the abuse of his authority a little far."

VIII. A President's Odyssey

In the meantime, what had become of Lavarède?

Waking up later than the others, his head weighed down by the previous evening's libations and chemistry, it took him some time to take account of his situation. Where was he? What was he doing there? The chimeras of his dreams were still haunting his mind.

A ray of bright sunlight, however, warm and dazzling, irrupted into his room and brought him back to reality. He remembered Bouvreuil's threats, the peril that Aurett was about to run, and hastened to get up. There, a surprise awaited him, comical at first, and then annoying: no more clothes; no more weapons.

After the astonishment came the indignation "Those mozos, perhaps the soldiers...the thieves!"

Then came the reflection. "Of course, it's a rogue's trick...so find the rogue...no one but Bouvreuil."

And the anger: "It's the thirteenth of June. Oh, is the thirteenth going to bring me misfortune?"

Then Lavarède calls out. Concha responds. He asks her what time it is. It's nearly eight o'clock in the morning. He learns that the others left at daybreak.

"Your Grace is presently alone in the rancho," Concha tells him.

"But I can hear voices out there below my window."

"Oh, those are the soldiers guarding Your Grace."

"Solders? What an honor! And what precaution!"

"Yes, with Hyeronimo the Brave."

"Hyeronimo the muleteer."

"The same."

In the other hemisphere, as in our old world, women are inclined to be chatty, especially when talking to an elegant cavalier, even in a summary costume. Lavarède was therefore able to talk at his ease with the genial Concha.

"Tell me, lovely ranchera, do you know why they call Hyeronimo 'the Brave.'?"

"Oh, everyone in these parts knows that."

"But I'm not from these parts."

"It was after one of our revolutions, a year ago. He was the one who gave the signal for the pronunciamento."

"Ah!"

"Yes, and two months ago, when President General Zelaya was sent packing, in order to bring back President Doctor Guzman, he was the one who fired the first shot of the musket."[26]

"His rifle's a repeater, then..."

"I don't understand."

"It doesn't matter. He makes revolutions come and go...but the fellow's only a muleteer."

"Oh, Señor, he has a sensitive soul; he wouldn't hurt a guinea-pig. He always fires into the air. Besides which, it's well-known that in Costa Rica, we're not as bloodthirsty as people in the other neighboring Republics. Our revolutions never shed a drop of blood."

Armand could not help smiling on hearing that history lesson, given by such a gracious professor. Leaning out of the widow, however, he saw a fourth individual chatting with those he referred to in jest as his "guard of honor."

"Jesus Maria!" said Concha. "That's General Zelaya!"

"The former president?"

"In person!"

"The one before Dr. Guzman?"

"Of course—there aren't two..."

"Does he want to come back?"

"That, Señor, I don't know...but I'll run to welcome him, for he's much loved."

"What! Why was he overthrown, then?"

"Because he refused to promote all the colonels. He thought there were enough generals."

"How many were there?"

"Three hundred."

"And how many soldiers in the army?"

"Five hundred."

Lavarède burst out laughing—laughter that Concha's astonished expression rendered even louder. However, she left in order to place herself under the general's orders, leaving our friend scantily dressed but furnished with the complete baggage of a Costa Rican politician. At present, he knew his Republic as well as anyone. And he lent an even more attentive ear to the conversation that was going on in the courtyard between the general and his guards.

This is what he heard:

It was ex-President Zelaya who was speaking. "Hyeronimo, our party is counting on you. That wretch Guzman, come in the name of *los serviles*, hasn't kept any of his promises, and what's more, he wants to bring back the Jesuits!

---

[26] These characters are fictitious, but at the time the novel was written, the president of Honduras was José Zelaya and the El Salvadoran minister serving as that country's representative in the U.S.A. was named Dr. Guzman.

Last year, the signal for the revolution went out from the province of Nicoya. Let it go out this time from the Golfo Dulce, and let it be, as always, Hyeronimo the Brave who gives it. But what's the matter with you? You seem hesitant..."

"Excellency," the muleteer replied, "I'm not refusing absolutely, but I need to be better informed...will there be any danger?"

"None. Cambo, José's residence, as well as his 'château,' as the European pompously calls it, are populated with our friends. Our party is ready. You know full well that when *los libres* stir things up, it's because they're certain of success."

"But what do I, personally, stand to gain from this new revolution?"

"You can ask for whatever you want, for you and these two men—doubtless your servants?"

"No, Excellency; we're guarding a Frenchman; José wants us to keep him away from the Château de la Cruz all day."

"Leave the Frenchman in peace; José's affairs are only of interest to him. I'm counting on you, and I'm taking the road to the capital to prepare the movement."

And, throwing him a purse full of piastres and dollars, Genera Zelaya left. But he had not only sown the seeds of revolt among his own people; one remark had revived Lavarède's suspicions.

Why did José want to keep him away all day. Obviously, to accomplish some villainous enterprise against the young Englishwoman, his friend. It was necessary, at all costs, to catch up with her and reach the Château de la Cruz.

But how?

After a moment's reflection, he smiled. He had it.

He immediately went down to the courtyard, in his primitive costume, after having picked up a chair, and addressed himself to the muleteer.

"My friend," he said, "I heard everything, and if you wish, I'm yours. Let's march against Don José."

To his great surprise, however, Hyeronimo shook his head. The soldiers made gestures of fatalistic resignation.

"No, Señor," said the muleteer, with a certain practicality. "This time, I won't give the signal. First of all, you can take it for granted that Don José will resist—the general warned me of that without suspecting it. He hasn't yet received his salary, and he'll never go empty-handed. And then, we can't think of it. He's lived in Europe; he's armed; he'll shoot at us. He's not an old Costa Rican like us. Blood will be shed. We're determined that it won't be ours."

"Well then, I offer you mine..."

The three men looked at him in amazement. They did not think him chivalrous, but slightly mad. Is there not, in any case, a seed of madness in heroism, a noble but certain folly?

But he brandished his chair in a somewhat menacing fashion. It was a good bamboo chair, solid and flexible: a dangerous weapon in the hands of a determined man. The indigenes, without needing to consult one another, fell into accord. It was necessary not to annoy the European. While accepting the sacrifice that the new adherent of their part proposed, however, the idea occurred to them to take a few sage precautions, inspired by the spirit of reason.

"That's all very well if Zelaya's conspiracy succeeds," said the muleteer, "but if he fails…Don José won't forgive me for having let you escape in order to go to Cambo to give the signal for the revolution."

"Nor us," added the two soldiers.

Lavarède frowned, and struck the ground with his chair. Immediately, one of the warriors, a Terraba Indian by birth—they are very peaceful agriculturalists—had a practical idea.

"If the French seigneur would care to tie us up, or at least hobble our feet, it would make it impossible for us to pursue him, and it will be obvious that we aren't his accomplices."

"All right," said Armand, "but time is pressing. Tie one another up at the first sign of bad news you receive, and that will suffice."

"Your grace is too kind."

"As for you, Hyeronimo, I'll take your mule—the best one."

"Oh, Señor, my bread and butter?"

The chair quivered.

"Take it, take it!" the arriero hastened to add. "The best one is Matagna. Look at him—one would think he were an English horse."

"Good. I'm lacking more than one respectable garment. I can't see me starting a revolution in cotton underpants., even in a warm country."

"Your Excellency doesn't want me to take off my clothes!"

Tranquilly, the journalist raised the bamboo chair, his arms taut. "Exactly so—my excellency wants nothing else. It's the best means of protecting you in case of reprisals. Come on—I'll strip you whether you like it or not."

"You have two costumes," the Terraba observed. "One of leather underneath and one of embroidered velvet on top."

That was the custom when a convoy of muleteers had to traverse mountainous country where the temperature is subject to abrupt changes, as in that region. Hyeronimo looked at the Indian askance, darted a glance at the chair, and finally took off the broad trousers with laces and his leather waistcoat-cum-jacket, which Armand immediately put on. A sombrero borrowed from the ranchero completed his metamorphosis.

Our Parisian looked every inch the indigene. "By the way," he said, "what is the signal that I have to give?"

"The same as last year—three gunshots."

"Give me your revolver, then."

"But I don't have one! And even if I had one, I wouldn't give it to Your Grace!"

"Why not?"

82

"With your bad European habits, you'd be capable of shooting at people."

"Right!" said Armand, laughing. "I'll have to find a rifle that speaks for itself. Let's go!"

Having mounted Matagna, Lavarède urged the mule to a rapid trot, and set off through the mountains toward the gold and quartz mines. Already alerted by Zelaya, groups were waiting along the way. They recognized Hyeronimo's mule and gave him an ovation.

"Hurrah for the liberator of the people!"

Good! Now I'm a liberator, Lavarède thought, and thought it necessary to give them a little speech as he passed by.

There are phrases that always succeed, and he employed them.

"Hyeronimo the Brave is on his way to rouse the peoples of eastern Costa Rica," he said to then, in substance. "I'm rousing the peoples of the West. Follow me to La Cruz, and lets overthrow the tyrants!"

"*Vivan los libros!*" replied the conspirators.

Lavarède was applying a slight twist to the truth, but even philosophers recognize that it is sometimes necessary to lie to people, when it is for their own good.

Now, nothing encourages people to rise up against tyrants like knowing that others are already doing so. At every hacienda and every rancho he went past, a few more partisans joined his troop. At every pueblo he passed through, the crowd grew. A few kilometers from La Cruz, Lavarède found himself at the head of a respectable number of people, inflamed by his enthusiastic words—which proves that, if it is good to know the English language when one goes traveling, it is also good to know the Castilian language.

His small army was hindering him slightly, however, because he was constrained to slow his mount to the pace of a troop on foot, and he was in haste to the place where Aurett might be in danger.

He used a stratagem. "My friends, we're going to split up here and you're going to penetrate into the Château de La Cruz in small groups. Our brothers there are also in groups—recognize one another. I shall go on ahead, alone, in order that none of you will be running any risk. It's the job of the leader to go the first into danger! Follow me prudently, and wait to act together when I give the agreed signal.

No leader of a conspiracy had ever operated thus before. Lavarède—which his Costa Ricans pronounced "La Bareda"—was saluted with loud cheers.

"Long live the liberator of the people!"

The echoes of the Cordilera sent the cries from the Llanura Alta to the Canas Cordas—and while the Señor Liberador urged Matagna to a rapid trot, other partisans descended from the nearby slopes to join the military promenade from which a revolution would surge forth.

In his haste to fly to Aurett, Armand forgot to furnish himself with a revolver.

He reached the Château de La Cruz.

At the very moment when the mule penetrated into the courtyard, José had just gone back into the room on the ground floor where poor Aurett was a prisoner.

"Choose," he said, "to condemn your father to death or become my wife."

On the sonorous pavement of the courtyard the mule's hooves made a kind of appeal, to which the young Englishman responded unconsciously. Instinctively, she ran to the window. It was providential aid that was arriving…at a trot. She recognized the rider.

In spite of the efforts of José, who grabbed hold of her, she shouted: "Armand!"

In her desperate situation, rigid British virtue forgot the rules of etiquette; she did not shout: "Monsieur Lavarède!"—but without her meaning to, that single word sprang from her heart, encapsulating everything: "Armand!"

With one bound, Lavarède leapt over the window-sill and into the room. His vigorous hands seized José and sent him flying to the far side of the room, away from his miraculously saved victim.

"Monsieur," he said to him. "You are a rude blackguard, but while I'm alive, you shall not touch a hair on this young woman's head."

José, yellow with anger and rage, took refuge behind a table, his right hand clenched on the butt of a revolver that he had just pulled from his belt.

A luminous idea crossed Lavarède's mind. *I don't have a weapon. That revolver…he's the one who'll give the signal!* And gaily, he added: *A revolution for Miss Aurett!*

Then, recovering all his composure, although he was unarmed, he began jeering at his armed adversary.

"Be careful, José. You're very pale. You're afraid and you're going to miss me."

The fake aristocrat extends his arm and fires. A cry from the young woman responds to the detonation, but Armand has not flinched.

"I told you so."

He is smiling, his arms folded, still sneering at the American. The latter takes aim again, doubtless better this time.

"Missed again," says the Frenchman, who nevertheless twitches slightly.

A trickle of blood runs from his left shoulder. Aurett has seen it. She runs forward to cover him with her body.

José hesitates; he dies not want to hit the young woman with the millions. Armand sees that apprehension. With a gesture, he thrusts his friend aside and resumes his provocation.

"Coward!" he shouts at José. "Fire one last bullet, then! Do you dare? A third, I tell you! Poltroon!"

The wretch straightens up in response to the insult, as if it were a whiplash. Livid, he takes aim, slowly, straight at the heart. As he presses the trigger, his pale face brightens in an evil smile.

He fires!

This time, Lavarède, a living target, ought to be dead—but a hand has sent the bullet astray. Aurett, at the risk of her life, has launched herself at José. With a rapid movement she has knocked his right arm upwards, and the third bullet hits the wall. She has saved Lavarède.

A glimmer of joy lights up their faces. On the part of Aurett, it is the joy of having preserved hr friend's life. On his part, it is another triumph altogether.

In response to the third detonation, tumultuous cries have resounded outside. The revolution is beginning. And Armand, quitting the passive role that no longer serves any purpose, leaps upon the terrified José and disarms him.

Immediately, men rush into the room and take possession of the governor. Others invade the courtyard. Through the ground-floor window, they see Lavarède and cheer him. They are the ones who have traveled with him on the road, and who recognize him as their leader. But emotion takes hold of them. Their friend La Bareda is covered in blood. He faints.

Aurett hastens toward him in order to care for him. Fortunately, the wound is only slight. José's bullet has only grazed his shoulder; a rapid bandage stops the bleeding.

In two minutes, everyone in the château has heard the news. He has been wounded; his blood has been shed for the good cause.

That is sufficient; they all rally, of their own accord, and place themselves under his orders. There and then, he is qualified as a general by the partisans of Zelaya and Hyeronimo. He is General La Bareda, the liberator of the people, the martyr of the revolution, and anything else he pleases!

Recovered from his momentary faint, he thinks about Aurett's father, and gives the order to free him. The four soldiers set to guard him bring him immediately. A good idea occurs to him.

"Take hold of that man," he orders, designating Don José, "and tie him up securely with the same cords that bound the victim of his tyranny."

There is no good revolution without compensations of that sort. The palaces remain the same, as do the prisons; only the tenants change.

The four men were carrying out their orders conscientiously when Murlyton stopped them with a gesture.

"What's the matter? What do you want."

"Oh," said the Englishman, "before you tie him up, I want to box him."

"So be it," said the liberator. "Box away..."

So saying, he accompanied that gesture of condescension and authority with one of the superb movements that King Solomon must have made when rendering justice.

In a blink of an eye, everyone moved into the courtyard. A circle was formed, with Lavarède sitting on an elevated seat, and Miss Aurett beside him.

And, to the great amazement of the audience, Don José received a formidable hail of punches, administered according to the strictest rules of the art. His cheeks swollen, his flesh bruised, his eyes puffy and bloody, he finally escaped from the Englishman's vengeful fury. The latter, whose anger was obviously concentrated, had not departed from his habitual calm.

"I'm satisfied," he said, with great phlegm. "My dignity is avenged."

"And my honor is saved," added Aurett, in a low voice, "thanks to our friend Monsieur Lavarède."

"Oh! He's every inch a gentleman!" And the Englishman went to shake his hand cordially.

While they were shaking hands there was a hubbub at the gate of the château. A man was trying to slip away. When challenged, he had not responded. Then, two or three mountain men had run after him and brought him back by force. Quite naturally, they brought him before their general.

The Liberator emitted a frank burst of laughter. The prisoner was crestfallen and tremulous.

"Ah, Master Bouvreuil!" said Armand. "Well, what do you say? From one day to the next, the roles can change in these parts."

"I saw you just now, when that crowd was acclaiming you...my one thought was to get away."

"To avoid my just wrath! But you don't know a word of Spanish. You wouldn't have got very far."

"Alas!"

"Tell me, my dear Monsieur Bouvreuil: yesterday you had me arrested—what if I were to have you shot today?"

"Oh! Oh! Lavarède, my kind friend, you wouldn't do that! Look, here's your unpaid bills, and here's the withdrawal of my claims, my banknotes...everything! Whatever you want...would you like my daughter too? Take it all, but don't take my life."

The Costa Ricans did not understand this dialogue, conducted in French, but they understood the gestures perfectly.

"What do I want with your fortune?" replied Lavarède, with a gesture of refusal. "I have five sous, as you know very well, and that's enough for me."

There was no misunderstanding that pantomime. A disinterested leader of a revolution is rare enough to enthuse a crowd in any latitude.

To excite them further, Armand cried, this time in Castilian: "We're not thieves: we're free citizens!"

An immense hurrah replied to him. If he had lifted his finger, Bouvreuil and José would have been lynched on the spot, with Captain Morales, who had obeyed them a few hours earlier, taking the lead. But the Liberator decided otherwise. He had made that revolution uniquely to save his young English friend, and now that was accomplished, he did not want to obtain any other profit from it; he wanted it to be free of any crime, exempt from any human sacrifice.

"No," he said, majestically, to Bouvreuil and José, "I don't want you dead. This slight wound that I've received, I bless, for it has made me the leader of all these brave men, and you won't pay for it with severe reprisals. However, you'll understand that I don't want you getting in my way again. I have too great an interest in continuing on my route not to want be rid of you. Captain Morales, you're going to take these two gentlemen, under a strong escort, over the mountains to the Atlantic shore. Go to Puerto Limone, and have them embarked on the first departing ship, in no matter what direction, provided that it's a long way from Costa Rica. It will surely take you a fortnight to carry out that order, after which you'll return to the capital of the Republic at San José, where you'll receive the recompense that your mission merits. I promise you that it will be as considerable as the service rendered. Here are our written orders. The money we're leaving to your two prisoners will pay for their passages and to maintain the escort under your command. I have spoken. Go! And *Vivan los libros!*"

"Our lives are saved," murmured José to Bouvreuil. "Nothing is lost yet. I know the country, and I guarantee that we'll find ourselves face to face with that overconfident Frenchman again."

Somewhat restored after his temporary disturbance, Murlyton took account of the service that Lavarède had just rendered him, as well as his daughter. The latter, for her part, had understood immediately. So their gratitude was increased, along with their amity for the fine fellow, and the destiny that had attached them to him for an entire year. For them, it as a simple matter of conscience to remind Lavarède that he was not here simply to overthrow Don José and his prefectoral throne.

"Your voyage," said the Englishman, "ought not suffer such delays. Honestly, I'm ready to discount from the duration the days lost here for our personal salvation."

"Not at all," said Armand. "There are minor incidents that it's necessary to anticipate when traveling without money. It's the necessary compensation."

"All right—but what are you going to do now?"

"Continue what I've begun here, of course."

"The revolution!"

"Certainly. Where will I find a better opportunity than in this lost corner of the American Cordillera to make a little progress? I can't execute any more advantageous task than that of revolutionizing the country. Besides which, I wouldn't want to fail in my obligations. These people have no other objective but to march on the capital; I'm their leader, so I must follow them, as Ledru-Rollin said in 1848.[27] Think about it, anyway. In acting thus, I remain within my

---

[27] The opportunist politician Alexandre Ledru-Rollin (1807-1874) was one of the prime movers of the 1848 Revolution, but had to go into exile thereafter be-

program; the capital, San José, is in a northerly direction. I need to go north in order to reach San Francisco. In consequence, I shall march at the head of my troops; I shall address myself to the new president, and ask him for the means to continue my voyage."

"Have you thought about the difficulties that await you in trying to reach San Francisco?"

"No. I'll encounter them soon enough."

"But you'll have to traverse the entire American isthmus, which isn't rich in roads capable of accommodating carriages, nor in railways, crossing Nicaragua, San Salvador and Guatemala. Then there's the entire length of Mexico to cross. You'll never get there..."

"Especially," Lavarède interjected, cheerfully, "if I don't begin. So let's make a start!"

And, having given is partisans the signal to depart, the general mounted his mule and set forth.

As faithful historians of this adventure, we must recognize that he was not running any great peril. Wherever he arrived, there was nothing but acclamations and hurrahs. As he went by people lit fireworks, and competed for the honor of lodging and feeding him and his retinue—which is to say, Murlyton and Aurett. Already, the rumor had spread among the men of his army and the regions through which they passed that they were his wife and father-in-law, and some of them repeated that to others with little knowing looks and significant nods of the head that only our three voyagers did not understand.

In the end, Aurett wanted to clarify the matter. The troop was heading toward the province of Guatarez, they were on foot following a path at the foot of Dota Mountain, and the hazard of the road had lodged the general staff of the little colony in a hacienda, the Cascante, where Mademoiselle Luz, an amiable señorita, did the honors. While Lavarède was changing the dressing on his shoulder wound, with the customary assistance of Murlyton, the two young women chatted, and Aurett learned everything from Luz's lips.

"An article in the constitution of 22 December 1871 specifies that the President of the Costa Rican Republic is elected for four years, not re-eligible; he has to have a capital of fifty thousand francs, be at least thirty years old, and be married."

Good, thought the young Englishman. *Monsieur Armand is the necessary age, in is the process of earning four millions, and his friends believe him to be married. I ought not to dissuade them. I'll continue to pass for his wife, and it will be very amusing, quite a joke, to see him acclaimed as president.*

She accompanied her reflections with a mischievous smile, which, involuntarily, said much more than she thought. That was because she had conceived

---

cause of his opposition to Louis-Napoléon Bonaparte, even before the coup of 1851.

a tender sentiment—of friendship, certainly, but a very profound friendship—for her young and courageous defender.

The journey continued under the same auspices. Less than twenty days after the departure from Golfo Dulce, our friend made a triumphant entry into San José, where public rumor had announced his arrival. With the aid of telegraphic dispatches, and unexpected coup-de-théâtre lay in wait there for General La Bareda. The bells rang out at top volume, the city's two cannons thundered, the people cheered, and the townsfolk of every rank waited, resigned, sensing that there was no point struggling against popular pressure.

Having left Cambo two hundred strong, the friends of the Liberator of the people numbered six thousand on arrival at San José. In the central square the army was waiting, lined up on one side—about a hundred and fifty men—with delegations from the towns of Puntarenas, Orosi and Angostura lined up on another side of the square. The delegates from Cartago, the rival city, who had come to salute the Liberator, were particularly noticeable. Facing the army stood authorities of every sort, and generals and colonels in large number. The fourth side of the square belonged to the leaders of the victorious troop.

The people were crowding every issue, shouting at the top of their voices. A howling crowd was swarming over the roofs of the Law Courts, the Presidential and National Palaces, and the churches of La Soledad, La Merced, Dolores and Carmen, protestant and Masonic temples, the seminary, the University, known as the College of Sion, and the orphanage—in brief, everywhere where there was room for anyone to perch. The ordinary population of the capital had doubled, and thirty thousand voices cried:

"Long live General La Bareda! Long live the Liberator of the People! Long live our President!"

"What are they saying?" said Armand, anxiously.

The president of the twelve deputies of the Republic advanced.

"They are saying, illustrious General, that by virtue of your French origin, you are Latin, as they are, as we all are; and that popular acclamation has designated you to be the President of Costa Rica, which you have delivered from tyrants. Long live President La Bareda!"

This time, our friend fell from the clouds.

"Oh good! Now I'm a president. What a pity I'm not mounted a black horse—that would complete the picture!"[28]

"What do you mean?" asked Miss Aurett, who had not left his side.

"Nothing, Miss…a memory of my country."

The constitutional bodies then came to present their homages to the young Englishwoman. She was addressed as "Madame la Presidente" from all sides. She was delighted, and infinitely amused. Murlyton was about to sketch a pro-

---

[28] The reference is to General Boulanger, a populist presidential candidate in 1888, who rode around the boulevards on a black horse rallying support.

test, which would have been vain in any case—it would have been lost in the din of the universal tumult—but Aurett stopped him.

"You mustn't do anything to thwart Monsieur Lavarède's actions, Papa. Don't say a word; it would be a disloyalty."

Somewhat abashed, Murlyton remained open-mouthed before the multi-colored spectacle, sparkling and extremely noisy, made to astonish his calm, gray and dull English eyes and ears.

An officer approached Armand respectfully. "Excellency, the army is waiting for you to do it the honor of passing it in review."

"I'm coming," said Lavarède, in a dignified fashion, urging his mule Matagna to a trot.

The small number of soldiers bearing arms surprised him at first; he remembered the lesson given to him by Concha.

"But Costa Rica," he said to the officer, "can mobilize five hundred men in peace time. Where are the others?"

"These are the only ones that remain, Excellency. The others are over there—colonels or generals, according to whether they have been more or less fortunate in the previous pronunciamentos."

"Perfect," replied the President, retaining his seriousness. "We'll sort that out." And, having placed himself facing the troop, he said in pure and sonorous Castilian: "Soldiers, you did not want to fire on the people; you are our brothers. It's necessary that this day should be joyful for everyone. Ask me what you will. As I have not promised you anything in advance, I shall give you more than the others. Speak—what do you desire?"

"Promotion!" replied a unanimous chorus.

"Very well, I appoint you all generals. Pass to the right, and long live Liberty!"

"Viva La Bareda!"

That cry was not only uttered by the soldiers, who broke into a run to cross the square and join the other fortunate individuals who had been promoted previously, but by all the people, who, from the height of rooftops, terraces, windows and balconies, had seen and understood that scene, in which Equality was not a vain word. Lavarède, having satisfied the desires of the soldiers, went into the Presidential Palace with his entourage, where had apartments had been prepared. As dusk fell, the entire city lit up with white electric beams. At first he thought it was a special display, but not at all. San José had been illuminated by electricity for five years.

"So," he said to Councilor Rabata, who occupied the position of his private secretary, "my capital isn't as backward as one might have thought."

"Much less so than you suppose; for if Your Excellency would care to listen to what is said to him over the telephone, he will find that a plot is already being woven against him."

"A plot to kill me?"

"Here! Oh, never—a plot to send you into exile.

"Oh, of course! I'm in on that plot! Today, I've made the joy of everyone who's approached me, and I haven't wasted my day. But since I can do anything, I suppose that I can also go away..."

"Everything except that. The president can't leave the territory. That's prohibited."

Armand grimaced. Instead of facilitating his voyage, his grandeur had become an obstacle."

"Let's see, my dear secretary, night is falling, my new subjects are gathering in the hippodrome of Mata-Redonda, and then everyone will go to bed. You've conducted me to this palace; I'll do the same as everyone else, after the banquet—for I assume that one is nourished like a president?—and we'll talk again about my departure immediately afterwards, for I have to intention of going moldy here."

"But what about the Constitution?"

"Like those of every country, it's made to be violated. First of all, I'm not naturalized."

"Parliament has voted."

"Secondly, I'm not married."

"The people have ratified the vote."

"Damnation!" Lavarède swore, in jest. "However, I don't want to stay here. I'd lose too much—four millions! Anyway, night brings counsel. Come and talk to me tomorrow when I wake up."

"I shall obey, Excellency—but before going into the banqueting hall, where the authorities and our family are waiting..."

"Not my family, my friends."

"So be it...as I was saying, before then, don't you want to know about the conspiracy? The director of your police force is still on the line."

"Oh...that's true. Let's listen to the telephone."

The electrical messenger invented by Edison connected the palace to the residence of the ex-president, Dr. Guzman, which was situated near the promenade of the central park. There men were gathered in a room there, holding an animated discussion; their voices resonated on the metallic plate.

"It's your fault, Guzman," General Zelaya was saying. "If you hadn't made concessions to the black party, if you hadn't thought about bringing back the Jesuits, expelled so many years ago, you wouldn't have been overthrown so easily."

"But it's even more your fault, General," riposted the doctor. "If you hadn't prepared the movement, thinking that it would turn to your advantage, and if you hadn't stirred up the workers and demoralized the army, this foreign adventurer wouldn't have succeeded in his conjuring trick."

"And as for me," moaned Hyeronimo, in a lamentable tone, "if I hadn't entrusted my mule Matagna to him, which all the people know, if I'd given the signal myself, today it would be me who'd be the president in his place!"

Suddenly, they were interrupted; the telephone bell rang resolutely.

"Hello! Hello!" said a voice. "You're in communication with the Presidential Palace."

The malcontents went pale. They thought they were doomed.

"What do you want?" asked Genera Zelaya, going to the apparatus.

"To offer you support in overthrowing La Bareda."

"You're in the President's entourage, then?"

"I'm very close to him."

"Who are you?"

"La Bareda himself."

IX. The Guatusos

The next morning, Councilor Rabata, in his capacity as the President's secretary, was admitted to his presence as soon as he woke up. His Excellency had slept admirably in the sheets of State; the taxpayers' chocolate had already been served to him, and he had enquired after Murlyton and Aurett, who, for their part, had obtained a well-earned repose in the apartments reserved for them. Rabata came in, bringing the president his first month's salary, as was customary. Lavarède started violently, and made a dramatic gesture.

"I don't want that money," he said. "I've served the cause of liberty for its own sake, not for a few filthy dollars. Allocate that sum to the budget for public education."

General La Bareda's fine response did not take long to be known throughout the city, and only increased his popularity. Parliament met in public session. The twelve representatives voted unanimously to award him, as a national recompense, the highest grade of the Order of the Star of Costa Rica, a saber of honor and a muleteer, similarly of honor, charged with caring for the mule Matagna and, if necessary, the president. That post was awarded to Agostin, the Indian of the rancho, and he was immediately sent with secretary Rabata to ask La Bareda whether there was anything more he desired.

"Yes," he replied, after reflection. "I want to be given a good revolver and a hundred cartridges. If you would care to add to that a case of sea-biscuits, that would give me pleasure, now that I have a mule to carry it. Finally, what I would like most of all is to leave."

On learning of that untimely desire, the public powers smiled, and the people groaned. Magnanimous liberator, they had said when he refused the salary. Bad citizen, they said when he wanted to leave the palace.

The partisans of Guzman and Zelaya had even begun to respond to strange rumors—echoes of the telephone call we have heard. The hero of Cambo, as he had been nicknamed on the twenty-third of June, was suspected of high treason on the twenty-fifth, two days after his elevation to the presidency. He was accused, in whispers but persistently, of conspiring against the security of the Republic.

That slight rumor, spreading risforzando and crescendo, like any good calumny, soon took on such proportions that the Parliament, yielding to the movement, decreed a special guard, commanded by the patriot General Zelaya, to watch President La Bareda closely and incessantly. Like Masaniello[29] he knew

---

[29] The nickname of Tommaso Aniello (1622-1647), a fisherman who became the leader of a popular revolt in Naples against its Spanish rulers in 1647; it did not end well.

about the redoubtable changes in popular opinion in a matter of hours, and our friend, thus kept out of sight in the company of the English duo, cursed the grandeur attaching him to his capital.

"How are you going to leave, since they're refusing your resignation?" asked Aurett.

"Trust in Providence, which has already got me out of more than one tight spot."

Scarcely had he pronounced that philosophical and fatalistic sentence than, in spite of the nobility of his function, the President of the Costa Rican Republic lay down full length on the floor of the drawing room in which he was chatting to his friends. In that scarcely majestic posture, the groaning Murlyton and the laughing Aurett swiftly joined him.

"What is it?"

"It's an earthquake, of course: one of the sixty annual oscillations I mentioned to you."

"The palace seems to be rocking gently."

They tried to stand up, but it was impossible for them to remain standing. Shaken like a salad in a basket, they sat down in the Turkish fashion, at a distance from the shaking and tumbling furniture. The nearby sound of breaking crockery mingled with the distant moaning of the frightened crowd. The only devoted servant remaining, the Indian Agostin, came in at that moment and found the entire presidential society crouching.

"Excellency," he said, "don't stay in the palace a minute longer—it's about to collapse."

"To get out of here!" exclaimed Armand. "I'd like nothing better—but General Zelaya's guard will stop me!"

"The guard has dispersed and the general is far away. We natives know that the movements of the earth are augmenting in number and duration. Look—everyone is running way; the volcanoes are fuming more than ever. It might be an even stronger earthquake than the other three!"

With a promptitude that is easily comprehensible, our three voyagers fled, leaving the capital San José and the presidency of Costa Rica behind. Agostin had saddled the mules, and tied on the case of sea-biscuits, a national gift. Everyone, armed and equipped, had leapt on to their mounts in a matter of seconds, and the little caravan set off, guided by the Indian.

He was right, that son of the American soil; the palace collapsed behind them with a frightful din.

Animals and people alike had panicked. The mules pricked up their ears before the danger that they could not see, about which their instinct alone warned them. The catastrophe was so sudden that no one, in the general peril, noticed the president's departure; they were solely occupied with the wrath of nature. Humans become small in such circumstances, and more than one brave man trembles.

After two hours of frantic galloping, having leapt over new crevasses, crossed torrents that had become dry roads and roads that had been transformed into torrents, scarcely recognizing the landscape, chaotically transformed by the rapid change of perspective, Agostin slowed the hectic pace that they had maintained since San José. It was evident that they had emerged from the zone in which the cosmic upheaval had taken place. They could get their breath back and take account of the situation. In order to assess it, Armand could only count on Agostin's experience.

"In what direction are we headed?"

"South-East, away from the volcanoes."

"Which is to say that we're heading toward the Atlantic."

"Yes, toward our ocean, the Indian Sea."

"What's that big town ahead of us?"

"Cartago."

"Doesn't the railway go through there?"

"The engineers' route, indeed."

"What do you mean?"

"I mean the road traced by the English on tracks of iron and steel. Nothing prevents you from taking it and reaching Limon via Orosi and Angostura. There you can embark, since you want to leave."

"Certainly I want to, but that's not the route I would have liked to take." Turning to his friends he added: "I'll be no further forward than on arrival in Colon, since we're about to find ourselves back on the Atlantic shore."

"The main thing, however, was to get out of San José," replied Murlyton, sagely.

In Cartago, the effects of the earthquake had been felt with a little less violence, but the populace was no less agitated, and in the universal peril in which every inhabitant was playing his part, no one took any more notice of the four travelers. The general panic was such that Agostin was able to load the mules and baggage into an empty wagon, where Armand and his friends joined them without attraction attention; he escaped the other danger of being recognized, like Louis XVI at Varennes.

The train moved off. At the foot of the enormous volcano of Turrialba, which is no less than twelve thousand English feet high, at Tucurrique station, Miss Aurett suddenly threw herself into the interior of the wagon. She was pale and trembling, and pointed her finger at a group of people who had just arrived.

"Don José!" she said, in a strangled voice.

"Him—the rogue!" exclaimed Lavarède, on the point of launching himself forward.

She stopped him gently. "You're not afraid of him, I know, but if he's still in the country, if he's come back, it's to get his revenge on you. Like everyone else, he must have leaned from telegraphic dispatches that you were being kept out of sight in the presidential palace. If he sees one of us, you'll be identified and taken back to the capital."

The reasoning was just. Armand yielded to those observations, and the stage was completed without any obstacle—but Lavarède resolved to leave the railway constructed by the English engineers sat some intermediate station.

Agostin was consulted. According to him, it was easy to stop near Calabozo, and as he had understood that they wanted, above all, to void being seen and recognized, he suggested that they resume the journey by mule and traverse the land of the Talamanca Indians.

"That's the most deserted region in the entire territory," he said.

"It'll be beginning again, as with Ramon, but at least it's liberty. Mr. Murlyton, I think it's necessary, for a while, to say farewell to the roast beef of old England; we're going back to the paradise of cassava pancakes and maize tortillas."

The caravan got down, as Agostin had advised, at an unmanned level crossing, thus avoiding the pecuniary demands of the Company, and, heading south-east, followed the lower slopes of the mountains, trying to catch a glimpse at least once a day of the sea to their left, in order not to lose their direction.

What our friends did not notice at Calabozo, however, was that Don José, having perceived them at Turrique, had boarded the same train, and was observing them prudently.

Having seen them head toward that almost uninhabited country on the Atlantic slopes, knowing the country as he did, he knew how many days it would take to find them again, and where they would eventually arrive. He certainly was not thinking about obeying the Constitution and taking the fugitive President back; it was to obtain his own vengeance and serve Bouvreuil's interests that he was in Costa Rica.

Aurett was slightly mistaken in thinking that he had come back; he had not left. Forcibly embarked on a Mexican coaster, he and his companion had stopped at the first port of call after Limon, at the mouth of the San Juan de Nicaragua. Then, having sent Bouvreuil to wait in Colon, with which communication was easy along the whole of that section of the coast, he had entered northern Costa Rica, furnished with a large sum of money exacted from his accomplice. There he had made contact with the chief of the Guatusos, Indians living between Nicaragua and Costa Rica. We shall soon discover the consequences of that step.

During the first few days of travel, the incidents of the journey made by Lavarède and his friends included nothing disquieting. The only material difficulty was crossing the torrential streams that ran down the mountains; the aid of the Indians and their rafts was precious.

On the third of July they reached the first foothills of the Montes Negros, avoiding the towns of Bribri and Cuabre, on the right bank of the Rio Dorado, because Lavarède had no wish to encounter any Costa Rican authorities.

"I prefer the savages," he said. "At least they don't build prisons."

Having found a kind of ruin on the side of a steep hill, which must have been a rancho in the previous century, long since abandoned, they had spent the night there when the mules began whinnying in a peculiar fashion at daybreak.

Agostin, with his Indian flair, declared that there must be danger in the vicinity. He examined the landscape and soon designated a distant point.

"Far away to the north-west, almost on the tracks of yesterday's journey, I can make out another caravan. It seems numerous. There are at least thirty horses and mules."

Lavarède was gripped by anxiety. "Are they soldiers?"

"No…I seem to recognize Indian accoutrements."

"No danger, then?"

"Not if they're shepherds or nomads traveling as a tribe. I can see them a little better now—they're almost all armed with rifles. That astonishes me, for the natives of the Talamanca aren't great hunters; they do more fishing than hunting."

A few more minutes went by. The four travelers had their eyes fixed on the distant group, which was drawing nearer, and which the rays of the rising sun were beginning to illuminate. Suddenly, Agostin went pale. Until now, he had not seemed easy to frighten, but now his teeth were chattering and he gave signs of the greatest fear.

"What is it? What's the matter?"

"They're Guatusos!"

"So?"

"The terrible Guatusos, the Indians with pale faces, blue eyes and red hair."

"One might think they were English by that description," said Murlyton.

"Alas, yes. They're the descendants of a band on English pirates cast away a hundred years ago on the banks of the Rio Frio, who imported ferocious and bloodthirsty mores into the tribe that took them in."[30]

"What are you saying?"

"The truth, unfortunately. The Guatusos, or Pranzos, are capable of the greatest cruelties. If it's us that they want, we're dead!"

"But how is it," Armand asked, "that these savages, who live north of the Poas, have come here to the south of the territory?"

"I can't explain that, Excellency, but they'd kill their fathers for a little money and a drink of *aguardiente*."

"Money? What if they were given some to go away?" hazarded Murlyton.

---

[30] This myth, inspired by the Guatuso people's unusual appearance, was still current in the late 19th century, by which time the tribe—whose bloodthirsty reputation was equally mythical—was on the brink of extinction. The last remnants of the people in question are nowadays known as the Maleku.

"You're forgetting that we have none in our pockets, and they won't take checks."

"No, no," murmured Agostin. "Don't attract their attention, and above all, don't move. If, by good fortune, they pass by without suspecting that we're here, I'll gladly offer a sacrifice to the Great Spirit."

"But aren't you a Catholic?"

"Yes, Your Grace, like all poor Indians—but that has never prevented us, when we're in danger, or among ourselves, from also praying to the Great Spirit Tule, the god of our fathers an our homeland."[31]

In his terror, he admitted what, by tradition, the indigenes had always carefully concealed, for fear of the Spanish conquerors.

At that moment, our travelers were able to make a troubling observation from their hideaway. To the appeals of their mules, other appeals had responded. First, the thirty Guatuso riders stopped; they seemed to hold a conference; then, changing direction, their compact group, preceded by a dozen spaced out as scouts, headed toward the rancho, scaling the hill on which Lavarède and his traveling companions were camped, with a surrounding maneuver.

If they had been able to conserve any doubt thus far as to the intentions of the Guatusos, no hesitation was any longer permissible. Aurett, who had aimed her binoculars at them, went pale and said: "The physical appearance of those Indians corresponds to the description given by Agostin. Furthermore, I've just recognized our enemy Don José in their midst."

"What are we going to do?" asked Murlyton coldly, without his voice betraying the slightest disturbance."

"The only thing we can," said Lavarède, resolutely. "Resist. We have weapons; we need to use them and take away the bandits' desire to get too close to us."

The roles were immediately distributed. The three men took cover behind fragments of wall, Agostin armed with his rifle, Armand and Murlyton with their long-range revolvers. They waited until the first riders were no more than two hundred meters away, and all three opened fire simultaneously. Two Indians fell; the horse ridden by a third reared up, no longer obedient to its rider; it had been wounded and staggered down the hill.

The uphill movement of the assailants did not stop at that first skirmish. It required two further salvos, which claimed another five victims—as many horses as Indians—for the aggressors to decide to beat a retreat and place them-

---

[31] Tule, as previously noted, simply means "people," in the language of the Kuna, or Guna people of Panama and Colombia. In Mexico, a certain reverence was attached to the "Arbol del Tule" (Tree of Tula), reputedly of significance to the Aztecs; although that Tula has no connection with the Panamanian Cerro Tula, it might have encouraged the confusion manifest here, which appears to be original to the authors.

selves, at a gallop, out of gunshot range. But they remained in sight, scarcely hidden by a crease in the terrain and a clump of tropical bushes.

"Their surprise attack has failed," said Lavarède. "Let's watch them attentively, for they won't leave it there."

With the aid of the Englishwoman's binoculars, they could see what was happening distinctly. The dead and wounded, five in number, were laid under a tree next to a small stream. One Guatuso guarded them and cared for them. Agostin perceived two horsemen placed as sentries to the left and the right in such a way as not to lose sight of the rancho.

With the exception of those two, the others had dismounted and engaged in a "palaver." By their gestures designating the hill, it was easy to guess that they were planning a new aggression, doubtless more prudent. Our friends redoubled their surveillance, remaining on their guard.

To their great astonishment, however, the entire day passed in that fashion. The two groups observed one another.

Agostin made the remark that the strength of animals and men needs to be sustained.

They had a few tins of food, plus the national gift, the case of sea-biscuits. The four diners did considerable honor to those provisions. As for the mules, they were given crushed and moistened biscuits. There is no shortage of springs in the mountains; ten meters behind the rancho a thin stream of limpid water emerged from the rock.

Meanwhile, night was falling. When the shadows extended over the landscape, Lavarède feared an attack. It was agreed that everyone would take turns on watch. They were four; Murlyton and Aurett would sleep while Armand and Agostin watched, relieving one another every two hours.

Attentive as the watchers were, nothing seemed to be moving in the valley. They heard the sound of regular footfalls, indicating that the enemy surveillance was continuing.

The Guatusos did not attack.

At daybreak, however, the besieged group understood that the Indians had changed tactics. The direct assault having failed, the Guatusos were employing another means.

They were mounting a blockade.

Instead of a single group, our friends distinguished six of them, each composed of only a few men, but controlling all the issues to the north, south and east; a single Indian on horseback at each post kept watch on the surrounded rancho.

There was no possibility of escaping westwards; behind the hill where their modest fortress stood, the Cordillera was sheer, overlooking the plain all the way to the sea.

The defenders held a grave council. They took a census of their provisions. For four people and their mounts, there was enough for five days.

The second day of the siege passed almost cheerfully. Lavarède's good humor never flagged.

"All the same," he said to the Englishman, "In promising not to leave me, and to watch me incessantly, you had no suspicion of what was going to happen to you."

"Certainly not."

"If you had, you wouldn't have started?"

"Probably not—but now I'm accustomed to your character. Your adventurous spirit interests me, and, being gentlemen, we must aid one another."

"Oh," Aurett interjected, "Monsieur Lavarède doesn't bargain. He's already saved me from so many perils that I'll never be able to repay him."

Armand smiled, and, pointing to the horizon where the Guatuso sentries were silhouetted, he said: "So far as we can anticipate, this time, we'll be running the same dangers together, and it will be very difficult for me to preserve you from them." In a grave tone, he added: "It's for you, most of all, that I tremble."

"It's necessary not to tremble for me or for yourself, Monsieur Armand. Who knows whether, one night, we might be able to escape our besiegers?"

"Well, that remains to be seen. What do you think, Agostin?"

The Indian did not reply. His gaze obstinately fixed on the south-east, he seemed absorbed.

Armand tapped him on the shoulder. "What are you looking for out there?" he asked.

"Salvation. The road by which to flee…to go toward friendly tribes."

"There are some in that direction?"

"Yes—the Bizeitas; then, further way, the Chiriquis. But how do we get away from the Guatusos? I don't know all the paths."

And he resumed his silent reverie, staring into space.

From time to time, a Guatuso advanced toward the rancho on reconnaissance, as if to make sure that the besieged were still there. A gunshot informed him immediately. The besiegers lost another two men playing that game.

They had a meal after one of those petty alerts. Only Agostin, preoccupied, his eyes still directed at the slopes of the mountain, did not eat.

Smiling, Aurett said to her father: "In spite of your banknotes and checks, without the assistance of our friend we'd have died of hunger two days ago."

"That's true. Monsieur Lavarède has nourished us, not only here but during the time of his presidency."

"You can put it on account," said Armand, in jest.

With the utmost gravity, Murlyton opened his notebook and displayed the notes he had already made. "You can see that it's already done."

"Oh! You're a very precise man."

"I'm an Englishman," he replied, simply.

Suddenly, Agostin climbed over the wall forming the parapet and let himself slide down outside. He followed the southern slope of the hill, almost crawling, trying to see something in the distance without being seen by the sentries.

He did not succeed. Rifle-shots rang out and a hail of bullets fell around him.

Hidden behind rocks, he heard the bullets striking the stone, but continued his route anyway. He did not stop until he was on the crest of a ravine. There, lying down at full length, his head leaning over the void, he observed, fixing in his mind a map of the terrain he had just surveyed. When he got up again, his ordinarily impassive face was illuminated with joy. Then he came back to the rancho.

The fusillade from the besiegers relented then. Evidently, the besiegers only wanted to prevent him from escaping.

"Well?" said Armand. "What were you doing? What did you see?"

"I was looking for a route, but all the paths are guarded. We can't get away from here."

"However," said Lavarède, "just now you seemed satisfied."

"Yes; I was glad that the Guatusos' bullets couldn't reach me—but that's all."

"Ah!"

And Agostin went to sit down with the mules, going to sleep—or pretending to do so.

Soon, a further incident woke him up and put all the besieged under arms. From the bottom of the valley, a Guatuso climbed up straight toward the rancho. Having arrived a few hundred meters away—within rifle range, that is—he waved a piece of white cloth.

Lavarède, who was on watch, revolver in hand, said to his friends: "In every country in the world, the white flag signifies that one wants to negotiate."

"Yes," said the Englishman, "But I don't trust these savages. Isn't it a trap?"

Agostin was watching attentively. "No, he's alone. It's obvious that he's asking to approach without our firing at him."

"Well, how do we reply?"

"By employing the same language as him. Wave a white handkerchief, and he'll come forward."

"It was immediately done and immediately understood. The Guatuso was holding something in his hand, which he held up at a distance. It was a piece of paper; they could make it out clearly with the binoculars. He came forward another hundred meters toward the white handkerchief that Miss Aurett was waving, and then stopped. He placed the piece of paper ostentatiously, pierced by the tip of a yucca leaf, pointed to it with an expressive pantomime and then ran back down hill, not at all reassured until he was covered by a dip in the ground further down the mountain.

Agostin went to fetch the message and bring it back to the rancho. It was written in the Castilian language: an ultimatum from Don José, thus conceived:

6 July 1891.

To Their Excellencies, Sir Murlyton, esquire, Miss Aurett Murlyton,

The prefect of Cambo, governor of the district of Golfo Dulce in Costa Rica has the honor of informing your excellencies that they are not the ones he is pursuing. In consequence, Your Excellencies may freely resume their route and remain in the territory of the Republic with their weapons, mounts and baggage. They will have the right to our protection. They may even take with them as their servant the soldier Agostin of the Terraba Indian tribe, whom we deem to have yielded to the injunctions of the French adventurer unduly calling himself General La Bareda—the man whom the public powers have declared to the stripped of the title of President of the Costa Rican Republic, which he had usurped, by virtue of an insurrection fomented by him and henceforth vanquished. It is him alone that I and my faithful soldiers wish to capture and punish. The Prefect-Governor gives Your Excellencies twenty-four hours to comply with his orders and withdraw to wherever they please. If they fail to obey within that time, they will incur the same penalties as the adventurer, their companion, whom we have resolved to capture dead or alive.

Signed: Don José Miraflores.

The reading of this document, which Armand translated for his friends, plunged them at first into somewhat somber reflections. Lavarède was the first to break the silence, addressing the Indian.

"You're free, Agostin, and you can go. You were right, as you see, to fear the Guatusos so much."

"Make no mistake, Your Grace," he replied. "The Guatusos are not soldiers of the government and Don José was lying when he wrote those words."

"You think so?"

"I'm sure of it. But I don't understand why he's consenting to let His Excellency and the young lady go. I divine a ruse, but I don't know what."

"We know," said Aurett. "And for my part, I'm determined not to put myself in the hands of that man again."

"Yes," added Murlyton. "Under the cover of politics, the wretch is pursuing a private vendetta against you, Lavarède, and an abominable design against my daughter."

"It's obvious," said Lavarède, "that he's seeking to divide us in order to weaken us, and that the Guatusos in his pay would like us to emerge from our impregnable fortress. You'd be their prisoners, exposed without defense to José's schemes—a soldier of fortune who dares to call me an adventurer! And I'd doubtless be murdered by the cruel Indians."

Armand's conclusions were accurate. The besieged had only once course to take, therefore: to fight until the last cartridge. That resolution made, the journalist made sure that the weapons were in good condition. As for ammunition, there was no shortage yet...

The day passed without incident, except that the blockade was tightened. Night fell. When it was Lavarède and Agostin's turn to stand guard, the Indian began speaking in a low voice, so as not to disturb the sleep of the English duo.

"Tomorrow will probably be hard," he said. "The chief will need a strong body and an alert mind. Sleep tranquilly then, all night. I'll keep watch for two."

Lavarède, exhausted by previous sleepless nights, accepted the soldier's offer and slept profoundly. When he woke up, daylight was visible on the horizon. He darted a rapid glance round. Aurett and her father were watching the plain, but the Indian had disappeared. A suspicion crossed the Frenchman's mind.

"Where's Agostin?" he asked.

"I don't know," said the Englishman. "We haven't seen him this morning."

Armand shook his head and murmured: "I should have suspected it."

That was all. He understood that the Indian, a stranger to the interests in play, had thought of saving himself and abandoning his friends of a day. Moreover, Agostin had shown himself to be prudent but not treacherous; he had left his rifle and cartridges behind, in full view.

"In sum," the young man concluded, "that's one soldier less to nourish. We can prolong the defense of the location."

With those words, the trio resigned themselves to doing without the fugitive. Certain of no longer having anyone to count on but themselves, they drew a new energy from that conviction. From that moment on they rationed themselves. One of the mules was set free, as an unnecessary mouth.

The animal, in any case, did not abuse its situation. Released outside the rancho, it stayed almost all day browsing the sides of the hill. Toward dusk, a Guatuso captured it with a lasso. In the rancho, cries of joy were heard rising from the Indian encampment.

The twenty-four hours given by Don José ran out. An attack was therefore to be feared. That night, therefore, they modified their habitual tactic. Two defenders slept while only one stayed awake; each watch only lasted an hour. That way, they each had two hours sleep out of three.

In the morning, the Guatsos' sentries had drawn closer. Lavarède was able to shoot one of them with Agostin's rifle.

The seventh of July passed slowly, seemingly interminable, but the men used to rapid action were running out of patience. The next day, their intention to put an end to it became clear. They began firing on the rancho as soon as a head became visible. None of their bullets reached the Europeans, however.

Once again the Guatusos modified their tactics; by night they dug holes in the flank of the escarpment and went to earth.

Lavarède was troubled. "They're establishing an Indian trench," he said. "Invisible, they'll get close to us without losing a man. It's necessary at all costs to make them show themselves. The mules will help us."

The animals were tied up on the side of mountain, in a kind of sheltered space. He brought them to the front and attached them on long tethers, which permitted them to reach the natural embrasures formed by the ruins. Instinctively, the animals put their heads through, in order to breathe the open air and gaze into space. The besiegers lent themselves to the strategy, and opened fire on the new targets. One mule was wounded in the head and throat, but in order to fire the Indians had to reveal themselves sufficiently to mark their hiding places. Murlyton and Armand fired in unison.

Aurett, who was watching attentively with the binoculars, saw two Guatusos roll down the mountain; one of them did not move again, the other was carried away by his comrades. Furious, the enemies came together at the bottom of the hill. By their disordered gestures and the cries of wrath whose echoes reached the rancho, Armand divined that the attack was imminent.

"Monsieur Lavarède," said Aurett, "You can see that I'm very calm. Entrust your revolver to me, while you take Agostin's rifle. I've shot at targets, and you'll see that I'm not unskilled."

"If one can hit a target, one can kill a Guatuso." Murlyton, still placid, supported his daughter's proposal in those terms.

Lavarède, more emotional than either of them, placed his valiant companion in the best position, the mule Matagna making her a rampart with his body. Without suspecting it, the Englishwoman was imitating the maneuver of Cossack cavalry, which consists of covering the rider with the mount, behind which, well sheltered, the cavalryman can fire at will.

Scarcely had these preparations been terminated than howls resounded. The Guatusos advanced in a compact group toward the improvised fort. In the rear, a few Indians slightly wounded in the preceding skirmishes formed a kind of reserve. In the middle of them, their chief and Don José could be seen, the latter recognizable by his large sombrero. They were keeping out of danger, encouraging the others vocally and with gestures.

The three defenders waited for the enemy to come well within range. Then they opened fire. The assailants charged *en masse*, at full tilt. In a matter of seconds, six cadavers lay on the ground. As many wounded fell back toward the reserve.

The Guatusos beat a retreat. The assault had been unfruitful.

The garrison of the rancho had suffered slightly. Murlyton, grazed on the forehead by a bullet, escaped with a bandage made from his daughter's handkerchief.

The assailants, their ardor cooled by the vigorous reception of the Europeans, had reached a small gully protected from the fire from the rancho. But the respite granted to the besieged did not last long.

Shouting, howling and firing, the Guatusos reappeared. This time, instead of advancing in a group, they formed a thin, enveloping line of snipers. Each of the three defenders had to fight against six or seven adversaries.

Their weapons spat bullets relentlessly, but in vain. They killed or wounded those in front of them, but in vain.

"There are too many of them," said Armand, furiously.

His gaze met Aurett's. There was a kind of veil over his eyes, but he had no time to express tenderness. The Guatusos were only a few meters from the wall of the ruins. Their faces were grimacing with hatred: a frightful vision! It was the charge of a troop of demons.

They had dropped their rifles; they were brandishing the terrible machetes that they usually carried in their belts. They reached the breach in the wall. At point-blank range, Lavarède felled one last attacker; he smashed another on the head with the butt of his weapon, on the retrenchment itself.

By his side, Murlyton, transforming his revolver into a club, stunned the Indian nearest to him, took possession of his long-bladed knife, and plunged it into his heart.

But Aurett was not built for that savage hand-to-hand combat. A Guatuso advanced toward her, his features contracted. Panicked, she wanted to flee, but her legs were paralyzed; her feet refused to leave the ground. Uttering a terrible scream, she tottered, and fell in a faint.

In response to her appeal, Armand, struck by terror, hurled himself in front of the Indian, but his emotion was injurious to the accuracy of his thrusts. His adversary's machete descended upon him and he fell to the ground, beside Aurett, who was splashed by his blood.

The savages were on the point of triumph: the vanquished were theirs, the men for scalping and the woman for an even more odious torture.

Suddenly, however, a fusillade burst forth from outside. Bullets whistled like deadly birds into the troop of Guatusos.

Stupefied, the latter stopped, and looked round. A second discharge cut through them. This time, they took to their heels, abandoning the rancho where the wounded Lavarède and the unconscious Aurett lay side by side, and the petrified Murlyton, covered in blood, contemplated them, as yet unable to understand the unexpected diversion that had just occurred.

X. From the Atlantic to the Pacific

The diversion that saved the three Europeans simultaneously rehabilitated the Terraba Indian Agostin. The wily soldier had not fled, abandoning his friends; he had gone to seek help from outside, sensing clearly that, if they all remained in the rancho, left to themselves, the final outcome of the struggle was not in doubt.

Such is the hatred that the ferocity of the Guatusos inspires in the other Indian tribes that Agostin's word quickly found an echo. A few Vizcitas and Tervis, Chirripos and Blancos joined him. But if the Guatusos are hated, they are also feared, and the brave men who followed the Terraba were too mild in their mores to be very dangerous, until hazard gave them a vigorous leader.

Perhaps you will remember the Indian Ramon, who had accompanied Lavarède as far as the Colombian border. Since then, having retired with those of his tribe to the slopes of the Chiriqui, he had, like them, been fishing for turtles in the Carib Sea.

Peaceful by custom, and issued from the same family, Indians take little notice of the lines of geographical demarcation established by the descendants of the Spanish conquerors. For them, it is still the ancient Tule land, the other country, whose shore is bathed by an ocean in which God has traced no frontiers—with the result that the fishermen of the Chiriqui and the Talamanca live together on very good terms in the vicinity of the island of Drago, although they do not belong officially to the same State, the former being Colombian and the latter Costa Rican.

Thus, Ramon and his relatives had been mingling for a while with their placid neighbors when Agostin came in search of resolute men to save "La Bareda." Like everyone else, Ramon had heard mention of the political adventure of the "General of the Liberty of the people," but he did not know that the liberator was his friend from Panama.

After a few words from the Terraba Agostin, he was no longer in any doubt. Energetic and courageous, habituated to command during the work of piercing the isthmus, he was soon ready to make a decision. Instinctively, the others recognized him as their leader, and it was thus, after two days march, that Ramon's troop put the José's Guatusos to flight and were able to save Lavarède, Murlyton and Aurett.

Bloodthirsty as the Guatusos were, they fled as soon as possible on this occasion, for, only fighting for the sum of money that their cacique had received, they had not put much ardor into it. After all, some of them had been killed and others wounded; they had earned their money, and they bade farewell to Don José.

The latter, gripped by fear in his turn, headed rapidly toward Puerto Viejo, which was once flourishing but is nowadays virtually abandoned. There, he embarked on a coaster and returned to Colon in order to report the failure of his enterprise in Talamanca to Bouvreuil, who had funded the affair.

Meanwhile, Ramon and Agostin had arrived in the rancho that had been so valiantly defended. A lamentable spectacle awaited them.

With a gaping wound in his right side, Armand is lying there, bathed in his own blood, which has flowed abundantly. He is pale, his face bloodless. He is no longer giving any sign of life. Next to him, Aurett, unconscious, seems to be wounded too, so much blood has her defender shed upon her.

While Murlyton, who has only been slightly wounded, recognizes Ramon, Agostin perceives that the young woman has only fainted. The tribal physician is there; he makes her breathe a vigorous revulsive.

She finally opens her eyes and gazes fearfully at the Indians pressing around her. The memory of the Guatusos returns to her. In a troubled vision, she has seen one of those terrible men hurl himself on her friend. Then nothing more…except a cloud.

Her first word is for her defender, "Monsieur Armand?" she demands.

Her father points to the body lying next to her, whose head Ramon lifts gently.

"And you, Father? Oh, forgive me! You're hurt?"

"Me…it's nothing, my daughter. But him, our brave friend…alas…"

"My God!" she cries, sitting up and leaning over. "Is it serious? Oh! Ramon, I recognize you! Well, tell me, I beg you. I'm trembling."

To these emotional words Ramon only replies with a silent and eloquent gaze, indicating the savant Indian who is examining Armand's wound.

After a pause, the other only says: "Dangerous—especially if the machete was poisoned."

Then Aurett uttered a cry that went straight to her father's soul, and Ramon's, so much dolor and emotion did it contain. If Lavarède had been able to hear that cry, it would have revealed to him the secret of the tenderness contained in the young woman's heart.

The Indian physician was touched himself. He took a dried herb from his satchel, reduced it to a powder, which he dissolved in water, and washed the edges of the wound. Anxiously leaning over them, his features were seen to pass through various expressions: anguish, expectation, and finally tranquility.

"Don't worry, young lady—and you too, Ramon. There was no poison on the Guatuso's weapon." There was a double sigh of relief and joy. "But the cut is nevertheless deep," he went on, "And threatens your friend's life…"

"All the blood that he's shed, his life has flowed away with it, no doubt?"

"No, and it's even fortunate that he's shed so much outside…he'd have died stifled but for that. The water of the stream is nearby; first I'm going to wash the wound with abundant water."

The Indians placed the body as he indicated—which is to say, with his right shoulder in the direction of the current—in such a way that, by its natural flow, the clear cool water of the spring was constantly renewed. Then the healer prepared a liquid with the juice of medically precious herbs, the astringents and antiseptics that nature gives to primitive peoples.

The poor journalist had still not recovered consciousness. Murlyton forced a strong dose of tafia rum between his lips. The cordial was scarcely able to render a few feeble beats to the heart.

Armand was grievously wounded, and Aurett repeated in a soft voice: "Once again, it was for me…it's always for me."

They could not remain in that remote spot, however. It was necessary to think about transporting Lavarède to some place where more complete care could be given to him.

Ramon and Agostin, Murlyton and Aurett consulted one another. The Indian's dressing would suffice for the time being; in any case, they had the means to renew it for several days. But they had to reach the nearest city outside Costa Rican territory without delay. That was Colon, on the Atlantic. Only there would the necessary enlightened care and tranquility be found. A means of transport was necessary, however, that would not jolt the wounded man excessively, under the penalty of losing all the effect of the medicinal plants.

If the wound did not close up, it would reopen, and that would be mortal.

On the other hand, fever and delirium would soon arrive, when the invalid recovered his senses; at all costs it was necessary to make haste.

Agostin quickly organized a kind of improvised stretcher with branches and a sheet of solid fabric, which was hitched to the mule Matagna. The wounded man was gently laid upon it, and then, with his escort of friends, he was taken down to the coast along the Rio Tervis. It only required a few hours to reach the shore of the sea, which was as deserted as the rest of the region.

Poor Aurett did not quit her beloved patient for a moment. When he was laid down in the bottom of a *champan*, a flat-bottomed boat moored to Ramon's canoe, which took it in tow, she was the one who made a cushion with her knees on which to rest Armand's head, which she inundated with her tears.

Murlyton did not raise any protest in the name of propriety; there was no need, since Lavarède was almost a cadaver, devoid of consciousness, only breathing very feebly; the last breath of life might have flown away at any moment.

The Indians stuck close to the coast in order to avoid the impact of the waves. As they approached the Bocas del Toro, they found smooth water in Almirante Bay. In sum, the crossing, which took six days, was exempt from any accident.

Lavarède did not open his eyes until the third day—although, as the Indian physician had warned, he had no consciousness of himself. He was alive; that was all. Delirium began to take hold of him, though, and without him being aware of it, unable to take account of it, he was transported into a room on the ground floor of the Isthmus Hotel, where Murlyton had stayed for the first time two months earlier.

"All that fatigue, all that courage expended," Aurett murmured, "has achieved nothing. By devoting himself to me, Monsieur Armand had lost long weeks without advancing by a single step."

The Englishman had not hesitated for a moment to take charge of everything: doctors, surgeons, the hotel; the invalid wanted for nothing—not even the renewal of his wardrobe.

"I would do as much, as a gentleman," he said, "and out of humanity, even for a stranger that I found in this situation. All the more reason to do it for our valued companion."

Aurett had more than that in her young head, and one day, she opened up to her father. "That wound has not only put Monsieur Lavarède's life in danger, but also his future, if we're fortunate enough to cure him."

"What do you mean?"

"That he'll inevitably lose his chance of gaining Cousin Richard's four millions, since it will take him weeks to get back on his feet, and since he's back in Colon, as on is arrival from Europe, having lost two months in the American isthmus."

"My daughter, those are the contingencies of our young friend's crazy enterprise."

"But his blood, sacrificed to save me, his life generously given for mine— are those, Father, *contingencies*, as you call them, of which we can't take account?"

"I'm no more unaware than you are, my dear child, of Monsieur Lavarède's qualities of courage and devotion. But what more can I do than I've done? Aren't we lavishing all the cares upon him that we'd give to one of our own?"

"That's not sufficient. We have other duties to fulfill toward him."

"You know that I'm a man of honor and an affectionate father. If you want me to fulfill them, at least tell me what these duties are that your enthusiastic tone suggests to you…and which I can't see very clearly with my reason alone."

"Well, here they are: not only do we owe it to him not to hinder him in his task, but we ought to help him accomplish it, because it's for us—for me—that he's stopped. It's necessary, for me at least, that he advances, even unconsciously, toward the goal he wants to attain."

"What do you mean?"

"This, my dear father: his goal, taking the overland route, was to reach San Francisco. The overland route is closed; there remains the sea route. I've obtained information. In two days, an American steamer, the *Alaska*, leaves Panama for San Francisco, and we have a strict obligation, at least out of gratitude, to embark our savior upon it. The crossing takes thirteen days, fourteen at the most.

On board, we'll continue to care for him, and complete his recovery. The surgeon, our compatriot, told you today that wounds inflict by a blade are followed by a rapid convalescence when the essential organs have not been attained. Such is Monsieur Armand's case. He isn't yet taking account of his situation; let's take advantage of that to carry out my plan. I'll be profoundly grateful to you, Father."

"My dear child, you seem to be more hot-headed than is reasonable for a cool Englishwoman…but the sentiment that inspires you is too honorable for me to not to forgive what seems to me to be exaggerated. It's agreed; all three of us will take passage aboard the *Alaska*. I'll only point out to you that our invalid is presently in bed, and that in order to catch your steamer it will be necessary to get him to the other side of the isthmus. Is that possible?"

Murlyton having yielded, Aurett became tender and seductive.

"Of course it's possible. I've met Monsieur Gérolans again, Monsieur Lavarède's French friend, who is employed on the canal works, and we chatted together with the surgeon. Our invalid—I'm delighted to hear you say 'our'—is transportable in this way: he'll remain in his bed; his mattress will be placed on a flat-bed wagon from Colon to Panama: seventeen or eighteen French leagues to cross by railway…and he'll be hoisted aboard the American ship, still on the mattress, which it will be sufficient for us to add to our hotel bill. During the journey, we shan't be separated from him; there's only a slight risk of fever. The calm of the subsequent voyage in the Pacific will give us the time and the means to soothe any such bout. Within three weeks he'll be on his feet, having gained ground, ready to continue his route. You can see that we'll have done a good, honest deed, of which, in consequence, we shall never have to repent."

"I find that you have all the practical qualities of our nation, my dear Aurett; you've planned everything, anticipated everything. Let it be done as you desire…and may God guide us…"

With a head like Aurett's and an arm like Murlyton's, one passes rapidly from words to action. While Gérolans and Ramon, who came every day for news, proceeded with the installation of the wounded man—still feverish, but who had periods of placid calm from time to time, fortunate presages of his imminent recovery—Aurett perceived the perfidious Bouvreuil, who, having been resident in Colon for some time, had kept himself informed of the misadventures of the man whom he called, mentally, his "son-in-law," with inflexions both ferocious and tender.

"Well. Mademoiselle, what has become of your excellent friend? I dared not go to seek news of him myself, but I obtain it second hand, and I've learned of your devotion."

"I'm simply seeking to acquit my debt to Monsieur Lavarède, who has saved me from ambushes…to which you are perhaps no stranger."

"Oh, Miss, can you have such an idea? I've been here for nearly a month, since the President"—he uttered a mocking laugh—"expelled me from his Estates. But I'm glad to see that your efforts have been crowned with success; Lavarède must be better, since he's left the hotel."

Aurett understood that it was necessary to put Bouvreuil off the track. In the most ingenuous tone, mixing enough truth in it to make the lie plausible, she replied: "On the contrary, he's not getting better; the air of this marshy country is very unfavorable to him, and by order of the physicians we're transporting him inland, to a village high in the Cordillera, where the pure atmosphere will be better for his health."

So saying, she took her leave, and ran to the train, leaving Bouvreuil somewhat nonplussed.

A few minutes afterwards, the latter was rejoined by a person who had hidden from the Englishwoman until then, Don José, whose presence so close to her she had not suspected.

To begin with, the two master blackguards congratulated one another on the relative success of their machinations.

The adventurer was the sorrier of the two. "If I haven't been able to take possession of the little one and her millions," he said, "which would have given me a handsome share in the scheme, at least you have nothing to complain about—you're much better served. My Guatuso's machete-stroke has laid up your globetrotter for a long time—and that's well worth the thousand piastres it cost you."

"I don't say any different, but I'm still suspicious of that young English-woman. I fear that she's taking my traveler God knows where. What if she enables him to complete his world tour, even wounded?"

"And how far do you think she'll get with a half-dead man, traveling like a parcel?"

"The fellow's sturdy…and after all, I want him to escape in order that he'll confess that he'd defeated, on his knees, in front of Pénélope. It's an obsession now. After all the tricks he's played on me, I want him to marry my daughter."

That matrimonial vengeance made the Spaniard smile. He seemed to reflect. "Well, nothing's easier than for us to board the first departing train and find out where they stopped. A passenger lying on a mattress gets noticed, damn it!"

There was no passenger train for several hours. On the way, however, at the stations near the mountains, they were told that no one had seen an injured man corresponding to the description they gave get off. At Culebra, they saw Gérolans and Ramon returning to Panama, and questioned them.

"Enemies of our friend," whispered the Indian to the Frenchman. "Let me handle it." And he put them on a false trail: the train had supposedly stopped in the florid country overlooking the Pacific coast, but he did not know the name of the pueblo to which the sick man had been taken.

That was sufficient to make them waste another day in futile searching. When they arrived in Panama on the eighteenth of July, two days after their departure from Colon, it was just in time to watch the *Alaska* cast off and to see the silhouette of the blonde miss on the deck. It was impossible to catch up with the steamer...and there were only three regular departures per month.

There was an outburst of oaths and blasphemies from Bouvreuil and José that would have scandalized a Huguenot. A Jew who was passing by on the Old City quay—the Jews had taken a leading role in the city's commerce for some years—heard them and, sniffing an opportunity, since human passion was in play, enquired as to the motive for their anger.

José complained that a magnificent deal had gone awry because he and his friend had just missed the departing steamer. It was necessary, at all costs, for them to reach San Francisco at the same time as the steamer.

"At the same time isn't possible, but within a day or two, I can furnish you the means...if you have the money."

For a Colombian condor—equivalent to fifty francs in gold—the Israelite gave them the precious information that an attentive reading of the Mexican and American maritime schedules would have given to them gratis. It was sufficient to return as rapidly as possible to Colon by the isthmic railway, and there embark for Jamaica. That island is linked by a regular service with Havana, which is in constant and quotidian communication with Vera Cruz. There, nothing was simpler than taking the curious Camino de Hierro Nacional Mexicano, which leads to Mexico, traversing the three torrid, temperate and cool zones in twelve hours, showing the traveler tropical vegetation low down, linked to the snowy pine forest of the summits by a reminder of the European forests of medium altitudes. In Mexico, the Laredo Ruia would indicated the most direct route by *ferrocarril* to El Paso del Norte, in order to link up with the great American trains crossing the United States from east to west, and take one of the branches of the Southern Pacific Railroad to San Francisco.

All that would take a minimum of fifteen days, and they would need the departures of the steam-boats to link up, in order not to lose time *en route*.

Having furnished themselves with gold and banknotes in Colon, where he cashed a large French check, Bouvreuil began that fantastic chase, accompanied by the inseparable Don José.

Once the initial ardor had passed, however, the adventurer thought that he was not the one who would get the most profit out of all of that, and he took steps to equalize the chances of his profit. Bouvreuil had realized about twenty thousand francs. While crossing the Gulf of Mexico, José relieved him of three quarters of that sum and lost his accomplice while disembarking at Vera Cruz.

After a futile fit of fury and a complaint lodged at the Consulate, the landlord was obliged to continue his journey, thinking sadly about the phantom Lavarède, with whom he kept catching up only to lose him again every time.

Wouldn't it be much simpler and less tiring, he thought, *if he simply married Pénélope?*

While the artist in legal documents was crossing the seas, islands and continents of the American regions, the *Alaska* was sailing placidly, the Pacific Ocean having full deserved its name, carrying our friends.

The vivifying iodized air and tender and assiduous care worked wonders, and Lavarède was gaining strength from day to day.

As soon as his reason returned he asked how he came to be there, aboard an American vessel sailing for "Frisco," as they say out there.

Aurett had to confess everything, and when he protested, Murlyton interrupted him. "Permit me," he said. "I can't suffer being indebted to you. You've saved us, you've nourished us; in our turn, we're doing as much. This way, neither one of us owes the other anything."

That was precise and clear; but Armand exchanged a glance with Aurett, which meant: *He's mistaken; I shall always owe you gratitude, at least, for the tender fashion in which you've cared for me...*

And the young, energetic blonde miss responded with a squeeze of the hand that might have been translated as: *And I shall never forget that I owe you my honor, my life, and a hitherto-unknown sensation in my heart.*

Soon, Lavarède was able to get up. The ship's physician permitted it, and even ordered it, while forbidding him all effort and fatigue.

By day, he strolled in the shade, supported by Murlyton; in the evening, Aurett chatted with him or read to him.

All the books and newspapers in the first class saloon passed by in that fashion, but one reading cheered them up more than all the rest. It was that of the *Diario de l'Estado de Panama*, a newspaper that had appeared on the morning of their departure. Its correspondent in San José, in Costa Rica, gave an account of the "socialist attempt" by a French adventurer, who had succeeded in having himself elected as President of the Costa Rican Republic "by way of intrigue and corruption."

The triumph of the usurper, the emphatic *cronista* concluded, *was not of long duration. Heaven itself manifested its horror at that illegality; it provoked a catastrophe and the ancient soil of Costa Rica quivered on its foundations in order to expel the false liberator who wanted to forge chains for us. The public powers immediately met, and it was decreed that the man I question, whose true name in unknown. The criminal—for one does not hide one's identity unless one is culpable—will be exiled from the Costa Rican state henceforth, and forbidden to bear the name "La Bareda."*

"That reminds me," said Armand, with sincere laughter, "of a drama by Bouchardy[32] that I saw performed when I was young, and in which an unfortunate is, like me *exiled forever from the State of Florence and forbidden to bear*

---

[32] Joseph Bouchardy (1810-1870) was a popular writer of vaudevilles and melodramas. I cannot identify the specific play to which Lavarède is referring.

the name of Pietro. Well, at least it will be a picturesque memory of my voyage. I'll be able to say that I too was once the President of a Republic!"

Eventually, on the first of August, at four o'clock in the afternoon, the Alaska crossed the Golden Gate, maneuvered through the midst of the ships of all nationalities gathered in the port of San Francisco, and dropped anchor a cable from the North Pier.

A quarter of an hour later, the ship's launch deposited Lavarède and his companions on the quay.

XI. Frisco

San Francisco—Frisco for the Americans, economical with time and words—is the most important port in the American West, and it marvelous bay has been celebrated by many voyagers.

Of all American cities, it is the one that bears the least resemblance to "an American city." The crowds there are more variegated, less uniform, and the pleasures are more striking, less dissimulated. People are more "up front," less hypocritical. Its external appearance is more cheerful, less austere. It is evidently the abode most likely to please a European, who would end up dying of boredom in certain rigid and prudish cities of New England, for instance.

On the disembarkation quay, encumbered by barrels, crates and bales, a compact and noisy crowd was agitating: traders, sailors, Chinese coolies and Irish laborers were moving in all directions, so busy that they did not spare a glance for the new arrivals.

The latter had paused, slightly stunned at first, by passing abruptly from the calm of the open sea to the bustle of a great city. Armand thought, with a hint of sadness, about the days of the crossing, during which Aurett had lavished tender concern and conversation upon him. One rapidly gets used to letting life go by, especially in the company of a pretty girl. So it was almost with regret that the young man saw the moment arrive at which the struggle would be resumed.

"Where are we going?" asked Aurett.

The question made Armand shiver. He turned to Murlyton and said: "Do you know the city?"

"Not in the least."

"Then permit me to give you some advice. Take that broad street planted with trees that opens facing us—that's Kearny Street. Five hundred meters from here you'll see, next door to the Stock Exchange, the China Pacific Hotel; I recommend it to you."

"Ah!" said the Englishman, surprised. "You've been here before!"

Lavarède smiled. "Not exactly, but I've read a great deal..." He changed tone: "Now we're ashore, and I'm no longer suffering from my injury, I need to think about earning my living and continuing my journey."

"Just like that—right away," said Murlyton, at whom his daughter had just darted an expressive glance.

"To accept your hospitality any longer would be indiscreet." Tranquilly, he added: "You see that man over there surrounded by a heap of poor devils of all nations? He's hiring cargo handlers. He'll hire me. That will ensure food for two days, and time to reflect." He extended his hand to the Englishman

"Very curious," murmured the latter. "Head of State back there, dock laborer here. Very curious."

Aurett intervened: "You're forgetting what the ship's doctor said, Father. At the slightest violent effort, his wound might reopen. It would be inhuman and disloyal to allow Monsieur Lavarède to do that."

The gentleman slapped his forehead. "Oh, that's right! Listen, my dear convalescent: your condition demands care for another week. Accompany us to the hotel you indicated to us."

"What! The hotel?"

"Yes—it's included in the care that I owe you."

"And the beefsteak too?"

"Yes, that's the price of my daughter's life; I'm reimbursing you, that's all. Good accounts make good friends."

"And good adversaries," added Armand, smiling.

"I don't think," Aurett concluded, "that Monsieur Lavarède intends to impose on my father the humiliation of remaining his debtor."

The journalist had to give in. He went with his traveling companions along Kearny Street.

That street, the most beautiful in San Francisco, is lined with monuments: the old and new City Hall, the Customs, the Post Office, the Money Exchange, the Stock Exchange, the Commercial Library, all useful edifices; fifteen churches, alternating with theaters—the Baldwin, the Californian, etc.—banks and sumptuous ten-story hotels with balconies laden with tropical plants.

"Magnificent!" declared Murlyton.

"Especially," Armand replied, "When one remembers that this immense city has only existed for forty-five years."

"Is that all?" said Aurett.

"Not one more, Mademoiselle. In 1847 there was nothing on the coast but a town of a thousand inhabitants, Yerba Buena, founded in 1776 by Franciscan missionaries from Mexico."

"And today?"

"San Francisco counts three hundred thousand souls. The discovery of gold deposits brought a host of adventurers here; that fever has calmed down now; industry and agriculture have replaced 'claims'..." The Frenchman broke off. "But we've arrived."

Before them stood the China Pacific Hotel. They went into the office, where the "managing director," Mr. Tower, was seated majestically. Standing in front of him was a young man of about twenty, who was speaking to him animatedly. As the travelers arrived, the latter stepped away a few paces.

Mr. Tower bowed slightly, and addressed the Englishman: "I guess, gentlemen, that you would like rooms?"

"I guess" is a locution usual in America, like "I say" in England, "*savez-vous*" in Belgium and "*dis donc*" in France.

116

Murlyton replied to the question. "Indeed: three rooms. We expect to be staying for a week."

"All right, gentlemen. I guess your luggage is at the station."

"We have no luggage."

"All right. Let's say, then, three persons, fifteen dollars a day; eight days: that's a hundred and twenty dollars in all."

Murlyton took out his wallet and handed Mr. Tower banknotes to the required amount.

The unknown man who had been talking to the hotel manager a moment before had drawn nearer; he assumed a satisfied expression on seeing the Englishman settle his account. While Mr. Tower rang for a bellboy to show his clients to their rooms, the young man bowed to the Englishman.

"You're a foreigner, sir?" he asked.

"Not a foreigner, an Englishman."

The unknown man bowed again. Murlyton approved; the reverence flattered his national pride.

"So you have the honor of being English. Well, permit a simple nugget-hunter to give you some advice."

"I'll permit it."

"Beware of pickpockets." And the young man pointed at the pocket in which his interlocutor had placed his wallet.

"Pooh! To take that, it would be necessary to be..."

"Simply skilled. Don't forget, sir, that our pickpockets are also recruited in Great Britain."

With that reflection, the particular chauvinism of which did not seem to be much to the Englishman's taste, the unknown man went out tranquilly. At the same moment, a bellboy appeared. On Mr. Tower's instruction, he told the travelers to follow him. In a matter of seconds, the elevator deposited them on the first floor landing.

"Here we are," said their guide. "Rooms thirteen, fifteen and seventeen. The latter two have a connecting door."

"Thirteen's mine," murmured Lavarède. As Aurett pursed her lips, he added: "It's already brought me luck in Costa Rica."

The young woman smiled. Lavarède, leaving his friends to settle in, shut himself in his room, banal but comfortable, and proceeded to tidy himself up. Then, refreshed and convinced by a glance in the mirror that his recent ordeals had not altered his handsome appearance too much, the Parisian opened his window and contemplated the immense perspective of Montgomery Street and Kearny Street.

The luxurious houses that border those streets are constructed in red fir, but, coated with a special substance, they give the illusion of marble palaces. Carriages of all kinds, trams and omnibuses were passing along the streets incessantly, while busy pedestrians jostled one another on the sidewalks, and a buzz rose from the streets compounded out of cries, conversations and rolling wheels, which delighted Armand. The noise reminded him of "his" Paris. He would not have been a true boulevardier, however, had he not experienced the need, no matter where he was in the world to think that it did not have the same "cachet."

From comparisons he passed on to memories. He saw once again the Rue de Châteaudun, where, for the first time, he had encountered the charming young woman who was accompanying him around the world.

Suddenly, he was snatched from his reverie.

In the next room, occupied by Murlyton, the electric bells were ringing furiously and the sound of raised voices reached Lavarède. It required something serous for the impassive Englishman to utter such cries. Very intrigued, not to say anxious, Armand ran to the door of number 15. It was open.

In the middle of the room, his face scarlet, Murlyton was brandishing a wad of paper. Aurett seemed to be trying to calm him down.

At the moment when the journalist arrived, a bellboy ran into the room.

"Mr. Tower!" cried the Englishman, as soon as he appeared. "Tell him to come immediately—right away."

The frightened bellboy drew away.

"Ah!" said the gentleman, beckoning to the Frenchman to come in. "I'm furious. My checks, my banknotes…all blank paper!"

"Pardon! What do you mean?"

"My father has been robbed," Aurett put in. "Instead of his wallet, he only found a wad of blank paper."

"Yes, exactly—robbed," Murlyton agreed, with increasing anger. "And with the wallet, my watch, my razor—everything!"

Mr. Tower came in. "I'm informed that you're asking for me."

"Sir," declared the Englishman, trying to recover his composure. "I've been robbed I had my wallet when I arrived here—you can confirm that."

"Indeed—you took the payment for the week out of it."

"Well, since that moment, I've spoke to three people: you, the gentleman to whom you were talking, and the bellboy. One of the three is my thief."

With all the tranquility in the world, the hotelier replied: "Very accurately deduced, sir."

"No compliments. On whom do your suspicions fall?"

Mr. Tower smiled. "My conviction is firm, sir. You were relieved of your cash by the person who was in my office."

The travelers looked at one another, astonished.

"What!" stammered Aurett, expressing her companions' thinking. "You're accusing that person? But you seemed to be on the best of terms with him."

The stout Tower raised his index finger in the air. "That merits explanation. You're European, Miss, and you're not aware that in San Francisco, the police are impotent. The prairie begins seven miles from the city, where everyone who has committed a crime takes refuge."

"That's no reason to open the house to them," remarked Lavarède, "or to shake hands with them."

"Wait a moment. The city's robbers have formed a syndicate, and have established an Insurance Company against themselves."

"Insurance!" exclaimed Murlyton.

"Yes, gentleman—the idea is practical. We Americans understand practical ideas, and the Company functions to general satisfaction. Thus, in return for an annual premium of two hundred dollars, I can insure that no theft will be committed to my prejudice."

"It doesn't show," jeered the Englishman.

"Let's be clear, I beg you. I don't insure travelers, but only my own property...and I gain by it, because our robbers are so skillful that they'd steal the house and me inside it, without me perceiving it. That young man is the cashier of the thieves, and he came to collect his premium."

And with that conclusive speech, Mr. Tower withdrew, without anyone thinking of retaining him.

The travelers looked at one another silently.

Lavarède, struck by the comical side of the situation, was the first to recover the power of speech. "A nice country," he murmured, "where the thieves are syndicated and the police ridiculed."

"Ah!" said Murlyton, lugubriously. "I greatly regret having come here...nowhere else would such a situation be tolerated."

"Pardon me, but it exists all over the world. Don't the Tuaregs of the Sahara form a veritable syndicate? The first tribe to encounter a caravan levies a right of passage, after which, the merchants, their animals and their baggage have nothing more to fear. A few horsemen escort them or precede them, in order to acquaint other desert raiders that the right of passage had been acquitted. In Asia Minor, numerous Kurdish peoples proceed in the same fashion, to the general satisfaction. Finally, in the heart of Europe, isn't the association of Italian bandits, the Mafia, prosperous?"

Aurett listened, smiling.

"Very well," she said, finally. "So my father has been robbed in America just as one might be in Africa, Asia or Europe—but that doesn't alter the fact that for the moment, we're completely deprived of money."

"I don't have a farthing left," agreed the gentleman, with a piteous grimace.

"I have five sous," said Armand. "That's already a trifle tight for going around the world on one's own; for three people, it will surely be insufficient. And that's annoying: as you can't continue to follow me, I'm immobilized here; I'll lose time."

The Englishman looked at him. "You're right. I'll go to the nearest telegraph office and cable my banker, as they say here."

He sat down, drafted a telegram and read it aloud, as if to request the approval of his listeners.

"*To Harris, Goldener and Sons, Gracechurch Street, London, England. Folio 237. Send two thousand pounds by return telegraph mandate China Pacific Hotel Kearny Street, San Francisco. Edward Murlyton.*"

The telegraph office in Sacramento Street was nearby; the three of them soon arrived there—but a further disappointment awaited them. It was definitely a day of bad luck. The clerk who received the dispatch asked for a dollar a word for the transmission, which came to twenty-eight dollars. Murlyton explained his situation, gave his address, and affirmed that Harris, Goldener and Sons would hasten to honor his signature, but it was in vain. The clerk did not want to hear it.

"For twenty-eight dollars, I'll send it. The company doesn't give credit." And with that, he closed his grille in the faces of the discomfited travelers.

Night was falling when the Englishman returned to the hotel, deeply afflicted. Aurett was almost as depressed as her father, and the anxiety painted on her face extinguished any whimsical amusement on the Parisian's part.

Their meal was silent, and when the last mouthful had been swallowed, Murlyton and his daughter retired to their rooms. Lavarède whiled away half an hour in the lounge, among strangers of all nationalities, and went back to his room in his turn.

The next day, at nine o'clock in the morning, Aurett was drinking a cup of tea dolefully, into which she was dipping pieces of toast. She had just met her father, who had not slept any more than she had. Both of them were pale, and one irksome thought kept coming back to them.

We're four thousand leagues from home, without a penny in our pockets.

"And as well as that," the young woman continued, aloud, "if the young man finds the means to continue his voyage, we don't have the right to retain him."

"Oh, if only that telegraph clerk has consented to give me credit!"

"Yes, but he didn't want to, and that was his right."

"It's very embarrassing. I don't know what to do. Go to see our consul? But the thief has stolen my papers as well as my banknotes. Enquiries will have to be made—it might take a fortnight. And yet I don't have any other means."

At that moment there was a discreet knock on the door, and one of the stewards appeared. "Monsieur Armand Lavarède," he said, "asks whether, in spite of the early hour, Sir will receive him. He would like to speak to him about an important matter."

Murlyton looked at his daughter. Aurett's eyes expressed hope. The very name of the Frenchman made her feel better.

"Send him in," he said.

A moment later the young man made his entrance. He was smiling. Everything about him testified to his contentment. The young Englishwoman thought that if Monsieur Armand appeared satisfied, it was because he had found a means to put an end to their troubles.

"I'll get straight to the point," Lavarède declared, after a rapid handshake. "Courteous adversaries, we were making the tour of the world together. Now, when I was wounded, incapable of continuing on my way, you cared for me, pampered me and transported me; I'm therefore in your debt."

"Not at all," the Englishman interjected. "I was making restitution. You had been wounded protecting my daughter."

Armand raised his arms to the heavens, with a desolate expression. "That's irrelevant. I have the right to expend a little blood along the way; Cousin Richard's will only requires me to be economical with money. Now, accepting your hospitality is almost failing in that requirement, so I beg you to permit me to find you the twenty-eight dollars you need to cable London."

Murlyton stood up, emotionally. "What! You want...you can...?"

Aurett did not budge. As soon as her traveling companion had arrived, had she not divined that he had come for that reason? But her large eyes fixed on the young man with an exceedingly tender expression.

Meanwhile, Lavarède replied: "I can procure you that sum. It's in my interest, in any case. I can't stop long in this city and my departure is dependent on yours..."

"But how will you do it?"

"I'll do what I promise by the most simple means in the world. Modern alchemy will permit me to transform into good dollars the five sous that my cousin's generosity accorded me, and which my enemies didn't think of taking from me when they stole my garments at Señora Concha's rancho. They didn't know what I can do with twenty-five centimes, but I know, so I've saved them preciously."

"But what alchemy?"

"Oh, sir, respect my secret. I'll take care of the matter after lunch. I authorize you to follow my steps at a distance, for it might perhaps shock your prejudices a little. There, now we're in accord, it's necessary for you to suspend your worries until three o'clock, and let's talk about something else. Let's talk about the city where we are."

"Until three o'clock?"

"Exactly. To occupy you, allow me to show you around Frisco."

What can one do without money, except wander? So they went to look at the villas of varied architecture constructed on the heights, Montgomery, North Park, and the Cliff House, from which one can see the most admirable panoramas in the world. Here, the city dominated by its three railway stations, Oakland, South and North Pacific, which link it to New York, Mexico and the territories of the Dominion; there, the busy harbor, the fort of the Presidio, the sea

121

dotted with the white patches of sails and the gray plumes of steamers; Seal Rock emerging in the distance, with its herds of seals protected by the federal government.

Lavarède explained everything.

"Do you see those strips of verdure cutting through the thickets of houses? They indicate the location of the cemeteries of Lone Mount, the Freemasons and the Old-Fellows. It's there that lovers go to talk about the future among the stones that seal the past…as they do in the Orient."

As Aurett made a moue he added: "What do you expect, Miss? Everything is strange here. Consider that islet of buildings where the houses seem pressed against one another. That's Chinatown."

"Tell us about Chinatown, my dear cicerone."

"Between Lafayette Square and Alta-Plaza," Armand hastened to continue, "there are thirty blocks of houses constructed in the Chinese fashion, separated by narrow streets cluttered with filth. Those houses now lodge ten times as many people as before. It's the seat of the six great Immigration Companies. Oh, those Companies! In France people complain about employment agencies. What would they say about the subjects of the Son of Heaven? Those societies have agents along the entire coat of the Middle Kingdom, who impress emigrants, employed here as coolies, servants, artisans, launderers, etc. They're embarked on the sole condition that their bodies will be repatriated if they die. The Companies have their own laws and tribunals, before which all conflicts between Celestials are judged, without appeal."

It was time to return to the hotel. After the meal, voluntarily prolonged, a short siesta in the lounge took the travelers to the time indicated by the Parisian.

"Three o'clock!" Aurett and her father exclaimed.

Armand conceded, and five minutes later, all three were walking along the sidewalk of Kearny Street. The Frenchman was marching in the lead. He seemed to be inspecting the terrain.

Having arrived in front of the Stock Exchange, besieged by a compact crowd of speculators, he made a gesture of satisfaction.

Then Murlyton and Aurett witnessed a spectacle that was incomprehensible to them. Lavarède took his handkerchief out of his pocket, unfolded it, shook it, and finally laid it out on the sidewalk with the absorbed air of a man performing an operation of capital importance—after which he walked around the batiste square murmuring unintelligible words and waving his arms.

Rummaging in his waistcoat pocket, he took out the five sous that comprised his entire baggage, one by one, and deposited them in a sinuous line on the handkerchief.

This performance attracted the attention of people nearby. One passer-by stopped, then two, and then ten. When the Parisian had finished, a circle had formed.

Graciously, he bowed, and made a little speech, in excellent English.

"Originally from this free land, I was brought up in France. It was there that I made the marvelous discovery with which I have come to endow my fatherland. Throughout the Middle Ages, scholars, then named alchemists, searched for the philosopher's stone, the metamorphosis of base metal into pure gold. Well, that for which those admirable toilers searched in vain, chance has enabled me to discover. Yes, gentlemen, in my hands bronze become silver. One cent is transformed into a dollar. Look: here's a French sou; you're going to witness the curious experiment. But if I'm to deliver you my secret, please encourage the operator. Go on, put your hands in our pockets—take advantage of the opportunity, gentlemen."

"Eh!" remarked a speculator who had just slipped into the circle. "If the method were infallible, the inventor would have no need to make appeal to public generosity."

Lavarède looked at the interrupter, and was dumbstruck. It was Bouvreuil, in person.

Aurett had recognized him immediately. "Father," she said to Murlyton, with a hint of fear. "There's that vile man!"

How did he come to be there? In the most easily explicable fashion. Having arrived that morning by the Southern Pacific Railroad, Pénélope's father, who still had nearly four thousand francs and his letters of credit had reasoned thus:

Monsieur Armand is a boulevardier. It's therefore on the busiest street, on the local boulevard, that I have the best chance of finding him.

He had made enquiries, and, as you can see, events had proved him right.

A murmur of approval had greeted his observation, although, having been made in French, someone had been obliged to translate it. But the Parisian had recovered all his aplomb, and the superiority that the use of the language of the country gave him came to his aid.

"Gentlemen," he cried, "the man who has just spoken does not have the soul of a philanthropist. He has no understanding of delicacy. If I'm asking for your obol, it's in order not to appear to be giving you alms. He doesn't see that; he doesn't want to let go of a cent. He's one of those people who expects to receive without giving. He's probably a usurer!" And, in a loud voice: "He is one, gentlemen! See the characteristics of the race: the flat nose, the fleeting gaze, the thin lips, opening over the teeth of a jackal. Oh, what an odious and base physiognomy!"

The audience laughed. Bouvreuil, who understood enough to think it a good idea to leave, went to observe from some distance away.

"Joke, my friend," he muttered. "I've found you again. I'll soon be able to make you regret your gibes."

Having laughed, the curious paid. The cents tumbled on to the ground, a rain of copper that Armand picked up carefully, encouraging the hesitant.

"Come on gentlemen, another ten cents…another five, three, two…!"

Two more coins clinked on the ground. The young man then picked up his handkerchief, his sous and his receipts, put them in his pockets and said, gravely: "The experiment is concluded. As you see, with a sou, I've just procured a dollar. The exercise that you've just witnessed is what Parisians newsvendors call *La Postiche*."[33]

Silvery laughter greeted this speech. It was Aurett. To anyone who had told her, three months earlier, that she would admire a French journalist in such a circumstance, she would have responded with a categorical denial. British etiquette did not permit such an aberration. And yet, impossibly, implausibly, it had happened, without her sensing any revolt in her inner being. It is true that she was a long way from correct English society, and that Lavarède was playing the charlatan on her behalf.

The gaiety of a charming young woman is infectious. The audience dispersed with smiling faces.

"Good trick!" they said.

Only one man, with an unkempt red beard and mud-stained clothes, a "placer-scraper," as people out there call the latecomers who glean the rare gold dust forgotten in the abandoned deposits, drew his revolver and said, in a hoarse voice: "Equal shares, my businessman. I threw you a cent; I'm counting on half a dollar profit...for the alchemist, if you please."

He took aim at Armand.

The Englishwoman saw the movement and uttered a scream. Murlyton took a step forward in order to interpose himself, but the Parisian stopped him with a gesture. Drawing his own revolver, he faced up to his adversary. The latter pressed his trigger. A bullet whistled past the journalist's ear and went through the hat of a passer-by—a true American, who turned round, grumbling: "What a bore these fellows are who settle their differences in the street!" and then passed on, smoothing the nap of his hat.

Armand fired in his turn, so accurately that he smashed the butt of his aggressor's weapon, whose hand was traversed by the bullet.

"Is that enough?" he asked.

"Yes!" cursed the wounded man. "All right!"

Nodding his head slightly, Lavarède drew away. He was in a hurry to rejoin his friends, who were standing ten paces away, as if nailed to the ground, the gentleman very red and the young woman very pale. A further incident delayed him again, however. A Chinaman, who, by virtue of his blue tunic and his cap surmounted by an amber globule was recognizable as a literate of the second class, barred his way. The Celestial had been one of the first to stop next to the young man. He had watched the entire scene with an ardent satisfaction.

"You have a cool head, sir," he said, in nasal English.

The Frenchman looked at him, smiling. "Is this another quarrel?"

---

[33] i.e. "the sham," or, in American, "the con."

"No, merely a question. You're courageous and in need of money?"

"You have a proposition to offer me, then?"

"Exactly."

"Do it quickly; my friends are waiting for me."

"It's a matter of dangerous work, but well paid."

Armand hesitated. He had to reason to launch himself into a hazardous enterprise, for now, with the dollar he possessed, he was sure that he could procure the sum promised to Murlyton. A secret instinct, however, interested him in the Chinaman's proposal—and he would not be risking anything by going to see.

"I remain free to refuse if the conditions don't suit me?"

"Yes."

"What do I have to do?"

"Come this evening, at ten o'clock, to the southern corner of Alta Plaza Square."

"On the edge of Chinatown?"

"That's right. You'll be taken to the place where you'll learn what's expected of you."

"Ten o'clock—I'll be there." And to himself, he murmured: "Ugly brute! That's local color."

With that, the literate with the amber button went his way, and Lavarède went his.

"Ah!" cried Murlyton. "I wouldn't have let you try to get me the money if I'd known you were going to risk your life!"

"Let's not talk about that," the young man interjected. "Very picturesque, wasn't it, that duel in the street? It'll make an amusing article...when I get home. For the moment, let's go to the office of the *Californian Times*."

At the newspaper office, the Englishman, instructed by Lavarède, obtained, for the price of a dollar, the insertion of the following advertisement:

Certain method of winning on the horses. Write Box 271, Californian. Enclose ten cents.

"With that advertisement," said the young man to his companions, "we'll have what we need tomorrow, and more."

"That's quite possible," remarked the Englishman. "Human stupidity is limitless—but what's the certain method your promising?"

Lavarède shrugged his shoulders and said, laughing: "Only bet on the winners."

"Oh!" said Aurett, affronted. "That's not honest!"

The remark appeared to wound the Frenchman.

"You're mistaken, Mademoiselle. We need a few dollars; I'm borrowing them as best I can, with the certainty of not doing any wrong to anyone. Tomorrow we'll come to the *Californian*, and open the letters addressed to us until we have the twenty-eight dollars. Mr. Murlyton will cable London. Then, the response from your banker having arrived, we'll return ten cents to each of the opened letters that we've collected from the paper. Your father will then put in a new advertisement saying that the method of wining on the horses doesn't exist. Our correspondents only have to present themselves at the *Californian Times*, with identification, after which the sums they've sent will be reimbursed. Cost: three or four dollars. That will be my commission."

The young woman blushed on listening to this explanation. She was ashamed of thinking badly of him, and admitted it frankly.

"Will you forgive me, Monsieur Lavarède?" she said, extending her hand to him.

"Your susceptibility does you honor," the Frenchman riposted, having recovered his good humor. "I congratulate you on it, and am almost glad of the small mortification that it caused me."

On that reply, the Englishwoman's blush deepened further, but the travelers reached the China Pacific Hotel, and their thoughts changed direction at the sight of Bouvreuil coming into the lobby after them.

The landlord had followed them, and, certain of having found their lodgings, was about to take a room in the hotel, in order to be able to keep watch on his "son-in-law," as he persisted in designating Lavarède.

The latter looked the businessman up and down. "It's you again, Monsieur Bouvreuil?"

"It will always be me."

"You're determined not to leave me alone?"

"And to take you back to Europe, ruined and repentant—yes."

"Then you're still thinking of marrying me…?"

"To my daughter Pénélope, when you've failed in your mad enterprise. Exactly!"

"In that case, Monsieur Bouvreuil, prepare your legs. I intend to make you run."

"I shall run."

"I shall outdistance you—not so much to obtain my cousin's inheritance, as in order not to see you again."

And, turning his back on his enemy, Armand leapt into the elevator, in which the English duo had already taken their places, leaving Bouvreuil in a very bad humor. Reflection doubtless calmed the delegate of the Panama shareholders down, however, for an hour later, after having booked a room in Mr. Tower's office, he went to the telegraph office and sent a dispatch to his daughter at Sens (Yonne), saying: *San Francisco. Found fugitive. Am hopeful.*

XII. In Chinatown

That same evening, as ten o'clock chimed on the innumerable clocks of San Francisco, Armand arrived at the southern corner of Alta Plaza Square. He made sure that his revolver slid easily from its leather holster, and looked around. To his right rose buildings of American construction, tall and bare; to his left, Chinatown began, with its low buildings and its bizarrely-shaped roofs.

"So," murmured the journalist, "is the mandarin going to leave me standing here?"

As if to reply to his question, an individual who had been hidden in a doorway until then approached, gliding noiselessly in his felt slippers.

"You're brave and in need of money," he said, in the nasal tone particular to the Chinese.

"Bravo!" said Lavarède. "Everything in place, even the password. Lead on."

"One moment," the Chinaman said. "Who sent you here?"

"A literate with an amber button."

"Where did you see him?"

"At the Stock Exchange."

"Then it's you that is expected. Follow me."

With that, the two men started walking at a rapid pace, going into the narrow streets of the Chinese quarter. Armand followed his guide, whose moving silhouette furnished him with an indispensable point of reference, for, in the midst of the American city inundated by electric light, Chinatown was a patch of shadow. Here, as in their own land, the natives of the Middle Kingdom were refractory to progress. The streets ought to have been lit by oil lamps; the lamps existed but no one ever lit them. There were only grease-paper lanterns, and yet, nowhere would lighting have been more useful.

The roadways of trampled earth, divided in the middle by stinking trenches into which water drained, along with the ordure tipped in by the inhabitants, careless of interrupting the flow, offered pedestrians extraordinary facilities for breaking their necks. But Lavarède had researched San Francisco, so he prudently followed in the tracks of his guide, and, after only stumbling two or three times, reach Sacramento Street, which runs through the middle of the strange quarter. It is on that street that the habitations of well-to-do Chinamen and the offices of the Immigration Agencies are situated.

The individual that the Parisian was accompanying went to a nearby house, seized the brass door-knocker and rapped in a particular manner. The door immediately turned on its hinges. The visitors entered, and the door closed of its own accord, without anyone appearing.

"Very amusing," murmured the Parisian. "We appear to be acting in a melodrama in a well-tricked-out theater. While speaking, he looked around. He found himself in a rather large courtyard surrounded by low buildings.

He was not given time to pursue his inspection. "Come," said his guide, dragging him away.

Facing them was a doorway framed with red joist decorated with black threads, through which the first steps of a narrow stairway could be seen. They went up. On the first floor they went through a sequence of rooms vaguely illuminated by candles enclosed in paper lanterns. In the last one, where light was dispersed less parsimoniously, three men dressed in the latest Peking fashions were conversing in low voices.

All of them got to their feet when Armand arrived; the Parisian had no difficulty recognizing one of them as the Chinaman from the Stock Exchange, who said to his companions: "This is the brave man I mentioned to you."

The journalist bowed, seemingly unembarrassed by the searching gazes fixed on him by three pairs of oblique eyes.

"Sit down," said the literate with the amber button.

"Gladly," said Lavarède, taking advantage of the permission. Silently, he added: *What diabolical affair are these saffron faces going to propose to me?*

The guide had withdrawn discreetly. After a pause, the Celestial who had already spoken said to the Parisian: "You're not English, are you?"

"How did you know that?"

"You express yourself very well, but with a particular accent that convinces me that you were born in France."

"All right."

"That was what convinced me to arrange a meeting with you."

Armand nodded, waiting for his interlocutor to explain.

The other went on: "Five hundred dollars is good pay."

Five hundred dollars! thought the Frenchman. *All Chinamen are misers; their deal must be frightful.*

The Chinaman misinterpreted his facial expression. "Come on," he said. "Let's not beat around the bush. We're authorized to go as far as two thousand. That's the final offer. Do you accept?"

For that price, Lavarède thought, *they're going to ask me to blow up the whole city.*

"Well?"

"Well, it's agreed. When do I get the money?"

"In three days' time, at midnight."

"Ah!" There was disappointment in the exclamation. By receiving a part of the promised fee in advance, the Parisian would have been able to renounce the advertisement in the *Californian Times* that had displeased Aurett.

"What's the matter?"

"Nothing. I repeat: it's agreed. What do I have to do?"

"Attach a paving stone to the feet of a corpse and throw it into the sea."

"Ah!" said Armand, with a smile. "It's you who've made this corpse?"

The literate shook his head. "No, it's disease."

"So it's not a matter of concealing a crime? Then why offer me two thousand dollars?" Then he slapped his forehead. "I've got it...still melodrama...there's an inheritance?"

"No."

"Then I don't understand."

"Do you need to understand?"

"Since childhood, I've only acted when the objective seemed to me to be clear, distinct...and not criminal."

The Chinamen looked at him; they had a rapid discussion in low voices. The one who decided was the spokesman. "So be it," he said. "You'll be satisfied."

"Good."

"But remember that nothing in the world can protect you from our vengeance if you betray us."

"An unnecessary threat," said Lavarède, tranquilly. "If I were a coward, I wouldn't be here. Why would I betray you, since I'm not afraid of you?"

His interlocutor appeared to appreciate the reasoning, and he began, in a slow voice; "Our name is the White Lotus. Our name is *No hypocrisy*."

"Ah. Good!" Armand put in. "I have it—it's a matter of a political conspiracy. You're the revolutionaries of the Middle Kingdom. I like that better!"

The literate looked at him benevolently. "You're up to date—so much the better. But one word in your definition is inexact. We're no more revolutionaries than the people of this country who say 'America for the Americans.' We say: 'China for the Chinese.' Conquered by a Manchu horde, which holds power today, we intend to deliver our fatherland and establish a national Chinese government."

"And in order to work the trick you massacre Europeans in Shanghai, Canton and Petchili!"

"We deplore those massacres, without being able to prevent them. The lower orders remember that in 1860 European soldiers helped in crushing the Tai-Pings, devoted to the same work as us, and in their ignorance, they include all Europeans in the same hatred." The literate smiled and said: "But we're not here to give you a lecture on internal politics. Let's return to our sheep—that, I believe, is how the French express it?"

"Indeed," the journalist confirmed, amused by the turn of the conversation.

"This is it: there is a resident in this city named Kin-Tchang, of Manchu origin. Once, in China, he delivered two affiliates of the White Lotus to the authorities. Knowing that the Society avenges its members, he expatriated himself. He was safe here. The Unites States government is ill-disposed in our regard; we are forced to operate with great reserve. We intend, however, to punish his infamy. You know that we love our native soil. If we emigrate it is on the express condition that if we die, our mortal remains will be taken back to China.

"That's well-known. You even have the habit, which seems singular n Europe, of having our coffins made while you're alive. You place them in full view in your abodes, and put a certain coquetry into enlivening them with carvings and decorations..."

The man with the amber button nodded n satisfaction. "Exactly! Well, we have decided that the body of the Manchu Kin-Tschang will not return to the Middle Kingdom."

"Damn!"

In our way of seeing, such a punishment seems puerile, but the journalist understood that Chinese ideas made that exclusion a terrible punishment.

The literate continued: "He doubtless caught wind of our plan, for he took precautions. He died yesterday and his body, immediately taken away has been transported to the Pacific Box dock. Perhaps you're unaware that that's a shipping company?"

The journalist could not resist the temptation to show off his erudition, and, in a professorial tone, he said: "You'll see whether I'm unaware. Your compatriots are numerous in the state of California. Marcel Monnier[34] estimates their number at more than fifty thousand. Once, those who died in exile were repatriated by a Chinese junk that shuttled between the American and Asiatic coasts, with one departure every two months or thereabouts. There was a gap to fill, so a Yankee company was formed, and charted four steamers, one of which leaves every fortnight, with the late sons of Han—that's how you describe yourselves, isn't it?"

"Indeed," affirmed the delighted literate.

"As there isn't always a sufficient quantity of corpses, the Pacific Box Line steamers complete their cargoes by accepting merchandise, and even a few passengers that aren't frightened by those nautical hearses. There!"

"Good," said the man with the amber button, won over. "I can see that I made a fortunate choice."

Armand bowed.

"This is what we expect of you. Kin-Tchang's coffin bears the number 49. It's a matter of extracting the Manchu and throwing him in the sea with a stone attached to his neck."

"And you're offering two thousand dollars for so little?"

"It's more difficult than you might think. None of us could do it. For one thing, no Chinaman would carry out that sacrilege. Then too, the Company in on

---

[34] Marcel Monnier (1853-1918) was a Parisian journalist, associated with *Le Temps*, and member of the Societé de Géographie de Paris who wrote a number of travel books and cultivated a substantial reputation as a globe-trotter.

the alert, and the watchman at the dock would be suspicious of anyone resembling a subject of the Son of Heaven."

"Whereas he won't be suspicious of me, a European," the Parisian completed, "and I can take advantage of that to deplete his cargo."

"That's it."

"Furthermore," added Lavarède, "the Company is American, and in case of failure you wouldn't want to deal with the Union's courts. In fact, I'm beginning to understand the difficulties: breaking and entering, theft, sacrilege etc."

His interlocutor bit his lip, but immediately recovered his composure. "Well, two thousand dollars…ten thousand francs, in French money…"

"Is well worth running a few risks. That's my opinion. I accept the bargain. But how will the sum be given to me?"

"The dock is fifty yards from the harbor. Three nights from now, one of ours will be on watch. On showing him the cadaver, you'll collect the moment."

"A fair swap. That suits me. I only need to find a means to get into the dock."

"That's your business. I can give you one useful item of information, though."

"Go on."

"The employee who'll be on guard that night is a man named Vincent, Irish in origin. He takes his meals at the Oxtail Tavern in Susgrave Street, next door to the Box Line headquarters, opposite Oceanic Steamship."

"Noted."

"I'll add one more thing: it's indispensable to act at the appointed time, for the next morning, the coffins will be taken aboard the *Heavenway*, which will put out to sea that day."

The journalist's face lit up, and, unable to contain himself any longer, the happy fellow exclaimed: "Eureka!"

"What have you found?" asked the Chinaman, thus proving that he merited the badge of the literate.

"What I was looking for. Don't worry—you'll have your Manchu." Mentally he added: *Otherwise, he'd be in my way.*

Everything being agreed, the young man took his leave of his hosts and went back to the hotel, humming. He had evidently brought back a robust gaiety from the Chinese quarter, for the next day, at lunch, Murlyton and Aurett were astonished by his good humor. They remarked on it to him.

"Good," said Lavarède. "You'll understand my joy. Today, Monday the third of August, I have the honor of informing you that I shall be leaving San Francisco on Thursday the sixth."

"Ah!" pronounced a voice behind him that caused him to shiver.

He turned round. Bouvreuil was there, having approached silently after noticing his cheerful expression, and had overheard his final words.

For a moment, Armand had forgotten his enemy, but, disagreeable as is appearance was, he refrained from letting any annoyance show.

"Why, it's the worthy Monsieur Bouvreuil again," he said, smiling.

"In person. You mentioned your departure, and as the interest that I have leads me to forbid you to leave..."

"See how true the axiom is that is every love affair, there is one who loves and another who allows themselves to be loved. I'm the other one, and I'm counting on giving you the slip."

"Don't count on it. My daughter Pénélope is expecting..."

The name of the usurer's daughter had the gift of exasperating Armand."

"Monsieur Bouvreuil," he said. "Penelope waited for Ulysses while spinning. For the sake of prudence, I advise you to do likewise."[35]

His foot was tapping suggestively. The landlord drew away, not without launching an absurd item of repartee at the young man: "You're quick, but I'm tenacious. We'll see!"

Once rid of him, Lavarède told his companions about his expedition to the "land of the slippers." He told them the plan that had quite naturally germinated in his brain: to take the place of the mandarin Kin-Tchang and travel to China in coffin number 49, reserved for the dead man.

Murlyton protested. "But in that case, my daughter and I will have to book passage on this funereal ship, the *Heavenway*, and spend twenty days in company with the dead."

Aurett had paled slightly. Nevertheless, she hastened to interrupt the Englishman. "We don't have the right to raise any obstacle to Monsieur Lavarède's departure. That would be incorrect, Father."

"Undoubtedly, but..."

"You're exaggerating my nervous sensibility. I'm more intrepid than you seem to think, and the crossing on the Pacific Box Line steamer doesn't appear to me to be insupportable."

The journalist understood all that she was not saying. He tried to thank her, but she stopped him, smiling.

"You've seen death at close range for me; in my turn, I'll see the dead. I'm evening things up."

She said that delicately, with such good grace that Murlyton was convinced that his fears were unfounded. Nothing prevented him, thereafter, from reserving two cabins at the Shipping Company as soon as he received the money from London, and the incident was closed, to general satisfaction. Armand only

---

[35] The wordplay is based on the fact that *filer* [spinning] can also be used as an injunction to go away, as in the American phrase "get lost." The mythical Penelope was, of course, weaving her father's shroud while keeping her suitors at bay, but Bouvreuil is probably not as literate as the Chinaman, and might not take the inference that far.

132

begged his friends to make every effort to put the unbearable Bouvreuil off the track—and they all awaited the moment to present themselves at the *Californian Times* to discover the result of the advertisement that had appeared that morning.

That night they sent to the newspaper's office. The number of letters that had arrived at the relevant box number had reached five hundred, which, at ten cents per missive, represented fifty dollars, or two hundred and fifty francs, nearly twice the amount they required.

"O power of advertising!" declared the delighted gentleman, who, as had been agreed, contented himself with taking the twenty-eight dollars required for the telegram.

Fifty minutes later, he had cabled his bankers in London and he returned to the China Pacific, where the young couple had preceded him. He found them in the lounge, and, his serenity returned by the assurance of soon being furnished with money, he shook Lavarède's hand as if to break the bones and said: "I'm beginning to believe that you'll get your cousin's inheritance."

"We're not at the end of the voyage yet."

"Bah! You're the kind of man who won't spend your five sous, and will make a fortune on the way."

Armand returned the handshake and murmured: "There are ten thousand like me on the boulevard, who generally live in dreams. If we took it into our heads to make money, there'd soon be none left for the financiers."

XIII. The Pacific Box Line Company

Susgrave Street was a narrow street leading to the harbor. That was where the Oxtail Tavern was located, at which the Irishman Vincent, the Box Company employee identified to Armand by his two-thousand-dollar Chinaman, ate his meals.

On Tuesday, at midday, having brushed his suit, tailored in the English style and waxed his brown moustache, Lavarède went into the tavern, his eyes sparkling with joyful hope. Without looking at them, he went through the crowd of mariners, dock workers and petty clerks gathered at the tables, went to the counter and addressed himself to the proprietress, a stout red-faced matron who was bursting out of her dress.

"Pardon me, Madame, but could you give me some information?"

"Anything you wish, sir," replied the stout woman, simpering.

"A thousand thanks. Do you have, among your customers a man named Vincent?"

"Yes indeed."

"Is he here at the moment?"

The tavern-keeper looked around the room and, still simpering, said: "He is—over there, in the corner, the fellow sitting at the little round table."

"All alone?"

"Yes—he prefers that."

Armand shot the innkeeper a grateful glance that almost made her swoon with pleasure, and headed for the individual she had pointed out. He was short and fat, with reddish blond hair, installed in a corner of the room, eating gluttonously while reading a newspaper. His fleshy fists were moving back and forth without him raising his head, and he was so absorbed by his double occupation that he was probably the only person in the establishment who had not noticed the Parisian come in.

The latter calmly took a stool, sat down facing the Pacific Box employee, and put a hand on his newspaper.

"Is it to Mr. Vincent to whom I have the pleasure of speaking?" he asked.

The man looked the person disturbing him up and down. He was certainly discontented to be interrupted in his meal, but the journalist was unmoved by such trivia.

"You don't know me," he said, "which is quite natural…I've come from France. I'm looking for a cousin who lives in the city. His name is Vincent and he has the right to half of an inheritance. The fellow left the country many years ago. I've never seen him, so I'm running around Frisco visiting all the Vincents. Perhaps you're the right one?"

"Me?" growled his interlocutor.

"Well, it's possible. At any rate, we'll soon see. But I'll have lunch at the same time—it makes chatting more agreeable. Is the wine presentable here?"

Vincent's face brightened. "Yes, but it's dear."

"Bah! I don't mind the expense. You won't refuse to have a glass with me?"

This time, Vincent's face became almost amiable. How can one not welcome, in any case, a stranger who talks to you about an inheritance and good wine? On his order, the waiter brought a tray, and placed a labeled bottle and two glasses before them. Lavarède immediately filled them, and clinked glasses with the man opposite.

"To your health!" he said. "And may you be my cousin! No compliment— you have a physiognomy that goes with mine..."

The other blinked, drank a gulp of the wine that had been poured for him, and then clicked his tongue.

"Pretty good," he murmured. "A pity one can't drink it all the time."

"One could," said the Parisian, lowering his voice, "if one had the luck of an inheritance."

"Well, yes, only then. Go on, let's talk about the affair in question."

"I'd like nothing better, since I've made the voyage to America, but let me eat a little first. I'm dying of hunger."

The waiter had just served Lavarède, and for a moment, the journalist seemed to be absorbed in the digestion of the peppermint stew placed in front of him. Vincent watched him, with an impatience that he would doubtless have expressed if Armand had not take care to fill his glass several times. One does not hurry a man who distributes "the milk of the vine" so generously.

Finally, he judged that his subject was ready, and, starting on a second bottle that the waiter has presented to him with the respect due to a client who is spending good money, he said: "My dear Mr. Vincent, you'll understand that my investigation is delicate, and that, in order not to be the victim of some adventurer, I'm obliged to take precautions.

"Of course, but..."

"You can't be confused with the sharpers who are so numerous in the city. You're an honorable citizen, living on his labor, for whom my esteem is acquired. My only objective in coming here is to ask you to answer a few indispensable preliminary questions.

"You have only to ask; I'll answer."

They employee was visibly on tenterhooks, eager to know.

Good, thought Lavarède. *The fish is hooked; it only remains to reel him in.*

Graciously, he said: "Do you know where you were born, Mr. Vincent?"

The man shrugged his shoulders. "My God—what a question. I lived there until I was twenty."

"Where?"

"Ladbroke Hill, six miles from Dublin...in Ireland."

The Parisian simulated a joyful surprise. By reflection, Vincent's face brightened.

"Go on with the interrogation," he said, timidly.

"I believe you're the son of...?"

"Joseph William Vincent of Ladbroke, and Marie Pauline Crooks, of Noxleburg."

"Very good."

"Very good?" said the breathless employee. "Am I your cousin?"

"Almost..."

"What do you mean, *almost?*"

"There's still one point to clarify."

"Go on."

Excited by the thought of an inheritance, Vincent had such a strange expression that the journalist was on the brink of bursting into laughter, which would doubtless have compromised the success of his negotiation. He contained himself, not without difficulty, and continued: "Do you remember an old female relative who lived in Dublin? Rich and miserly, she never saw her relatives, doubtless fearing that the poor folk might want to borrow money from her."

The employee appeared to search his memory. "No," he said, finally, trembling that his reply might put an end to his golden dream, "but that's not surprising. My father died when I was twelve, and my mother followed him to the grave a few months later."

"Think hard: Aunt Margaret?"

"Margaret!" exclaimed Vincent, triumphantly. "I know that name!"

Of course, Lavarède thought. *It's common enough in Ireland.* Then, with a perfectly simulated gravity, the young man extended his hands to his interlocutor and said: "Cousin..."

The other did not let him finish. "Cousin," he repeated

"We are—there's no longer any doubt about it, so far as I'm concerned. Listen, then: Aunt Margaret died leaving eight thousand pounds sterling, to be divided between you and me, on condition that we both receive it at the same time. She must surely have wanted to repair her ill-treatment of the two branches of the family by that means."

And to the poor devil who was listening to him open-mouthed, he told the story of how, being pressed for money himself, he had decided to come in person to find his cousin. He told him that he was staying at the China Pacific Hotel on Montgomery Street—which made the needy Vincent open his eyes wide.

"At that rate," the latter remarked, "your four thousand pounds won't get you very far. Me, I won't play the great lord. I'll buy some land in Ireland and live by farming it..."

Lavarède had no interest in his pseudo-relative's plans for the future, and interrupted him to ask: "What time to you have to get back to work?"

"Two o'clock."

"It's five to."

"What does it matter now? I've a good mind to hand in my resignation."

Armand started. "Oh, don't do that!" he exclaimed. In an instant, he saw the plan he had so painstakingly contrived falling to dust.

"Why not?"

"Because..." He could not, however, reply: *Because I need you to get into the Company dock.* Searching for words, he said: "Because…legal formalities take a long time in the United States, where the lawyers will need to communicate with those in Dublin representing Aunt Margaret, and those in Paris charged with my interests. If you hand in your resignation today you might be penniless for a whole month."

"That's true—but it's a pity too, for I'd like to have avoided the chore I have to take on tomorrow."

"What's that?" asked the Parisian, with the most innocent expression in the world, while he thanked the God of voyagers mentally for having brought about the transition he desired so much.

"The night shift with the yellow sleepers…otherwise known as the dead Chinamen."

Lavarède put on the surprised expression of an ignorant tourist and allowed the employee to explain the functioning of Pacific Box.

"Brrrr!" he murmured, when Vincent had finished. "It must make a singular impression to spend the night in the midst of all those coffins."

"It's tiresome."

"Not banal, at least, as a tourist adventure, and I'd like to do it myself, if possible…in order to have a story to tell when I go back."

"It can be arranged," said his interlocutor, "if you really mean it."

"My word, yes."

"Nothing simpler. Tomorrow, I'll go in through the Administration; you wait outside and I'll open the door that gives access to the quay for you—that's the way the packages are brought in for embarkation. Neither seen nor known, we'll be at home until morning. Bring me whisky."

Armand had difficulty hiding his joy. His ruse had succeeded completely. The watchman was offering to let him into the dock personally. Now, it was a matter of leaving the Oxtail Tavern without opening his purse, since he still only had twenty-five centimes in his pocket.

"A proposition, cousin?" he said.

"Agreed in advance."

"As you're on duty tomorrow, can you get leave from your administration this afternoon?"

"Perhaps."

"Let's go together and ask. Afterwards, we can go back to my hotel, where we'll have dinner."

"I don't know…if I should," the employee stammered, excited by the idea of eating at a first-rate table.

"Go on."

"All right."

The Rabelaisian moment had arrived, but it had been prepared with a master hand, and when Lavarède, having searched, declared that he only had French currency, Vincent nobly assured him that he would settle the bill. He went further than that, and invited his new friend to have lunch with him at the Oxtail Tavern again, at his expense, the following day: a politeness to which Armand replied: "Agreed! But I'll entertain you in the evening at the China Pacific."

"Perfect! Lunch on me, dinner on you!" Delightedly, the fat man was thinking: *I'll come out of that very well, for it's better at the hotel and dearer*.

As he went back into the hotel, the journalist met Murlyton coming out. The worthy gentlemen was radiant. He had received a response from his bankers in London, collected his money from the Central Post Office and taken the letters he had opened back to the *Californian Times*, after having scrupulously returned the ten cents he had borrowed from the naïve correspondents. The advertisement indicated by Lavarède had settled the question definitively.

Lavarède abandoned his pseudo-cousin momentarily to say to the Englishman, in a low voice: "Take advantage of your stroll to book passage aboard the *Heavenway*."

"We're leaving, then?"

"Did you doubt it?" Indicating Vincent, he added: "This worthy fellow is furnishing me with the means—without suspecting it, of course. He'll tell you all about it at dinner. I've invited him for this evening and tomorrow."

"But two dinners will cost you more than twenty-five centimes," said Murlyton.

Armand shook his head. "Not at all. You paid Mr. Tower for eight full days."

"Yes, but I don't see…"

"Wait. We arrived on Saturday. The hotel therefore owes me meals until next Saturday. Now, I'm leaving on Wednesday evening, still having the right to Thursday, Friday and Saturday—five meals. I'm taking two of them in advance for that man. As for the other three, I'll take them with me. Mr. Tower will thus remain my debtor for the room, which will be vacant for two days before the appointed date."

"Very accurately reasoned," the Englishman declared. "I'll book the places with Pacific Box."

That evening, at dinner, Vincent, whom the Parisian had relate the story of their acquaintance, amused the gentleman and his daughter enormously. When he had gone, however, Aurett said quietly to Lavarède: "I feel sorry for the poor man. He believes in his inheritance, and the disappointment will be great."

"True, but I have a consolation in store for him."

"What?"

He hesitated momentarily, then made his decision. "Are you asking me to tell you the secret?"

Aurett looked him straight in the face and said: "Yes, I'm asking. There's a shadow in my thoughts: dispel it."

"I obey. I'm giving Vincent the two thousand dollars from my Chinese friends."

The young woman's face lit up with a smile. She extended her hand to her interlocutor shook his vigorously, saying simply: "Thank you."

Having returned to her room, she declared to herself seriously that she was very glad to be traveling the world in the company of Lavarède. By virtue of a bizarre reluctance, however, she said nothing about that to the honorable Mr. Murlyton.

XIV. Lavarède Plays Dead

The next day, at about ten o'clock in the evening, Armand emerged from the China Pacific Hotel with Vincent. The former was carrying a voluminous package wrapped up in strong paper. The latter seemed to be having difficulty supporting himself. There was nothing astonishing about that. During dinner, Lavarède had played the part of his guest's drink dispenser, and, with one of them filling the glass and the other emptying it, the employees mind had not taken long to become fuddled. Vincent was magnificently drunk.

Nevertheless, partly sustained by his companion and encouraged most of all by the confidence that the package contained, among other things, a bottle of excellent run, the worthy man arrived in reasonably good condition at what he called the funereal transport company's "public entrance." There, he parted from the journalist, and while the latter went along Susgrave Street as far as the quay, he went through the porter's lodge, crossed the courtyard with an unsteady gait, went through a sequence of offices and finally reached the hall of the dead.

The four bare walls formed an elongated rectangle, covered with a glazed roof. Two doors gave access to it: the one by which the employee had just entered and another set in the opposite wall, which served for the exit of the "merchandise." Fifty biers posed on trestles were lined up along the walls. On top of each one was a label bearing a registration number.

Vincent began by carefully locking himself in, then chose from a bunch of keys the one the opened the door to the quay, and went to let his dear cousin in.

A few moments later the two men were sitting side by side, watching a saucepan in which the rum, warmed by the flame of a spirit lamp, was giving rise to a sizzling full of promise. In spite of a certain embarrassment of the tongue, the "Watchman" talked a great deal, beginning stories that never ended, and only conserving in the confusion of his ides one clear thought. That being the only one, he expressed it frequently:

"By God," he said, "I have a throat as dry as tinder. Hurry the punch along, cousin, so that I can give it the accolade."

Finally, Lavarède declared that the mixture contained in the saucepan was ready, and served a large helping to the employee. But one might have thought that the beverage augmented Vincent's thirst even further. He swallowed glasses of punch with a prodigious rapidity, without perceiving that his companion was not drinking.

The effect of that surfeit of alcohol was overwhelming. The Irishman suddenly stopped talking; his eyes closed in spite of his efforts. He oscillated on the stool that served in as a seat, and would infallibly have fallen over backwards if Armand had not caught him in his arms.

Gently, the Parisian laid him down on the ground, where the drunkard lay supine, with a blissful groan.

"Oof!" murmured Lavarède. "I'm rid of him. Now, to work."

The tools necessary to repair any accidents that befell the packages—screwdrivers, a hammer, etc.—were set out on a table. The young man took possession of them and made a circuit of the room, consulting the labels on the coffins. Number 49 soon struck his gaze.

Lavarède stopped, prey to a singular emotion.

Before him stretched the bier of varnished oak, curiously worked, which contained the remains of the Manchu Kin-Tchang. The dead man had dreamed of sleeping the eternal sleep in that narrow dwelling. He had thought, thus protected, that he would return to his native land, from which he had been obliged to exile himself while alive—and at the idea of deceiving that supreme hope, of despoiling the nameless thing that had been a man, the Parisian felt his heartbeats accelerating, while a cold sweat pearled on his temples.

He was on the point of renouncing his expedition and fleeing, in order not to become the profaner of a tomb, but he pulled himself together. After all, the dead man was a Chinaman, one of those ugly apes at which Occidentals learned to laugh when very small—and then, in sum, what harm was he doing? Was the earth of the Middle Kingdom really preferable to the green shroud of the waters?

Brusquely, Lavarède took out the screws that were maintaining the lid on the coffin and uncovered the box. Inside, cushioned by blue satin embroidered with gold, and a kind of leaden hull, the Manchu appeared, his elbows beside his body and his arms folded in such a way that the index fingers were touching the earlobes. His wide open eyes—in China the eyes of the dead are opened, whereas, in other countries, they are closed—seemed to be gazing with a disquieting fixity at the landscapes of the beyond. At that moment, something akin to a murmur of voices became audible. Lavarède turned round, gripped by an inexplicable anguish, but almost immediately, a smile distended his features. The noise came from the direction where Vincent was asleep. The drunkard was dreaming.

To run to him, take his bunch of keys and return to the Manchu was the work of a moment. With a thousand precautions the journalist slid the coffin to the ground, and, overcoming his repugnance, he seized Kin-Tchang round the waist. With an abrupt effort he pulled him out of the box and, shivering at the contact of his lugubrious burden, he marched toward the door to the quay.

He had almost reached it when Vincent called: "Cousin!"

The young man stopped, his feet nailed to the ground, and turned his head toward the drunken man. In the course of that movement he found himself face to face with the corpse, whose head was resting on his shoulder. The Manchu seemed to smile. Certainly, if he was witnessing the scene from another fatherland, he would have been well avenged by his enemy's shock. Lavarède was subject to a kind of hypnotism; his eyes fixed on Kin-Tchang's eyes, his neck seemed paralyzed, and he could not turn his head.

A minute passed thus…a century…during which Armand, afflicted by the immobility of the man he was carrying, expected at any moment to feel Vincent's hand fall on his shoulder. But nothing moved. Gradually, the Parisian calmed down; his taut muscles relaxed…

A sonorous snore proved to him that the employee had not ceased sleeping, and he set about opening the door.

The quay was deserted.

"Sapristi! Is he going to miss the rendezvous?" muttered Armand. After a more attentive inspection, however, he murmured: "No; I believe I recognize the silhouette of that individual arriving over there."

Some distance away, in fact, a man was marching rapidly, without making a sound, thanks to his felt slippers. Lavarède propped the Manchu's corpse against the wall and went to meet the pedestrian. The latter watched him coming, recognized him in is turn, and asked him: "Have you succeeded."

"Perfectly. The traitor awaits your pleasure."

The literate with the amber button—for it was him—made a joyful gesture.

"In that case, let's move fast."

Emotionlessly, this time, Armand returned to the hall, loaded the unfortunate Kin-Tchang on to his shoulder again, and carried him to the edge of the quay. The mandarin leaned over the dead man.

"It's really him," he said, in a hateful tone. "The White Lotus is avenged."

He went down a few steps of one of the stairways integrated into the quay and picked up, with difficulty, a cast iron cylinder that he had doubtless hidden there in advance. A solid rope attached it to the waist of the cadaver, and the Chinaman tranquilly pushed the whole into the water.

There was a dull sound, followed by a splash; great concentric circles slowly extended from the bank, and nothing more. The liquid mirror became smooth again, effacing al trace of the funereal operation.

The literate handed a packet of banknotes to Lavarède. "Here are the two thousand dollars owed to you. Adieu, my companion. May the divinity favor you." And he drew away rapidly, doubtless anxious not to remain any longer in the theater of his exploits.

Armand followed him with his eyes, and when his silhouette had melted into the obscurity, he went back into the hall. A moment later, the lead sheath contained in the coffin went to join the remains of the Manchu, making more room.

Lavarède was no longer trembling. With the aid of a drill, he pierced a few holes in the wall of the box, in which he counted on living henceforth.

Those preparations terminated, he replaced the Company's tools and reattached the keys to Vincent's belt. The employee was still snoring. With a smile floating on his lips, the Parisian studied him, and then introduced the mandarin's banknotes into an envelope that he had prepared, sealed it carefully, and placed it in plain view on the stool that his pseudo-cousin had previously occupied.

Having done that, he gathered together the food with which he had charged himself before leaving the China Pacific Hotel, deposited it in the empty bier, replaced it on the trestles, and lay down in the funereal box, pulling the lid back on top of him.

Henceforth, until reaching the Chinese coast, Lavarède was "dead."

At dawn, when Vincent, his head heavy, opened his eyes, he was astonished to find himself alone. He immediately perceived the Frenchman's latter. The subscription left no doubt: it was addressed to him. He opened it, and his stout fingers trembled on contact with the banknotes.

He read:

My dear cousin,

Accept these two thousand dollars on account of the inheritance about which I spoke to you. Personally, I'm voluntarily renouncing life—but one sometimes comes back from the other world. If that happens to me, I'll hasten to inform you. Believe that in quitting this earth, I'm taking with me the most cordial memory of you.

The employee rubbed his eyes, reread the strange missive, and put his head in his hands—a gesture which, as everyone knows, signifies that one is giving up any attempt to understand. His mime terminated with a shrug of the shoulders and a single sentence pronounced in a tranquil one:

"He was crazy, but two thousand dollars is reasonable."

With that slightly cavalier funeral oration, Vincent left the hall without paying any heed to a stifled laugh that seemed to emerge from bier 49.

At the same time, Bouvreuil, sitting in his room, was having a conversation with one of the bellboys of the China Pacific Hotel, who was originally from Germany. In return for an honest retribution, the boy was keeping watch on the landlord's behalf on the movements of Armand and his companions.

"So you're saying that he didn't come back last night?" said Pénélope's father.

"No, sir. The guest in room 13 was out all night."

"Out! What about the others?"

"They're locked in their rooms."

"Locked!"

Bouvreuil leap out of bed and pulled his trousers on. "As long as they haven't left the hotel under cover of darkness!"

The young German shook his head. "It's improbable, because their shoes are still outside their doors."

The usurer breathed out. "Ah! That's good, my friend. Thank you."

Left alone, Bouvreuil reflected while getting dressed.

That devil of a man has disappeared, he said to himself, *but I have a means of catching up with him. If he's on the point of continuing his voyage, the English pair, obliged to travel with him, will surely catch up with him. It's just a matter of not losing sight of them.*

Hastily, he piled his not-very-extensive wardrobe into his valise, pell-mell and left the room. Murlyton and his daughter were still asleep. Their shoes, as the bellboy had affirmed, were lined up outside their doors.

Delighted, Bouvreuil went to hide in the office of the hotel, deserted at this early hour, where he could not be seen. The watch was beginning to become unbearable when Aurett and her father, arm in arm with, finally put in an appearance. They both went out into the street at the tranquil pace of two good bourgeois taking a leisurely stroll. Without the inexplicable absence of Lavarède, the landlord would certainly not have thought of following them, but his mistrust—which was in direct proportion to his duplicity—was alert. Luggage in hand, he followed the English duo.

The latter did not suspect that the usurer as so close to them. In the course of their walk they made the purchases indispensable to the long voyage they were about to undertake. Bouvreuil shuddered with contentment on seeing them equip themselves with a large suitcase and then pile underwear, toilet necessities and perfume into it. They were definitely about to depart, and he praised his perspicacity.

At the end of a street, the English duo having turned the corner, he hastened his steps to catch up with them. On emerging on to the avenue, however, he almost ran into their arms.

On perceiving him, Aurett uttered a little squeal. "Do you see that man, Father?"

"Ah!" said Murlyton, phlegmatically. "What's he doing here?"

"He has his valise."

"As we have ours."

"He's following us."

"Perhaps."

During this rapid conversation, Bouvreuil had crossed the street, and was standing on the opposite sidewalk, seemingly interested in reading a poster.

"It's necessary that we give him the slip, Father."

"Do you think so, Aurett?"

"Yes, out of delicacy toward Monsieur Lavarède."

"Then you shall be satisfied."

A hansom cab was passing by. At a sign from the gentleman, the carriage pulled in at the sidewalk. The English duo took their places inside. Already, however, attentive to their movements, the landlord had stopped another vehicle. The young woman waved her gist at him angrily.

"It's too much. He doesn't intend to let us out alone."

Murlyton shrugged his shoulders and showed a sovereign to the cab-driver, who was perched on the seat. "You see this?" he said, placidly.

"Yes, sir!"

"It's yours if you can lose that cab."

"Where are we going?"

"Wherever you like."

"All right!"

The man picked up the reins, enlivened his horse with a crack of the whip, and the carriage departed at a rapid pace. Bouvreuil's cab moved off and followed at the same pace. For a few minutes the two cabs maintained their distance.

Suddenly, a crowd of people blocked the way.

"Good!" grumbled the gentleman. "That's all we need. We're hemmed in."

The promise of a sovereign had perked up the driver, however. Raising his whip in the air he shouted, in a resounding voice: "Police!"

The crowd scattered immediately, only to reform again into a compact mass once the carriage had passed. Aurett clapped her hands in joy. Less adroit or less stimulated, Bouvreuil's driver debated with the crowd, which refused to let him through.

In the meantime, the hansom traveled rapidly, swerving into a side street, and disappeared. Bouvreuil was beaten. Deeply chagrined, he returned to the China Pacific Hotel. There was still a chance of catching up with the fugitives. That was to consult a timetable of ships leaving port, in order to know which vessels would take to the sea during the day.

As he arrived there, a man was emerging from the hotel. It was Vincent, who, having finished his shift, had come to ask Mr. Tower whether his pseudo-cousin had come back. On his negative response, he went away, shrugging his shoulders.

Bouvreuil recognized him: he was the guest that Lavarède had twice brought to the dining room, an individual who had intrigued him greatly. The opportunity was too good for him not to seize it by the hair—the "hair" in question being, in this case, Vincent's arm, which he grabbed as the Irishman was going past him.

"What the...?" said the other, not without astonishment.

"You're doubtless looking for your friend?"

"Yes."

"Me too."

"You?"

"Me. We made the voyage from France together. I'm very worried, and as he left the hotel last night in your company, I thought you might be able to reassure me on his account."

"Alas, no!" sighed Vincent, assuming an afflicted expression. "I think he's dead. At least, that's what he wrote to me."

"What are you telling me?"

"The truth. This is my poor cousin's letter."

"He's your cousin?"

"Yes...come all the way from Ireland expressly to see me."

At these words the landlord could scarcely suppress a movement of joy. His vague suspicions took on substance. He divined that he had his hand on the instrument of which the Parisian had made use. Why? With what objective? That was what it was important to know, and he would find out.

"Look," he went on, in a friendly tone, "you seem to me to be as worried as I am. Will you have a glass of port? We can have a chat, and perhaps the two of us can pick up some trace of him, for it isn't possible that he's already dead."

A glass of port is never to be refused. Vincent accepted. A few moments later the two men were sitting in Bouvreuil's room, in front of a bottle whose dusty coating testified to a respectable antiquity...and Vincent was talking...and Bouvreuil was listening...

Meanwhile, Aurett and her father, liberated from their stubborn pursuer, had been taken to a restaurant near the harbor, had eaten lunch and had then gone aboard the *Heavenway*. Its cargo loaded, the steamer was waiting under pressure for the high tide. Everything was ready on board and the swirls of smoke that were escaping from the funnels indicated that the ship was ready to take to the sea when the signal was given.

The young Englishwoman could not keep still. Standing hear the gangway she was searching the crowd swarming to the quay with her gaze, with an enormous dread that she might recognize Bouvreuil among the strollers. A short distance away, the captain of the *Heavenway*, a former merchant captain seduced by the high pay offered by the Pacific Box Line was also watching. It was scarcely probable that any supplementary cargo would present itself at this time, but one never knows, and the captain as prepared to be surprised.

With his massive head, his ruddy complexion and his face enlarged by russet side-whiskers, the master—after God—aboard the *Heavenway* was a Yankee in the full force of the term, not very amiable, not talkative at all, but as practical as it was possible to be, knowing how to utilize events and circumstances. His ship's tonnage as two thousand; he had found the means to take aboard that full weight of merchandise, plus the dead Chinese and the living passengers into the bargain.

The moment for departure had come.

"Are we under pressure?" the captain asked the first mate, who was standing on the footbridge.

"Yes, sir."

At that moment, a man in a hurry, valise in hand, raced on to the steamer and demanded, in an anxious voice: "Mr. Mathew, Commandant of the *Heavenway?*"

Murlyton and his daughter made a gesture of annoyance. The newcomer was Bouvreuil.

The usurer had talked to Vincent, and had concluded from his story that Lavarède must be aboard the steamer, for he was too interested in the Chinese for that not to hide something suspect. That supposition had become a certainty when he had perceived the English duo on the deck.

"Mr. Mathew?" he repeated.

"That's me," replied the captain, advancing toward him.

"Very good. Delighted to make your acquaintance!" And, handing him a printed sheet of paper, he added: "I'm going to make the crossing with you. This will prove to you that I've regulated it with the administration of Pacific Box."

Mr. Mathew nodded his head. "That's fine, Monsieur, but..."

"There's a but?"

"Yes. My ship isn't fitted out with passengers in view. I only have twelve cabins."

"That's sufficient," said Bouvreuil.

"However," the American continued imperturbably, "seven are presently occupied..."

"That leaves five, then..."

"Which have been reserved by gentlemen who are embarking in Honolulu."

Pénélope's father grimaced. "Which means?" he said, with visible anxiety.

"That as far as the Sandwich Islands, I can assure you of a cabin, but for the rest of the journey, it'll be necessary for you to make do with a hammock in the crew's quarters—unless you prefer to wait for the next departure."

"No, no, I'll be content with that," the landlord hastened to reply.

He was obliged to admit privately, however, that his sea voyages were not very successful, and he evoked the painful memory of the *Lorraine*.

Mr. Mathew raised to his lips a large whistle attached to the extremity of a steel chain and blew a long, shrill blast thereon.

At that signal, the steamer appeared to come to life, like a marine monster roaring and spitting out steam. The pistons slid progressively in the cylinders, with a dull purr. Smoke belched from the funnels. And under the pressure of its propeller, which was spinning in a whirlpool of white foam, the *Heavenway* drew away from the quay majestically.

Slowly, as if to allow the splendid panorama of the city to be admired, she traversed the harbor, crowded, as ever, by a veritable merchant fleet. She tacked across the bay, guided by the pilot between the innumerable vessels plying the local routes to Auckland, Sausalito and Fulton. Further away, she passed the island of Quarantaine, then San Rafael and Telegraph Hill. Finally, after the fortress of the Presidio, having passed through the Golden Gate, the ship paused to drop the pilot. The latter's coaster drew away.

Then, leaving Cliff House and Seal Island behind, the *Heavenway*'s bow cleaved through the waves of the Pacific Ocean.

The first days of the crossing passed without incident. The Pacific remained as smooth as a mirror, and the *Heavenway*'s passengers were able to stroll on deck without fear of being surprised by rolling.

Aurett and her father had decided that the other passengers—American cattle merchants or unimportant Chinamen—were not people worth frequenting, and they only exchanged a few words with Captain Mathew and his first made, Mr. Craigton. But those gentlemen, although slightly embarrassed in the presence of such correct persons, were only a feeble distraction for them.

On Sunday, after a Bible reading made in a loud voice by the captain, surrounded by his crew, Bouvreuil had tried to engage the English duo in conversation, but the young woman had responded so dryly to his first words that he had admitted himself beaten and had not persisted. From that moment on he had avoided going near her, limiting himself to watching all her movements from a distance.

He had an idea, that landlord. The Murlytons were aboard, so Lavarède must be here too. Except that the diabolical journalist was well hidden, and Pénélope's father had wandered all over the ship without spotting him anywhere. The engine-room, the food stores, the crew quarters—his future abode— were the object of scrupulous investigation on his part, which produced no result—but he stuck to his guns, stubbornly.

"He's here," he repeated to himself. "He'll have to show himself eventually. It's therefore a matter of not losing sight of the young miss. She's my *informer*."

And with that police epithet, which would have caused the person to whom it was applied to jump. Bouvreuil kept watch.

The days of the eighth and ninth of August passed without him being able to obtain the slightest indication of the presence of his enemy on board, and when he returned to his cabin, in a very bad mood, he lay down on his bunk, proffering the most terrible threats against Armand.

Fortunately, human strength has its limits; in spite of his exasperation, the usurer slept the profound sleep wrongly named the sleep of the just.

In the middle of the night he was woken up with a start by a loud noise resounding under the floor of his cabin. He raised himself up on his elbow and, very emotional, listened hard—but silence had fallen again. After a few moments, the landlord retreated under his sheets again, cruising.

He had had a nightmare; that was all. Beneath the cabins was the compartment reserved for the coffins. How could the noise possibly have come from there? The dead, lying in their biers, are quiet people and peaceful neighbors. No doubt was permissible, Bouvreuil had been dreaming. And with that affirmation, the delegate of the Panama shareholders went meekly back to sleep.

For once, his perspicacity was at fault; the noise really had come from the hold of the dead.

As one can divine, Lavarède, once enclosed in his bier, had soon become bored. From the shocks agitating his prison he had understood that he had been embarked. Then, the trepidation of the propeller's axle had indicated the moment of departure, and although he was narrowly confined he had breathed more easily when the rocking movement of the *Heavenway* had informed him that the steamer had reached the open sea.

No one came into his funereal compartment. The journalist was therefore able to emerge from his box and stretch his limbs, slightly numbed by his long immobility. The promenade between two rows of coffins was certainly not cheerful, and the atmosphere was impregnated by a particularly musky odor, but as the young man said to himself, he was not there to amuse himself.

Thus, the days of the seventh and eighth of August passed as well as could be expected. On the morning of the ninth, however, Armand observed, anxiously, that the provisions he had appropriated from the larder of the China Pacific Hotel had run out. All that remained were a piece of chocolate and a crust of bread—to accomplish a twenty-two day crossing!

He did not abandon himself to despair, and simply resolved to wait until night to slip into the galley and renew his provisions.

It was a long time coming, that night. The voyager's empty stomach protested against the slowness of the hours, but the objurgations of the organ in question did not influence the Parisian's determination. An imprudence might ruin everything. It was better to suffer a little and not to quit his hiding place until a moment when, except for the sailors on watch on the deck, everyone aboard would be asleep.

Finally, that impatiently-awaited moment arrived.

Armand left the compartment of the "repatriates," slid along the corridors, and reached the larder that, on modern ships, replaces the old food-storage lockers without a hitch. Biscuits, tins of corned beef and bottles of wine were piled up there in haste in a piece of canvas that our explorer found thee.

Having parceled up his booty, he took the route that had brought him there in reverse—but the luck that had protected his expedition thus far suddenly ran out. In the corridor of the cabins, Lavarède found himself face to face with a crewman. The corridor was narrow. The sailor looked at Armand and appeared surprised not to recognize him as, either as one of his comrades or one of the passengers.

"What are you doing here?" he asked.

"What I'm doing here...," the journalist began—but what he was doing there, he could not say. Only a stroke of audacity could get him out of it.

Abruptly, he leapt upon the sailor, who was as yet unsuspicious, tripped him up, and while the American was floundering on the floor he raced away in the direction of the coffin compartment. The furious man, however, leapt to his feet and launched himself in pursuit.

Armand turned his head without slowing his pace. Twenty feet separated him from his enemy. That was sufficient. With a final effort he reached the door of the compartment, bounded into his bier and disappeared therein, closing the lid with a bang at the very moment when the sailor appeared in the doorway of the hold.

The American stopped dead. At a glance, he had recognized the place where he was, and the sudden, inexplicable noise terrified him. Sailors are all superstitious. They brave the unchained elements fearlessly, but tremble at the mere thought of the invisible.

The man did not go any further. Carefully, he closed the door of the "chamber of the dead," into which he had darted a somewhat troubled glance. Nothing unusual had been evident. He went back on deck, somewhat shaken; there he confided his adventure to the men of the watch, and they all, without hesitation, declared that their comrade had encountered a ghost. They reached that conclusion by logical reasoning: only the dead live among the dead; without a doubt, they were in the presence of a soul separated from its terrestrial husk without being in a state of grace.

Impressed by the appreciations of his companions, the man who had pursued Lavarède no longer had any clear perception of the event. He eventually began to imagine that he had felt an object colder than ice applied to his calf. His self-respect was, moreover, satisfied by that. It was not a man that had knocked him down but a spirit...

In that regard, they recalled the struggle between Jacob and the angel, but in spite of Biblical citations and the detached air that a few sailors affected, fear floated over the ship.

On handing over the watch to their replacements, the sailors made them party to the marvelous incident, embroidering it slightly, of course. The men of the second watch trembled more forcefully than those of the first, and took back to the crew's quarters a nervousness that spread from man to man.

In brief, in the morning, while Lavarède, somewhat anxious about the consequences of his adventure, was keeping quiet in his cushioned box, there was not a single seaman who did not fell ill-at-ease when passing through the steamer's corridors, interrogating shadowy corners with an anxious gaze, fearful of seeing "the tormented soul of the *Heavenway*" suddenly loom up before him.

At an early hour, Murlyton and his daughter had gone up on deck. Captain Mathew had informed them that on that day, the tenth of August, the steamer would traverse the great Pacific current known by the name of Kuro Siwo, or the Black River. Leaning on the bulwark, they listened to the American's explanations.

"The name is the current is perfectly justified," he said. "It forms a veritable river, whose waters are darker in color. Eight or nine kilometers wide, on average, the Kuro Siwo frays a passage through the ocean waves. It's a true counterpart of the Gulf Stream, the Atlantic current."

"But does it have a similar elevated temperature?" Aurett asked.

"Yes, Mademoiselle, and if the southern portion of the territory of Alaska is covered in abundant vegetation, it's uniquely to the Kuro Siwo that the phenomenon must be attributed. Without that, like all the rest of the peninsula, the southern coast would be blocked by ice, and the flora there would consist of mosses, lichens and a few stunted birch trees."

"In sum, it's something like Roscoff in France."

"Precisely—except that the American Roscoff, which was once Russian, extends over a length of three hundred miles."

Murlyton was completing this information with the familiar theory of warm currents when Mr. Craigton approached, wearing an embarrassed expression.

"What's the matter?" Mr. Mathew asked his first mate. "You don't seem comfortable."

"Mysterious things are happening on board."

The captain started. "On my ship?"

"Yes, sir."

"Explain yourself."

"I'd like nothing better, Mr. Mathew. This is it. Last night, Seaman Fivecreek met a being with the form of a man in the corridor of the cabins."

"The form of a man!" exclaimed the captain. What do you mean, the *form* of a man?"

"I mean that it was only an appearance. Fivecreek didn't recognize him as either a passenger or a crewman, and he asked him what he was doing there."

"And?"

"He felt sick," Craigton continued, "because he suddenly heard words spoken in an unknown language, and then a terrible cold. One might have thought that a block of ice had been applied to his skin. The impression was so powerful that he fell over."

Mr. Mathew shrugged. "Fivecreek was drunk. He was dreaming."

"I don't think so, sir. When the first moment of stupor had passed, the fellow got up and ran after the singular stroller, but the other went into the chamber of the dead and vanished with a clap of thunder."

The young Englishwoman looked at her father, half serious and half smiling. She had guessed who the author of the panic was. She laughed at the thought of Lavarède becoming a ghost for the crew; but, realizing that the young man had emerged from his hiding place to renew his food supplies, she experienced a muted anxiety. Had he succeeded in his expedition, and might he not be suffering from hunger at that very moment?

The captain was silent for a moment. Evidently, he was embarrassed. Maritime regulations made no provision for the introduction on board of a ghost. What ought he to do? The response to the question did not come, and rather than be found wanting, Mr. Mathew judged it politic to affect the most complete incredulity.

"Mr. Craigton," he said, in a mocking tone, "I can't believe that you, a serious officer, are making yourself the echo of such tales. Go and tell Fivecreek that if he has any more marvelous adventures I'll put him in irons to calm his imagination."

The second-in-command bowed, but remained bent over, without completing the gesture he had commenced. A voice had cut in, saying: "My opinion is that the sailor wasn't dreaming. I was woken up myself last night by a loud noise that appeared to be coming from the place where the coffins are."

Everyone turned to the man who had spoken. It was Bouvreuil. Having come up on deck a few minutes before, he had listened to the mate's report without being noticed. The young Englishwoman's anxiety had not escaped him, and, vaguely scenting a correlation between the sailor's adventure and the disappearance of his undiscoverable "son-in-law" he had intervened in the conversation.

The captain looked the passenger up and down. "You claim to have heard...?"

"Yes Captain, I repeat: I was woken up be a frightful noise."

"And did you notice what time that happened?" asked the mate.

"It might have been about midnight."

Craigton nodded his head. "That's the time indicated by Fivecreek."

Mr. Mathew was no longer laughing. Not a strong mind at all, having only an elementary education not much superior to that of his subordinates, the Captain, outside of his métier, which he knew well, was ignorant of everything. There was nothing astonishing in the fact that he shared his sailors' superstitions. He had tried to jeer at first, but the testimony of a passenger gave the incident a character of undeniable authenticity.

The ship was haunted. And Mr. Mathew thought, with an inexpressible malaise, that before reaching Honolulu, the steamer's first port of call, it would be necessary to live for seven days in a narrow space in which a being from the other world had taken up residence. The prospect had nothing attractive about it.

Aurett followed the thoughts on his visage. She tried to deflect the worthy man's opinion with an indifferent tone. "I think that a poorly secured item of cargo must have fallen," she said. "That would explain the noise that woke this man up."

She indicated Bouvreuil. The latter had not taken his eyes off the young woman and is suspicions had acquired substance. His strategy was to contradict the young Englishwoman, so he hastened to respond: "Indeed, but that doesn't explain Seaman Fivecreek's encounter." Then, in an amiable fashion, he added: "It seems to me that it would be easy enough to find out what's going on."

"Ah!" said Mr. Mathew. "How, pray?"

"The fantastic being disappeared in the hold of the Chinese. It's sufficient to place a sentry at the door of the hold. Either the young lady's supposition is correct and nothing abnormal will happen, or the mariner really saw something, and the mysterious visitor is among his own again. Our doubts will be transformed into certainties, and we'll no longer have to do anything, if the circumstances require it, but say a few prayers to ensure the repose of the errant soul, and ours."

Aurett had paled slightly. With the compartment of the repatriates guarded, Lavarède would be condemned to die of starvation or confess himself beaten. Either alternative seemed tragic. And yet Mr. Mathew delighted by the solution proposed by the usurer, turned to the first mate, rubbing his hands.

"You understood that, Mr. Craigton?"

"Perfectly, Mr. Mathew."

"Well then, arrange for the door of the yellow compartment to be kept under constant watch."

Bouvreuil launched a glance of triumph at the young woman. The latter turned her head away, but the usurer had time to observe that her eyes were moist. In fact, Aurett had experienced a painful emotion on hearing the captain give the order. A crazy desire to leap upon the landlord and wring his neck had possessed the gentle girl, and the concern for "propriety" always present in a British mind had almost been vanquished.

It was not merely antipathy that she felt toward Bouvreuil but a furious sentiment bearing a strong resemblance to hatred. She would have seen Pénélope's father at grips with the most abominable adventures without any displeasure. In brief, anger lent a ferocity to the innocent creature, who had thus far only known smiles and generosity. The lamb was enraged. And as a repercussion, the young woman, who had until then only admitted timidly that she felt "a certain amity" for Armand, declared frankly to herself that the word *amity* was insufficient.

Her frankness was immediately rewarded by a disturbance so delicious that she no longer hesitated to consider it as a duty to assist the journalist. She was obliged to recognize, however, that in acting in that way she would be going against the interests of her father, and thought it only decent to obtain his consent. That was easy. The gentleman adored his daughter. He accepted without overmuch difficulty the somewhat specious reasons with which she bombarded him.

"Well, so be it," he said to her, by way of conclusion. "Humanitarian duty, duty of gratitude…act as you please. I give you *carte blanche*."

The lunch bell brought the officers and passengers together on the quarterdeck.

The Englishwoman had resumed hr smiling expression, but the rosy tint of her cheeks was slightly accentuated and her eyes were sparkling with malice, like those of a kitten to whom chance has granted a tête-à-tête with a cream cheese.

Bouvreuil made all those observations, not without a certain anxiety. Aurett did not even look at him. Tranquilly, she sat down in her usual place, chatted as usual about the minor incidents on board, and appeared to have forgotten what had happened that morning. When the fuming coffee had been poured for the diners, however, she suddenly interrupted Captain Mathew in the middle of a dissertation about frigate-birds, the admirable birds that one encounters in the open sea, five or six days from the coast.

"By the way, Captain, what about the famous ghost?"

"It hasn't been seen again, Miss."

"Really! Your sailors must be reassured."

Mr. Mathew grimaced. "Pooh!"

"What! They're still trembling? A spirit guarded by a sentry is, however, no longer to be feared." She laughed as she spoke.

Her mocking tone cut the captain to the quick. "Well, Miss, the sailors are courageous when it's a matter of a known danger. Tempests and lightning don't prevent them maneuvering the ship. But against…otherworldly things, impalpable beings, the bravest man can do nothing."

He had lowered his voice as he spoke, thus proving that he was not sheltered from all disquiet. Aurett's gaiety seemed to augment it.

She went on: "You don't have any English mariners in the crew?"

"No, all Americans—why?"

"Because they'd have given heart to the others."

The antagonism that exists between old Albion and young America, between John Bull and his son Jonathan, is well-known. Nothing could be more disagreeable to the Captain than the young woman's remark.

"An Englishman," he said, in a surly tone, "wouldn't be any different than the others."

"Oh, but yes!"

Mr. Mathew went crimson. "Well, I'll wager…," he began—but stopped, and continued, more calmly: "I was about to say something stupid, since there's no seaman of your nation aboard."

"That doesn't matter. What will you wager?"" the young woman asked, privately delighted to see her interlocutor exactly where she had wanted to lead him.

"No, it's pointless."

"Please."

"To oblige you, then: I'll wager that an Englishman wouldn't be any more tranquil than my men. As you see, the wager is platonic, since there's no British national aboard my ship."

Aurett's expression had become grave. "I'm only a young woman," she said, affecting a great seriousness, "but I accept the wager. I'll do what none of your sailors will do, and I hope thus to reassure them."

"You!" cried all those present, astonished.

"Me."

And as the diners interrogated her with their gazes, the Englishwoman went on: "Is it a bet?"

"Yes, Mademoiselle."

"Fix the stake yourself."

"Ten dollars."

"Good. So, Captain, would you care to assemble the crew on deck and make them the proposition that I've just submitted to you."

Mr. Mathew seemed nonplussed. "It's agreed, isn't it, Mademoiselle, that you'll only request possible things?"

"Naturally, since I'm prepared to do what I demand of your men. You don't suppose I'd deliver myself to fantasies at which a well-brought-up person would blush?"

Reassured by that declaration, the Captain promised, and once the coffee had been drunk, he went up on deck, followed by the passengers, curious to know what was about to happen. The latter, moreover, following the American custom, began to lay bets in their turn. Mr. Mathew's ten dollars set a thousand in motion.

On the order transmitted by the first mate, the bosun's whistle summoned the crew "on top." From the mast and between decks, the mariners responded to the appeal and placed themselves in two rows, facing the group formed by the officers and passengers. Then Aurett leaned toward Mr. Mathew's ear and pronounced a few words in a low voice.

The Captain made a gesture of surprise, and then, making his decision, he addressed the sailors.

"Lads," he said, "last night, one of you encountered an individual who ought not to be aboard."

A murmur went through the ranks.

"Perhaps he was the victim of his imagination. It's necessary to test the proposition, in order to spare you the chore of mounting guard on the door of the Chinese compartment."

The sailors sketched smiles. Evidently, the suppression of the sentry duty did not displease them. Encouraged by that welcome, Mr. Mathew continued.

"The affair is simple. Designate one of you who will spend tonight in the yellow room. That way, at least we'll know whether or not one of the dead walks by night. You can say in a little while what you've decided. Break ranks!"

All the faces had darkened. The sailors conferred with one another. After five minutes, the oldest came o the captain, his beret in hand.

"Well?" asked Mr. Mathew.

155

The man shifted his weight from one foot to the other, with an embarrassed expression.

"Apologies, Captain," he said, finally, "but the comrades would prefer you to order one of them to do it. No one wants to challenge the spirits, inasmuch as bad things happen to those who scorn them. If the service is ordered, someone will obey; otherwise, we can't reach an agreement."

"I've won the bet, Captain," said Aurett, joyfully. Turning to the seaman, she added: "Tell your comrades not to worry; no sailor will have to go into the chamber of the dead."

The sea-dog interrogated his Captain with his eyes, and, seeing that the latter approved the passenger's words, went to rejoin his companions. In the meantime, the Englishwoman, with her softest smile, declared to those around her that she would spend the night in the midst of the coffins.

Everyone praised her courage, Bouvreuil along with the others—but he drew away murmuring: "That explains everything. It's a method analogous to the one he employed between Paris and Bordeaux. This time, the box is a bier. I believe I've finally got him—and Pénélope's marriage is making progress."

XV. The Chinese Freemasons

Happy the man who, still young, pales to his doom
And falls to eternal repose in the peace of the tomb.

"Imbecile rhymer, pretentious philosopher! Nice repose, adorable peace! Which of the two has given me the commencement of lumbago?"

Lavarède spoke thus while stretching his limbs, dolorously impressed by too long a station in the Manchu Kin-Tchang's box. All day long he had not dared to emerge from his hiding-place. He feared a surprise. He had heard the comings and goings of the sailors replacing the sentries placed at the door of his domicile, and, suspecting the cause of that stir, had remained impassive. Even though the rectangular box was cushioned, however its lack of breadth made it an uncomfortable bed. So, weary and cramped, the journalist had quit it toward nightfall.

He was certain that no one was making a round at that moment, and the contraband voyager promised himself to spent the night sitting up, in order to recover from his long horizontal station. After taking a tin of corned beef that he had removed from the galley the night before from his bier, transformed into both a bedroom and a dining room, he had begun to eat with a hearty appetite, when footsteps sounded in the corridor.

Good, he thought. *The passengers are all returning to their cabins. Oh! Have I frightened them?*

He stopped abruptly, the footsteps having paused at the door; almost immediately, a key grated in the lock. The young man only just had time to throw himself behind a coffin. A flood of light penetrated his compartment.

A patrol! That's it! I'm caught!

Imprudently, he had moved away from his hiding-place, and it was now impossible for him to get back to it without being seen.

Twenty-five seconds went by, measured by his heartbeats. Suddenly, there was the sound of a soft voice.

"Thank you, Captain," it said. "These candles will give me light, this book sufficient distraction. I don't believe in fantastic apparitions; I'm certain that nothing supernatural will occur, and I'll win my bet entirely."

"Nevertheless, a sailor will stand guard in the corridor, Mademoiselle...."

"No, no, I'm not in any danger. Please just give me the key... Thank you—and now, good night."

There was a momentary rustling, and then the door closed again. Advancing his head slightly, Lavarède perceived Aurett standing with a candle in her hand, her body slightly inclined forward, carefully listening to the people who had accompanied her draw away. Finally reassured by the silence, she approached the coffins with a visible repugnance and consulted the brass plates bearing the registration numbers fixed to the lids.

"Forty-nine," she murmured, in a low voice. "Where's forty-nine?"

Very surprised to see her alone in such a place, the tenant of that number immediately replied in the same tone: "Have no fear, Mademoiselle; number forty-nine is taking a stroll."

She shivered at the sound of his voice, but immediately pulled herself together.

"Is that you, Monsieur Lavarède?"

"In person." Emerging from hiding, he added, with the utmost seriousness: "To what good fortune do I owe the pleasure of your visit?"

The circumstances gave the question a burlesque character. The young woman smiled, and the ice was broken.

At the first moment, the young woman had experienced some embarrassment, but it had dissipated now, and it was as a good comrade that she cheerfully related the story of the revenant. She became more serious to tell him about her anxieties, and he method of procedure she had used in order to get into the Chinese compartment, in order to bring the prisoner provisions. Like the practical person she was, she concluded by taking, from a bag hidden under her dress, chocolate, biscuits, port wine, and even a superb joint of cold roast beef, carefully wrapped in silk paper.

"This way," she declared, "I'll be tranquil. They'll no longer be keeping watch on this sinister place, and I can renew your food supplies."

Armand listened with a very tender satisfaction. On her last words he took her hand and raised it to his lips. As she seemed embarrassed, she said: "Have no fear, Mademoiselle; that's how our ancestors marked their respect for princesses. At this moment, you see, I'm touched by the interest that you're taking in me, and the perfect courtesy of Mr. Murlyton—for he has surely authorized you?"

She moved her head in a mutinous fashion.

"My father permitted…without positively permitting…but he had given me *carte blanche*, and I used it."

"He's not unaware of your presence, though?"

"Oh no—but he didn't know that I had the intention of coming here when he gave me a license to help you." After a slight pause she went on: "I ought to add that I've been severely scolded on this occasion."

"Scolded, you?"

She assumed a contrite expression. "Yes, Monsieur Lavarède. After the incident on deck, my father took me aside and said: 'I suppose, Aurett, that you're not going through with your plan.'

"'Why not?' I replied.

158

"'But don't you think that this nocturnal tête-à-tête with my loyal adversary is rather improper?' I confess that the reflection embarrassed me. I hadn't thought of that."

"Nor had I," affirmed the journalist.

She clapped her hands. "Nor had you—as I insisted. Finally, my father gave in, for he holds you in high esteem—but he wants you to give a formal promise to keep silent about our 'shocking interview.'"

"Oh, Mademoiselle, he can't think me capable of wanting to harm you?"

"Harm me?" she repeated. "He was right then: this would be compromising?"

"No, no, my dear and benevolent little sister, there's nothing in this but great amicability and kindness. The only sentiments I experience are gratitude and respect."

Perhaps the tone was not entirely in accord with the words—Armand's voice was trembling slightly—but Aurett, who, in posing her question, had yielded to a momentary coquetry, was infinitely grateful to him for his reserve. What did it matter henceforth that she was alone with him? A sister has nothing to fear from her brother. She thought that with that single word he had reduced to nullity any trace of malevolent accusation that might be produced. Both of them, in any case, were conscious that the terrain was red hot. They changed the subject. For a long time, they discussed various means of returning to Europe once they had reached China.

Lavarède planned to reach Shanghai and engage himself as a sailor on one of the steamships bound for Great Britain. That would be easy, for the Chinese authorities were making every effort to retain their own mariners on land, especially since the rebuilding of the navy has been the order of the day in the Middle Kingdom. The crews of steamships arriving from Europe were rarely complete when they set out on the return journey.

Aurett approved the plan, which seemed easy to realize. It was the only one that seemed practical, in any case, as Armand remarked. It was, indeed, impossible to reach Europe overland. It would be necessary to travel nearly seven thousand kilometers across little known regions, in the midst of hostile populations or icy deserts.

Having exhausted that subject of conversation, the young people only exchanged rare words. Miss Murlyton was feeling drowsy; her heavy eyelids were closing involuntarily. Lavarède perceived that.

"Go to sleep," he said. "Go to sleep, little sister."

She smiled to him, and confidently went to sleep under the protection of her friend.

She was woken up in the morning by her father's voice. Annoyed at not seeing her, the gentleman had knocked forcefully on the door of the compartment. With a rapid glance she made sure that Armand was back in his hiding place, and, reassured on that point, opened the door.

159

"What time is it, then?" she asked Murlyton, who was accompanied by the first mate.

"Six o'clock. It's broad daylight and I was beginning to worry..."

"Truly, have I slept for such a long time?"

Mr. Craigton uttered a cry of amazement. "You were asleep, Mademoiselle? Oh!"

"But of course." And fixing her clear gaze on her father, she added: "I even dreamed that the spirit on board shook my hand and called me *sister*."

Murlyton nodded his head approvingly and escorted his daughter back to her cabin. She did not escape the admiration of the crew, however, and for the rest of the day, when she strolled on deck, she was able to see the sailors bow as she went past with superstitious respect.

In sum, her intervention had succeeded marvelously. The sentry-duty outside the "yellow chamber" was suspended and the Parisian, no longer blockaded, was no longer running any risk of being defeated by starvation. She was, therefore, in an exceedingly good mood, to the extent that she even deigned to reply to one or two observations emitted by Bouvreuil.

How she would have regretted her condescension had she suspected that the usurer had quit his cabin during the night and had spent an hour with his ear glued to the wall of the Chinese compartment! And her regret would have changed to terror if she had heard him, after that patient espionage, murmur while rubbing his hands together—his favorite gesture when he was hatching some nasty scheme for his fellows—"Flirt, pretty Miss; it's not the one who flirts who marries."

Life on board had resumed its monotony. There was not a cloud in the sky, not a wave on the surface of the ocean. The sun darted its rays at the steamer implacably. The passengers, numbed by the heat, sought out the bands of shadow cast by the funnels or the footbridge, and there, lying in deck-chairs, they dozed, plunged in a kind of torpor.

The *Heavenway*, silent in the midst of the mute immensity, took on the appearance of the phantom ship that, according to maritime legend, wanders incessantly in the oceanic deserts, manned by a crew of dead men.

If Lavarède was bored, he was by no means the only one. Even Aurett's gaiety seemed dubious—which disappointed Mr. Mathew, because the young woman, since her "exploit," was the object of a particular veneration on his part. He compared her naively to all the celebrated women whose biographies were in a book he had on board: Ophictalis the Assyrian; Amnoser of Egypt, who defended Thebes; the Armorican Arreda; Jeanne d'Arc; Sonia Kvercedja, burned alive by the Tatars, who had been nicknamed the Muscovite Jeanne.[36] Such a heroine, bored! The worthy man was in despair.

---

[36] I have reproduced this list exactly as it appears in the original, as none of the names, except that of Jeanne d'Arc, appear anywhere else, so far as I can tell.

Fortunately, on the fifteenth of August, sharks appeared around the ship. They accompanied it, ready to snatch anything that fell into the sea. For want of any other distraction, shark-fishing is not to be disdained. The officers and sailors were delighted to be able to offer the spectacle to "their" young lady.

After half an hour of efforts, one of the monsters was hoisted aboard. It was a hammerhead shark, thus named—obviously—because of the shape of its head. It measured nearly seven meters, and the witnesses shivered on perceiving its enormous mouth armed with two rows of triangular teeth, as sharp as steel blades.

After the capture of one of those terrible denizens of the ocean, it is customary to open up their stomach. One generally finds there absolutely indigestible objects that testify to the prodigious voracity of the species. The mariners of the *Heavenway* had no intention of failing in that custom, and their fidelity to tradition was rewarded by the discovery of a tin-plate cylinder, hermetically sealed, which was handed to the captain.

"Ah!" said the latter. "It's doubtless a document confided to the sea by castaways."

Those words excited the curiosity of the passengers, who surrounded Mr. Mathew. The officer removed the gutta-percha stopper sealing the cylinder and took a sheet of paper out of the receptacle on which symbols were aligned.

Captain Mathew made a gesture of disappointment. "It's in Chinese," he complained. "It's impossible to decipher the hieroglyphs."

"Let me see," said Murlyton, taking the piece of paper.

More fortunate than the passengers of the *Heavenway*, we can give a translation of this curious document. Beside a triangular symbol, and three dots similarly arranged in a triangle, it was headed: *Universal League of Freemasons, Society of Haven, Earth and Humankind*; and the text read:

To the Tien-Tai.
I (neophyte) give my life, and consecrate my will to the expulsion of the usurpers; to it alone I belong, and I have no other terrestrial relative.
The Tien-Tai accepts you, Varga-Carfos, Grandmaster.[37]

---

[37] This text is reproduced diagrammatically in the original, following an illustration that claims to be a reproduction of the original Chinese characters, allegedly copied exactly—according to an authorial footnote—from a "certificate of freemasonry" brought back from China by "Lieutenant Carpier" (who remains as mysterious, if not as implausible, as the strangely-named "grandmaster"). The symbology of the covert organizations in question gave rise to the modern designation of Chinese criminal gangs as "triads." What was supposedly known about the organizations in question in the 1890s had been related at length in Jules Lermina's feuilleton *La Bataille de Strasbourg* (1891-92; tr. as *The Battle of Strasbourg*, Black Coat Prress, ISBN 978-1-61227-324-2) along with this

The Englishman examined the characters for some time, and finally said: "I don't know what these lines signify, but there are some signs that I recognize."

"Which ones?" asked the passengers.

"This triangle and the three dots placed at the top left. They indicate that we're in the presence of a document emanating from the freemasons of China."

Everyone protested: "Freemasons among the Celestials—get away!"

"They exist," Murlyton affirmed, "and not only do they have the same emblem as our freemasons in Europe and America, the triangle, but also the ordeals of admission employed among us, which seem to have been borrowed from the far more ancient Chinese society."

"Really?" said Mr. Mathew, very interested. "And you can tell us how the yellow men proceed?"

"Yes, thanks to a very studious publication that has appeared in England. My knowledge is limited, but this is what I can tell you, in broad terms..." A movement of attention passed through the audience, and Murlyton continued: "The League of the Tien-Tai, or the Society of Heaven, Earth and Humankind already existed in the second century of the Christian era, and all the 'images' of European freemasons were invented by it.

"So, when a neophyte wishes to be admitted into the Tien-Tai, also known by the name of the Triad, or the Universal League, he must go to the 'camp of the faithful' and introduce himself at the 'Eastern Gate.' It is there that the executor of important works is stationed, whose naked blade is ever ready to fall upon the heads of profane individuals audacious enough to introduce themselves without authorization into the sacred enclosure.[38]

"The newcomer is dressed in white; in principle, he ought to wear a new one, but if he is too poor, the Society spares him that expense, on the sole condition that he has his ordinary costume cleaned with the utmost care. His right shoulder and knees are bare; instead of plaiting his hair, he allows it to hang down loosely over his nape, in order to show that he is protesting against Tatar domination. Before crossing the sacrosanct threshold, the neophyte pays his subscription, which is equivalent to seventeen francs fifty centimes. That indis-

---

text; Lermina had scrupulously admitted drawing the information from article in the American *Harper's Magazine* ("Chinese Secret Societies" by Frederick Boyle, in the September 1891 issue). Boyle and Lermina do not draw any analogy between the "Ten-Tai" (actually Tian-Di) triangle and the Freemasons' pyramid, but the notion of the society as a "Chinese Freemasonry" has been bandied about extensively in more recent times.

[38] The entirety of this account is paraphrased from *La Bataille de Strasbourg*— Lermina also cites the entry fee in French as 17 francs 50. The parallel passage appears on pp. 231-32 of the Black Coat Presss translation of the Lermina text.

pensable formality accomplished, eight members of the league have him pass under a vault of interlaced blades."

"Most curious," declared the passengers, with a common voice."

Delighted with the effect that he was producing, the Englishman continued.

"The fanatic advances tremulously into the mysterious enclosure. He arrives at the Pavilion of Red Flowers, where the faithful purify their souls in water taken from the river Sam-Ho, on the banks of which the 'five ancestors' took refuge who were persecuted by the ingratitude of the emperor and the intrigues of his unworthy favorite Tan-Sing.

"The neophyte then passes through the Circle of Heaven and Earth and crosses over the Bridge of Two Planks guarded by the Red Young Man, armed with a spear destined to transpierce the profane who escape the vigilant eye of the guardian of the Eastern Gate. On the other side of that redoubtable passage are the Market of Universal Peace, the Temple of Good Fortune, the City of Willows and the Garden of Peach Trees; it is the seat of the Grand-Master.

"At the moment when the ceremony begins, the spectacle becomes imposing, the arch of swords forming again over the neophyte's head. He kneels down, takes an oath with thirty-six articles and declares that all his relatives are dead. In the language of initiates, that formula signifies that a member of the league no longer recognizes terrestrial bonds.

"After making that declaration, the fanatic prostrates himself at the foot of the Grand-Master's throne, and the eight blades that were interlaced above his head are touched to his bare shoulder. He is presented with a cup of arrack; he mingled a few drops of blood with that beverage, which he causes to flow from his arm, the epidermis of which has just been subjected to a slight prick, and then he drinks it all in a single draught, and the Tien-Tai counts one adherent more."

"Good," Aurett put in. "I observe that there is ridiculousness in all countries."

The smiles of the listeners proved that they shared the young woman's appreciation, but Murlyton shook his head.

"You're wrong, Aurett," he said. "You're judging lightly. This mummery, designed to strike the minds of simple individuals, conceals projects that are terrible for the Chinese government. Every adherent of the Tien-Tai swears never to have recourse to the Chinese authorities, or even to appear as a witness before any tribunal. He must only claim justice from the Grand-Master of his lodge. The sentences pronounced by that dignitary are executed by the affiliates, and the power of the Society, which numbers its adherents in the millions, is such that the mandarins dare not take action against it. Understand that it is necessary not to mock an association whose declared aim is to expel the Manchu conquerors, and which has already inspired such dread in its enemies that its members are assured of impunity."

"My God!" exclaimed the Captain. "I can think of no better way to thank you for your lecture than to ask Mademoiselle to keep the document; it is an interesting curiosity, not to mention that postman who brought it aboard is not banal."

Aurett accepted without being begged. The Chinese parchment would go well with the collection of souvenirs that she had gathered, like every English traveler, and Mr. Mathew was right: the fashion in which it had come aboard gave it a real value.

A week later, the passengers heard with joy the announcement of land. The *Heavenway* was in sight of the port of Honolulu, the best mooring in the Sandwich Islands, or Hawaii.

XVI. From the Sandwich Islands to the Chinese Coast

Guided by a pilot, the *Heavenway* came through the dangerous pass traced through the reefs and dropped anchor in the port of Honolulu.

The city rises up in semicircular stages around the bay. It is a delightful spectacle for eyes fatigued by the invariable horizon of the high seas. The houses appear in the midst of clumps of coconut palms, amaranths and halapepe, giving the impression less of a city than an agglomeration of pleasure resorts.

The steamer not being due to take to sea again until the next day, Murlyton and his daughter decided to spend the day on land. A long walk would do them good. They could also deliver themselves without any danger to the pleasure of walking in that fortune land where snakes are unknown. Even batrachians do not exist in the Sandwich Islands, and everyone remembers the German missionary whom the natives declared to be mad because he made reference to an old feudal custom of beating the waters of castle moats in order to impose silence on the croaking population.

This, the English duo, after having wandered through a few streets of the city reached the banks of the River Kanaha, the mouth of which is nearby, and went upriver into the valley of Nouhouhanou.[39] They went at a steady pace, admiring the cultivated fields, limited by rows of pandanus, breadfruit trees, cassia and sida. The warm air, incessantly refreshed by the sea breezes, was laden with aromatic perfumes.

After walking for an hour, they found a veritable wood of arborescent ferns. Those light plants, which always retain small dimensions in our climes, grow there a height of eight or ten meters, forming a vault of verdure under which the deep buzz of scarab beetles resonates. In foliage hanging down like long blonde hair, fern-flowers mingle with bright tufts of hibiscus, a strange tree whose flowers, white in the morning, become yellow in the middle of the day and red in the evening.

Beyond the ferns the ground rose up. The travelers had reached the foothills of the mountain that, in the Sandwich Islands as in all the islands of Oceania, occupies the center of the emergent lands.

---

[39] This name does not appear anywhere else other than the present text. The same is true of several others in the chapter. I have corrected a couple of odd references that seem to arise from misprints, but numerous others are simply invented, and from now on, many of the place names and other supposedly local terms scattered in the text are completely fictitious, mingled with a few items drawn from rather cursory research.

At that moment they encountered a Papolo, a Kanak of the poor class. The native, although his face was tattooed red and blue, seemed perfectly at ease in a linen suit and a superb panama hat. He greeted the newcomers.

"Good morning, Signor; *je vous salue*, Señorita."

That greeting, in several languages, made Aurett smile. She did not know that the Hawaiian Kanaks, incessantly in contact with the Americans and Europeans who handle all the commerce of the archipelago, have accepted their language as well as their money. In the same way that French louis, pounds sterling, American dollars. Italian lire, Russian roubles and Mexican piastres all clink together in their pockets, words of various nationalities are confused in their speech, which, adding in the autochthonous dialect, gives birth to the most amusing patois. A traveler can say with reason that the modern Hawaiian language is an Oceanian volapük. In any case, it constitutes a kind of sabir, easy to speak and understand, as the sabir of the Mediterranean shores is for Latins.

In the same flowery idiom, the Papolo continued: "Are you going to see the Kahunas?"

"The Kahunas?" Murlyton repeated.

"Yes—the priests of the goddess Pélé."

"So they still exist?" asked the gentleman. "I thought that the ancient religion had completely disappeared, replaced by Protestantism, and even, since King Kalakaua, by atheism."

The indigene shook his head. "We no longer sacrifice to Pélé since our queen Ka'shumanu, widow of Kamehamaha convinced her son Prince Lihohilo to violate the taboo on the same day that he put on the mantle of royal plumes, but the priests consecrated to the goddess have not deserted her and we make them offerings as of old."

"Yes, I understand," Murlyton murmured. "You're Christians in name and worshipers of Pélé underneath."

The Papolo made an energetic gesture of negation. "No, no, Monsieur, don't think that. We respect the Kahunas because it pleases the old ones, but our amity is to Christ, for it was him who put an end to the tyranny of the chiefs and gave us universal suffrage."

In a bizarre fashion, the Kanak was telling the truth. The inhabitants of that distant land lost in mid-ocean enjoy the universal suffrage that Belgium has not yet been able to attain.

While chatting thus the travelers were scaling the side of the mountain. The trees of the plain had been succeeded by gigantic myrtles with gnarled branches, covered in white flowers.

"We're arrived," said the Papolo.

He emerged with his companions on to a plateau covered with short thick grass, bordered by a perpendicular wall of rock. In the granite, the patient chisels of vanished generations had hollowed out figures illuminated with red ocher. An irregular arch opened in the foot of the rock, hollowing out a hole of shadow in the sun-drenched wall.

"The temple of Pélé," said the indigene, simply. And as the English duo stopped, looking curiously at the red lines traces in the rock, he added: "Come—the taboo is not observed, and the Kahunas give visitors a good welcome."

Some sixty years before, a stranger would not have traversed the plateau on which Aurett and her father were standing with impunity. The taboo, or taboos, consecrating a location to the Divinity punished profaners with atrocious tortures; but today, the customs of old have fallen into desuetude and little remains of the ancient Kanak religion but a temple, the deserted dwelling of a dethroned god.

The English duo went into the temple after the Papolo. It was a succession of caves that extended into the mountain, linked by narrow corridors, sometimes level and sometimes steeply sloping, into which steps had been roughly hewn. Everywhere, granite needles studded the ceiling and rose from the floor, blocks with strange forms to which the sacred illuminators had given the appearance of fantastic monsters. In obscure corners, the silhouettes of warriors, leaning on their spears, seemed to be mounting eternal guard in that dwelling of eternity. Once, victorious soldiers had dedicated the weapons thanks to which they had won their battles to the goddess.

Murlyton and the young woman followed their guide silently and thoughtfully, experiencing, if one might express it thus, a retrospective emotion. It seemed to them that the wheel of the years had spun backwards, and that they were about to witness one of the terrifying sacrifices of which the vaults of the temple had so often been witness. Their ears filled with a buzzing, like a distant echo of the sacred drums, and they imagined that they could perceive, in the half-light, the mysterious procession of priests and virgins going to the hall of the supreme sacrifice.

Suddenly, they stopped. At the elbow of a dark corridor, they found themselves on the threshold of the chamber known as the "cave of victims." Vaster and more densely populated with stone monsters than the preceding ones, it seemed grandiose. In the vault, a fissure bordered with rubescent vegetation allowed a roseate light to filter through, which added to the supernatural appearance of the place.

Almost immediately, a voice bade them welcome. A Kahuna clad in a kalauhi—a kind of chasuble open on one side—had risen from a stone bench where he had been dreaming of disappeared splendors and came toward hem. He was very far from the savage worshipers of Pélé. He guided the tourists as if he were a professional cicerone, and when the visit was concluded, he asked prosaically for a "tip," which Murlyton granted him in the English manner—which is to say, sufficient but not generous. The Papolo stayed in the temple, but having taken his leave of the English duo, he said to them: "Hurry back down to the plain, because the moumoukaou wind might well blow soon, and on the mountain it's dangerous."

"What do you mean by moumoukaou?"

The indigene extended his arm in a north-easterly direction. That is, in fact, the direction from which the tempests blow, which sometimes ravage the archipelago. The Hawaiian name of the wind says a great deal about the disasters it causes: moumoukaou signifies "destruction."

The English duo resumed the road to the city at a brisk pace. As they approached the cultivated region, they perceived ahead of them, on the shore of the sea, a large area dotted with small huts, veritable cottages, brightened by clumps of trees and well-raked pathways—but the whole was enclosed by palisades and ditches. In response to a question they asked, a passer-by made a gesture of fear and murmured: "Mai Pake."

The Kanak words meant nothing to the English, but the indigene combined a mime with his explanation, and he found in his polyglot vocabulary the horrible word for which he was searching: "Lepers!"

In fact, leprosy, the terrible affliction that desolated Europe in the Middle Ages, has been rife for thirty years among the "little golden people" of Hawaii, who call it "the Chinese disease." Two per cent of the population are afflicted by it. Once, it had been considered sufficient to attach bells to the necks of the sick to warn of their presence, and to avoid any contact, but since the white population had been afflicted too, the precautions had become sterner, almost ferocious. The lepers, for whom an annual commission searched carefully, were confined, some of them—"the protected"—in a leprosarium near Honolulu, the others on Molokai island, the "land of misery" from which no one ever returned. It was the sole means that civilization had found to prevent contagion.

On Molokai, a priest, Father Damien, Belgian in origin, won the admiration of all, spending a heroic apostolate in the midst of the unfortunate for sixteen years, and died of the disease at the age of thirty-three, like Christ.[40] Marcel Monnier has seen the most indifferent, fanatical protestants, dogged in their hatred of papists, take their hats off emotionally when pronouncing the name of the consoler of the plague-ridden. That is very good of them, but no Englishman has taken over his post, vacant for three years.

"The poor folk!" said the Englishwoman, to whom her father had given a rapid explanation. "Don't you think it's very cruel to treat them like that and take away all hope?"

"Certain cruelties are necessary, my child, in the interests of all," the gentleman replied. "Five hundred years ago, leprosy invaded the Christian countries. If the sick hadn't been confined in special places, from which they could

---

[40] Father Damien, born Jozef De Veuster (1840-1889) did, indeed, spend sixteen years in the Molokai leper colony, eventually contracting the disease, but was considerably older than 33 when he died. He was canonized in 2009.

168

only emerge equipped with a rattle whose sound warned their fellow citizens to flee, Europe would be a vast ossuary today. Humanity spends its time defending itself. When one danger is averted another surges forth. Thus, the present scourge of our civilization is alcoholism; it will be necessary before long to take energetic measures to eliminate it, because it leads to epilepsy, madness and sanguinary decompositions of every species.

Saddened by these morose reflections, the walkers reached the city. They were just in time. The sky had suddenly darkened; a heavy warmth lay upon the land, from which a kind of m mist as rising that was shrinking the horizon by the minute. A distant noise was audible, which had some analogy with a cannonade, and suddenly, a furious squall passed over, decapitating trees and shaking the houses. The moumoukaou wind was rising.

There was no possibility of getting back to the harbor during the squall. Murlyton and his daughter were hurled against a wall, near to a doorway. Stunned by the shock, the travelers asked to take shelter in the dwelling

It was a modest villa occupied by a reformed pastor; the most amicable welcome was given to his compatriots, but they arrived during the middle of a sermon, and they were invited to sit down and listen. Before an audience a dozen strong, the Reverend Zacharias, brandishing a piece of paper, was thundering against an invisible enemy.

"Yes, my brethren, this evening all of Honolulu will bear witness to this damnable spectacle and risk their eternal salvation. You, at least, will not see this envoy of the demon, this instrument of Hell, this apocalyptic being which has only the form of a woman, and whose name, with its Hebraic and Dutch consonants, only appears to me through Biblical fears."

The printed paper that the reverend's hand was striking incessantly was nothing other than a program for the theater at which Sarah Bernhardt's company was putting on a performance that evening during her world tour.

Aurett found a means of taking possession of it while taking leave of their ghost momentarily. "This will amuse Monsieur Lavarède," she said to her father. "From the depths of his Chinese tomb he'll be able to catch a glimpse of his beloved Paris."

The next day, when the *Heavenway* left the port of Honolulu, heading toward Japan, the last port of call before the Chinese coast, she carried a few more passengers: the Chinamen mentioned by Captain Mathew when they left San Francisco. In accordance with the agreement made, Bouvreuil was now accommodated with the crew.

Now, if the presence of the Celestials left Murlyton and his daughter indifferent, the relative distancing of the landlord gave them a certain satisfaction. The latter, moreover, did not show himself much. One might have thought that he was striving to spare his traveling companions the displeasure of seeing him. If he came on deck, he kept well away from the place where they were relaxing, absorbed in contemplating of the distant horizon. At meal times, he only opened

169

his mouth in order to eat. In addition, his physiognomy was modified. It had taken on a paternal expression, and no trace of anxiety was any longer visible in the usurer.

In fact, he had none, as one could easily be convinced by reading the cablegram sent from Honolulu that Mademoiselle Pénélope Bouvreuil received at Sens on the evening of the nineteenth of August, as she was finishing dinner. That dispatch caused her a joy so profound that the emotion in her rugged virgin heart was communicated to her stomach and she thought that she might die of indigestion. It read: *En route for Taku, China. Impossible to go any further. Marriage assured.*

At the precise moment when Pénélope, feeling very queasy, went to bed. Aurett, on the other side of the world, quit her own and went up on deck to cast an eye at Gardner Island and the Maus and Krusenstern reefs,[41] which the steamer's route skirted. The previous evening, the young woman, accompanied by her father, had paid Lavarède a visit. She had shown him the Chinese document brought aboard, quite involuntarily, by the shark, and the journalist had tried hard to decipher some of the symbols.

"Like Egyptian hieroglyphs," he said, "the first Chinese characters were simple reproductions of natural forms. Then time moved on and the necessity of rendered impalpable things in symbols led to a first complication. The same character represented an entity and its dominant quality: the horse and speed, the old man and experience. To avoid confusion, the original sign underwent a slight alteration. According to circumstances, it was augmented or reduced. The evolution of the human mind continued. Every day, more numerous ideas gave birth to new graphical inventions, to such an extent that the primitive types, tortured, mutilated and contorted, became unrecognizable. With patience, however, one can sometimes work out the original design—the 'root' design—and thus disentangle the filiation of the character that one has before one's eyes, and divine something of the enigma posed by the writer."

"My word," the Englishwoman had relied. "I'd like to assure myself of the correctness of your theory. I'll leave the paper with you on two conditions."

"They're accepted in advance."

"Firstly, that you make me party to the results of your research."

"Gladly, as you know, Mademoiselle."

"Secondly," the young woman had continued, without appearing to notice her interlocutor's caressant tone, "you'll take care not to lose my Celestial document, for on my return to London, I want to place it in a glass case with the caption: *Freemasonic Chinese document found in the stomach of a shark near Honolulu.*"

---

[41] Gardner Island is now known as Nikumroro, in Kiribati; the reefs cited have not maintained the names given, if they ever had them, although the second is presumably named after the famous Russian explorer Adam Krusenstern.

"And all your friends will envy you such a souvenir.

"You said it."

Thus engaged, the conversation had moved on quite naturally to China, the mysterious empire of the sons of Han, where four hundred million people of the yellow race were preventing European penetration by the sheer force of numbers.

"A strange people," said Armand. "First of all, they raised themselves up to a high level of civilization, and then they remained stationary, permitting Occidental barbarism to overtake them. I won't talk about the compass or gunpowder, known in the Middle Kingdom several centuries before the white race discovered them, but the hypothesis of the Earth's sphericity indicated an advanced scientific reasoning, doesn't it? Like me, you know that the presentiment of that verity didn't see the light of day until the fifteenth century,[42] and in 1492, when Christopher Columbus left Spain with his three caravels to furnish the experimental demonstration by going in search of what he believed to be the Asiatic Indies, the majority of the scientists of the day mocked him agreeably. Well, the proof was made in the year 203 of our Era, when the Asiatic Columbus Li-Pai-Chun[43] departed adventurously in a large junk and landed in the Gulf of California. Seduced by his tales, his compatriots formed a second expedition in the year 206, but the ships composing it were dispersed by a tempest and Li-Pai-Chun ran aground on Krusenstern reef near the Hawaiian islands, where he died miserably."

That story had interested Aurett. So, learning that the *Heavenway* was to pass to the north of the reef, she had wanted to cast an eye over the rock, incessantly beaten by the waves, that had been the melancholy tomb of the Chinese voyager. Then again, it was the last land she would see until the Japanese port of call of Nagasaki, for the steamer's route would leave the Anson and Magellan archipelagos far to the south.

On the following days, no incident troubled the monotony of the crossing. The uniformly blue sky resembled an immense lazuli bowl overturned on the emerald tray of the ocean. The young Englishwoman seemed nervous and aggravated; in vain Murlyton, still impassive, as befit a veritable gentleman, did his best to urge her to be patient; he was wasting his time. Aurett appeared to

---

[42] This is nonsense. Empedocles measured the diameter of the spherical Earth fairly accurately in the fifth century B.C., and Christopher Columbus set forth on the basis of an erroneous recalculation that suggested that the distance to the Indies travelling westwards was considerably shorter than it was. The most famous document of the European Renaissance, Dante's *Divine Comedy*, clearly recognizes the sphericity of the Earth, placing Purgatory in the middle of the hemisphere he wrongly assumed to be almost entirely covered by an ocean.

[43] This name is one of the many that do not appear anywhere else than the present text.

have caught sunstroke, for her visage only became serene again at the moment when the radiant star, having completed its course, disappeared over the horizon in a crimson apotheosis.

When dinner was over she took her father to the stern and there, leaning over the bulwark, she watched the elongated waves raised by the pressure of the propeller in a seething phosphorescence. She pretended to recognize letters in the rapid gleams snaking over the somber water. Which ones? The young woman did not explain herself on that score, but she certainly loved to study them, for her contemplation lasted a long time. And when the ship went to sleep, with only the men on watch protecting the security of all, she said to her father, in an untranslatable tone: shall we go down to the Chinese compartment?"

"Every evening! Why?"

"To find out what we'll encounter tomorrow. Monsieur Lavarède is marking the ship's route on the map I gave him, and if there's an islet or a rock he'll let us know about anything remarkable that happened there. The captain of the ship doesn't know anything."

The father approved benevolently, and they both went down to the coffin hold. For an hour they chatted with Armand, forgetful of the dead whom native piety was returning to their homeland. Eventually, Murlyton stood up and said, with an entirely British phlegm: "It's late. Monsieur Lavarède must need to sleep."

"No," replied the journalist, looking at Aurett.

"I beg your pardon, but to prolong our visit would be indiscreet, and I'd never forgive myself."

With which they shook hands and wished one another goodnight, and while he English duo went back to their cabins, Armand lay down philosophically in his coffin, murmuring words that were probably not intended for the gentleman.

"She's an angel! Never, without these too-brief meetings, would I have had the courage to continue this tedious crossing."

As for Aurett, her past nervousness in the place of the dead made her smile, and she confessed ingenuously that no part of the ship appeared to her to be as agreeable as the "chamber of sleep." That was the euphemism by which she designated the compartment in question.

Meanwhile, the *Heavenway* continued to make progress. On the fourth of September it entered Van Diemen Strait, situated between the extreme tip of Kiu-Siu island, the southern limit of Japan, and the Chinese islands of Liu-Kiu. The following day, they would reach Nagasaki, and the young Englishwoman rejoiced when Mr. Mathew gave her that news. If there were no hitches, the crossing was almost over.

Night fell: a dark, moonless night. As usual, Aurett had taken her father up on deck to await the hour when it would be possible to go down to see their friend—except that the passengers did not seem inclined to go to bed. Leaning on the bulwark, they were watching the surface of the ocean. One might have thought that they were awaiting some phenomenon that was slow to appear.

The young Englishwoman sought enlightenment, but before the person she had interrogated could answer, a voice rang out: "There it is! There it is! All right!"

Darting her gaze at the sea, Aurett understood. The *Heavenway* was sailing through the midst of a sea of molten gold. Momentarily separated by the passage of the ship, the waters joined up again behind her, forming a whirlpool of luminous foam—and the eddies were propagated, inundating the crests of every waves with a glittering diadem. The phosphorescence, with the presence of a particular alga renders frequent in that region, was augmenting in intensity with every passing minute, and a carpet of light extended over the black waves.

Seamen came up to the deck, carrying objects of no value—pieces of scrap metal and empty bottles—and threw them overboard. At each impact, the liquid droplets rose up like a swarm of fireflies.

For more than two hours the phenomenon continued. Passengers and sailors alike forgot sleep in the presence of the marvelous spectacle offered to their eyes. Then the sea went dark, and everyone, their heads slightly heavy and their eyes fatigued by the luminous debauch went back, either to their cabins or the crew quarters. Aurett and her father would willingly have followed them.

"Wait," she said. "Let's not forget that Monsieur Lavarède is counting on our visit."

"It's very late," remarked Murlyton, "and I believe it would be better to put it off until tomorrow..."

But she protested: "Do you think so? Imprisoned as he is, he can't have any idea of what's happening. What would he think of us?"

The Englishman shrugged his shoulders imperceptibly, but made no reply. He knew that a woman, being able to talk twice as fast and for much longer than a man, always ends up getting her way.

In fact, Aurett was right. Lavarède was astonished to have been abandoned by his traveling companions. At first he had thought it a slight delay caused by an unimportant incident, but time passed, and he had become nervous, then anxious, and finally sad. With the aid of imagination, he had supposed that an accident or an illness had retained one of the English duo in their cabins. At the risk of being seen, he was about to quit his refuge when Murlyton and the young woman appeared.

In a few words, they brought him up to date.

He was glad to observe the inanity of his dark presentiments—so glad that he approved the gentleman when the latter remarked on the late hour and the necessity of cutting short, that evening, the duration of the quotidian conversation. He shook Aurett's hand, perhaps for slightly longer than usual, and accompanied the visitors to the door.

Suddenly, he gripped them by the arm and murmured: "Listen!"

A thin partition separated the compartment of the dead from the corridor, and through that frail obstacle the slightest sounds were perceptible. What had attracted the attention of the Parisian was a rustling outside. One might have thought that a hand was sliding over the partition.

The English duo had heard it too. They had stopped, holding their breath.

"Ah!" whispered Murlyton. "Someone's walking on tiptoe in the corridor."

"Yes," said Lavarède, "and coming this way."

"Who can it be?"

"I don't know. But in that uncertainty, it's best to hide, in case a sailor comes into the room."

With infinite precaution, all three of them moved between the coffins. Then the door opened slowly, and several men came in, almost brushing the concealed Europeans.

The door having closed behind the last, one of the mysterious newcomers lit a kind of little lantern, which projected an attenuated gleam in the compartment, like that of a night-light.

Aurett scarcely retained a cry of surprise. Five individuals were there, and she recognized the Chinese passengers who had embarked at Honolulu.

Until that day, those individuals had pretended not to know one another. With what objective had they come together in this fashion, in the middle of the night, is a place where nobody went?

Murlyton was asking himself the same question. As for the journalist, he was watching curiously, awaiting for the mystery to explain itself.

Brothers Han, Jap, Tung and Li," began the one who appeared to be the leader, "listen to me." He was speaking in a muted voice, but the Europeans could hear him.

Ah! thought Armand, nonplussed. *Do I understand Chinese now?*

"Two of you," the speaker continued, "have been brought up by the white priests. You do not know the language of the sons of Han, so I am expressing myself in Hawaiian patois, for we must all understand."

"Good, good," muttered the Parisian. "That explanation reassures me."

Aurett placed her hand on the young man's arm to bid him to remain silent.

"Tomorrow, brothers, we reach Nagasaki, where Jap, Tung and Li will descend to land, in order to reach the Chinese coast by the first merchant junk that presents itself."

The Chinamen nodded.

"You know why our supreme leader has recalled us. Our Society, *No hypocrisy*, merits its name. The least of our adepts knows why and against what he is fighting. Each of us represents a detachment that must unite in Peking on a date that I shall give you."

"It will be done," replied the others, in unison.

"Good. Now, these are our Grand-Master's orders, and the facts that motivate them. We sons of Han wish to render to the Chinese and expel the Manchu invaders who hold power. Their leader, whom they qualify proudly as the Son of Heaven, senses his throne trembling under the pressure of a people marching to liberty. Frightened, he is extending his hand to the foreigners from Europe, hoping that they will defend him against our enterprises. He has already permitted them to establish trading posts on the coasts; now he is thinking of letting them into the interior of the country."

A growl interrupted the man who was speaking. His listeners had made the same gesture of menace, and their yellow faces, contracted by anger, were frightening.

"One man," the leader continued, "a German, Dr. Keyser, has come to the Emperor and said to him: 'With a bag of silk that I shall fill with gas, I shall rise into the air and navigate there. Grant me permission to attempt the experiment in the idle of the capital, and to circulate above the lands submissive to your domination.' The Emperor has consented, and on the twenty-second of October, this Keyser will rise up with his machine, which he calls a 'dirigible balloon.'"

The Chinaman paused; then, in an insinuating voice, as if to communicated his conviction to his listeners, he continued: "Such is the official version. But here, as always, the people are being deceived. Dominating the land, this German will study the roads, the rivers and the canals, in order that when the time comes, the European armies will know our means of communication precisely, and will take advantage of it to crush us. But we are alert! To the enterprises of our enemies, we shall oppose the will of an entire nation. We have the numbers and the devotion; let us prove that we also have the intelligence. The Europeans, discouraged by the massacres, are following the honest invasion with the dissimulated invasion. Let us destroy their apparatus and thus demonstrate that we are not people who can be fooled."

"Yes, yes: we will obey."

A shiver shook the fanatics, jealous of their liberty to the point of considering civilization as a danger.

"Now, brothers," the orator concluded, "return to our cabins. Jap, Tung and Li will leave first. Han and I will spent a few more moments here, and then depart in our turn."

The individuals designated extended their hands to the leaders, and then, after putting them to their breast and head, they left the compartment of the repatriates.

The man who had transmitted the orders of the Grand-Master of the secret society *No hypocrisy* turned to the affiliate who had remained it him and said, softly: "Han, I asked you to remain because I need something else from you."

"Command," said his interlocutor, simply.

In a clear voice, the leader let fall words that caused the young Englishwoman to shiver in her hiding place: "It's necessary, after the port of call at Nagasaki, to throw coffin number 49 into the sea."

Han shrugged his shoulders. "It will be thrown."

175

"You're not asking why?"

"What does it matter to me? You speak; I obey."

"I want you to know, however. A fortnight ago, the Committee of San Francisco advised me that a Manchu traitor, condemned by the secret tribunal never to rest in Chinese soil, was about to succeed in eluding the sentence, thanks to the diligence of the Pacific Box Line, and quit America."

"Well?" interrogated the man named Han.

"I have received no new communication since then. The coffin is, therefore, on board, and I must conform with the instructions of the committee."

While speaking, he had picked up the lantern and directed the luminous ray over the coffins. Each one, it will be remembered, was marked with a brass plaque bearing the registration number.

"Here it is," said the leader, stopping in front of Lavarède's bier. "The day after tomorrow, we'll throw it into the waters of the gulf of Petchili."

"Why not immediately, since we're here?" said Han.

"Because the floating box might perhaps be picked up by another ship. In Nagasaki, I'll equip myself with lead weights, which will drag the corpse of the Manchu and his final dwelling into the abyss of the sea. Do you understand?"

"Yes, chief."

"Good. Let's go to sleep, and the day after tomorrow, the traitor will meet his fate."

"May thus be struck forcefully all those who resemble him," recited the Chinaman Han.

"Yes, all!"

"And may the Middle Kingdom return to its legitimate possessors."

The door of the compartment closed with a slight click; the conspirators disappeared, and, with a little effort, the three spectators of that strange scene might have imagined that they had just been dreaming.

The reality of the adventure was not in doubt for anyone, however, and Aurett, deeply affected, asked in a trembling voice: "Did you hear that, Monsieur Lavarède?"

"Yes, Mademoiselle," the Parisian elide, tranquilly. "The saffron-faces intend to plunge coffin number 49 into the ocean depths. The Honolulu Committee is lagging behind the Frisco Committee. It's very amusing."

"You think so?" Murlyton put in.

"Indeed!"

"You have a curious character, Monsieur Lavarède, I'm pleased to recognize—but after all, in the circumstances, the resolution of these people seems very dangerous to you."

"Dangerous? Do you think so?"

"At least from the viewpoint of your cousin's inheritance."

"How is that?"

176

"I assume that you won't be in coffin 49 when those conspirators take it away."

"Be certain of it, my dear Mr. Murlyton."

"But without that utensil, it will be impossible for you to disembark at Taku, and then..."

Armand smiled. "It's evident that if they deprived me of my bier, my voyage would be compromised."

"That's what I said."

"Only, they won't deprive me of it." As the English duo looked at him with amazement, he finished: "You'll soon understand why—it's as simple as saying *bonjour*, thanks to this pen-knife."

He had taken a small pen-knife with a tortoiseshell handle out of his pocket. He opened it, and went to the coffin in which he had been domiciled. He introduced the blade into the groove of one of the screws retained the numbered brass plate.

"What are you doing?" asked Aurett.

"As you can see, Mademoiselle, I'm unscrewing this plate."

At the same moment the second screw came out. The Parisian recommenced the operation on the next coffin.

"Ah!" said the young woman. "I understand."

"I'm changing the number: with my neighbor's plate on my coffin I'll be number forty-eight; with mine on his, he'll be number forty-nine. It's him that his compatriots will ballast with lead and send on the submarine excursion with which they were threatening me."

A few seconds later, the substitution had been made, and the delighted Lavarède wished his adversary *bonsoir*. The pressure of Aurett's hand lasted even longer than on the previous day. The terrible Chinamen had frightened the gentleman's daughter so much that it was excusable for her to forget her slender fingers in the hand of the amiable man who got himself out of the most difficult situations as if it were a game.

On the fifth of September, under relaxed steam, the *Heavenway* doubled Cape Long, which masks and shelters the city of Nagasaki, the chief place of the ken, or government, of the same name, and one of the seven Japanese ports open to Europeans.

Like all young women, Aurett had read the work of Pierre Loti. She smiled on perceiving the agglomeration of minuscule houses composing the city, and which, surrounded by verdant hills, seemed ridiculously cramped. Small habitations small people, apartments formed by movable paper partitions; red fish invariably made of paper, suspended from rods as a sign of rejoicing—in brief, everything making up Japanese life—filed before her eyes as she remembered her reading. Soon, however, she became serious. That was because, alongside those risible details, she sensed the effort of an intelligent and laborious people, possessed of the desire to catch up with the civilizations of the Occident.

To begin with, at the entrance to the harbor, there is the Ojesaki lighthouse, whose beam is visible forty-two kilometers away, as Mr. Mathew explained to her. Then, along the quays, there are the immense docks where the coal extracted from the mines of Takashima is piled up. Everything indicates the tendencies of a nation marching toward progress under the orders of its emperor, the Mikado, once an absolute autocrat, now a constitutional sovereign.

Then, opposite, as if to serve as a contrast to those edifices erected by the new Japan, are the landscapes once bloodied by blind fanaticism: Takabuko Island, or the Long Spear, Daika Point, and, above all, Pappenberg Mountain, where, in 1858, four thousand Christians had been hurled into the sea.

Once disembarked, the English duo are able to take even better account of the spirited movement revolutionizing Japan. The man of the people, wearing the national smock and the conical coiffure, rubs shoulders with the functionary buttoned up in his black frock-coat and coiffed in a top hat. The functionaries are slightly awkward in their European costume, doubtless unhabituated to it as yet. Their spouses, clad in the latest Paris fashions, look more comfortable. Out here, as everywhere, women fashion themselves more rapidly to new customs.

The narrow shop, of the ancient model, contains the modern store, whose full-length mirrors excite the admiration of passers-by.

Even the frightful parliamentary politics has taken root in the empire of the Mikado. The travelers acquire proof of that on seeing the walls covered with multicolored electoral posters. One day, perhaps, the Japanese might regret that European import, and, in their defense, will recall that Europeans also brought them the kiss. The most tender of caresses was unknown to the inhabitants of Kiu-Siu and Nippon, in fact; it was replaced by a complex ceremony. Once again, the women had the glory of being the first to understand.

The English duo wanted to have dinner before going back aboard. Alas, the national cuisine, like the nation itself, is in a period of transformation, and the diners were able to eat rhubarb croquettes fried in rice-oil, roast chicken dotted with the eggs of red ants and fish à la vinaigrette seasoned with brown sugar, triumphantly served to them by an indigene in the small waistcoat and white belted apron of a waiter in Parisian café. To foodstuffs imported from abroad the Japanese cooks add a few autochthonous condiments—brown sugar in the vinaigrette, ants' eggs in the roast—with the result that, in that unfortunate city, the local inhabitants and travelers are equally incapable of having a good meal. In the name of progress, people tighten their belts.

A singular land, moreover, which displays at the same time a police soldier, a samurai, striking the European prince that he is charged with protecting, and the little Japanese lady, sitting in her coquettish tchaia built on stilts, smiling at all the foreigners, who she salutes with a rouitshiva, a generous *bonjour*; where there are already railways, but one can be carried in chairs by porters. The transition of mores is also manifest in the attire of the soldiers of the Imperial Guard, imitative of the uniforms of the Second Empire.

We would be wrong, moreover, to laugh at those valiant, intelligent and passionate little people, for, in spite of our recent defeats, it is not German influence that is dominant there; France is still loved there, for preference.

Tired by their excursion, Murlyton and his daughter returned to the harbor. The *Heavenway*'s launch was at the quay. They took their places in it. Almost immediately, two men came running up. Aurett could not repress a shudder on recognizing the two Chinese passengers whose conversation she had overheard in the compartment of the dead. Each of them was carrying a long package, of considerable weight, to judge by the bearers' efforts.

"Do you recognize them, Father?" the young woman asked.

"Yes, of course," the gentleman replied. And as the young woman pointed out the objects to two individuals were holding, he added tranquilly: "Probably the lead weights that will drag their deceased compatriot to the ocean bed."

Aurett looked away. She thought that, but for a providential hazard, Lavarède would have had no warning of the Chinamen's plan, and then...

She imagined the men slipping by night into the hold, attaching their lead weights to the coffin where the Parisian was sleep, and letting the whole fall into the black water, which would close silently over its swallowed prey.

"What's the matter, Aurett?" asked Murlyton. "You're very pale."

"It's because I was thinking about...what can no longer happen."

The Englishman looked intently at the young woman; then his eyes went back to the Chinese. That movement brought the color back to the cheeks of the pretty voyager; she sensed that her feelings had been divined, and experienced a delicate impression. Certain sentiments want no confidants, and the dearest father in the world is sometimes wrong to look into his daughter's soul.

When the boat had drawn alongside the ship, the English duo strolled along the deck silently, waiting for the hour when they could go down to visit Lavarède without fear of being seen. They had to see Armand that day, since the Chinese had chosen the next day to immense coffin number 49. An encounter with the initiates of the White Lotus would have been disastrous, and it would be prudent to abstain.

The visit was prolonged well beyond the usual limits. The gentleman was obliged to indicate the advanced hour several times before convincing Aurett to return to her cabin. She was very drowsy, however, for she fell profoundly asleep as soon as she lay down in her bunk.

When she opened her eyes again the *Heavenway* had left Nagasaki and was cleaving the waves of the Blue Sea. The lunch bell had just rung. As she went to the dining room the young woman perceived land on the horizon, the jagged silhouette of which was outlined against the pure sky.

"What is that mountain?" she asked of Mr. Mathew, who was nearby.

"Mense Island, Miss," the American replied. "We'll have doubled it this evening and we'll enter the Yellow Sea, which Korea and the Chinese coast enclose ever more narrowly until the gulf of Petchili."

"Blue Sea, Yellow Sea. So many colors!"

"The names are justified, Miss."

"You're joking, Mr. Mathew. Blue, fine—but yellow?"

The captain smiled. "You'll see that tint. The explanation of the phenomenon is simple. The sea is quite shallow, and the rivers that flow into it pass over alluvial deposits known as 'yellow earth.' The mud they carry is very fine and remains in suspense in the water—hence their particular hue."

The young woman listened to that little geographical lesson distractedly. She was counting the days that still separated her from the end of the crossing, and it was of scant importance to her whether she was telling those rosary-beads of twenty-four hours over waves of one color or another.

If she was morose, however, Bouvreuil was becoming exuberant. The arrival in port had filled him with joy—quite naturally, the passengers thought, given that life in the crew quarters could not be restful.

The day seemed interminable to the Englishwoman. The idea that when night fell, it would be necessary to shut herself in her cabin without giving an amicable handshake to Monsieur Lavarède caused her a veritable chagrin. The steamer had never seemed so ugly, the ocean so insipid; the immutable blue of the sky grated on her nerves.

As Murlyton, a born observer, had understood by certain twitches of the nostrils the internal storm that was raging, he carefully refrained from speaking to his daughter. He launched himself into a long discussion with the first mate about fisheries in Newfoundland, and the best kinds of bait to catch lobsters. On such themes, and Englishman and an American can argue for weeks, provided that the brandy never runs out. Thanks to that stratagem, the gentleman was able to reach dinner time without Aurett having any opportunity to vent any of her irritation on him.

When dusk fell, it was necessary to go back on deck. Murlyton was apprehensive of that moment, but, to his great surprise, Aurett proved to be amiable and cheerful. Her bad mood seemed to have dissipated completely along with the sunlight. She stayed on deck quite late, lying limply in a rocking-chair, to which the movement of the steamer communicated a gentle sway.

At about eleven o'clock she declared that she was tired, kissed her father tenderly on the cheek, and retired to her cabin without having pronounced the journalist's name. So the Englishman shut himself in his own, delighted to have avoided the anticipated squall, and yielded to the consolations of sleep.

He would have been less tranquil had he known what idea had calmed his daughter down.

She had decided resolutely to keep watch on the Chinamen during the accomplishment of their funereal task. When everyone was sleep, she slipped into the dark corridor.

Almost immediately, light footfalls became audible at the other extremity. A muted gleam permitted her to perceive two vague silhouettes. That was sufficient. She had recognized Han and his chief by the light of their lantern.

The gleam suddenly vanished. Aurett understood that the Celestials had gone into the compartment of the dead, and, gripped by an irresistible curiosity, she slid silently to the door. Han had left it ajar. The Englishwoman darted a glance through the gap.

The affiliates of the White Lotus had placed their lantern on the floor and were occupied in sliding coffin number 49 off the brackets that were supporting it. A false movement caused the oak coffer to bump on to the floor. Already troubled, Aurett could not suppress a slight gasp. Immediately a muscular hand seized her wrist, and before she could take account of what was happening, she was dragged inside the room of the dead.

Han had bounded forward at the sound she had uttered and he bought her to his chief. The latter fixed a penetrating gaze upon the young woman, and, like a bird fascinated by a snake, she tried to turn her head in order to escape the motionless eyes that were hypnotizing her. Behind her, barring the door, Han awaited his companion's orders.

Finally, the chief shrugged his shoulders. "So much the worse for her. Go!"

With a rapid gesture, Han drew his dagger and raised it over the Englishwoman. She was doomed—but suddenly, the Chinaman spun around like a top and was slammed, with a groan of pain, into the corner of a neighboring bier.

Lavarède had just loomed up alongside the young woman. Forewarned of the visit of the Celestials and wanting to watch their little task, he had hidden—and then, quite naturally, he had hastened to the aid of the blonde miss. Now he was in front of her, covering her with his body, confronting the menacing Chinamen.

The battle was about to commence. Aurett had a fleeting intuition that her friend was about to sacrifice his cousin's inheritance for her. The noise would certainly attract the mariners; the journalist would be discovered. And if, by chance, no one came, the situation was no less desperate. The Parisian's secret was no longer safe. The two Chinamen knew it—not to mention that the brave fellow might be killed in the unequal combat.

She looked at Armand. He smiled.

"Let's see," he said, employing the Hawaiian sabir. "Why do you want to murder this young woman, who is my friend?"

The man whom Han called the chief looked at Lavarède in surprise, but did not reply.

"Oh," the latter continued, imperturbably, "you fear being compromised. As if I didn't know that you're here to throw coffin number 49 into the sea." And, as his listeners started in amazement, he said: "Charged with the same mission, I've been living in bier 48." At the same time, he lifted the lid of his prison, and showed the bewildered Chinamen that it was empty.

The chief recovered the power of speech. "Who are you, then?"

"Who am I? Look."

Overcoming, with some difficulty, the urge that he had to laugh, Armand held out to his interlocutor the tin-plate cylinder found in the shark's stomach.

The mere sight of the receptacle plunged the Chinaman into astonishment. He opened it, read the parchment, and then handed it back to the journalist.

"You're one of our brothers, and you answer for this European woman?"

"Since San Francisco my sister has come by night to bring me the food without which I would be similar today to those who surround us."

"Good. She'll remain silent, won't she?"

"As myself."

"That's good. Han, let's resume our operation."

Shortly afterwards, the Chinamen left, carrying the former number 48, who had become, by virtue of the Frenchman's will, the 49 vowed to the execration of the White Lotus.

"Now, Mademoiselle," said Lavarède, gallantly, "go back to your cabin and sleep. Excuse me for not escorting you back, but as you know, my health forbids me to leave the room."

She squeezed his hand for a long time, and withdrew.

The next day, as she was alone on deck, Han came to lean on the bulwark two meters away, and without looking at her or making any gesture that might betray their complicity, said: "Sister of one of ours, you had a fright last night. Forgive us. You are going to the Middle Kingdom. Accept this. The chief sends it to you."

He was holding a metal flower depicting the white corolla of a lotus.

"Place it in your corsage; that flower will spare you the brutalities of the mandarin police and will enable you to find friends wherever you go."

Like a passenger weary of admiring the ocean, the Chinaman turned away, made sure that no one was looking and dropped the flower deftly at the young woman's feet. Having done that, he drew away tranquilly.

After a moment, Aurett picked up the emblem of the powerful secret society and slipped it into her pocket. Almost involuntarily, she murmured: "I might, perhaps, be able to be useful to him."

Meanwhile, the voyage continued. The *Heavenway* drew closer to the Korean shore, allowing towns and villages to be seen. Mr. Mathew recounted the strange customs of the land, where hospitality is more than Scottish.

Finally, on the evening of the tenth, they came within sight of Taku.

It was too late to go into the harbor, and the *Heavenway* was obliged to lie to under low steam in order to wait for daybreak. For the last time, the English duo went down to visit Lavarède. They agreed to meet again the following evening at the hotel booked by the Pacific Box Line. During the day, Armand would find a means of eluding the vigilance of the Company's agents.

And, full of confidence, the competitors who had become friends shook hands vigorously and repeated: "Until tomorrow!"

XVII. Complications and Chinoiseries

On the eleventh of September, at ten o'clock in the morning, Mr. Saxby, the director of the Taku Office, representing Pacific Box in China, was in his office, a vast room in which the wide open windows were letting in the sunlight, the perfume of flowers and birdsong. He was opening his mail, assisted by a young employee who testified to his respect for his hierarchical superior with a cheerful awkwardness.

Mr. Saxby handed the other a letter. "Look, Howdin, take note of this: the Pali-Ma family, from the village of Tien-Be, will come this morning to reclaim the body of the late Li-Mua, deceased in San Francisco and repatriated by the *Heavenway*. Consult the on-board register and have the coffin brought here, in order that the recognition can be carried out swiftly. Otherwise, we risk being late for lunch."

While the employee ran out, bumping into the door, the director added, to himself: "Such haste is incredible. The ship has scarcely come into port and these people are claiming their package. The public are becoming more and more demanding. One doesn't have time to breathe."

After a pause, he added: "I have a good mind to send round a circular, specifying that people can only take delivery twenty-four hours after the arrival of the transpacific."

At that moment, someone knocked on the door, and a little groom, correctly dressed in brown cloth, appeared on the threshold.

"What is it, Bridge?"

"A man is asking to see the Director, sir."

"What sort of man?"

"A passenger brought by the *Heavenway*. He says that he has an important communication to make."

"Good! Another demand! At any rate, he's a client of the Company; I have to see him. Send him in."

The groom disappeared, and then announced: "Monsieur Bouvreuil."

The usurer came in, smiling, and bowed to the irritated Mr. Saxby, who replied with a nod of the head.

"Monsieur," he began, "I'm a Frenchman, a property-owner, a millionaire twice over, President of…"

The director stood up, as if moved by a spring, and said, in an engaging one: "Please sit down." When Bouvreuil was seated, he went on: "How may I have the pleasure of assisting you?"

"In no way, Monsieur. On the contrary, I have come to render you a service."

"You, Monsieur?" Mr. Saxby was visibly astonished.

"Indeed, yes," Pénélope's father continued, in a paternal tone. "Like all those who know risks of large-scale enterprises, I have a horror of fraud. Now, your Company is the victim of a fraudster."

"You astonish me. Our surveillance is unassailable, as I have written in my most recent report to the central administration."

"I don't say any different; however, one of my compatriots has introduced himself into the compartment reserved for the repatriates and has crossed the Pacific without paying for his passage."

"How was he able to do that?" complained the bewildered director.

"I don't know, but I can affirm to you that he did it. The man must still be aboard; I haven't seen him come ashore, and I've been watching carefully, I can assure you. You can catch him, and demand the reimbursement of the sum of which he has cheated you—and that will be that."

Howdin came back in.

"Sir, the Pali-Ma family is here. They're waiting for you for the opening of the coffin and the signature of the delivery note."

"I'm coming. Will you excuse me for a moment, sit—I'll come back."

"Oh, I'll go," Bouvreuil declared. "My mission is concluded." And, rubbing his hands, he added in a low voice: "Like my dear son-in-law's voyage, also concluded."

The two men went into the next room, where several people were surrounding a bier placed on the ground. All Chinese, the newcomers were wearing silk garments, to which were fixed broad horizontal pink and white bands, as a sign of mourning. An old woman was weeping. Two professional mourners were uttering shrill howls, lugubriously cadenced. The family must have been well off, because the employees in question were not sparing the ears of the onlookers.

The old woman came to meet Mr. Saxby. "I am Pali-Ma, the mother of Li-Mua, dead at twenty-two years of age. Here is the certificate from the mandarin of my village."

"Good," said the director. "Let's go!"

The agents of the Company who had brought bier number 48 prepared to unscrew the lid, but they had scarcely touched it when they leapt backwards with a cry of fright. A man had suddenly stood up.

"Lavarède!" cried Bouvreuil, while the Chinese recoiled, bewildered. He turned to the director. "There's your fraudster!"

Mr. Saxby briskly drew the revolver that, like every good American, he always kept in his pocket, just in case, and took aim at Armand, who was surprised to find himself in such a numerous company.

"You're caught! Make the slightest move and I'll shoot."

"No need," replied the journalist. "I understand that immobility is necessary."

At a sign from the director, the agents of the company approached and took hold of the voyager.

Mr. Saxby examined Armand. His good looks were in his favor, so it was in an almost amicable tone that he went on: "I guess, sir, that all this is nothing but a joke. I won't make any fuss, then, merely asking you to settle the price of your passage. In view of the smallness of the cabin you were occupying, I'll even consent to a twenty-five per cent reduction."

Lavarède bowed. "It would be impossible to be more amiable, but..."

"Ah! There's a but?"

"Yes. Even reduced, the passage is still too costly for my purse, for I only possess twenty-five centimes."

Mr. Saxby's arms agitated desperately. "Five cents! And you dared to embark on one of our steamers!"

"Permit me, Monsieur: I was embarked, after having been treacherously enclosed in a coffin with a few provisions. I intend to sue the Pacific Box Company for damages."

The director suddenly became annoyed. "You're mocking me. So be it— I'll have you arrested."

"One moment," Bouvreuil intervened, having stood aside thus far. "There's a means of sorting everything out. I'll gladly lend the gentleman the small sum that he needs."

"Ah, the worthy Bouvreuil!" the young man exclaimed. "I would have been astonished not to see you here."

The American interrupted. "Borrow the money from this gentleman, and it's all settled."

"But I can't borrow it from him!"

"What do you mean, you can't?"

Ceasing to laugh, Armand said: "No, and he knows it full well, for reasons that it would take too long to explain—but I'll make you a proposition."

"Pooh!"

"You're intelligent, that's obvious. As an American you're practical. Good. By traversing the Pacific as I have, I've put your Company at a loss."

"That's right."

"Isn't it? You see, we understand one another already. That loss, it's impossible for me to redeem, but, by way of compensation, I can give you a means of realizing a profit greatly superior to the price of the crossing."

"What profit?"

Lavarède darted a mocking glance at Bouvreuil, who was listening in amazement. The American was at the point to which he wanted to bring him.

"Permit me, Monsieur Director—if I give you the means, will you cancel my debt?"

"Of course," said Mr. Saxby, after a moment's reflection.

"Listen to me, then. You possess four ships. Each one undertakes approximately six voyages a year, with a average of fifty repatriates. Thus, transport assured of twelve hundred Chinese..."

"That's true, but I don't see what it has to do with..."

"Follow my reasoning. Of those twelve hundred passengers, only one in six has enough money to buy his coffin while he's alive. There remain, therefore, a thousand deceased to whom you furnish the double container of lead and wood. Now, you use good oak—I've been able to ascertain that—and the bier must cost you five dollars."

"True."

"If it only cost you three dollars, that would be a net profit for you of ten thousand francs a year."

"Oh," growled Mr. Saxby, "We've thought of that—but the clients want oak."

"You'll give it to them...or at least, you'll give them the appearance."

"What do you mean?"

"Silver fir, first washed with sulfuric acid diluted with water to a fifth, and then hydrochloric acid, diluted to a sixth, causticated, and finally varnished."

"Quite simple, but are you sure of what you're saying?"

"Keep me prisoner until you've done the experiment. It doesn't take long."

Mr. Saxby held out his hand. "In truth, Sir, you'll have paid for your passage, and the Company will have a good deal. I'm delighted to have made your acquaintance."

And to Bouvreuil, chewing his bit, Lavarède murmured, with his most gracious smile: "You see, my dear Monsieur Bouvreuil, that with a little chemistry, one can clear the awkward obstacles from one's route."

The Chinese, gathered in a corner, made no protest—and with good reason—against the agreement debated in English. Everything seemed to be arranged, when a newcomer appeared in the hall.

By his blue tunic bordered by a green stripe and his somber coiffure surmounted by a jade button, they recognized a police officer, With him was a young man from the Pali-Ma family, who had disappeared immediately when the coffin was opened. The latter pointed at Lavarède and pronounced words in Chinese, which the Frenchman did not understand.

The policeman ran to the door and uttered a guttural exclamation. Immediately, ten men dressed in the same fashion irrupted into the hall and took hold of Armand.

"I regret to have to inform you," Mr. Saxby said to him, after a conversation with the leader of the troop, "that you're in serious trouble."

"Why?"

"You're accused of having destroyed the remains of young Li-Mua in order to take his place. Sacrilege, profanation of a sepulcher, and all that. In all probability, you'll be condemned to death."

Lavarède shuddered slightly, but immediately got a grip on himself. "Thank you for the information," he said.

"Be assured that I'm very sorry," said the director, "and that I'll do what I can to help. Do you have any relatives or friends to whom you want to bid farewell? I can forward your letters."

The journalist hesitated momentarily. The sweet image of Aurett passed before his eyes—but then he shook his head. "I'm obliged to you, but I don't want to announce my death to anyone yet...except, of course, the worthy Monsieur Bouvreuil, who's listening to us; as I've saved his life, the news will give him pleasure."

Bowing to the visibly troubled Bouvreuil, he placed himself in the hands of the policemen again, and left under their escort, to be taken to prison.

As they went through the city of Taku, a few groups formed around the path of the procession, but they were immediately dispersed by the policemen's sticks, manipulated with a dexterity testifying to abundant practice.

Chinese cities are not very clean. The streets, divided in the middle by ditches into which the inhabitants throw excrement, affect the senses of sight and smell disagreeably. In its quality as a port, Taku is even dirtier than the cities of the interior. Of monuments, there are none. The greater number of the houses are built of mud and clay. At intervals, a richer habitation displays its façade, ornamented with multicolored faiences depicting complex arabesques, animals and flowers. Only one promenade exists, on the bank of the river Pei-Ho, at the mouth of which the morose Chinese township is located—and even that unique place of pleasure is saddened by the prison, which it borders. It is there, too, that the Ti-Tou, the governor of a Hsien, or third-class city, has criminals executed.

Armand was unaware of these details, so, on arriving beside the river, he uttered a sigh of satisfaction. He had been stifling in the narrow and stinking streets; here he could take deep breaths. In front of him extended the estuary of the Pei-Ho, three kilometers wide, with its yellow waters, running between low, gray, dismal banks—but at least there was no lack of space, and the eye could roam the surrounding landscape. Under the overlapping branches of the enormous plane trees that sheltered the promenade, Armand marched with an impression of relief. Why? His situation was no less critical, his guards no less attentive, but a purer air was reaching his lungs, and that was sufficient for confidence to return to our valiant Parisian.

He went pale however, on perceiving two familiar faces in front of him. Miss Aurett and her father, still tourists, were visiting the city while awaiting the hour at which Lavarède had promised to meet them at the hotel, and chance—an unfortunate chance—had brought them to the bank of the Pei-Ho at the right moment to cross the captive's path.

The young woman put her hand on her heart. She wanted to speak, but hr emotion was too strong; the words would not pass her lips. Murlyton asked, in

English in order not to be understood by the guards, said: "You've been caught?"

"Yes, on Monsieur Bouvreuil's denunciation."

"Oh, the vile man!" exclaimed Aurett, suddenly finding her voice.

One of the policemen threatened the journalist with his sword. It was an invitation to silence. Everyone understood it, and the Englishman drew his swooning daughter away.

"Courage, child," he said. "Let's find out where our friend is being taken. Perhaps our consul will be able to do something for him."

Lavarède, who turned round in order to be able to continue looking at his friends, saw the following his escort at a distance. When a wooden door with red cross-pieces, decorated with bronze plaques depicting fabulous animals close behind him, his gaze met that of the blonde Englishwoman, wild and staring—and at that terrible moment, when everything was separating them, he understood that, by mutual consent, they would be able to nullify the testament of his parsimonious cousin by means of a marriage.

Preoccupied by that thought, following his guards, he traversed a brick courtyard distractedly, climbed the steps of a wooden perron covered with a blue awning and found himself in a dark room where a young Chinaman was writing on a long strip of paper with a paintbrush.

The chief of the escort approached the scribe and said a few words to him. The latter immediately stood up and went out, returning a few moments later with a fat man so bloated that his hooded eyelids scarcely opened. The policemen bowed profoundly, raising their hands alternately to the level of their ears.

Good, thought Lavarède. *He's the governor of the prison.*

The fat man demanded a few explanations from the policemen, and then made a gesture, as if to say: "Go!" Two policemen immediately took hold of Armand, while the Chinese scribe emptied his pockets with marvelous dexterity.

"There's a clerk," murmured the prisoner, "that pickpockets wouldn't disown."

That was all. He perceived that in the Middle Kingdom, as in Europe, a captive is deprived, as soon as he arrived, of everything he possesses.

The searcher had spread the objects out on his desk, if a kind of easel supporting an inclined tabletop could be called by that term. The pen-knife and the five sous constituting the voyager's fortune were the object of a prolonged examination; then the governor's gaze fell upon the tin-plate container brought by the shark into the waters of Honolulu.

Lavarède made as if to pick it up. "That's not mine..." he began—but his guardians shook him brutally. It occurred to him that French is not widely spoken in China, and he abstained.

The clerk opened the container and took out the parchment that Armand had tried to decipher. Calmly, with a pretentious gesture—pen-pushers are the same the world over—he unrolled it, but scarcely had he glanced at it than he dropped it on the table, making a frightful grimace.

The governor picked up the sheet of paper and immediately put it down again, blowing into his cheeks—after which he passed his hand over his forehead, looked at his clerk and then the chief of the police squad, and took a few steps, breathing hard.

"Pooh! Pooh!"

He came back to the man who had arrested the Frenchman. An animated discussion began. With his short arms, the functionary described broad gestures, but the impassive policeman did not appear to be moved. He replied briefly, maintaining a cold expression. Obviously, he was refusing something that his interlocutor was demanding insistently.

That lasted for a quarter of an hour without Lavarède being able to determine what it was about. The two men doubtless fell into agreement, for the captive was taken to a room and locked in.

Left alone, Armand reflected on his sad situation. Momentarily amused by the grotesques that had appeared in front of him, he now thought that he was locked in a Chinese prison, accused of sacrilege. He knew, from the stories told by missionaries and voyagers, about the inflexibility of the country's laws and the cruelty of its tortures, and he was obliged to admit that, barring a miracle, his goose was cooked. The old adage of the sons of Han came to mind: *To punish a guilty party is good, but to strike a European barbarian is delightful.*

Those morose reflections put a melancholy mask on the prisoner's face, and he was not astonished that a tear blurred his vision when he pronounced a name dolorously:

"Aurett!"

That sweet, joyful name, as bright as a ray of dawn light or the skylark's prelude, lent the jail an appearance of mockery. More unfortunate than Tantalus, who could at least devour with his eyes the fruits that incessantly drew away from his lips. Armand would never see the young woman again.

So, the gay Parisian was in a deep depression when the door of his prison opened, causing him to start. Gravely, with courteous gestures, the fat governor appeared, leading a young girl by the hand. Bring up the rear, the scribe appeared, carrying a table laden with dishes. He placed it ceremoniously before the captive, along with two bottles containing a liquid similar to wine.

The governor smiled, and with a gesture, invited Lavarède to eat. Then he pushed the Chinese girl forward. The latter, very intimidated, fixed her dark eyes on the journalist momentarily and blushed, which gave her lovely lemon-hued skin an orange tint.

In a low voice, in French, she said: "I am Diamba."

"Eh?" said Armand, surprised.

"I am Diamba," she repeated.

"I understand—but how is it that you speak the same language as me?"

190

"The white bonzes taught me."

"Right! You were brought up by missionaries!"

She nodded her head by way of affirmation.

"And you've been permitted to come to relieve the prisoner's tedium somewhat?"

"That's not the reason."

"Then I don't understand."

The girl lowered her eyes. "I have to talk to you."

"I'm listening, child—go on."

Diamba looked at the governor and exchanged a few words with him in Chinese, after which she addressed herself to Lavarède.

"Chun-Tze, the governor of the prison of Taku, says this: 'I regret keeping you captive, but as a humble functionary, I must obey the Ti-Tou who governs the city. Otherwise, I would be sent the sword with which I would be obliged to open my belly. Save for liberty, I will give you anything you request: good food, exquisite wines, fist-rate eau-de-vie, the emperor's tea, picked by virgins with gloved hands in order that the leaves remain immaculate. Finally, if you desire to write to your friends, your letters will be forwarded faithfully.'"

His eyes wide and his mouth open in an O, Armand listened in amazement.

The governor Chun-Tze bowed, and smiled in the most engaging fashion.

Diamba continued: "Chun-Tze, knowing who you are, and who your brothers are, wanted to set you free; he has made the request of the Ti-Tou, but he refused."

"Ah!" the journalist was finally able to exclaim.

"Your people, he claims, are showing too much audacity. An express dispatch is departing tomorrow for Peking, and the Son of Heaven himself will decide your fate. Chun-Tze, here present, begs you to notice that he has tried to save you. He begs you also, when you correspond with our friends, to affirm that he admires them and that, in spite of his function, his good wishes are with them."

"What friends do you mean?" asked the captive, confused by the strangeness of the conversation.

Diamba folded her arms over her chest, inclined her body in a very respectful bow, and then straightened up and used her finger to describe a triangle on her forehead."

Lavarède slapped his own. He had understood. The certificate of freemasonry found on him was having its effect.

The prisoner was benefiting from the terror inspired by the secret societies; they were looking after him in order not to fall victim to the sect to which they supposed him to be affiliated.

All his good humor returned. With a noble gesture, he extended his hand to the Chinaman, and, giving his tone a melodramatic pitch appropriate to the role in which he found himself cast, he spoke,

191

"Diamba," he said, "Chun-Tze could not have chosen a more gracious messenger. Report my words to him. Let dread be distanced from his mind. Those who respect the members of the Universal Lodge have no reason to tremble; they will be protected, if necessary. Let him continue to show himself attentive and courteous, and, far from being threatened, he will be shielded."

The governor's face brightened. The fat man even sketched a genuflection, and withdrew with forceful protestations, which Diamba had difficulty translating.

Again the journalist was left alone, but hope had now illuminated the darkness of his spirit. His jailer had been transformed into a domestic.

XVIII. Aurett's Anguish

On seeing Lavarède disappear into Taku prison, Aurett had asked: "What is that building?"

"Probably the prison," Murlyton replied.

The young woman stamped her foot. "The prison! And you say that so calmly! The Chinese dare to lock up a citizen of a free nation in dungeons reserved for criminals; if order isn't restored, that could happen to you or me tomorrow."

"No," said the gentleman, "because we're traveling correctly."

An indignant stare from his companion shut him up.

"I hope, Father," Aurett went on, in a strangely calm tone, "that you're not going to reproach that young man for certain...irregularities for which you alone are culpable."

"Me!" protested the Englishman.

"Undoubtedly, you. By accepting the ridiculous clause of an insensate testament, you've constrained our...friend to do the same. You have, in a way, forced him outside the law, and I consider..."

She stopped momentarily.

"You consider...?" her father repeated, very upset by those reproaches, which he deemed to be undeserved.

"I consider that it would be appropriate for us to do our utmost to obtain Monsieur Lavarède's release.

Murlyton looked at her with a bewildered expression. "How? I don't know anyone in this diabolical country. I'm incapable of making myself understood to the inhabitants..."

"Oh! Because you don't want to..."

"What? I don't speak Chinese because I don't want to?"

"That's not what I meant."

"Then explain yourself."

He was visibly yielding. Aurett ceased scolding him. She became gentle and persuasive.

"Let's see, Father," she went on, in a caressant voice, "when an Englishman is in trouble, anywhere in the world, what does he do?"

"He appeals to his consul."

"Exactly. Well, don't you think that his intervention will never have been so justified?"

"Yes, except that Lavarède isn't English."

"He's our friend—that's sufficient. Since the departure, he's saved my life ten times over."

"In fact, why not? Let's go to the consulate."

Fundamentally, Murlyton would have been very glad to get his companion on the world tour, for whom he experienced a very keen amity, out of trouble. He therefore put his daughter's idea into action.

The consul listened to his story, promised to take the steps necessary to have the journalist set free, and arranged to meet his compatriots again the following day. It was necessary to give him time to mount a rapid investigation, in order to establish the facts clearly.

An hour before the appointed time, the young Englishwoman and her father arrived at the consulate. That untimely haste was, of course, attributable to Aurett. The result, however, was a long wait on the bamboo chairs in the antechamber. Finally, they were introduced to see the consul. The latter's face was gloomy.

"I've busied myself with your affair," he said to Murlyton, "but your protégé is in a bad situation. The director of the shipping company told me everything, and the governor, whom I visited, has informed me that the sacrilegious individual would have been beheaded this morning if he had not the good fortune to be affiliated to the Universal League of Heaven, Earth and Humankind."

Urged by his daughter, the gentleman explained how the act of adhesion to the League had fallen into their hands, and how the Chinese aboard the ship had committed the sacrilege of which Lavarède was accused, but the consul stopped him.

"Refrain from saying anything about all that. Let it be believed that the prisoner is a member of the secret society. All the functionaries are trembling before him. The governor is afraid of him. He dared not take responsibility for the execution, and he had sent to Peking for orders. Oh, if the Pali-Ma family had not been rich and powerful, you can be sure that your protégé would be free by now. Unfortunately, one of the Pali-Mas is the mandarin Te-Tchong—which is to say, the military leader. You understand? Caught between the Pali-Ma and the freemasons, the governor has decided that he won't decide anything himself. He prefers to leave all responsibility to the Tsong-li-Yamen, the Council of Ministers, and the sovereign."

"What can we do, then?" asked the Englishwoman.

"Wait, Mademoiselle."

"How long?"

"Three weeks, perhaps four."

She raised her eyes to the heavens with an expression so desolate that the consul felt obliged to offer her a few words of consolation.

"I think, Mademoiselle, that it will all end well. In this country, when a guilty party isn't killed straight away, he has every chance of escaping death. I've spoken about it to my colleague, the French consul, who thinks as I do. I promise you that I'll seek information, and keep you up to date with what happens."

And with that vague promise, he dismissed his visitors.

They both headed back toward the hotel in silence, absorbed by their thoughts, not noticing that young men were following them. Armed with sticks, treading the ground with bare feet, the Chinese looked threatening.

As Murlyton and his daughter turned into a side-street, a stick whistled through the air and came down hard on the gentleman's shoulder. At the same time, a furious clamor erupted, and the compact group of assailants moved forward rapidly.

"What's happening?" asked the young woman.

"Chinese hospitality," said the Englishman, phlegmatically. "Its motto is nice and simple: *Death to foreigners*."

While speaking he had drawn his revolver, and he faced up to the enemies. Even armed, however, the struggle was unequal now. Two hundred fanatics where howling threats. He was about to fire even so when Aurett retained his arm. Like lightning, the memory of Han, the Chinaman encountered on the *Heavenway*, returned to her. She remembered what he had said when throwing her the lotus flower: "With this sign, you'll find friends everywhere."

She was carrying the flower hidden in the pleats of her corsage. To take it out and show it to the assailants was a matter of a second—and the clamors suddenly died down; the sticks raised to strike were lowered.

Before the gentleman could ask for an explanation of the abrupt reversal, the street was empty; the enemies had vanished.

Aurett was amused by his astonishment. She told him about her adventure. She had hidden it from him until then, but it had just had such a useful epilogue that even a father much more severe than Murlyton would have forgiven her. He did not reproach his daughter for her excursion to the chamber of the dead, and only growled: "I don't like this country. Too many secret societies."

The reflection did not lack justice. Affiliations are the scourge of the Middle Kingdom. A state within a state, they maintain a perpetual agitation, and the courageous missionaries who seek to extend European influence out there by means of religion and language, see their efforts paralyzed by an occult power. They are fortunate when they and their pupils are not torn apart by savage mobs.

From that day on, the English duo were able to circulate through the city. No one hindered their progress, but they sensed instinctively that they were being watched. They had the proof that they were not mistaken. In one of their walks they got lost. Very embarrassed, they were trying to find their way when an indigene approached them and invited them by means of gestures to follow him. He guided them back to their hotel, and when they arrived, he went away without accepting he silver coin that the gentleman offered him.

The young woman became restless, however, and very anxious. What had become of Armand? When she interrogated herself, that was what she invariably called him. All her British prejudices had melted away in the face of the mortal danger he was in, Instead of resisting her sentiment, as etiquette required, she allowed it to carry her away, glad and rather proud of the new soul that she was discovering, and softly, she repeated the philosophical question: "Why love, if there is death? Why death, if there is love?"

After a week, she wanted to see Lavarède. Since her lotus flower pin appeased the masses, it was necessary to try its power on the functionaries. With Murlyton, deeply affected by recent events, she went to the prison.

All her eloquence failed, however, against the passivity of Chun-Tze. The fat governor took refuge behind his orders from the Ti-Tou; all that he could do was permit the young lady to write to the prisoner. He would take him the missive and come back with the reply.

Diamba, naturally, served as interpreter. On the governor's orders she had remained at the prison in order that the prisoner could converse with someone who spoke his language.

No one noticed the attention with which the Chinese girl studied the Englishwoman, but after the visitor's departure, she went to sit in Armand's room and murmured, in her concentrated voice: "She's beautiful, your fiancée." And when Lavarède shivered, she continued: "She's beautiful, and her soul is yours."

That was all. In those simple words rang a kind of resigned sadness. Perhaps the Chinese girl had associated the journalist with a red dream—red being the color of dreams of marriage in China, and only employed for bridal costumes.

Clutching in her hand the piece of paper on which Armand had scribbled a few affectionate lines in haste, Aurett left the prison. Murlyton seemed discontented with the partial success of their move.

On the quay of the Pei-Ho, they found themselves face to face with Monsieur Bouvreuil. The usurer seemed embarrassed at first, but, pulling himself together, he bowed ceremoniously to the English duo and said in a penetrating one: "You've doubtless been to visit the prisoner."

Murlyton and his daughter made a detour to avoid the unwelcome intrusion, and continued walking without replying, but that was not to Bouvreuil's liking. Turning on his heel, he caught up with the walkers.

"Perhaps you're judging my conduct a trifle severely. Be certain that I didn't foresee what has happened; I merely wanted to stop Monsieur Lavarède in order to ensure his marriage to my dear Pénélope."

Aurett spun around as if she had been bitten by a viper. "Mademoiselle Pénélope will not marry Monsieur Lavarède," she said, coldly.

"Oh! What?" stammered the usurer, slightly perturbed by the tone in which the words had been pronounced.

"One does not give one's name to the daughter of an informer," the Englishwoman continued, gradually becoming excited. "It would require the excuse of passion to enter into a family as poor in honor, and Monsieur Armand is far from loving you and that demoiselle. The result of your maneuvers is that your victim despises you a little more every day, and I am obliged to tell you that my father and I share his opinion."

196

Bouvreuil, suffocating, tried to protest. The Englishman did not give him the time.

"Miss Murlyton has spoken well. I will add that no relationship can exist between us and an individual of your sort. Now go away—and note this: henceforth, my mouth will not open to reply to you, but my fists will close."

And the gentleman presented the landlord with a boxer's fist so menacing that the latter took a step backwards. He abstained from retaining people with whom conversation had become so difficult.

Deep down, Bouvreuil was experiencing a very real chagrin. Not that remorse was gripping his conscience—he had rid himself of that *impedimentum* a long time ago, appropriate at the most for stopping honest men on the road to fortune—but he understood that Pénélope's marriage was more hypothetical than ever. Furthermore, he was familiar with the amiable character of his heir, and returning to Paris without the expected fiancé appeared to him to be a prospect devoid of charm.

Undoubtedly, the usurer had rubbed his hands at the idea of forcing Lavarède to pay for his passage on the *Heavenway*, but his joy had been transformed into despair when the Chinese authorities had got mixed up in the affair. He had immediately taken account of the gravity of the situation. He had taken action, visiting functionaries, offering large bribes to the secretaries of mandarins. Those employees had taken the money but had not freed the prisoner.

Discouraged by such costly checks, Bouvreuil had fallen back on the consulates. Then he had heard the portentous words pronounced that had made his flesh creep: sacrilege; violation of a sepulcher. He had been told inexplicable things: Lavarède was a conspirator, a Chinese freemason affiliated to the League of Heaven, Earth and Humankind.

He had made enquiries about the secret societies, stupefied to see the journalist mixed up in the internal politics of the Middle Kingdom—with the result that, no longer understanding anything, he had plucked up the courage, from his very mental confusion, to approach Murlyton in order to obtain some enlightenment from him. The gentleman's reception had not matched his expectations. So, once the English duo were too far away to hear him, the unhappy landlord vented a fit of fury compared to which the rages of Homer's heroes would have seemed mere twitches of impatience.

No man's nerves, even those of a usurer, can remain eternally taut. Bouvreuil, therefore, eventually calmed down. Having become more placid, he held council with himself, and decided that, as circumstances did not permit him to do otherwise, he would wait and see what happened. Assuming that Aurett's presence in the prison might conceal some plan of escape, however, he decided that it was necessary to watch the young woman carefully, in order to pursue his "son-in-law" if he succeeded in deceiving the surveillance of Taku's jailers.

Two weeks went by without him discovering the slightest indication suggestive of an impending flight. The Englishwoman went out with her father.

Every day she was a little paler, and chagrin was imprinting blue rings around her soft gaze. She made three visits to the prison, but came back from each one sadder than before.

"Sapristi!" said Bouvreuil. "This isn't getting and further forward. What are they waiting for?"

The month of October began. Until the fifteenth, life retained its monotonous, tedious, heart-rending course; but on the evening of that day, terrible news arrived.

It was the English consul who brought it to his compatriots, as they were silently taking tea at the Pacific Box Line hotel.

On seeing him appear in the lounge, Aurett ran to meet him, with her arms extended and her eyes dilated by an ardent interrogation.

"The emperor's decision has been notified to the Ti-Tou this afternoon."

"Ah!" was all that the young woman said.

"And what has His Grace decided?" asked Murlyton, getting to his feet."

The consul lowered his head. A poignant emotion gripped his interlocutors.

"What?" they stammered. "Monsieur Lavarède?"

"Will be taken to Peking laden with a cangue, and decapitated in the usual place of executions, near the Bridge of Tears."

Aurett closed her eyes and tottered. Not only was the man she loved to be given to the executioner, but he would be subjected to the torture of the cangue: an atrocious torture! The cangue is a sort of portable pillory formed of planks three or four centimeters thick, bound together by leather thongs. The victim's head and hands are passed through holes in which they are secured. The unfortunate must walk with that heavy apparatus, which hinders his movements, tearing his neck and wrists.

The young woman saw Armand, thus tortured, following the dusty roads of the province of Petchili. For five days, bruised and breathless, he would have to walk long stages before reaching Peking. And there, horribly, the end of his troubles would be brutal death! A blow of the sword would cast his intelligent head upon the ground. His sweetly cheerful gaze would be extinguished forever.

Suddenly, the Englishwoman raised her head. The consul had withdrawn, discreetly, leaving those to whom he had brought such terrifying news alone.

"Father," she said.

"Courage, my child," replied Murlyton, in an emotional tone.

"Courage? I have it—but I also have a plea to address to you."

"Speak, my dear daughter."

She looked the gentleman full in the face, revealing the moist periwinkles of her eyes, and then she continued: "I had dreamed of becoming Monsieur Lavarède's wife, Father. A long time ago, I recognized that I love him. Forgive me for not having confessed it to you sooner. A wager had been made; I had to remain quiet until fate had made a decision. Today, alas, it has spoken. He is going to die. I want to be there, beside him, to protect his body against the insults of the multitude, to assure him of a sepulcher, and afterwards..."

She stopped, strangled by emotion.

"Afterwards?" the gentleman repeated, anxiously.

Her only response was to throw herself into his arms and burst into sobs.

By virtue of eloquence, Murlyton succeeded in rendering her some hope. Perhaps Lavarède could escape on the way. In a prison, in the midst of numerous guards, flight is more difficult than on the roads, where a thousand incidents occur of which a determined man might be able to take advantage. Since she desired it, they would go to Peking.

Aurett appeared to forget her dolor in order to occupy herself with the preparations for the departure. With her father, she set out in quest of a vehicle of some sort, but the city had very few, and all those it possessed had been retained by functionaries and rich merchants. Those people were going to Peking to witness unprecedented celebrations. A dirigible balloon, said to be an airborne ship, was to make an ascent. The announcement of that marvel had stirred the apathy of the inhabitants, and throughout the ken of Petchili there was not a single carriage or junk for hire.

By dint of searching, however, the Englishman discovered a Korean coolie who, in return for the exorbitant price of one tael per day, consented to carry the travelers in his sail-barrow. The tael is a gold coin of variable value. As for a sail-barrow, it consists of a kind of square table pierced in the middle in order to let through the single wheel that it possesses. At the front, when the wind is favorable, a mast permits the hoisting of a sail. At the rear are two shafts, between which the conductor of the bizarre vehicle trots, serving as a rudder. Not very stable, such vehicles expose tourists to frequent collisions, but it is necessary to be content with what one can get.[44]

Murlyton and Aurett reached an understanding with the Korean. He would come to pick them up at the hotel the following day, the sixteenth of October, at eight o'clock in the morning. The gentleman gave him two sapeks—small coins—by way of an advance, and went back with Aurett, for the last time, into the establishment owned by Pacific Box.

---

[44] The sail-barrow, like the cangue, had been featured in Albert Robida's *Aventures de Saturnin Farandoul* (q.v.), from which the authors of the present text probably borrowed both motifs.

XIX. The White Lotus

Daylight had scarcely made its appearance when Lavarède was roused from his sleep by the processional entrance of Chun-Tze, followed by his clerk, Diamba and an individual in the blue and green uniform special to agents of the police.

He sat on his bed and considered the visitors. The governor was sponging his brow; Diamba's eyelids were reddened by tears. The clerk and the policeman remained impassive. The Chinese girl informed the prisoner that he was to be transferred to Peking in order to be executed there, and that Fonni-Kuen, an esteemed police officer, would escort him.

At first the voyager welcomed the news with satisfaction. The prison was weighing upon him; but when having gone down to the courtyard his neck and writs were trapped by the planks of the cangue, he began to think that change is not always an amelioration.

Ten Toas, or policemen, were delegated to guard him.

After amicable farewells to Chun-Tzi and poor tearful Diamba, the prison doors opened and the cortege set forth. The guide Fonni-Kuen headed upriver.

Soon, the little troop emerged from the city and moved into the countryside. Peasants had brought in the harvest of maize and sorghum, and the land, deprived of its ornamentation of plants, extended in the gilded yellow expanses particular to the region.

At about ten o'clock they stopped in a small village, where the men of the escort took their meal. Very weary, bruised by the contact of the wood of the cangue, Lavarède was squatting like a tailor, in such a way that the lower portion of the hideous instrument was supported on the ground, which offered temporary relief to his pain-racked neck.

He was alone. One of the policemen came over to him, holding planks under his arm, which seemed to the journalist to form another collar. The newcomer put a finger over his lips, recommending the prisoner to remain silent, and them with marvelous skill, relieved him of the cangue, which he replaced with the one he was carrying.

To his great surprise, Armand perceived that the second was much lighter. In addition, the edge of the wood pressing on the neck had been fitted with a horsehair cushion, which muffled the pain of the contact.

Having completed the operation, the agent opened his tunic and bared his chest. With a gesture he indicated a lotus flower tattooed on the skin, and drew away precipitately. The Parisian smiled: another one who took him for a freemason and was doing what he could to offer him relief.

After the siesta, they set off marching again. That evening, at nine o'clock, the detachment entered the town of Tien-Tcheng, softly couched on the bank of the Pei-Ho. After a few detours in the streets, they crossed the marble bridge ornamented with a dozen giant figures of Buddha that linked the two halves of the town, and reached a police station situated on the left bank. Lavarède was locked in a fairly spacious cell, where the cangue was removed. That ornamental torture was reserved for public display.

The young man lay down. In spite of the substitution carried out during the halt, he was suffering from a violent crick in the neck, and his wrists were swollen and painful.

Another four days of marching," he muttered. "I'll be in a fine state on arrival."

The door opened then, and the policeman with the lotus flower slipped into the cell. He was carrying a box full of reddish ointment.

"Zoueng-Mao," he said, in a low voice. And as the prisoner looked at him uncomprehendingly, he repeated, in a slightly louder voice: "Zoueng-Mao!"

A memory crossed the journalist's mind. He recalled an episode in the story of Marco Polo living at the court of Kubla Khan, in which the celebrated voyager recounted that convict in labor camps obtained a few hours of rest by rubbing their skins with Zoueng-Mao.

That preparation, Marco Polo said, renders the flesh violet, covers it with pustules and gives it the appearance of the fiercest inflammation—an appearance only, for a person who makes use of Zoueng-Mao suffers no distress.[45]

The policeman pointed at the box and hen at Lavarède's feet. The latter understood. The trick, centuries old, still worked. In Chinese society, stagnant in the midst of people making rapid progress, everything is eternal, tricks as well as customs, ideas as well as errors. He made a routine gesture of thanks. He, the Parisian avid for the "tomorrow" for which steam was too slow, admired the cart immobilized by the rut.

In order to show his protector that he had grasped his meaning, he took his shoes of and coated his flesh with the ointment. The agent seemed satisfied, and withdrew.

In the morning, when they came to look for him in order to continue his route, Armand showed the Toas his swollen feet, marbled with red blisters. The latter shook their heads and went to obtain orders from their chief. Half a hour later, Armand was carried out on a stretcher and taken aboard a junk, in the bottom of which he was comfortably installed—after which, the boatmen deployed sails of plaited straw, and, pushed by a brisk wind, the boat sailed up the Pei-Ho. It was thus that the prisoner made his journey, which would have been charming but for the anxiety regarding its end.

With his habitual mental activity, however, Armand took an interest in the landscape. He admired the numerous natural canals that linked Lake Amilo to

---

[45] The ointment in question is not mentioned by Marco Polo and is completely fictitious,

201

the river. It was a veritable pleasure to see monuments file past: the palaces and the pagodas of Tientsin, a city of a million inhabitants, the capital of the province of Petchili. He remembered that Peking, the administrative city and residence of the emperor, is only the principal place of a department of the province in question, the department of Shantung. He greatly regretted that there were no English troops in the place, where, in 1860, the war against China had been concluded by a treaty that opened up the cities of the coast to Europeans.

"Oh, they'd have been able to get me out of the hands of these clowns," he murmured. Then his robust confidence got the upper hand again. "But I'll get out of it anyway," the valiant young man concluded.

They spent the night in La-Min, some distance beyond Tientsin.

The next day, the junk took the escort all the way to Bac-Nou, a small town that serves as a trading-post for the large city of Pao-Ti.

Eventually, at dusk on the third day aboard, they reached Tungchow.

The travelers were to travel the eighteen kilometers that still separated them from Peking by land. Armand was enclosed in a large portable chair requisitioned by the chief of the escort, and then, in spite of the late hour, the troop set out again.

It was about midnight when Lavarède made his entrance into the official capital.

Ah! he thought. *We're arriving. I won't be sorry to get some sleep.*

That wish was only to be granted after two hours walking through the city. The streets, deserted at that time of night, bordered by brick walls that served as enclosures for the gardens that surround all the houses of the imperial city, had a lugubrious appearance. At each of their extremities extended chains stopped the march of the policemen, who had to detach them and then reattach them before continuing their route.

Several times, police agents came to challenge the travelers. They announced their presence at a distance by striking redoubtable blows on wooden cylinders, with which those functionaries were equipped. After a few minutes of discussion, they withdrew. It was thus that Lavarède progressed slowly through the Chinese city and reached the broad highway that runs along the wall of the interior city, or imperial city. The Street of Tranquility, Tchang-Nagai-Kini, is the name of that avenue, from which one can perceive, beyond the wall that circles the habitations of the Son of Heaven and his court, roofs covered in yellow or red tiles, according to whether they sheltered the members of the imperial family or mere aristocrats. Gray tiles were the prerogative of private house.[46]

---

[46] Although the orthography is often idiosyncratic, and many of the supposedly Chinese names are invented, the geographical features of Peking mentioned in this chapter appear to be ultimately derived from a description of the city published by the Jesuit Antoine Gaubil (1689-1759), who lived in the city from 1722 until his death and sent back numerous documents for publication, which

In front of one of the three gates that link the King-Chung, the city of the court, with the Ouei-Chung, the city of the subjects, the policemen prostrated themselves. It was the Nyang-Ting-Men, or Gate of Peace, through which the allies had entered in 1860.

Finally, the vehicle in which the prisoner was becoming impatient penetrated beneath a black vault and stopped. They had arrived. After a few clerical formalities, Lavarède, taken to a somber cell, was able to lie down on the planks that served as a bunk, and fall profoundly asleep.

A shock woke him up. One might have thought that something had struck his leg. He reached out with his arms instinctively. His hand encountered a hand.

"Who's there?" he demanded, not without emotion.

"A Frenchman!" exclaimed a voice, with a joyful inflexion.

"Two, to judge by your language."

"Yes, two, Who are you?"

"A prisoner…and you?"

"Also a prisoner, and a Catholic priest."

Wearied by the journey, Armand had not perceived in the darkness that his cell already contained an inhabitant, who had been asleep, as he explained to the voyager.

He told him his story: he was a missionary persecuted by the authorities. Arrested without any reason after the affiliates of the White Lotus, during a day of rioting, had burned the mission and massacred his companions, he had been brought to this prison, where he appeared to have been forgotten. And when Armand became indignant, the priest murmured softly:

"Almost all of us end up like this, but recriminations would be unjustified. In coming to China, we know what we are risking and we pardon them in advance. The poor people do not know what they are doing. Would you believe that even the literate accuse us of collecting children, not to bring them up but to kill them and use their bodies in magical operations? Their eyes are particularly useful to us, the mandarins say, to manufacture collodion for photography."

"That's insane."

"Isn't it? But that ignorance, which condemns us, is less painful to me than the disunity of the nations of Europe. Civilized writers have no hesitation in approving of the acts of savagery committed by the crowd, with the tacit collaboration of the functionaries."

"Oh!" cried Lavarède. "Not French journalists, I assume!"

"Far from it. It has been written that the massacres were uniquely directed against the French and the Catholics, and I have in my pocket a copy of the proclamation that was pinned up in Ho-Nan a few days before the attack on our mission. This is what it said: 'Let us burn the dwellings and temples of the for-

---

were much quoted in scholarly circles thereafter. Their proximal source was probably Lermina's *Bataille de Strasbourg*.

eigners. Let us tear of Christianity by the roots. Let us punish the Chinese trai-
tors who have embrace that religion. Let us banish their families to America.
Germany is with us.'"

A silence followed those words. The missionary was the first to break it.

"Let's leave that sober subject. God has his purpose in permitting those
crimes. Let's talk about you—and if my question isn't indiscreet, tell me what
unfortunate circumstances have led you to this hell."

In order to recount his odyssey, Armand recovered his good humor. The
priest listened attentively, and when he had finished, said: "The secret societies
are evidently protecting you; the substitution of the cangue and the voyage in the
junk prove that. Perhaps you will be saved, which I hope, for France has need of
men of heart and spirit."

"A faint hope. I'm to be executed tomorrow, the twenty-second of October."

"Then let us pray to God that the Chang-I-See and the Kin-Tien-Kien declare the day inauspicious and forbid the emperor to go out."

"What does that mean?"

"That's true—you're not familiar with China. The assemblies I've just
named are the colleges of rites and astronomy, which are the only ones that can
authorize the sovereign's excursions."

"What has that to do with my case?"

"Oh, if the head of state remains confined to the Red City, there will be
few soldiers on the Bridge of Tears, the place of execution. A strike of some sort
would be easy, whereas..."

"Whereas," concluded Lavarède, philosophically, "if the emperor quits his
palace, he'll oblige me to quit the earth. The system of compensations. O
Azaïs!"[47]

Although pronounced in a light tone, those words darkened the mood of
the two men, and they stopped talking for some time.

Slowly, the hours of the day fell through the sandglass of eternity. Armand's only distraction was to be taken before a mandarin, who, with cruel politeness, informed him that the following day, he would depart for the land of the
ancestors, his had separate from his body. And from the prisoner whom he considered to be already dead, the functionary did not hide his hatred of Europeans.

"I would like," he told him, "all those of your race to be in my hands, in
order to crush all the enemies of my country at the same time."

With those encouraging words, the journalist was taken back to his prison.
He experienced a great weariness. Discouragement weighed upon him. Death

---

[47] The reference is to the philosopher Pierre Hyacinthe Azaïs (1766-1845),
whose most important work was *Des Compensations dans les destinées
humaines* [Compensations in Human Destiny] (1809), which argued that happiness and misery retain an essential equilibrium in all circumstances.

itself did not frighten him, and yet his breast was compressed by anguish. Putting little value on his life, he regretted his sweet dream. The blue-tinted lightning of the executioner's blade was about to separate him from Aurett forever.

That night, he slept badly, often woken up with a start by imaginary noises, and in the morning, when they came to fetch him to march him to the scaffold, he was exhausted; his limbs, stiffened by curvature, almost refused him service. He embraced the missionary, who whispered words of hope into his ear.

"Perhaps the emperor won't go out! Have faith in God, my son, my brother..."

Then he followed the policeman charged with taking him to the executioner.

They left the prison. In the street, Armand understood that he was lost. The absolute master of four hundred million Chinese was about to travel the streets. Everything offered proof of it: the closed houses hung with white sheets, the unusual movement of the soldiers, the square pieces of cloth that passers-by were holding in their hands, in order to cover their heads as the emperor went by, looking at him being punishable by death.

A crazy idea occurred to the Parisian. *If I encounter my cousin in the other world*, he thought, *he'll be very glad to have played such a trick on me.*

Meanwhile, with the cangue around his neck—the real one, this time—and surrounded by his guardians in blue and green costumes. Armand marched. As if through a veil, he glimpsed the Gate of Submission and the Gate of the Dawn. Momentarily, the sight of Lake Tai-y-Tche, covered in lotus flowers, rested his eyes.

As they moved forward the crowd became denser. Regular soldiers in celestial blue uniforms, forming a hedge, maintained a free space in the middle of the road, pushing the curious back against the houses.

Is it really my presence that's exciting the city to this extent? thought Lavarède.

When they arrived at the canal that serves as the outflow of Lake Lien-Koua-Tche, however, that vain thought faded away. In front of him opened the Bridge of Tears, under military guard. On the opposite bank a vast square opened, one of whose corners was isolated by a palisade. Above the enclosure, an enormous yellow object was swaying, elongated in the form of a cigar. One might have thought it a marine monster, but Armand was not deceived. He recognized the dirigible balloon immediately.

Manchu warriors in multicolored vestments, with luxuriously ornamented weapons, were arranged around the square.

At that sight, the condemned man forgot his situation for a moment, but once the bridge was crossed he escort stopped abruptly, and he was recalled to a sentiment of reality. To his right, on a raised platform, the executioner of Peking and his aides, wearing a blue tchepa with wide sleeves, with a yellow dragon embroidered on the chest, was waiting, motionless, for the moment to go to work. Next to them, the bench was visible on which the condemned man is laid down, and the wooden cages designed to receive the criminal heads. Several already contained their prey, and the sight of the bloodstained faces grimacing death at the crowd was lugubrious.

Lavarède went pale, but Gallic pride immediately made him raise his head. Since death was inevitable, it was necessary to welcome it cheerfully, like an expected friend, and show the Sons of Han how a Frenchman can die.

On the orders of the Toas of the escort, he sat down on the bench of the condemned. There, crushed by the weight of the cangue, his ears buzzing, he waited for the fatal moment to arrive.

Suddenly, he shivered, and his gaze became fixed. The line of soldiers had just opened up, and in the reserved space, Aurett had appeared, leaning on her father's arm.

The sail of the barrow inflated by a favorable wind, the English duo had left Taku. The terrestrial skiff moved at a good pace, the Korean coolie trotting between the shafts.

On the evening of the first day they reached Tientsin, where the English resident, Mr. Grewbis, insisted on inviting them to dinner. The amiable man was delighted to spend an evening with compatriots, and when he learned about their plan to reach Peking his joy became delirious. He was going there himself, to the celebrations for which the launch of the balloon was the pretext. It would be a pleasure for him to give his guests a place in his carriage, a good vehicle constructed in Europe, bearing no resemblance to the primitive carts that jolted the indigenes. He thought, however, that he ought not to conceal it from Murlyton that the imperial city was particularly dangerous.

"The Chinese," he said to him, "are people of routine. Our compatriot Mr. Hart[48] founded a gas factory in Peking, which closed for lack of clientele. Dr. Kasper,[49] this German aeronaut, has reopened it in order to inflate his dirigible. That has caused considerable effervescence in the population. The secret societies are always looking for pretexts to riot..."

"That's precisely what interests us," Aurett declared, squarely.

"In that cause, I'll only think about one thing: the pleasure of traveling in your company."

Murlyton, therefore, dismissed the Korean coolie and his barrow, but not without having paid the wily Korean the price of the whole journey. At daybreak the latter took the road back to Taku.

---

[48] Sir Robert Hart (1835-1911) was the Inspector General of China's Maritime Customs from 1863 until his death, and attempted to introduce numerous modernizations to the capital, with limited success.

[49] The authors have apparently forgotten that the aeronaut was previously called Keyser.

Two li from Tientsin, the man met a pedestrian who seemed to be in a very bad mood. It was Bouvreuil.

Less fortunate than the English, he had not been able to procure any means of transport. He witnessed their departure and, fearful of losing track of them, decided to travel on foot the hundred and thirty-five kilometers that separate Peking from the sea. After thirty kilometers—or, in local terminology, thirty-seven li—he stopped, exhausted, in a town. When he met the coolie he had just set out again, his feet and back aching. He seemed to recognize the driver of the barrow. He interrogated him, understood that he was free, and immediately struck a deal with him in sign language to carry him to the end of his journey.

A businessman, like all his peers, the Korean only agreed at the exorbitant price of two taels a day. The price having been accepted, he applied himself diligently, and on the morning of the twenty-second of October, Bouvreuil entered Peking.

He was somewhat disfigured, of course. In his haste, the barrow-man had spilled his client on several occasions. The swollen nose and bruised forehead of the landlord offered evidence of the solidity of the roads of Petchili.

Since the previous day, Murlyton and his daughter had been staying with Mr. Grewbis' colleague. Straight away, Aurett had enquired about Lavarède; without paling, she heard the resident reply to her that the execution would take place at ten o'clock at the Bridge of Tears. She even found the strength to smile and thank her compatriot—but she did not sleep that night.

The most insensate projects formed in her brain. Slower to be moved, the women of the north surpass those of the south in audacity in the execution of their plans. The practical sense that their race possesses transforms their imaginations into realities, and an act of insane temerity that would remain a dream on the part of a Neapolitan or Andalusian will be carried out by a lovestruck Englishwoman—and Aurett was in love with her entire soul, her entire youth.

Scarcely had she got up than she detached a sharp knife from a panoply, made sure that her revolver was in working order, and then went into her father's room. The gentleman, kept awake by a double anxiety, was already up and about. He looked at his daughter. She seemed calm, but her blue eyes, shining with a feverish gleam, expressed a cold, implacable will.

"What are you going to do, Aurett?" Murlyton asked.

"Go to where he is, Father," was all she said.

The Englishman nodded his head. He sensed that his daughter's life was at stake at that moment, but, gripped by a sort of fatalism, he did not resist. He gesture to indicate that he was awaiting Aurett's instructions. Then, it was as if a trigger has been released in the poor child. She ran to her father, embraced him for a long time, and then, without saying a word, drew him to the door.

In the street, an agitated population was swarming. The Bridge of Tears is not far from the Residence. The English duo soon reached the square, the middle of which was isolated by a double line of soldiers. Behind them was a dense crowd, noisy and variegated, which seemed to be looking forward to the spectacle with great pleasure. On looking closer, however, one would have seen that some of them were exchanging rapid signs. Ardent gazes were fixed on the soldiers, and sometimes, beneath the shot blouse of a passer-by, the hilt of a curved dagger was visible.

Aurett did not see anything. She headed for the corner of the square, where the bench of the condemned stood, careless of collisions and recriminations. There were murmurs at first, but then a word had circulated: "Lien-Koua!" the idlers repeated, making way for her.

Lien-Koua! Lotus! Indeed, fixed in her corsage, the pin that had already protected her in Taku was glittering in the sunlight. The rumor reached the soldiers. One of them extended is sword to bar the young woman's passage, but his gaze fell upon the lotus flower and he lowered his weapon. Aurett and her father penetrated into the reserved enclosure.

It was at that moment that Lavarède saw them.

Like the first, the second line of soldiers opened before them. They reached the platform, climbed the three steps that gave access to it, and, passing in front of the stupefied executioners, approached the bench of the condemned. It was assumed that the Europeans had been given special permission.

Armand had risen to his feet. Aurett gripped the hands passed through the cangue, and, giving herself entirely, with the simplicity of those in love, said: "You were expecting me, weren't you?"

He studied her, hesitating over a reply, but his gaze encountered the moist gaze of the gentleman, and like a torrent breaking its dykes, the words flooded from his lips.

"Yes, I was expecting you, as one expects the light on the threshold of darkness. I was expecting you because..." He paused, but resumed almost immediately in a breathless voice: "Here, I can speak. The executioner is watching me. Adieu does not measure its terms, for it is the end. In a moment, the guilty mouth will be closed forever. The expiation and the sin will almost be confused. I was expecting you because I love you."

Aurett closed her eyes. A red flush invaded her face.

"Forgive me," the unfortunate continued. "You too, Mr. Murlyton. It's a dead man who is speaking. What does it matter, at this moment, whether or not I'm in love?"

The young woman repeated, dully: "What does it matter?"

"Ah!" Murlyton muttered. "It would have been my daughter's happiness."

And as the journalist interrogated her with his eyes, Aurett murmured, so softly that Armand could scarcely hear it: "I love you too."

The condemned man's visage was transfigured. All terrestrial joys blossomed in his features. Suddenly, however, he became somber again.

"The executioner has gone to ask the commander of the soldiers for orders; he's coming back to separate us, and as the Manchu warrior strikes the mortal blow, I can only cry out: 'Adieu, Lien-Koua, my White Lotus!'"

It was a cry of pain and desperation that the young man uttered.

"Lien-Koua! Lien-Koua!"

A confused echo repeated that word, pronounced audible. A muted growl escaped the attentive crowd. Aurett paid no heed to it. She had turned to look at the approaching executioner.

The man was already climbing the steps of the platform. It was over. The hour of violent separation was sounding. She had a frightful vision of the torture. A flood of hatred or those who had condemned her to mourning surged through her brain. She seized the dagger she had taken from the resident's panoply, sliced through the leather thongs linking the different components of the cangue, and handed the revolver to the liberated Parisian.

"At least let's defend ourselves!" she cried.

Instinctively, Armand shot the executioner, who fell.

Stupefied by his daughter's action, Murlyton drew his weapon mechanically, and all three struck menacing poses, dominating the people from the height of the platform—which the frightened aides had left vacant.

But a strange phenomenon occurred. A swell agitated the people; the line of guards broke up, and a roar burst forth in the air: "Lien-Koua!"

Lavarède heard, and understood.

"The White Lotus is saving us!"

A howling crowd ran toward the scaffold, knocking down and killing the soldiers and the executioners. Armand and his companions were carried way, as if by a human tide, and they found themselves, without knowing how, a few paces away from Dr. Kasper's balloon.

Inflated, reading to depart, tugging at its moorings, the apparatus seemed to be impatient to lift off. It was an invitation to flee. With one bound, Armand was in the nacelle, calling to his companions. They joined him, and set about helping him to cut the ropes retaining the dirigible to the ground.

At that moment, the Manchu regulars, recovered from their shock and rallied by their mandarins, attacked the affiliates of the White Lotus who were forming a living rampart for the fugitives. The latter gave way. Lavarède cut the last rope, and the balloon rose up slowly.

"Saved!" cried the Parisian.

But the upward movement of the aerostat was suddenly interrupted. The three passengers looked at one another.

"What's happening?"

"Another mooring-rope, no doubt."

Leaning over. Armand attempted to see what was impeding the fight of the balloon.

Clinging to the anchor hanging down from the side of the nacelle, a man was holding back the airship. It was Bouvreuil again.

Having arrived in Peking that morning, he had witnessed the entire scene. He had followed the fugitives, but at the idea of being separated from them he had lost his head, and attached himself desperately to the nacelle that was carrying away Pénélope's beloved.

At a glance, Armand understood the danger. The better armed regulars were slowly driving back his saviors. Already, the last ranks had been driven back inside the enclosure reserved for the aerostat. Numerous cadavers were littering the ground, more men of the people among them than soldiers. A moment's hesitation might ruin everything.

The young man looked around. There was a large crate in the bottom of the nacelle. What did it contain? Weapons and food supplies, undoubtedly, since Dr. Kasper had announced that his apparatus would remain in the air for several days. With a superhuman effort, Lavarède lifted up the enormous package and threw it out.

Suddenly unballasted, the balloon leapt up three hundred feet, and, seized by an air current, fled toward the south-south-east, while the furious battle around the Bridge of Tears continued.

XX. China From Above

Bouvreuil had uttered a scream of fear when the aerostat rose up abruptly. Instinctively, his grip on the anchor tightened, and now he remained suspended in the void, his face convulsed by the fear of a vertiginous fall.

Out of humanity, Lavarède, aided by Murlyton, hoisted the unfortunate into the nacelle, where the usurer avoided a disagreeable confrontation by losing consciousness. He was left to come round without anyone paying any more heed to him.

In any case, there was a visible embarrassment between the passengers. With the sentiment of security, calm had re-entered Aurett's mind. Her excitement dissipated, the young woman blushed at the thought of the confessions exchanged near the Bridge of Tears. For his part, Armand, anxious not to abuse the situation, avoided saying anything to her, and for the sake of appearances, he began, very seriously, to take notes.

Peking, he wrote, *has almost the same circumference as Paris: thirty-six kilometers instead of thirty-two; but as each of its houses shelters a single family and is surrounded by a spacious garden, its population cannot exceed six million souls.*

The journalist's preoccupation did no harm to his accuracy. His estimate was closer to the truth than those of voyagers reporting the number of Chinese inhabiting the imperial city as between one and three million. That petty labor soon bored him, however. He leaned on the edge of the nacelle and watched the landscape go past beneath his feet. The wind had freshened and the balloon, traveling at the speed of an express train, was passing over hills, villages and, watercourses, hardly giving the tourist time to recognize them.

With the aid of an excellent map and a compass that he had found on board, however, Lavarède was able to take account of the distance traveled. He perceived Tientsin to the east, noted the Pei-Ho in passing, and then the imperial canal linking that river to the Hoang-Ho and the Yang-Tse-Kiang, over which the famous bridge of Palikao extends where, in 1860, the "tigers"—Chinese warriors—were crushed by the Franco-English artillery.

That distraction exhausted, the Parisian made an inventory of the objects contained in the nacelle. There were scientific instruments—the compass of which he had already made use, barometers, thermometers and orometers—garments, and a certain number of electrical switches and wires, doubtless designed for maneuvering the aerostat, but which, not knowing how the apparatus was constructed, he judged it prudent not to touch.

One depressing observation resulted from his census, moreover: a total lack of food. It was necessary to make his friends party to the situation, and especially to dispel the constraint that existed between them. It was not at a time

211

when everyone might need all their energy that they could indulge in vain prejudices.

Armand decided to explain himself frankly. Aurett was sitting next to her father at one end of the nacelle. Lavarède approached them.

"Mr. Murlyton," he said, "And you, my dear Miss, listen to me." His grave tone impressed them. They interrogated him with their gazes. "I'm constrained to raise a delicate subject. This morning, at a supreme moment, we exchanged words…" The Englishwoman sketched a modest gesture. "Oh, don't worry, I have no intention of taking advantage of them. On our return to Paris, I shall remember them, with your permission, but until then, we are adversaries, and only the tone of challenge is appropriate."

The gentleman smiled. Aurett nodded.

Armand went on: "Presently, our interest is the same. We are captive in a balloon floating above inhospitable territory, where we must not land. You're not unaware of the sentiments of the local people with regard to Europeans. In Petchili, that was still possible, but we have now quit the territory where the White Lotus flourishes. The masters of this region are the sectarians of the Society of the Elder Brother, the most bloodthirsty of all, and if we fall into their hands…"

A clicking sound interrupted the young man. He turned round. Behind him he saw the white face of Bouvreuil. His unconsciousness dissipated. Pénélope's father had propped himself up against the side of the nacelle. He had heard everything, and his teeth were chattering in terror. That was the sound that the voyagers had heard.

Armand shrugged his shoulders and turned back to his friends.

"Two solutions are now offered to us. If the wind holds, we'll arrive during the night at Shanghai, a Europeanized coastal city, and will then be out of trouble. If not, we'll continue floating over territory where we can't land."

"Bah!" relied Aurett, lightly. "This aerostat is constructed in such a way as to remain in the air for several days—so Mr. Grewbis told me, at least."

"Agreed—but we can't remain in it."

"Why is that?"

"Because the crate that I threw overboard at the departure contained the food supplies, and we haven't an atom of nourishment."

Without speaking, the Englishman displayed his flask, filled at the hotel the previous day. That might sustain them for one day, but would not nourish them. Their expressions darkened. The idea of possible death by starvation, within sight of rich fields the approach to which was forbidden by fanaticism, was not cheerful, and Bouvreuil expressed the general opinion by groaning: "That's all I need! To die of hunger!"

His enemy's voice brought back the Parisian's sense of humor. "No, my dear Monsieur you won't die of hunger. You've fortunately reminded me of your presence. I was mistaken when I said we had no food. You're here."

"What do you mean, I'm here?" asked the usurer, nonplussed.

"Sent by Heaven, my dear Monsieur Bouvreuil, to save three Christians in a tight situation from death." He addressed Aurett, on whose lips the smile had reappeared. "Don't worry, Mademoiselle, that excellent man will furnish us a good fifty kilos of flesh. A little tough, no doubt, but in our situation, we ought not to be too demanding with regard to quality."

Pénélope's father leapt to his feet. "Oh!" he cried. "Do you intend to eat me?"

As tranquilly as could be, Armand replied: "Exactly, Monsieur Bouvreuil." He interrupted the usurer, who was about to protest. "You're not a regular passenger here, but an intruder. Furthermore, if I'd left you outside the nacelle, you'd have fallen after a few minutes. I've saved your life, so it belongs to me, and if necessary, I won't hesitate to take back what I conserved for you."

"But that's not possible!" Bouvreuil objected, desperately. "You can't do that—it's savagery."

"It's hunger, my brave Monsieur. After all, you have only yourself to blame. Did we invite you to take passage on the nacelle of the *Medusa?*"

Aurett and Murlyton had difficulty suppressing their desire to laugh. Fundamentally, they admired the Parisian, whose anxiety had not taken away his Parisian love of joking. The landlord was not amused, though. At the fatal name of the *Medusa*, evoking the memory of the crowded raft populated by cannibals, he felt his hair standing on end. He paraded his fearful gaze around him. Oh, how he would have liked to get out!

One thing, however, should have reassured him. Far from slackening, the wind was becoming stronger. The aerostat left behind the large city of Tsi-Nan, once washed by the Hoang-Ho, and which the change in the curse of the capricious river had been unable to bring down. On the horizon, the vast lake of Kai-Foung, three times as large as Lake Geneva, displayed the blue expanse of its waters.

Although hunger pangs were appealing in all stomachs, no one complained. Bouvreuil's face merely changed from white to green. The usurer was frightened by his hunger.

Every pang I feel, he thought, *must be shared by the others, and brings the moment closer when Lavarède will cut my throat.*

No longer calling him his son-in-law now, he cursed Pénélope's caprice.

She could have married someone else, after all. There are plenty more handsome than he is...and at least I'd be sitting tranquilly by my fireside, instead of dangling between heaven and earth, with the prospect of being devoured by that savage.

Suddenly, he had an idea.

I'm saved, he thought. *Let's make a sacrifice.* Addressing himself to Lavarède, he said: "Monsieur, I'm not a surplus guest, as you suppose. You have nothing to eat, and, as chance would have it, I have a cake in my pocket, bought this morning from an ambulant merchant in the crowd. It's a matter of human duty to share it with you."

As he spoke, he took out a pancake made from manioc and rice.

Armand weighed it in his hand. "Four parts, a drop of rum… that's another two days of life, Bouvreuil," he said, majestically. "I grant you mercy for forty-eight hours."

Good, thought the businessman. *He who has a delayed payment owes nothing.*

Chim-Ara, Yung-Ve, Bai-Tzem and Wei-Lion filed before the voyagers' eyes. By night, Armand recognized the marshes of Ken-Tchao, where the imperia canal cuts the Hoang-Ho delta—but the sky was cloudy; under the pressure of the wind, they continued their journey in pitch darkness.

They were all emotional. Deprived of reference-points by which to judge the distance covered, it seemed to them that the balloon was immobilized in a sphere of shadow. No one slept. Their eyes staring in the direction of the ground, they sought in vain for a glimmer of light

At one moment, they glimpsed numerous luminous dots. Murlyton contemplated his watch; it was two o'clock in the morning.

"We're probably floating above Tchin-Kiang," Lavarède declared. "Within an hour, we'll reach Shanghai.

Aurett started. "Listen!" she said.

Armand cocked an ear, and uttered an anxious exclamation. A regular splashing sound was audible down below, where the ground ought to have been.

"It's the noise of the sea," murmured the gentleman, as if frightened by his own words.

Suddenly, a strident ripping sound vibrated in the air, the dazzling broken line of a lightning-flash cleaved though the cloud, and by its fleeting light the aeronauts perceived hectic waves beneath them, climbing on top of one another in a furious rush, as if to scale the heavens.

"We're being drawn out to sea," Armand shouted. "At all costs, we need to climb higher and find an inverse current to bring us back to land."

The observation was just. Every time a wind rises, the displacement of the atmospheric layers and their different densities determine the establishment of a current in the opposite direction. The necessity was to rise high enough to reach the point where the phenomenon was manifest.

In an instant, the nacelle was pillaged. Everyone had understood. Even Bouvreuil joined in. Fearful and panic-stricken, the landlord seized everything that came to hand and threw it into the void. Lavarède had great difficulty wresting the compass away from him that served as a guide to their aerial course.

Lightened, the balloon rose up, higher and higher. It entered the region of the clouds. In the midst of a thick mist, streaked with lightning flashes, deafened by detonations of high no human artillery can give any idea, Armand observed that the aerostat had leveled off in the very heart of the electric storm. Blue-tinted flames were running along the ropes, and the rain that was striking the taffeta of the envelope rebounded in fiery splashes. They were at risk of being struck at any moment. They had to get out of that uniquely dangerous zone at any price.

"Throw off more weight," the young man ordered, hoarsely.

"There isn't anything else," replied Murlyton.

"Nothing more!"

The Parisian looked at Aurett. He saw that she was pale, her eyes widened by fear, hanging on to a rope with both hands.

Nothing more! It was death for her. No—never! He would save her.

With a rapid movement, he put his leg over the edge of the nacelle—but the Englishwoman had understood; with a single bound she was beside him, holding him back.

"Together or not at all," she said, simply.

"All three, then," said someone next to them.

They shivered. Murlyton was there, as calm as if he had been in a drawing-room. "What do you think?" he added, placidly.

Lavarède had a desperate expression, but his eyes encountered Bouvreuil. He went to him, grabbed him by the collar, and shouted: "Jump, Monsieur Bouvreuil—the common good demands it!"

He shook him, shoving him toward the edge of the nacelle. Bewildered, the landlord was unable to reply, but his attitude spoke for him. He clung to the side-wall, al his energy concentrated into a single thought: not to be hurled into the void.

At that decisive moment, he let out a cry of joy. "Not yet…the plank!"

"What plank?"

"Look!"

Armand bent down, and experienced an intense stab of pleasure in his turn. On the wicker floor of the nacelle a loose plank had been set, supporting the banquettes. Quicker than thought, the plank was torn from its groove and thrown overboard.

A shock cause the aerostat to quiver, and it launched upwards out of the stormy zone.

Now the involuntary aeronauts were above the tempest. They looked down at the clouds racing after one another, amid a deafening racket. Around them the air was calm, without a breeze. But as they relaxed in the contemplation of the sublime spectacle that the storm provided for them, there was a violent shock.

They were all thrown, pell-mell, into the bottom of the aerostat's nacelle. Struck by the reactionary current, it was borne away westwards with a vertiginous, incalculable rapidity, for a time of which they could not take account...

None of the voyagers had the courage to get up. A kind of torpor nailed them in place. Eyes closed, penetrated by a terrible cold, they remained immo-

215

bile. They had difficulty breathing; their lungs seemed to lack air. They did not have the strength to put their lips to the flask, in which almost nothing remained.

"Ah!" Lavarède moaned, recognizing the symptoms of altitude sickness. "We're at a height of at least six thousand meters."

He shook himself, trying to dispel his numbness, but fell back inertly alongside his companions. They all seemed to be dead. Pale and rigid, with droplets of blood forming in their nostrils and ears, they remained recumbent, unconscious on the floor of the nacelle, which an irresistible force was driving toward central Asia.

Day succeeded night without their being able to move. Again, shadow spread over the earth. Then a shiver shook the passengers in the balloon; their eyelids reopened, and feeble voices asked: "Where are we?"

"I don't know," replied the young man, who had just succeeded in sitting up, "but we're obviously going down."

"How do you know?"

"Because we're breathing more easily. We're able to talk."

"Very true!" Murlyton approved.

He had taken his daughter in his arms and was trying to bring her round. She was the one who drank the last drops of cordial, under the envious gaze of Bouvreuil. However, the danger of perishing of cold having passed, another presented itself. Into what country had the aerostat drawn them? What welcome awaited the voyagers on the surface of the globe? Question marks loomed up menacingly.

In vain, Lavarède tried to pierce the veil of shadow that imprisoned the apparatus. No indication announced the approach of the ground, and yet, at any moment, a rock or a tree might emerge in the path of the balloon, rip its envelope and transform the descent into a mortal fall.

Finally, the sun appeared over a horizon of high mountains. The Englishman addressed a questioning gaze to Armand. The latter shrugged his shoulders.

Everywhere, on all sides, as far as the eye could see, there was a chaos of granite. Peaks crowned with ice succeeded one another, rocks piled up. Everything attested that this point on the terrestrial sphere had been the theater of one of the most rightful convulsions in the life of the planet.

The balloon descended slowly into a valley with slopes covered with fir-trees, closed by a lake whose opposite bank was marked by high cliffs. Glaciers reflected the sunlight, throwing a dazzling cloak over the mountain ridges, but the giant rocks and the severe and grandiose panorama were effaced when Aurett said, in a concentrated voice: "People!"

In the valley, several hundred indigenes, noses in the air, were following every movement of the balloon. Clad in long robes, over which were thrown wide-sleeved cassocks, and coiffed in fur bonnets, the people were pointing at the aerostat with emphatic gestures. With every passing minute, more curious individuals arrived to swell the crowd. The balloon was still going down. It was no more than three hundred meters from the ground.

"It's not possible," murmured Lavarède, who was studying the singular individuals attentively.

The English duo and Pénélope's father enquired in unison: "What isn't possible?"

"It's a fortuitous resemblance."

"What resemblance?"

Armand shook his head. "I'm imagining it…it's too implausible. We would have had to traverse China from east to west during the storm."

"Come on!" exclaimed the gentleman, with slight impatience. "Explain yourself!"

"Gladly. You know that Gabriel Bonvalot,[50] the illustrious explorer, who accompanied Prince Henri d'Orléans on the Deken mission, was guided by a son of a Tekke king,[51] by the name of Rachmed, through the high mountains of Tibet."

"Yes," declared Aurett. "I read the account of his journey through the icy desert, four or five thousand meters above sea level, according to the geographers."

"You read that in my newspaper," said the Parisian. "Well, that story was illustrated by photographs taken by the prince. One of them represented a group of mandarins in Lhasa, the capital of the country."

"Good. So?"

"And it seems to me that I recognize them."

A salvo of musket-fire interrupted the conversation and returned the attention of the voyagers to the ground. The members of the curious crowd were indulging in vivid demonstrations of joy, extending their arms toward the nacelle with prolonged cries, repeated by the echoes of the terrain. A few of them, armed with rifles, were firing into the air while leaping about incessantly.

Aurett made a movement of fear.

"Don't worry," the journalist hastened to say. "The disposition of these worthy people seems to be excellent. Here, as in Africa, they make powder talk to honor the guests that hazard brings them. All of this is a good omen."

---

[50] Gabriel Bonvalot (1853-1933) was one of the first Europeans to reach the Tibetan plateau, in 1889. An account of his journey was published *La Terre Illustrée* shortly before Lermina's *La Bataille de Strasbourg* began serialization there, in March 1891, and a fuller account appeared as a book in 1892. He was accompanied by Prince Henri d'Orléans (1867-1901), whose father, the Duc de Chartres, financed the expedition, and the Belgian missionary Father Constant De Deken (1852-1896), who spoke Chinese. They crossed the plateau, but were not allowed to enter Lhasa, which thus remained tantalizingly mysterious.

[51] The Tekke are a Turkmen tribe.

"And they're not cannibals?" Bouvreuil put in.

"No, Monsieur Bouvreuil. I believe that these Tibetans, if that's what they are, nourish themselves, like all herdsmen, on the flesh of their livestock, sheep and yaks—those oxen with horse' tails, which are both beasts of burden and edible animals. They haven't yet promoted landlords to that rank."

The usurer did not notice the sarcasm. His fear set aside, he was feeling hungry. He and his companions had been deprived of nourishment for more than fifty hours.

"Do you think that the Tibetans will give us something to eat?" he asked.

"Certainly. In that regard, a piece of advice: if you value your precarious existence, eat sparingly. After the fast you've just undergone, the slightest indigestion might be mortal!"

At that moment, the wind having dropped completely, the nacelle gently touched down on the grass that carpeted the valley.

XXI. The Land of the Lamas

Immediately, the voyagers were surrounded by a noisy, gesticulating crowd. In the mist of the repeated cries and disordered movements, however, there was a hint of veneration in the manner in which the indigenes approached the voyagers. That respect was manifest in a rather comical manner. All the people, at the sight of the aeronauts, stuck out their tongues while bowing their heads. Aurett nearly burst out laughing, but a remark from her friend stopped her in time.

"Don't laugh! They're Tibetans, no doubt about it; that childlike grimace is, among them, a profound reverence."

Priests, whom Lavarède immediately identified to his friends as "lamas," the local term, helped them to climb out of their aerial prison. After their hands had served to assist the newcomers they put them to their lips and embarked on complex reverences, mingled with genuflections.

Armand looked at the English duo, and they looked at him.

The people were speaking an unknown language, and indulging in an incomprehensible pantomime, giving them a slightly crazy appearance.

"Pooh," said the journalist, by way of conclusion. "There's no need to know what they're saying. These people seem well-disposed; let's try to take advantage of it to get something to eat."

He clapped a lama on the shoulder, who immediately prostrated himself, and then pointed at his mouth several times to indicate that he was hungry. The priest directed the young man's attention to a large wooden construction situated a short distance away, and invited him to follow him there, with his companions.

The latter did not have to be begged. Leaving the balloon under the guard of warriors, who were placed as sentries around the nacelle, they drew away, preceded by the lama, while the inhabitants bowed in passing, touching the ground with their foreheads.

Introduced into the palace, they went through several courtyards surrounded by buildings. The last one, planted with a garden, was bordered by a larger house with a more richly ornamented façade. A sculpted doorway opened before them. They went into a vast hall in which the light was filtered by windows whose glass was replaced by boards sliced into fine lacework.

At the back stood an enormous green marble cube, looming over two granite steps. The lama pointed at it, with a sort of embarrassment. Lavarède went up first. He thought he had divined that the priest wanted him to climb on to the pedestal, and, assuming that he was obeying a local custom, he took his place there.

The Tibetan uttered a guttural: "Hagh!" which attracted several of his colleagues, and they all took boxes from their pockets, from which they extracted a white powder. They filled a receptacle hollowed out in the marble with the powder, and hen ignited the preparation; thick fumes of myrrh and incense made Armand sneeze. Then, without paying any more attention to the English duo and Bouvreuil, the lamas disappeared, announcing by gestures that they were going to bring the voyagers something to eat.

"What does all this signify?" asked the journalist, when they had gone. "Has my renown as a former president of the Costa Rican Republic spread all the way here?"

"It's unlikely. Anyway, incense isn't part of the reception of presidents."

"That's true. One offers them a banquet washed down with good wines—that's the custom that would suit me best today—while the vapors of incense, disagreeable to respire, are reserved..."

"For gods."

"Uniquely for gods. Perhaps 'Lavarède' means Buddha in Tibetan."

"They don't know your name."

"Then I'm at a loss."

Two by two, marching in step to the chimes of a gong, the priests came back in. With a sacerdotal gravity they were carrying silver trays and water-jugs.

"Like a procession at the Porte-Saint-Martin," the Parisian muttered.

The lamas did not understand that disrespectful reflection. Following an extraordinarily complicated ritual, they presented everything to Armand, shoving aside his companions at the foot of the pedestal.

Before serving himself, the journalist demanded that the English duo should take their share of the honey, fruits and meat making up the meal. He did not touch it until afterwards, and finally offered the remains to Bouvreuil. The landlord could not reasonably expect his "debtor" to go to any expense of amiability in his regard.

Lavarède's simple action had a bizarre repercussion in the minds of the priests, however. From that moment on they resumed their obsequious attitude with regard to the gentleman and his daughter, but they did not put themselves to any inconvenience for the usurer, who was very discontented with that inequality of treatment.

Armand was enormously amused by his enemy's discomfited expression. Alas, he was soon to envy his fate. When the meal was over, a large circular grille was brought out, which was slotted into holes accommodated in the flagstones forming the floor of the hall, and the respected guest found himself in a cage.

He became annoyed, swore and complained, but the priests drowned out his voice by intoning a strange liturgical chant, and recommenced burning increase, almost to the point of asphyxiating him. Then the faithful filled the pagoda. Everyone bowed down to the ground, raising their left arms above their heads, clutching wooden sticks, on which cylinders covered in bizarre symbols pivoted.

"No more doubt about it," groaned the Parisian, between two sneezes provoked by the odorous fumes with which he was being lavished. "I'm really passing for a god. Those are prayer-mills."

And that continued until dusk. After nightfall, the exhausted Lavarède's prison was removed and he was allowed to savor a well-earned meal.

"If I'd known," he said to his friends, before going to sleep, "I'd have hoisted Monsieur Bouvreuil up on to the marble table. He could play Buddha in my place. In fact, why not impose the role upon him."

"Ah! Good idea!"

"But I daren't disabuse my worshipers. If I tried to correct their mistake, they'd treat me as an impostor. It's atrocious to be adored like this. The best thing is to decamp, without any fuss."

A glance darted outside, however, demonstrated that it would be difficult. Warriors were stationed around the pagoda. All precautions had been taken to prevent an escape.

The next day, the journalist, not finding sufficient satisfaction in treating Bouvreuil as domestic, tried to refuse to be caged—but then, with a great profusion of reverent gestures, the lamas took hold of him, bound his ankles and wrists, and exposed him in that fashion to the worship of the Buddhists.

Several days went by like that. As long as the journalist lent himself to the admiration of the ever-increasing crowd, he was pampered, stuffed with the most delicate foodstuffs, and given excellent wine from the valley of the Ganges to drink. If he tried to escape the prayers, however, the lamas tied him up, very respectfully, but very tightly.

His exasperation was indescribable. The English duo shared it; like him, they were prisoners. Bouvreuil was the only one having a good time; he was free to come and go; no one took any notice of his actions.

"Come on, my dear Monsieur," he said, when the Parisian got carried away, "have a little patience. The year fixed by your cousin is already considerably diminished. As soon as it has run out, I'll employ my liberty to secure yours. Imagine that you're serving a brief term in prison for debt."

The landlord, of course, only indulged in that kind of facetiousness when the bars of the age ensured him of impunity.

Once, however, in a bad mood and holding a considerable grudge against him, Murlyton unleashed one of those punches whose secret is known to his compatriots. The lamas immediately concluded that the servant, to whom they did not deign to pay any heed, had offended the powerful lords thanks to whom the pagoda was receiving such considerable benefits, and administered a considerable beating with clubs at the food of the marble altar where Armand was enthroned.

That was a pleasant distraction for Lavarède, but did not alter the fact that he was still a prisoner.

Aided by his companions, he attempted to get his guardians drunk in order to evade the vigilance of the sentries, but only succeeded in rendering the surveillance of which he was the object more obsessive.

A sadness mingled with impotent rage took possession of him, and it is impossible to determine to what extremities he might have been driven…when, on the evening of the twenty-fifth day, an incident gave him hope.

Night was falling. One by one, the faithful had retired, and the grinding of prayer-mills was no longer troubling the religious silence of the pagoda. Armand calculated that within an hour, his cage would be opened and he would finally be able to go back to his "apartment," where he would at least be able to lie down on his cushions and rest his weary limbs.

A man came into the sanctuary. He was wearing the katpalba, a dark-colored blouse secured at the waist, and the broad trousers of the Iliuks of the Siberian frontier. In his hand he was holding an astrakhan bonnet.

Well, well, thought Lavarède, habituated to Tibetan costumes. *Where has he come from?*

Aurett and her father considered the newcomer curiously. Slowly, the man approached the pedestal. His regular features, his expressive dark eyes and the grey-tinted beard that framed the lower part of his visage testified to his japhetic origin.

Having arrived at the green marble cube, he prostrated himself, rotated his prayer-mill, and pronounced a few words in a low voice.

"In what European country were you born?"

Lavarède was startled. The man was speaking French.

"Who are you?" he asked.

"Rachmed of the Tekke race."

"Rachmed?" the journalist repeated. "Rachmed the guide of…?"

"The great scholar Bonvalot, yes."

"Why are you here?"

"When I left him, I came back to live in this land. My dwelling is five days march from Lhasa. I learned from pilgrims that Buddha had descended from heaven into a pagoda of Tengri-Nor—the large lake that you can see."

"Buddha!" exclaimed the Parisian and his friends.

The Tekke nodded his head. "Yes. From the description of your aerial chariot I recognized a balloon, and, certain that visitors from Europe were prisoners of the lamas, I set forth to help them escape. Bonvalot and his companion, a king's son like me, have taught me to love all the men of Europe."

Aurett address a gracious smile to the unexpected savior, and, after having made sure with a rapid glance that no priest was present, she questioned him. "But how did you know that we were prisoners?"

Rachmed looked at her mildly. "I knew the sacred legend."

"What legend?"

"You don't know the prophecy, then?"

"Absolutely not."

"A sacred text says that in the near future, Buddha would descend from the heavens among the Tibetan. So long as he resides on the high plateaux the country will be prosperous and will dominate the nations. The lamas are to retain the god with rich presents, sacrifices appropriate to his grandeur, and not permit him to go away. The most frightful misfortunes will fall upon the people, deprived of their divine protector."

Everyone was listening. The adventure now became clear. The wording of the sacred text had been sufficient to enlighten the voyagers.

Distant footsteps sounded on the flagstones. Rachmed resumed his attitude of prayer, murmuring: "Someone's coming. You'll see me again tomorrow."

The priests liberated Armand and escort him to the rooms that they had given him as a residence, leaving him with the English duo to discuss the Tekke's revelation.

Bouvreuil was not there. They agreed to say nothing to him. Given his inclinations, the usurer might well have sought to raise an obstacle to the prisoners' plans; it was better to leave him in ignorance.

The next day, Rachmed, after a brief discussion with the English duo, presented himself to the Tag-Lama, the leader of the community, and offered to attempt to talk to the god who had descended from the heavens. During his voyage with Monsieur Bonvalot and Prince Henri d'Orléans, the Tekke had served as an interpreter, and the mandarins of Lhasa had conceived a high esteem for him. The priests therefore granted him permission to converse with Lavarède, and the news soon spread through the locality that the Buddha, thanks to the collaboration of a literate Asian skilled in making use of the language of the heavens, would be able to enter into communication with the humble inhabitants of Tibetan soil.

From then on, an interminable procession was engulfed in the pagoda. People came to consult the god about anything and everything. One wanted to cure his sick wife; another feared for his yaks or horses; a third, a hunter on the high plateaux, enquired as to the length of the commencing winter—and the journalist, ever ready to reply, alternately played the physician, the veterinary and the astronomer.

The last responsibility seemed to be easier to fulfill than the others. The snow was falling more frequently and numerous ice-floes were already floating on the surface of Tengri-Nor. To announce a rigorous winter was easy in those conditions.

His consultations were expensive. Warriors offered him their most beautiful weapons, pastors yak-hides, town-dwellers garments, and hunters begged him to accept their thickest and warmest furs.

Armand made a fortune, as he said in jest, but did not take a single step closer to liberty. Even Rachmed was discouraged. The lamas were too well aware of the holy prophecy, and the most unusual precautions were being taken to prevent the escape of the false Buddha.

The faithful became the accomplices of the priests. The departure of the Celestial voyager would bring down all misfortunes on Tibet; his slightest movements were noted by anxious eyes and discussed by people who could have matched the wiliest Europeans for cunning.

The Tekke, for example, was not allowed into the temple without being carefully searched. The same ceremony as repeated when he left.

Two more weeks went by. Murlyton, Aurett and Rachmed were excessively irritable. The struggle against the inevitable was depressing them, and the tranquility of Bouvreuil—who, since his correction, no longer permitted himself to mock overtly—drove them mad.

Bizarrely enough, Lavarède was calmer than his friends. Evidently, his imagination had discovered a path to follow. From time to time, an enigmatic smile strayed over his lips, and he addressed mocking glances to the crowd, but he made no reply to the English duo's questions.

As the fifth week of his captivity drew to close, he called Rachmed back as the latter, as was his custom, was about to return to is dwelling in the wake of the last of the faithful.

"Tell the Tag-Lama that I desire to have you at my table this evening. You'll only depart after the meal."

"Why?" asked the Tekke, surprised.

"Do it and you'll find out."

The high priest granted his Buddha's request willingly, and a few minutes later, the Parisian, the English duo and the interpreter were sitting on mats around a round lacquered table, eating with a hearty appetite. In a corner of the room, Pénélope's father was eating alone.

The dishes were placed in front of the diners; the aimanas—novices charged with menial tasks—had withdrawn.

Armand designated Bouvreuil with his gaze, and, leaning toward his friends, pronounced a few rapid words in a low voice. Surprise was legible on the faces of Murlyton and Aurett. As for Rachmed, he shook his head.

"They'll never agree to that!"

An incredulous smile from the god greeted that appreciation. "You're mistaken. They'll consent."

"Why is that?"

"Translate my words well tomorrow, and you'll see."

"What are you going to say?"

"I don't know yet, but I'm determined to get around these worthy lamas, and we'll soon see whether a citizen of the Boulevard des Italians can't get the better of these parchment-faced apes."

When the dinner was over, the Tekke, unconvinced, took his leave of the voyagers, and they all experienced a singular emotion in saying: "Until tomorrow!"

Winter is the Tibetans' most terrible enemy. On the plateaux whose lowest regions are at the height of Mont Blanc, the cold reigns supreme from November to April. The rivers freeze; the obstructed springs hollow out subterranean courses. The temperature drops by night to minus forty degrees, and a few leagues from Lhasa all vegetation disappears. Any man audacious enough to set forth into the icy desert will not encounter any tree to aliment his camp fire. He has to search the tracks of the summer caravans assiduously and collect yak droppings, the only combustible substance in that accursed country.

The rare valleys lost in the solitude of the high plateaux also suffer from the cold. The trees, hollow poplars and firs, split and die under the action of the frost; livestock perishes and the inhabitants sometimes lack the basic necessities, because the caravans that resupply them wait for the first warm days of April to set out. The Tibetans are, therefore, accustomed, at the commencement of the desolate period, to implore the clemency of Buddha.

On the first of December Lavarède, dressed in splendid clothes, and coiffed in a bonnet ornamented by a diamond almost as fine as the Régent de France, was exposed on the marble altar to the supplications of the crowd. The living god had bought about a recrudescence of piety throughout the region. The pagoda was overflowing with people, and the lamas, superficially impassive but inwardly delighted, banked the presents heaped up at the journalist's feet.

Suddenly, the latter put out his hand.

"Rachmed," he said, "translate my words for the people beloved by Heaven."

At the sound of his voice all heads were raised; the prayer-mills stopped turning, and the priests, amazed to see such an incident, unforeseen in the eleven thousand seven hundred and forty articles of the rite, pricked up their ears. Armand spoke, and the Tekke translated his words faithfully.

"Valiant men of Tibet and your wives, their incomparable companions, listen. With your welcome, with your faith, my divinity is pleased. Rolled in the blue sails of the infinite ether, I saw approaching, with regret, the predicted time of my voluntary exile on the terrestrial globe. Now I no longer regret the celestial abode; the fire of your souls illuminates for me this earth of dazzling light."

In spite of the sanctity of the place, an approving murmur greeted that flattering speech.

The Parisian exchanged a glance with Aurett, who was sitting with her father beside the malachite cube, and went on: "I want to make of the frightful season into which we are entering a mild spring, and its glacial winds into warm zephyrs. I want to render to the denuded trees their green finery, sow the hardened soil with smiling flower-beds and spread joy, abundance and love among you."

225

At that enchanting picture, a long frisson shook the audience. Rachmed looked at Armand anxiously. The latter did not seem to notice and raised his voice.

"The djinn, rebels against my authority, have armed themselves with scourges that desolate the world. The hour has come when they will be annihilated. Lamas who are listening to me, have the aerial chariot that brought me here brought into the pagoda. With my companions, I shall return it to a condition to effect the great voyage, and my servant"—he pointed at the bewildered Bouvreuil—"will go into space and bring back the invincible talismans accumulated during the centuries by the benevolent spirits, in anticipation of that struggle."

"What? What?" protested the landlord. "Me, in a balloon, alone—never!"

A blow with a stick cut off his speech. The Tag-Lama recalled him to propriety.

A hubbub had risen, and in the buzz of voices, Armand was able to murmur in such a fashion that only Aurett heard it: "Like Buddha, I believe I'm something of a symbolist."

Meanwhile, the god's promises were circulating. There were outbursts of loud cries of delight outside.

Skeptical by nature, the priests were nevertheless obliged to yield to popular pressure. That same evening, Lavarède recovered possession of his aerostat.

The envelope was in a pitiful state. Long tears striped its brilliant surface—but an attentive examination demonstrated that the damage as reparable with thread, needles, gum…and patience.

From that moment on, the journalist, the fake master of Heaven, Aurett and the gentleman spent their time restoring the silk of the aerostat—an ingrate task not designed for enjoyment. In the evening, however, when they were gathered around the bronze brazier that warmed the apartments, our voyagers looked at one another with joyous gleams in their eyes.

On the twenty-fourth of December, the balloon was ready. The envelope, supported by a rope extended between two poles, was swaying in the courtyard, above the nacelle stocked with weapons, warm clothing and various provisions, gifts from the pious Tibetans. Beneath the inferior opening a receptacle had been fixed designed to contain rice alcohol, the combustion of which would produce the hot air necessary to the ascent. For want of hydrogen gas, the journalist had selected that primitive means; the aerostat had become a Montgolfier.

The false Buddha had announced during the day that his servant would rise up into the air the following day, and had invited the faithful to witness the ceremony.

The lamas, very anxious to begin with, were reassured. They now believed Armand's fallacious promises, and proved it to him by more profound bows and more prolonged prostrations.

Enclosed with the English duo and Rachmed, the young man said to them: "No one is suspicious of us now. The priests will go back to their cells and the pagoda will be deserted. At midnight, the Tag-Lama will come to see me in response to the request that I made." He smiled. "We need to confer as to the surest means of defeating the djinn!"

"However," Murlyton objected, cutting to the heart of the question, "while the balloon is ready, we're locked in our rooms."

"It's precisely to open them up that the Tag-Lama is coming."

"Ah!" said Aurett. "I understand now."

"This is my plan. I strangle that venerable person a little, just enough to ensure his neutrality. We slip outside. In the nacelle are the flasks of rice alcohol that I requested. We fill the receptacle, ignite it, and bid farewell to our jailers."

Rachmed was listening. He was spending the night in the pagoda in order to serve as the Tag-Lama's interpreter in his conversation with the Buddha.

"Can you take me?" he asked, not without anxiety. "With you gone, I won't be safe here."

Lavarède became pensive. "Damn!" he said. "There are already four of us." Then he changed his mind. "In fact, there'll be four of us, including you. Bouvreuil has a horror of excursions in the clouds; he can stay."

Those final words had scarcely been pronounced when the usurer came in. He wanted to beg his ex-debtor to dispense with the ascent with which he thought he was threatened. That request summoned a smile to all lips, and the gentleman was obliged to restrain himself in order to conserve his gravity when the god assured Pénélope's father, generously, that he would strive to give him satisfaction.

The night wore on. Outside, the wind was howling, chasing thick clouds before it that did not allow any moonlight to filter through.

Ten o'clock, and then eleven sounded. Bouvreuil had retired to his room, and the others, their hearts hammering in their breasts, waited for midnight. If they succeeded in their enterprise, they would be free! If not, they would be condemned to an even narrower captivity in that desolate region.

Suddenly, they became immobile, as if frozen. The door creaked and grated on its hinges.

The Tag-Lama appeared—but he was not alone. Behind him marched an officer of the Chinese police, recognizable by his blue and green uniform.

Lavarède was not mistaken about that, and a sudden pallor spread over his face. What had the policeman come to do?

"Most worthy Buddha," said the high priest, "to err is the prerogative of humans. Forgive me in advance for what I have to say to you."

"I'm listening," replied the Parisian, recovering all his composure.

After a salutation, the lama continued. "A white freemason like you, condemned to death by the Tsong-Li-Yamen, escaped from the imperial capital by stealing a flying machine."

"Ah! And you want to take him back?"

The question asked by the god appeared to confuse the visitors.

"It's not that..."

"No," declared the Tag-Lama, in a piteous tone, "but the mandarin Sandyama, here present, chief of police of the secret road of Yunnan, has received orders to mount a search in order to discover the fugitive. Rumor of your miraculous arrival reached him, and he has come here. In spite of the rites that forbid nocturnal entry to the pagoda to the profane, I received him, so pressing was his plea. His soldiers are in the courtyard. Permit me to show him your aerial chariot in order to remove the doubt from his mind."

Armand reflected. Suddenly, he looked fixedly at Rachmed and the English duo, and then, approaching the Tag-Lama, he placed a hand on his shoulder.

"What is the point of this visit?" he said. "It would have been sufficient to ask me where the thief is, and I would have told you."

Rachmed had also stood up. In order to translate the false Buddha's words, he had moved between the priest and the policeman.

"That's true," murmured the Tag-Lama. "You consent, then...?"

"To put you on the right track? Yes, certainly."

Sandyama rubbed his hands together.

"Where is he hiding, powerful lord?"

"Near here."

"Truly?"

Lavarède addressed a glance to the gentleman, who had stood up in his turn.

"Show me the place," implored the policeman.

"Gladly. He is within easy reach of your grasp."

"O Buddha, prove that to me!"

"You wish it?"

"I implore you."

"Well then, be satisfied."

And, launching himself forward with his fists raised, he struck the officer full in chest, who uttered a muted groan. Before he had recovered from his surprise, the Parisian had knocked him to the ground. Rachmed, meanwhile, had knocked down the Tag-Lama.

"The ropes, quickly!" Armand ordered Murlyton.

Since repairing the balloon, cords were languishing in every corner. The Tibetan and the Chinaman were soon bound and gagged.

"What are we going to do?" asked Murlyton. You heard him—the courtyard is full of policemen."

"Put on the priest's costume. I'll put on the policeman's. And you, Miss, turn round."

The young woman obeyed. In a few minutes, the two men had undergone a metamorphosis.

"Now," said Lavarède, "let's go down. Miss Aurett, the sister of the Buddha, will give the necessary explanations to the Tag-Lama and the suspicious policeman Sandyama."

He made the astonished gentleman, the Englishwoman and the Tekke go ahead of him, then carefully closed the door and went down to the courtyard.

Some thirty or forty men were grouped around the balloon. Their silhouettes were discernible in the gloom.

"They're going to discover the trick," said the gentleman, softly.

"No, no," replied the journalist. "We'll ask them to step back in order to facilitate our little ploy. To Rahmed, he said: "Instruct these men to retire to the extremity of the courtyard. The sister of the Buddha will not consent to speak before the profane. Only Sandyama is authorized to approach."

The Tekke smiled. He understood Armand's plan. He transmitted the order in a sonorous voice. The agents, thinking that they recognized their chief and the Tag-Lama in the darkness, hastened to obey and moved away from the immediate vicinity of the aerostat.

A few moments later the fugitives were installed in the nacelle. Aurett poured a liter of alcohol into the receptacle designed for that purpose and ignited the liquid. A blue-tinted flame illuminated the wooden quadrilateral with a fantastic glow. Prudently, Lavarède and Murlyton turned their backs to the group of policemen. The latter watched uncomprehendingly, as if witnessing some magical ceremony. Meanwhile, under the influence of the warm air, the envelope dilated. The silk swelled, with slight creaking sounds. Soon, an oscillatory movement was produced.

"Drop the poles," said Lavarède, in a low voice.

With a kick, the interpreter cast the pieces of wood on the ground. Free now, the balloon tightened the ropes that linked it to the nacelle. With an iron rod, Armand activated the flame. Suddenly, a kind of quiver shook the apparatus. For another second, the aerostat appeared to hesitate as to whether to quit the ground; then, abruptly, it rose to the height of the roof of the pagoda.

A howl rang out. Finally realizing that they had been tricked, all the policemen ran across the courtyard, raising their bows and rifles in order to shoot at the fugitives.

"As long as they don't rip the envelope," muttered the Parisian.

But the clamors ceased—or, rather, changed. A sinister crack shook the atmosphere. A portion of the temple roof collapsed, and through the gaping opening shot a jet of flame. The police had other things to occupy them than the Montgolfier.

"Fire!" cried Lavarède. "We're saved."

Then, through one of the skylights fitted into the upper part of the edifice, three summarily-dressed individuals surged and started running over the roof, uttering cries of fright.

"The lama!" said Armand

"And the Chinese police chief!" added Aurett.

"And Monsieur Bouvreuil!" added the Englishman.

The three individuals, in their underwear in spite of the glacial cold, were indeed the voyagers' enemies. In the brief struggle with the officer, Lavarède had knocked over the brazier serving to heat the room. In their haste to get away, neither he nor his companions had paid any heed to the accident, and the fire, finding abundant aliment in the wooden palace, had propagated rapidly.

In response to the cries of the Chinaman, tied up but poorly gagged, Bouvreuil had woken up and come running. He had freed the two poor devils. The walls and the door leading to the courtyard were already ablaze. The three men had climbed up from one floor to the next, pursued by the roaring flames, and had reached the roof just in time to witness the departure of the authors of their woes.

While a rescue was being organized, the aerostat continue to rise, and was engulfed in the clouds that cushioned the sky, disappearing from all eyes.

In the morning, nothing remained of the temple but a heap of charred debris, still smoking on the frozen bank of the Tengu-Nor. A search was mounted for Bouvreuil, but he had disappeared. Sensing that after what had happened, his position was no longer tenable, the landlord had taken possession of some priestly garments, had taken flight and headed directly southwards, in the hope of reaching Hindustan or English Burma. His wallet had remained with his garment, consumed in the fire, and he had only been able to pick up a few papers.

Running all the while in order to combat the intense cold of the night, he thought: *Robbed by José, stripped by the fire, my voyage has cost me a hundred thousand francs…and my ungraspable son-in-law is presently soaring through the realm of the birds. And I'm going to die of hunger or be murdered! No, my poor Pénélope will never know how difficult it is to get a young woman settled!*

Leaving Lhasa to the east, Bouvreuil followed the icy bed of the Irarudnambe, and plunged into the gorges of Palhe, striving with the aid of the stars not to lose his direction.

XXII. The High Plateaux of Tibet

Pushed by a moderated wind, the Montgolfier floated above an ocean of cloud which hid the earth.

"Provided that we're heading southwards," said Rachmed, "we'll soon find ourselves in the admirable lands that extend between Calcutta and the mountains of Manipur."

"Very close to the sea," Murlyton completed. "Whereas, if we're heading eastwards, we'll come down in China again, and if westwards, we'll cross the plateaux of Kashmir and Pamir—the roof of the world."

"That would still be better than northwards, Monsieur."

"Why?"

"Because in that direction we'd encounter nothing but the Gobi, the interminable icy desert. With Bonvalot, it took us two months to cross that land of hunger."

A joyful exclamation from Lavarède interrupted that conversation. He had put the compass close to the aerostat's "heater" and was consulting it by the vacillating light of the alcohol.

"We're flying south-eastwards, my friends," he declared. "Tomorrow, no doubt, we'll be within sight of English establishments."

Everyone was reassured, and they decided that they could take turns to sleep. The passengers would work in shifts to maintain the fire, for the balloon would now only stay airborne on condition that it was always inflated with warm air. Cooling is rapid at those heights, and it was necessary to avoid landing in the mountains, from which the march to India would be long and difficult.

The Englishman offered to take the first watch. His companions wedged themselves as best they could against the walls of the nacelle, piling furs on top of hem, and the airship, carrying its sleeping crew, sailed on under the care of the gentleman.

The cold was biting. Murlyton's breath froze in his beard in icy stalactites, and, although the worthy man was muffled in a yak-hide, he felt the bitter wind penetrating to the marrow of his bones.

One after another, his drowsy companions experienced the same impressions, and it was a relief for them all when the sun appeared on the horizon. They felt a painful surprise, nevertheless, on seeing themselves suspended between the clouds and the blue vault of the heavens.

"Where are we?" they repeated. "Above what region?"

They let the fire in the burner die down slightly, and the aerostat descended slowly through the thick clouds that hid the ground.

Anxiously leaning over, they all ought to pierce the mist. Finally, the ground appeared.

The aeronauts exchanged anxious glances. In the distance as far as the eye could see, the rocky plateau extended, from which long peaks, sometimes isolated and sometime grouped, launched toward the sky. There was not a single green patch indicating vegetation: nothing but the gray hue of granite everywhere.

Suddenly, Armand extended his arm. "There, to the west," he said. "Water! One would think it were a great round lake."

Indeed, in the direction indicated, there was an expanse of water, circular in form, whose icy surface effected the sun's rays with an unsustainable glare.

Rachmed said nothing. His eyes wide, he turned to all four points of the compass-rose. His visage expressed an indescribable surprise. He leaned toward the journalist.

"Are you quite certain that we have been heading southwards?"

"Undoubtedly. Why?"

"Because I'm the victim of an unexpected resemblance. It seems to me that I'm on the coast of Lake Montcalm, at the central point of the Tibetan plateau. Those masses of rocks down there, which affect the appearance of a recumbent elephant, sheltered the Bonvalot expedition from the Siberian wind."

Lavarède interrupted him. "That's not possible. We can't have returned to the north of Lhasa. In any case, look at the compass."

The Tekke considered the instrument. It did indeed indicate a south-eastward route.

"I'm mistaken," murmured the guide. "It's strange, however, that two landscapes can be similar to that extent."

"And strange too," Murlyton murmured, "that we're not yet within sight of English territory."

Meanwhile, the balloon, warmed by a low fire, was maintaining a height of three or four hundred meters from the ground. All the reliefs had a singular vigor. That phenomenon, due to the rarefaction of the air, made Armand anxious, for it demonstrated that the ground was not getting any lower. Now, according to his approximate calculation, the Montgolfier ought at that moment to be overlooking the fertile plains extending to the east of the Ganges delta.

Toward midday, a volcano in ignition appeared to the right of the line followed by the aerostat. Nodding his head, Rachmed pointed it out to the young man. "The Reclus volcano," he said, simply.[52]

"Are you sure?"

"Impossible to be mistaken. It's the only eruptive cone between the Siberian frontier and the Himalaya."

"In that case, the wind is carrying us northwards?"

"Yes."

---

[52] The "Reclus volcano" was so named by Bonvalot, but the name did not stick, partly because there is a Reclus volcano in Patagonia.

"Rachmed, your eyes can be deceived, but the compass can't be deceived!"[53]

"Who can tell?"

The needle, imperturbably, marked north to the rear of the nacelle. In spite of their confidence on the magnetic pointer, the voyagers were troubled by Tekke's insistence. From time to time the latter pointed out some feature of the landscape.

"We camped there…one of our men died of cold and altitude sickness there…I went astray here; my companions lit a big fire on that peak to indicate their position to me…"

No one any longer replied. They all sensed that Rachmed was right. They should have emerged from the mountainous desert long before. But how, then, could the inverse indication of the compass be explained? In vain they took hold of it one after another, and shook it. The needle always returned to the same place.

The day was drawing to a close and the landscape had not been modified. The aerostat crossed a ridge that had masked the horizon. In unison, the Europeans uttered a cry of joy. In front of them extended a lake, whose open waters bore no ice.

"Hurrah!" cried the journalist. "We're entering into a more clement region. Water in a liquid state is the effect of a mild temperature."

But the Tekke shook his head and simply remarked: "The lake that never freezes."

Murlyton, Aurett and Lavarède had all read the account of the explorer Bonvalot's voyage. They had noticed that bizarrerie: a lake, the composition of whose waters rendered it immune to freezing. And that lake was more than eight hundred leagues from India! They were, therefore, being dragged fatally northwards. If any doubt had still remained, their conviction was firm now.

The balloon passed over the liquid surface like a bird, and on the opposite shore the granitic surface was renewed. At the same time, the wind became stronger.

"Well," said Armand, breaking the silence, "we'll return to France via Russia, that's all. For the moment, it's a matter of going higher. Night's falling, and an encounter with a peak would be disastrous."

"There are only two liters of alcohol left," the Englishman replied.

"The breeze has freshened; perhaps that will be enough to reach Siberia."

The Parisian's calmness reassured his companions, even though they thought they could perceive a shift in the wind. They ate at an altitude of four-

---

[53] It is surely amazing that none of the three men can take a bearing from the sun, and that none of them noticed, when it rose, that it was rising in the direction opposite to the one they expected on the basis of their compass reading.

teen hundred meters, and were getting ready to go to sleep when Lavarède uttered a veritable roar.

"What's the matter?"

"I beg your pardon. I've found it."

"Found what?"

"The reason why the compass is crazy. For there's no denying it—it's absolutely crazy."

That affirmation appeared to interest the gentleman, for he drew closer, saying: "And what is the reason?"

"Lightning, my dear Monsieur. Do you remember the tempest that took us to Lhasa? We took a veritable electric bath while traversing the stormy clouds, and since then, the magnetic needle hasn't known what it's doing, or what it's indicating."

"It's true, in fact—the phenomenon has often been observed."

"Yes," sighed the journalist, comically. "If we had realized that sooner, we would have been able to seek a more propitious current. Anyway, let's not weep for India—Siberia is calling us."

And, humming the Russian national anthem, he lay down in the bottom of the nacelle and closed his eyes.

Once again, Murlyton took the first watch; Armand succeeded him and passed the task on to Rachmed.

"Be economical with the rice alcohol," he said to him. "There's only half a liter left. Let's try to make it last until morning."

Nodding his head, the Tekke installed himself next to the heater. With the darkness, the intensity of the cold had doubled, and the guide felt numb.

His watch had lasted half an hour when the flame of the receptacle became paler and smaller. It required fuel. Not without difficulty, Rachmed shook off the torpor that had invaded him and bent down to pick up the funnel that they used when pouring the alcohol. He grunted and snatched his hand back sharply. The skin of his fingers remained stuck to the metal, leaving the flesh raw, with an almost intolerable sensation of burning.

Cold and heat produce identical effects. All polar expeditions report accidents analogous to the one to which the Tekke had just fallen victim. The application of the naked hand to a piece of metal chilled by the air provokes the same sensation as a scalding aspersion.

Dolorously surprised, Rachmed was not thinking clearly. The simplest thing would have been to wrap up his hand and pick up the funnel. He did not think of that. The receptacle was almost empty, blue alcohol flames were rising and falling abruptly, an indication of imminent extinction. Without reflection, the guide picked up the bottle containing the rest of the liquid and tilted it over the heater in order to fill it. Almost immediately, a strident click caused him to shudder. Under the influence of the heat, the bottle had broken and its contents had caught fire. Frightened, the Tekke let go, thus releasing half a liter of alcohol all at once.

There was a sharp sizzling sound, and a bright streak of fire licked the edges of the inferior opening of the aerostat. The silk immediately caught fire.

At that sight, Rachmed threw himself on to the companions, and snatched them from their sleep with the terrible words: "The balloon is on fire!"

They were all upright in a trice, and they looked up at the envelope. The terrible agent of destruction was gaining ground, cutting out an irregular circle in the fabric.

No one said a word. Fire is terrible on the ground, but it can be fought, and the hope of flight subsists, while in the air, with an abyss beneath the feet, caught between fear of the fire and the fear of falling, people lose all courage and initiative. A kind of fatalism grips the mind. Death is there, and people abandon themselves to it. It was as if they were all nailed to the spot.

"Adieu, Father! Adieu, Monsieur Lavarède!" said Aurett, in a faint voice.

Those words, which she had pronounced with clenched teeth, the supreme appeal of her feminine weakness, broke the spell. They tried to defend themselves. The rope linking the valve to the nacelle was untouched by the flame. Armand seized it and, with a dry click, activated the mechanism. They immediately felt a more rapid movement of descent.

The resultant upward air current, however, activated the work of the flame. The entire upper part of the balloon was consumed. The aerostat became a simple parachute bordered by a circle of flame.

Motionless, their chests tight, the passengers watched the disaster unfold. Their situation was frightful. They were lost in the darkness, with no way of knowing how far they were from the ground, sustained by a frail silk envelope whose diameter was diminishing by the second. No torture can give any idea of the mental torment of a person suspended in the void, waiting to fall.

There was a sudden impact; the parachute oscillated momentarily, and then, under the pressure of the wind, collapsed, darting a flame that was immediately extinguished to a considerable height. Rapid as its glare had been, however, the voyagers had time to glimpse a plain with a smooth and shiny surface.

"A frozen river," Rachmed declared.

"In that case," Lavarède replied, "let's get to the bank and wait for daylight."

So saying, he cut the ropes linking the nacelle to the debris of the envelope and, inviting his friends to imitate him, started hauling that vehicle of a new kind.

It's necessary not to lose our heads," he said. "Our provisions, our weapons, our furs, the tents—everything is in here."

With the aid of Murlyton and the Take, he brought the nacelle to the bank, at the price of a few falls, inevitable on ice that presented no asperity. The bank had a gentle slope, covered in hardened snow, which facilitated the voyagers' climb. A path snaked along the crest, beyond with was a high wall of rock.

After a brief search, they found that it led to the entrance to a cave. Rachmed improvised a torch with the debris of planks, and with that dubious illumination they went into the cave.

When they had taken the first few steps, the Europeans stopped dead, petrified by admiration. The high vault rounded out above their heads and the walls in which they were leaning seemed to be coated with topazes. Thousand of facets reflected the light, pricking the obscurity with yellow sparks.

"Marvelous," murmured Aurett, putting her hands together.

"What is it?" Lavarède demanded, quite astonished.

It was the guide who answered, with his usual laconism: "Gem salt."

He was right. It was, indeed, one of those caverns that one encounters, following a sinuous line from the Polish frontier all the way to the Great Wall of China.

The ground, covered with fine sand, offered a tempting couch for limbs exhausted by fatigue. Soon, with their eyes still full of radiance, they all rolled themselves up in their furs and soon lost the sentiment of existence...

Then shadows penetrated soundlessly into the cavern and approached the sleepers. Having arrived next to Aurett, they lifted her up, with a thousand precautions, and carried her outside. Then the young woman was attached to a horse, which, in company with several others, awaited the mysterious individuals.

A slight whistle was heard; each animal immediately had a rider, and the little troop moved away at a gallop.

The journalist and his friends had not heard anything. A piercing scream uttered by Aurett, abruptly woken up by the furious dash of her mount, did not succeed in extracting them from their torpor. Murlyton only turned over, yawned and resumed sleeping.

In the morning, a vague light illuminated the wall of shadow that veiled the depths of the cavern when Lavarède opened his eyes. In spite of his pelts and the protection of his rocky shelter, he felt numb.

He felt a prickling sensation in his nose and ears, as if thousands of needles activated by an invisible motor were plunging in and out of their cartilage.

"Brrr!" he said, shaking himself. "It's chilly."

He got up and adjusted his furs. At his feet, Murlyton and Rachmed, covered in heaps of animal skins, were still motionless.

"Why, where's Aurett?" said the young man. "Gone out already? How shaming for our reputedly stronger sex!" With those words he walked toward the entrance to the grotto.

He stopped momentarily. At the abrupt transition from dark to light his eyes had closed. The landscape was dazzling. All the reliefs of the ground were covered in crystalline ice; the nearby river seemed to be a stream of molten silver, multiplying the rays of the pale winter sunlight tenfold as it reflected them. One might have thought it a magical accumulation of diamonds sparkling on lamplight. There were flashes, an orgy of flamboyant rays leaping up from the ground—and by virtue of a strange optical illusion, the ground seemed to be drowning the sun.

Armand gazed, and then the thought of the Englishwoman returned to him. The path along the rocks was deserted, as was the river-bank.

Where, then, was the young woman hiding? He took a few steps and, a sudden anxiety biting his heart, called out to his gracious traveling companion. His voice died without awakening any echo.

He shouted more loudly. This time, someone responded. Murlyton, woken up by his cries, appeared and asked why he was shouting. At the first words he shared the young man's fear. His voice joined in to launch his daughter's name into space.

"Aurett! Aurett!"

They stopped occasionally to draw breath, Faces pale and brows furrowed, they listened—but they strained their ears in vain; they heard nothing but the incessant cracking of stressed ice.

They could not doubt it. Aurett had gone out, wanting to take a short stroll, and in that bizarre landscape she had gone astray. It was necessary to indicate the campsite to her. A big fire would fulfill that office, producing a column of smoke visible a long way off.

As they returned to the cavern, however, in order to break up the nacelle and transform it into firewood, Rachmed appeared before them.

"Miss Aurett?" the taciturn individual enquired.

"Lost...gone astray..."

He shook his head. "No."

"What do you mean, no?" exclaimed Lavarède.

"Not lost—taken."

"Taken? When? By whom?"

The Tekke's only response was to show them a small bag of embroidered silk that he was holding in his hand.

"What's that?"

"Sacred stones."

"Amulets?"

"Yes."

"Oh!" exclaimed Murlyton, impatiently. "Let's leave Rachmed and his fetishes! Think, Monsieur Lavarède, that my daughter must be searching for us, crying out in vain, her eyes scanning the horizon without finding any reference point to guide her." The gentleman's phlegm had vanished. It was the father who was speaking, hoarsely, with tears in his voice.

The Parisian, however, took his arm and constrained him to remain where he was. Then he said to the Tekke: "Explain, rapidly. You can see that he's suffering."

"This bag of amulets belongs to a warrior on campaign. He dropped it in the cave near the place where the young woman was lying."

The Englishman shivered. He understood now what the guide was saying.

"Go on," said Armand.

"They came last night. There were a dozen. They took the demoiselle away, attached to a horse, and took her westwards along course of the river."

How do you know all that?"

Rachmed smiled, revealing his white teeth, and pointed at the ground "The tracks."

On the crust of ice imprisoning the path, there were indeed slight scratches indicating the passage of living beings—but from that to recognizing their species there was a wide gap, and the faces of the Europeans expressed that so clearly that the Asiatic thought that he ought to say more.

"A former hunter of the Lob-Nor, I've followed the track of all animals. Today, I still feel capable of guiding you to the one you're regretting."

Lavarède and the Englishman shivered. To launch themselves in pursuit of Aurett's abductors seemed to lighten their dolor. Action consoles, because it supposes hope.

They wanted to set out immediately, but the Tekke shook his head. To venture on foot into that land, where cold reigns as master and every human is an enemy, it is indispensable to equip oneself with weapons and ammunition to defend oneself, fur tens to shelter by night, and provisions in order not to be at the mercy of problematic hunting.

Before quitting Lhasa they had filled the nacelle with everything that was useful among the presents offered to the god. Nothing was easier than to equip themselves. Understanding Rachmed's demands, Murlyton and Lavarède prepared the luggage that they had to carry, grimly.

On the advice of their companion, they organized it in such a fashion that they could carry it on their backs, in the fashion of soldiers. That way, their hands were free, and, in case of any troublesome encounter, their burdens would not hinder their use of weapons.

An hour was spent in preparations. Finally, with daggers and revolvers in their belts and rifles over their shoulders, the three men were ready.

Abandoning the nacelle and the objects it still contained in the cave, the three men took the route traveled by the young woman's abductors. Rachmed marched in the lead. With his eyes fixed on the ground, he advanced at a rapid pace, without hesitation. As a paleographer is able to translate an ancient manuscript, the Tekke was able to decipher the soil.

"Here," he said, "the bandits stopped. The demoiselle set foot on the ground."

Emotionally, the Englishman leaned over a scarcely-discernible scratch in the ice, which the guide identified as the trace of his daughter's foot.

Further on, Rachmed declared that a horse had stumbled. Even further on, he unknown enemies had eaten a meal.

"Let's have ours too," the Asiatic added. "In this temperature, it's necessary to save and maintain one's strength."

"No, let's keep moving. Every minute lost is a torture for my daughter—let's move!"

His eyes shining feverishly, Murlyton extended his arm westwards, as if to take hold of the warriors who had taken Aurett—but the guide had definitely assumed the leadership of the expedition, because his only reply to the gentleman's supplications was: "We need to stop and eat. If not, within an hour, the breath will die in our lungs, and we won't be able to go on."

While speaking, he squatted down. His companions were obliged to imitate him. Deep down, in any case, they understood the justice of Rachmed's observation. They were already experiencing the first symptoms of fatigue—difficulty in breathing, weakness in the limb—produced by the rarefaction of the air. They were aware that they would have to make frequent pauses, under penalty of being forced to renounce their enterprise.

The meal, consisting of strips of dried yak-meat and maize pancakes, revived them. They astonished themselves by eating avidly, forgetting that cold accelerates human combustion, like that of a hearth, and creates a need for abundant nourishment.

At a signal from the Tekke the pursuit recommenced. They marched until nightfall, and the voyagers stopped, exhausted, beside a warm spring, a certain number of which exist in the region.

From a kind of hollow excavated in the rock, hot water was escaping, the curse of which was marked by a line of floating mist. The air was warmed by it, and within a restricted perimeter, pale and meager grass covered the ground. Near the stream, in the disturbed soil, Rachmed showed his friends the tracks of the horses and the warriors. At one place he even discovered the imprint of the young Englishwoman's shoes. Murlyton did not say a word, but he shook the guide's hand.

The camp was set up, the fur tent erected. Everyone slid inside it with pleasure. The temperature had dropped abruptly; the thermometer with which the Englishman had equipped himself marked thirty-two degrees below zero. Lulled by the murmur of the nearby spring, however, the voyagers were falling asleep when a strange noose made them sit up again abruptly. It was a dull rumble, punctuated by shrill grating sounds that tore the ears.

"What the...?" murmured the Englishman.

"A cart," relied the Tekke, in a low voice.

Lavarède was on his feet immediately. "A cart! Then it has a driver."

Already he was about to emerge from the tent; Rachmed's hand stopped him. "Are you weary of living, that you want to expose your bare head to the cold? Put on your fur bonnet. Otherwise you'll fall down dead."

The advice was sound. In excessive frosts, congestion lies in wait for humans. The polar voyages prove that. How many sailors are asleep in the ice-sheet, having ignored the precautions recommended to crews? Armand did not know, but he only left the tent, with his companions, after covering himself up warmly. Outside, the cold reigned as master. On their cheeks, unprotected by fur, the voyagers experienced a sharp pain; it was as if a knife were digging into their flesh.

Meanwhile, the cart drew nearer. It had to pass close to the spring. Motionless, Lavarède and his companions waited, their hands clutching their rifles. Would those who were coming be benevolent or hostile?

Eventually, a black mass appeared in the shadow.

"Who goes there?" demanded Rachmed, whose knowledge of local languages naturally allocated the role of interpreter to him.

A series of guttural exclamations responded, and the cart stopped.

"Who goes there?" repeated the Tekke, in a menacing tone.

This time the driver replied: "A poor man delayed in the Kirghiz village of Beharsand, who is going home."

"Approach. If you're telling the truth, you have nothing to fear from us."

There was a pause; then footsteps resonated on the hardened ground and a man appeared. He was an old man, curbed, clad in a yak-skin. Beneath his fur bonnet, a thin face was visible, terminated by a long gray beard. "I'm not afraid," he said. "What could anyone steal from an unfortunate like me? Might as well scratch the rock to find nourishment there." Suddenly, however, he stopped. "Listen!" he said. "Death's envoy is coming toward us!"

"What does he mean, *death's envoy?*" murmured the Parisian.

Rachmed shook his head. "The gray bear of the mountains. If his ears haven't deceived him, we're going to suffer the assault of one of the most terrible beasts in creation."

In fact, the bear in question, similar to its American cousin, the grizzly, attains the size of an ox. Wandering the desolate heights, its stomach racked by hunger, it attacks everything unlucky enough to cross its path. Its vigor equals its voracity. When one meets it, one has to fight, because flight is impossible. In spite of its apparent ponderousness, the ferocious carnivore can run as fast as the most rapid horse, Tekke explained that rapidly to his companions.

In the meantime, the cart-driver lamented: "Cursed be this night! It's exhausted my yaks; the bear is going to devour them. My two animals, my only fortune! Who will pull the cart to the town now? Oh, I've lived too long, since I'm going to die of hunger."

Lavarède felt moved by that despair. He went to the man. "Be quiet," he ordered. "We have rifles to greet the bear."

"You'll defend me?"

"Yes, but where is it?"

"Listen!"

In the distance, a kind of muffled snoring could be heard.

"It's him," said the cart-driver. "He's hurrying. He's scented his prey."

Murlyton and the Tekke had joined the Frenchman

"Be careful," said the guide. "The gray bear is even more dangerous than a tiger. Aim at the head."

The growling became distinct; the animal could not be far away.

At that moment, the moon, veiled until then, appeared through a gap in the clouds and inundated the landscape with silvery light. Fifty paces away, a black form was moving rapidly over the surface of the ground.

"Here he comes!" cried the cart-driver, fearfully.

The three men arm their rifles. To the steely clicks the bear responds by grinding its teeth. It stops for a moment, considering its enemies, and then, with formidable growl, it rushes upon them.

Three gunshots ring out. A howl of pain proves that the animal had been hit, but it does not slow down.

The Englishman and Armand throw themselves to the side in order to let the bear pass by. Rachmed tries to do likewise, but a stone slips under his foot, and he staggers and loses his balance. He recovers, but too late—the beast is on him, and, with a thrust of its paw, the envoy sends him sprawling ten paces away.

A cry escapes the lips of the witnesses. The guide is doomed!

Rendered furious by its wounds, the carnivore is beside the inanimate body of the Tekke. It sniffs him, and turns round, clicking its jaws. It is about to crush the unfortunate man.

Then Armand forgets the peril; he only thinks about saving the man who had unhesitatingly put himself at his service. He runs toward the grizzly.

The ferocious animal tries to turn on the new enemy but does not have time. The Parisian reaches it and plunges his long Tibetan knife into the weak spot on the animal's shoulder. A shock lifts up the carnivore's body, and hurls Lavarède several meters away.

As rapid as thought, the young man is on his feet and assuming a defensive stance. No need! His blow has been struck by a vigorous hand. The grizzly totters momentarily on its enormous feet, and then falls to the ground, which its claws labor frantically. It is dead.

The Tekke is not much better off. Blood is flowing from his lacerated shoulder. But the cart-driver is grateful, He offers to take the wounded man to his dwelling. The tent and its contents are piled into the vehicle, where Rachmed is installed, and the caravans draws away into the night, abandoning the cadaver of the bear, already hardened by the cold.

XXIII. The Kirghiz Amazons

Dagrar's house—Dagrar was the indigene's name—was located in the depths of a narrow valley. A low, square habitation, with a stable destined for the yaks, and a hangar for the cart: that was what Dagrar referred to pompously as his "farm." At least it provided shelter from the cold, and the primitive hearth, place beneath a round hole cut in the roof, warmed the hosts while smoking them.

Rachmed had recovered consciousness. The violence of the blow had stunned him, but his wound was not very grave in itself.

"A night's rest," he said, "and we'll set forth again tomorrow."

In addition, Lavarède's enlightened care was not found wanting.

The next day, they held council. What were they going to do? The Frenchman opined that they should push on to Beharsand, which their guest had indicated as close by.

"You've picked up the tracks of a warrior band," he said to the Tekke. "It's probable that Aurett's abductors live in the town. In this country, it's not customary—which is understandable—to go far from the community to which one belongs. It's necessary to look for her there."

Murlyton agreed with that opinion. Having interrogated Dagrar, they learned that Beharsand was three hours march away.

"The Kirghiz," he added, "treat strangers rather harshly, but you have nothing to fear from them today; they're celebrating the feast of the Amazons."

"Amazons!" exclaimed he voyagers, surprised.

"I thought the last ones were in Dahomey," said the journalist

"The tribe whose fortress is Beharsand claim, like several others that remain, to be descended from a Scythian nation of warrior women, skillful in the use of the bow and he spear. Legend says that in a very ancient war against people from the Occident they were almost all exterminated. A few escaped the massacre and fled eastwards, reaching the high plateaux of Chinese Turkestan, where we are. In memory of their ancestors, the Kirghiz women become absolute masters of the town for one day a year. They bear the arms of the warriors, who occupy themselves with the housework. You encountered me in the middle of the night because I was employed until yesterday evening in the preparations for the feast. Have no fear of witnessing it; it will interest you and you won't be in any danger."

Armand shook his head. "At any other time, we'd be happy to celebrate with the Kirghiz, but today we have a task to fulfill. We need to find my friend's daughter, abducted by unknown horsemen."

He pointed at the Englishman. A tear was rolling slowly down the latter's cheek.

"His daughter," Dagrar repeated, in a low voice. He seemed to be questioning himself.

"Do you know something?" Lavarède interrogated.

The man pursed his lips in a sign of doubt.

"Speak!"

"No, I might be mistaken—and then, Lamfara is a powerful chief who does not pardon any treason."

He looked around fearfully, as if the person whose name he had pronounced might be able to hear him. But the Frenchman was not about to be content with half an explanation. He seized Dagrar by the arm and in a curt, menacing tone that rendered Tekke's translation almost unnecessary, he said: "Listen. We saved your life; we have the right to take it—and I swear to God that I won't hesitate if you refuse to reply." Then, suddenly softening, he went on: "I'm making threats, and that's wrong. We're not asking for your help—what would be the point? Just tell us what you suspect. We'll leave—and your name will never emerge from our lips, even if we're captured and attached to the torture-stake."

Asiatics are clairvoyant. Dagrar understood that he could trust him, and did not hesitate. "I'll speak, then—but remember your promise. Has the one you're looking for got hair the color of mountain grass at the end of summer?"

"Yes."

"She doesn't know the language of the country?"

"No, Where did you see her?"

"As I came out of the town. In the plain, warriors had set up their tent around a large fire. I was astonished when a woman ran toward me saying words that I did not understand. Suddenly, Lamfara appeared in his turn, forced the woman back inside, and told me to go away. He was doubtless waiting for everyone in Behardsand to go to sleep before taking the prisoner to his dwelling."

Armand exchanged a scintillating glance with the gentleman.

"And who is Lamfara?"

"He commands a hundred warriors. He's rich, and possesses more than five hundred yaks. He's also knowledgeable, as much as our physicians. He was brought up far from here, beyond the great lakes, in the country of the White Father."

"In Russia," Rachmed added. "The Tsar is the White Father to all the peoples of Asia..."

Lavarède cut him off. He could no longer stand still. Equally impatient, Murlyton armed himself in haste. They scarcely left the Tekke time to tell Dagrar where the nacelle was hidden and the numerous objects that they had abandoned with it. That was the price of the service he had rendered.

After a rapid adieu, they set off for Beharsand. They went past the warm spring again. Large vultures had already torn the cadaver of the gray bear apart; after one night, nothing remained of a terrible carnivore but a skeleton from which a few bloody shreds were hanging.

243

No one stopped. They were all in haste to reach the Kirghiz town.

Finally, after having climbed a small ridge, they perceived the settlement in a round valley formed by modest hills.

Beharsand has between three and four thousand inhabitants, but in the icy steppes of central Asia it represents one of the more important centers of population.

The Englishman held Armand back.

"Are we going into the town?"

"Why not?"

"It seems to me that we'd be putting our heads in the wolf's mouth."

Lavarède laughed. "Yesterday, your fears would have been well-founded; tomorrow they will be again. Today is something else." As the gentleman opened his mouth he went on: "No need. The feast of the Amazons is beginning. Let's take advantage of it."

With that, the Parisian pulled away and headed toward the nearest houses. His companions were obliged to follow him. He only responded to their questions with monosyllables. Doubtless he had an idea, but the moment to express it had not yet come.

The distance that separated them from the walls diminished. The line of fortifications, punctuated by square towers, loomed up before them. The Frenchman went straight to a gate where women wearing helmets, with round bucklers dangling from their belts, were mounting guard.

"Those are solid matrons," the young man remarked. "But for their braided hair and a few other clues, one might take them for true warriors."

The female guards made as if to stop the voyagers but Rachmed, in response to a whisper from the journalist, asked for directions to the house of chief Lamfara. Immediately, the women sketched their most amiable smiles, opening the mouths that divided their flat faces with prominent cheekbones.

"You need to go through Ameiraikhan Square," one of them aid, "but you'll have to wait, because the Amazon assembly is meeting there at present."

Armand uttered a joyful exclamation. "The women's assembly? Run, my friends."

"But why?" hazarded Murlyton.

"Why? You obviously don't understand the advantages that might be obtained from the emancipation of women."

Griping Rachmed by the arm, the journalist drew him aside and spoke to him volubly. Out of breath, having difficulty keeping ten paces behind, Aurett's father could not grasp a word.

In the streets, the Kirghiz women were showing off majestically, escorted by their husbands, who were, for that day, laden down with all sorts of cumbersome objects, ranging from large Chinese mirrors to children too young to walk. The walkers looked curiously at the strangers, and the resumed their conversations.

Finally, Lavarède and his companions emerged into Ameiraikhan Square. A strange spectacle awaited them thee.

Sitting on blocks of stone arranged in circles, women swathed in furs were listening to one of their compatriots. Perched in a more elevated seat, the woman in question was speaking in a guttural voice that was hard on the ears. The others were nodding their heads gravely, taking little puffs from long-stemmed pipes covered with metallic decorations.

Casually interrupting the speaker, Lavarède went into the circle. A clamor of amazement immediately rose up. Rising to their feet menacingly, the Kirghiz seemed ready to hurl themselves on the intruder. In Amazon memory, no man had ever disturbed the "Patich"—a reproduction of the council of female chiefs in the mother tribe.

"My God! What are you doing?" cried the Englishman, catching up with the Parisian.

The latter, as calm as a lecturer in the Salle des Capucines, turned to Rachmed, and said, quietly: "Go ahead!"

Immediately, the interpreter began to harangue the audience in a language unknown to the gentleman. He was repeating the lesson that he had just heard from Lavarède.

"Ladies," he shouted, "if we have troubled the deliberations of your powerful ladyships, it is to inform you of a crime of custom-violation committed by the men of this town."

Murlyton did not understand the meaning of the words, but he observed that he assembly became attentive.

"Today," continued the Tekke, "every woman is free; none can be detained against her will."

"*Voi! Voi!*" replied numerous voices.

"They're saying yes," Rachmed whispered rapidly to Armand. Then, resuming the local dialect, he continued: "And yet, a young woman is a prisoner in Beharsand. This is her father and her fiancé. They are asking you for justice. You will accord it to them, you who have perpetuated the memory of your valiant ancestors through the centuries."

A frenzied hurrah made the atmosphere vibrate. The Amazons wanted to know where Aurett was being held.

"In the house of chief Lamfara," Rachmed replied.

"To Lamfara's house!"

At that cry, all the women quit the Patich and, forming a tight column, set forth toward the designated place.

"Where are they going?" asked the Englishman.

"To free your daughter, my dear Monsieur."

"What! Why?"

"Because we're taking advantage of circumstances; I'll explain later. For the moment, let's get Aurett back from her abductor and let's get out of here as fast as we can. Tomorrow won't be a lucky day for us."

At that moment, Aurett was very pensive. An immense sadness was weighing upon her.

She saw herself once again tied across Lamfara's saddle, carried away into the darkness by the furious gallop of the Turcoman charger; then the halt during the day, and, when night feel again, the recommencement of the infernal journey. And with a constriction in her heart, she had thought that every stride of her mount was taking her further away from her father and Armand.

For a moment she had hoped. Among the tents set up in the middle of the second night a cart had appeared. She had run toward its driver, seeking a defender in the unknown traveler, but then her master had loomed up in front of her. Abruptly, he had dragged her back to the tent where she was resting, and the sound of the cart had gradually faded away in the distance.

Later, perched on the horse again, her escort had taken her into a strange town with widely-spaced houses. She remembered having passed under a triumphal arch made of stone, bizarre in form. Then her mount had stopped in the middle of a courtyard. Invited to step down, the captive had been locked in a low-ceilinged room.

In her mind, her despair at being separated from her friends was combined with the dread of finding herself confronted by the man who was keeping her prisoner.

What did the man want? A menacing question! No young woman can answer it, but they all quiver before the question?

Aurett imagined the Asiatic warrior she had scarcely glimpsed marching toward her, his gaze harsh and his gesture menacing. Hiding her head in her hands, she wondered what attitude to take in the presence of that enemy.

A man's voice caused her to tremble. She looked up. Chief Lamfara was standing before her. He had changed his clothes. A tunic ornamented with embroideries, red leather boots and a khanjar passed through his belt indicated his desire to please.

Bowing respectfully, his hands crossed over his chest, the chief spoke. Soft and sonorous syllables flowed from his lips, but their meaning escaped the prisoner.

Lamfara perceived that. He fell silent momentarily, seemed to be searching, and then resumed speaking—in English.

The young woman started in surprise.

"You understand now," he said, smiling. "Fortunately, in the country of the White Father one is not only taught Russian but other European languages. Don't reply, Miss, before having heard what I have to say. Out there, as a student in Moscow, I learned beauty as your race understands it, When I returned here, the young women seemed to me to be lumpen and graceless—let's say the word: hideous. As a rich man, all of them coveted my hand, but I disdained them. Why? Because I remembered European women, with their grace, their intelligence and their tyranny."

With a slight scowl, Aurett indicated that it was all perfectly irrelevant to her. She was reassured, however; the Asiatic's attitude was not threatening.

"I'll get to the point," the latter went on. "I was hunting with a few of my followers when I perceived a balloon on fire. My companions thought it a fantastic apparition, but I had recognized an aerostat. *Europeans*, I thought. Curiosity gripped me, and I watched the descent. Following you, I slipped into the cave, and there..."

He interrupted himself momentarily, and then continued in a strangled voice: "There I saw you. In this country, where I must live in order to conserve the fortune and rank bequeathed to me by my ancestors, you were shown to me: the living image of my regrets. I spared your companions, contenting myself with removing the treasure that I desired."

He was becoming gradually more excited.

"I am a feared and respected chief," he went on. "I possess many yaks and immense plains. No charger can resist when my knees press its flanks, and my bullet has never missed its target. Become my wife, young woman, and everyone will bow down to you. No one will look Lamfara's wife in the face."

A somber fire was burning in the khan's eyes. That nomad, who had been living for years with a dream brought back from Europe, obtained a kind of inspiration from his mania.

Aurett's fears were reborn. This strange person with the bizarre impulses, this barbaric khan complicated by civilization, was disturbing.

After his hesitation, Lamfara resumed: "Don't make a decision yet, I beg you. I know that your compatriots don't like to be constrained. I can wait!"

With those words, he went out.

Left alone, Aurett dissolved in tears. Beneath the apparent gentleness of the Kirghiz, she had sensed his implacable will.

How could she resist it? Alas, lost in the heart of the Asiatic massif, separated from her companions, who would never be able to pick up her trail, was she condemned to end her days in Beharsand?

How many mad projects presented themselves to her mind? How many desperate resolutions, which she abandoned one by one?

Suddenly, she heard a confused din outside. Curiously, the young woman ran to the window, opened it and looked out.

In the courtyard, chief Lamfara as arguing with a hundred women, in the midst of whom were Murlyton, Lavarède and Rachmed.

"Monsieur Armand!" Aurett shouted. "Save me!"

A great clamor responded to that appeal. The Englishman saw the chief make a gesture of rage, and the entire crowd was engulfed in the house.

A moment later, she was free. She was walking between her father and the young man, with an illumination of joy in her eyes.

"What's happening?" she asked.

"Later, later," Lavarède said, urgently. "We need to get out of this town. At midnight, nothing can keep us any longer from Lamfara's claws."

Following his advice, and through the intermediary of Rachmed, she asked the women of the Patich for permission to continue her journey. The latter, delighted to see the departure of the foreigner who had caused the insensitive heart of the rich Lamfara to beat faster, did not offer any resistance to her plea. They even put a small troop of yaks and food supplies at her disposal. They added, not without astonishment, in response to a request from the Englishwoman—made at Lavarède's request—an enormous sack full of all the shards of pottery, crockery and glassware they could find.

"Why load our animals with that unnecessary burden?" the gentleman asked Lavarède.

"Unnecessary, I grant you—but I think, personally, that it will render us a great service."

"What?"

"You'll see."

Escorted by the Amazons, the voyagers left Beharsand perched on four vigorous yaks.

Lamfara was following them at a distance. When they took their leave of the Kirghiz women, the khan made a sign to one of his servants, and said, curtly: "Don't lose sight of them As soon as this damned festival is over, I'll leave with my horsemen, and by Tamerlane, the European rose will belong to me!"

The man bowed, and, at an athletic pace, launched himself in pursuit of Aurett.

Meanwhile, Lavarède urged his companions on.

"Let's push our mounts, my dear friends; we won't be safe until we reach those mountains you can see to the west."

"What danger do you fear?" asked Murlyton, absorbed in the contemplation of his daughter.

"Almost none. Chief Lamfara, bound at this moment by a custom that I think admirable, for it has been useful to us, will no longer be bound once this evening is over. He will doubtless want to recover the treasure that we've stolen from him."

The Englishwoman's face expressed terror. Armand perceived it.

"Don't worry—he won't succeed, for by nightfall we'll have crossed the plain where the advantage is necessarily to numbers."

And all of them, whipping their mounts, hastened their pace in the direction indicated by the Frenchman.

XXIV. From Tarim to the Amu Darya

At dusk, the fugitives reached the first foothills of the great barrier that closes the plain of Beharsand to the west.

Murlyton proposed a halt. The yaks were showing signs of fatigue; their muscular legs had lost their energy. But the Parisian would not hear of it.

"Higher up!" he replied. "We need to be higher; we'll be attacked at daybreak."

And with his Tibetan kama he pricked the animals' rumps; the pain rendered them a temporary vigor. Finally, the overworked beasts lay down on a narrow plateau, at the entrance to a gorge,

"Perfect," said Lavarède. "Here we have the advantage of the terrain. Let's eat, and sleep.

He was obeyed. Such was the general lassitude that anxiety did not keep anyone awake under the fur tents.

The next day, as soon as the sun's red disk showed on the horizon, Armand got up and headed for the edge of the plateau. Beneath him, however, a veil of shadow still covered the plain, which the sun's oblique rays had not yet reached.

The cold was penetrating. The young man started walking back and forth to warm himself up.

For about half an hour he practiced that exercise, turning frequently toward Beharsand. Continuing its ascent toward the zenith, the sun launched its golden rays into the valleys, chasing away the darkness from its last retreats. The plain became visible. The journalist's eyes ran over the arid surface, speckled with dazzling patches of snow, and his gaze suddenly became fixed.

In the distance, in the mist, something was moving, advancing rapidly. It had no precise form, but Armand was under no illusion. He ran to the tents and woke the sleepers.

"Get ready! They're coming!"

In an instant, his companions were on their feet, the yaks were loaded and they set off along the gorge.

It was a narrow passage, a fissure in the granite caused by some geological crisis. Sometimes, the beasts of burden had just enough room to slide between the sheer walls.

The ground sloped upwards steeply.

At a bend in the path, the gorge became a ledge running along a perpendicular cliff overlooking an abyss.

"This is a good place," Lavarède murmured, with a smile. Addressing Rachmed, he said: "Hand me the sack with the broken crockery, please."

The guide passed it to him, and the Parisian emptied it methodically, in such a way as to cover ten meters of terrain with the heterogeneous fragments it contained.

"What does this ceremony signify?" asked the Englishman, who had followed the operation with surprise.

"You'll see in a little while—for now, let's get moving. Lamfara's warriors will be here in a quarter of an hour."

Indeed, the distant gallop of horses was audible to the voyagers. They set off on the march again. The path, obedient to the caprices of the rock, wound on sinuously. The little troop reached a point where it overlooked the place where they had paused. Armand raised his hand.

"Let's stop!"

"What about the Kirghiz?"

"They won't get as far as this. Look down—you'll laugh."

The enemy horsemen started along the ledge. Lamfara was in the lead. He perceived the Europeans and pointed them out to his men. A howl of triumph caused the echoes of the mountains to rumble. Aurett had gone as pale as wax.

"Have no fear," said Armand, again. "They won't get through."

With an unusual temerity, the horsemen maintained their mounts at a trot.

Suddenly, the horses stopped, producing a jam. Two animals lost their footing and tumbled down the slope, dragging their riders with them.

Lamfara, immobilized like his soldiers, was agitating furiously in his saddle, urging his horse on. It was wasted effort; the animal seemed petrified. Lavarède burst out laughing.

"You see. That's a memory of my military career. To stop cavalry, strew the ground with broken bottles. When going through a village, throw all the chairs into the street and not one horse will pass. In Africa, the zouaves obtain the same result with lead pellets cut into four."

While speaking he was loading his riddle.

"It's not enough to stop the enemy moving forward; it's necessary to oblige him to beat a retreat."

He fired. A man fell. Murlyton and Rachmed grabbed their rifles and, for a few minutes, a hail of bullets rained down on the Kirghiz band. Already demoralized by the abrupt halt of the horses, the cause of which escaped them, the warriors turned back, leaving a dozen dead on the ground.

Only the chief remained. Abandoned by his men, he did not want to give up. Leaping from his horse, he started scaling the slope on foot.

They all looked at him with a vague sadness. A courageous man marching toward death stirs even those who are about to strike him. Armand had placed himself in front of the young woman, shielding her with his body.

Fifty paces away, Lamfara raised his weapon and took careful aim. The Parisian hastened to do likewise. The two detonations were confused, and the Kirghiz, extending his arms, fell to his knees. With an abrupt effort, however, he got up again, sketched a kind of gesture of farewell with his arm, and fell backwards into the void.

While his body rolled down, rebounding from rock to rock, the voyagers instinctively put their hands to their hats, to render homage to a brave man.

"A fine death," murmured Murlyton, "but completely futile. That Asiatic wasn't a practical man."

With that very English funeral oration, the little troop continued its climb.

By nightfall, they had reached the summit of the mountain, and Lavarède, with satisfaction, pointed out to his friends the sacred formula of the Buddhists, engraved on a block of granite:

Om mane padme hum.

"That," he said, is as good as a signpost. It tells me that we're in the massif of the Celestial mountains, where those words, which a million of the faithful repeat every day, are carved into the rock an incalculable number of times. A brotherhood of lamas exists that has no other function than to cover the summits with it."

Not far from here, the voyagers discovered an *obos*, or mass of commemorative stones, which the people of the region, in the same way as the ancient Gauls and the Arabs, erect in certain places that it is important to recognize.

Everyone ate heartily. The next day, they came down the opposite slope from the heights, where they supposed that a less desolate landscape doubtless awaited them.

That hope was to be disappointed. For several weeks they wandered over a high plateau, having nothing to drink by melted ice, and nothing combustible except argol—which is to say, yak-droppings.

With great difficulty, they covered a few kilometers; then they were obliged to stop, exhausted by mountain sickness. Their legs weary and dolorous, their respiration halting, they slid when evening came into their tents and fell into a heavy slumber, from which they emerged even more fatigued. And always, the same landscape extended before them, of rocky masses and peaks, separated by frozen pools: a landscape so constantly similar that it was almost impossible to march in a given direction.

They all bore those ordeals courageously, which Rachmed's experience alleviated slightly. But Aurett, weaker had her companions, was deteriorating visibly. Her cheeks were hollow; her bruised feet would only carry her at the cost of sharp suffering. It was easy to see that, before long, she would be unable to continue the journey.

When the sun's radiance warmed the atmosphere, the young woman was hoisted on to one of the yaks, but those bright periods were rare. At any other time, by virtue of the rigorous cold that was rife, that immobility would have been fatal to her.

Armand went the extraordinary lengths, scouting the route, encouraging his friends, finding tender words to comfort the Englishwoman. She thanked him with a smile, but discouragement was slowly undermining her, and she became depressed.

The young woman found the permanent solitude oppressive. She was afraid of never getting out of that frightful country. And as if the voyagers' situation were not critical enough, a misfortune greater than all the rest fell upon them.

One evening, in a narrow valley sheltered from the glacial west wind, they set up the tents. The yaks, still laden, were a few paces away. Suddenly, bellowing madly, the animals suddenly took fright and fled at a gallop, climbing the slope of the ravine, and disappeared. In their panic, they carried away their masters' food provisions and ammunition.

Murlyton wanted to set off in pursuit, but Rachmed stopped him.

"You'll get lost," he said, "and a man lost in the darkness is a dead man. He must walk incessantly. If he stops, numbness nails him to the spot, his eyes close in spite of his efforts, and he goes to sleep, never to wake up."

"What are we going to do, then?"

"We won't eat. Tomorrow, we'll set out in search of our animals."

Although their stomachs were crying famine, it was necessary to yield to that reasoning. They all understood the danger of a nocturnal search in thirty degrees of frost. They lay down in a bad mood.

In the morning they set out hunting—but in vain. The searched the vicinity, but found no trace of the yaks anywhere. Under the influence of terror, such animals sometimes cover enormous distances. They must have been far away already.

Heads bowed, the voyagers returned to their camp. The argol collected on the way permitted them to light a fire around which they gathered, in melancholy fashion. They needed it. Deprived of nourishment for twenty-four hours, they were suffering doubly from the rigors of the temperature.

They remained facing the flame, immobile, their eyes vague, sunk in painful reflections. Very pale, and gripped by fever, Aurett seemed to forget the presence of her friends. Occasionally, her teeth chattered. Gradually, her eyes became anxious and red patches appeared on his cheeks.

Next to her, Murlyton and Lavarède, gazing at her, sensed with an inexpressible apprehension that a malady against which they had no armaments was taking hold. Already weakened by the difficult journey, the young woman had no strength left to resist privations. That evening, her companions had to carry her to her tent; her legs buckled beneath her. Even the men were conscious of their diminished energy.

"If this goes on for another day, none of us will see Europe again."

It was the gentleman who pronounced those discouraged words. Armand had a fit of anger. He reproached the Englishman for throwing in the towel. Why let himself go like that when critical circumstances demanded the collaboration of all their determination? But his vehement voice did not trouble his interlocutor.

With the phlegm that never left him, the latter contented himself with replying: "My dear Monsieur, we had nothing to eat yesterday, and no more today. I can feel ice in the marrow of my bones. In six, eight or ten hours, fever will lay me down beside my daughter, and it will be all over. If I'm experiencing any chagrin because of that, believe me, it's uniquely for her, poor child!"

The two men furtively wiped away a tear. Shaking off that instant of weakness, however, Lavarède said: "There's no cause for despair. Those stupid beasts have carried off our provisions, but we have our weapons."

"Only your rifle is loaded, Monsieur Lavarède, and it will be as useless as ours. What is there to hunt here? Crows forever out of range, wolves that will remain invisible until hunger has reduced us to impotence, and the occasional wild yak that a gunshot wouldn't bring down."

The sound of a voice became audible in the tent occupied by Aurett. Armand ran to it, followed by the Englishman. The young woman was talking.

Sitting up, having pushed away the garments with which her father had covered her, she was pointing at a point in empty space. Her rigid being was reaching out toward the place that her imagination was evoking.

"There…water…magnificent fruits. It's warm…another of those exquisite pears…"

"Delirium," murmured the Frenchman, dispiritedly.

Abruptly, he went out, picked up his rifle and approached Rachmed. "How many hours' fuel do you still have?"

"Until daybreak."

"Good. In that case, transport the fire to one of those high rocks that overlook the valley. I'll make arrangements not to lose sight of it."

"You're going out in the dark?"

"Yes. The wolves must be hungry too, and perhaps, by night, they'll dare to attack a lone man."

"That's madness."

"Possibly, but I also have a chance of bringing back other meat. Then again, is it wisdom to wait here until hunger and the cold have finished their work?"

The Tekke made a movement. "I'll come with you."

"No. Stay and guard the fire. Our companion is watching over his daughter."

And, having shaken the guide's hand, Armand plunged into the darkness. A few minutes later, at the top of a rocky spire, a bright flame lit up. The Tekke was illuminating the hunter's path.

The night was long. The gentleman knelt beside Aurett, following the progress of the illness with increasing anguish. The young woman no longer recognized him. Plunged into a comatose state, she only emerged from it during brief fits of delirium, but her strength as visibly running out. The crises became brief-er and less frequent. The sources of life were gradually drying up. Murlyton heaped up the covers in vain; the young woman's temperature went down. Death was extending its fleshless hand toward her.

At daybreak, Lavarède came back without having fired the single bullet that remained to him. No living being had come within range. Two kilometers away, the Frenchman had encountered a frozen stream with sheer banks. Stunted poplars grew along the banks. For a moment he had hoped. A group of wild yaks had shown themselves on the far bank, but the animals must have caught the man's scent, because they fled precipitately.

"Ah!" he said to Rachmed. "If I'd been able to bring down one of those beasts we'd have been saved thereafter."

The Take interrogated him with his gaze.

"Yes," Armand went on. A stream necessarily descends toward a plain. Provided with nourishment, we'd have been able to assemble a kind of raft with the wood of the poplars—or rather a sled—and abandon ourselves to the slope in order to get out of this frightful mountainous desert."

The guide stood up, his eyes shining. "It's a dangerous means, it's true, but what does it matter? Why not try it?"

"Oh, it's her that I would have liked to save."

Pensively, he went to Aurett's tent. He told the gentleman about the failure of his endeavor. The latter shrugged his shoulders and pointed to his daughter. A livid pallor covered the cheeks of the dying woman; her lowered eyelids had taken on a bluish tint; a halting breath was escaping from nostrils that were al-ready pinched.

But as they stood there, no longer able to find words, distressed by the idea of the inevitable, fatal denouement, a strange noise resounded outside.

Grave and sonorous, one might have thought it the call of a trumpet.

With one bound, Armand emerged from the tent. He bumped into Rachmed.

"That's the cry of a yak, isn't it?"

"Yes."

"Where is it?"

The guide extended his hand westwards. "Over there. It might be possible to take the animal by surprise."

With infinite precaution, the two men climbed the slope. At the top, the Tekke lay down, in such a way that only his head protruded over the crest of the escarpment.

The Parisian did the same.

A shudder ran through the bodies of the hunters. Fifty meters away, five yaks were grouped. One slightly part from the others—an adult, recognizable by its thick mane—was mounting guard.

"Aim well," said Rachmed. "All our lives depend on your rifle-shot."

Lavarède was well aware of that. Emotion caused his hand to tremble. He had to start gain twice over to line up the shot. Stiffening himself, he succeeded in quieting his nerves, taking slow aim at the isolated yak.

The detonation burst forth, resonating like a thunderclap in the echoes of the mountain. In the smoke, the hunters had leapt over the crest of the ridge.

The cattle ran off, bellowing madly, leaving behind their sentinel, which was exhausting itself in vain efforts to follow them.

"It has a broken leg!" the Tekke howled. "Daggers drawn! It's ours!"

Like wild beasts, both of them ran after the wounded animal. The latter, understanding the impossibility of flight, turned to face its adversaries, presenting its menacing horns to them. In the thick fleece that covered its head, its eyes were shining with bloody gleams.

"Be careful," said Rachmed. "You take the right flank; I'll take the left."

While running, the Frenchman carried out the required movement, and the yak, unable to defend itself, soon fell to the ground with a bellow of agony.

The Tekke lay down on top of it and, applying his lips to one of its wounds, avidly drank the blood that was escaping from it.

Armand shoved him away brusquely. "Think about the one who might die if we waste time!"

"Forgive me," said the ashamed guide. "I was so hungry!"

In a moment, the heavy cadaver was skinned. After having charged his companion with butchering the flesh of their prey, Lavarède, carrying the hide that was still warm, ran to Aurett's tent. Shoving the bewildered gentleman aside, he threw off the invalid's covers.

"What are you doing?" cried the Englishman.

"I'm saving her. Help me."

Feverishly, he stripped the young woman of her clothing, laying bare her virginal breasts.

"But that's not decent," hazarded Murlyton.

"Would you rather she died?"

And with that brutal reply he concluded his operation. After which he rolled Aurett up in the bloody and warm yak-hide, and lay her down again gently. Then he turned to the Englishman.

"It's a method of reanimating people struck down by cold. I've seen it when I was studying medicine. I remembered it just now, when I perceived the yak, and I've applied it. A little nourishment, now, and I'll answer for our companion."

He was right. That evening, reanimated by a few spoonfuls of meat juice, the young woman smiled at her savior. The fever had disappeared. The blood was running more warmly in her veins. She chatted, already making plans for the future. They would construct the raft imagined by the Frenchman; they would descend the course of the solidified river. Monsieur Lavarède would win his bet, and then..."

There she stopped abruptly. Her eyelids fluttered. She had been on the point of saying everything that she was thinking, of talking about her marriage, the delightful goal of her voyage around the world, during which she had learned to love.

Armand held out his hand; she put hers into it, closed her eyes and went quietly to sleep in the great silence of the desert. Even in sleep, with an unconscious grip, she kept her friend close to her.

Early the next morning the voyagers were able to transport their camp to the bank of the watercourse discovered by the Parisian, and they immediately set to work. Felling the poplars was difficult. They had to saw them with their Tibetan daggers, the only trenchant instruments they had.

Fortunately, the trees, filled internally with an inconsistent sapwood, did not put up an enormous resistance to the bite of the steel. It nevertheless took them no less than a week to establish a board six meters long and four wide.

The yak-skin, cut up into slender thongs, had permitted them to assemble the pieces of wood.

Long poles foxed to either side of the singular vehicle would propel it over the ice and serve to steer it.

Finally, the raft was, as Aurett put it, "set afloat," with the old tents and the new provisions solidly moored to its surface. Everyone took their places on board. The journalist and Rachmed took charge of maneuvering the directive poles.

And the descent commenced. Slow at first on a gradual slope, it soon accelerated in a series of rapids.

The improvised sled flew like an arrow between the steep banks, and the conductors had all the difficulty in the world avoiding the rocks protruding through the frozen surface, which would have shattered the apparatus like glass.

In the evening, taking advantage of a gentler slope, the friends pushed the wooden board to the bank and moored it there. The landscape was already less bare. The silhouettes of trees were profiled against the sky. For all of them, it was a joy to see black branches denuded of leaves. The vegetal replacing the stony was spring succeeding winter. Lavarède even adapted the old saying: "Trees, therefore humans." The sentence brought a smile to all faces.

"Would it give you pleasure to see people?" the journalist continued. "That's the solitary influenced of the desert. In cities, one only thinks about avoiding them. The desert, well applied, would suppress courts and tribunals, you see; it would it would be sufficient to have one law, thus conceived: *All peevish individuals will be condemned to a month on the high plateaux.* It would be the triumph of universal benevolence."

The young man had recovered all his gaiety, and even the Englishman applauded his witticism.

For two days the voyage continued without any other incident than the necessity of dragging the raft from time to time, by virtue of the temporary insufficiency of the slope. During the last few hours they had been moving between banks covered by forests. At night the thermometer only marked fifteen or sixteen degrees below zero, and Aurett joked about it, affirming that she was suffering from the heat.

The raft was still in good condition, the yak-skin thongs holding up marvelously.

That morning, Lavarède affirmed that the day would not pass without them encountering some habitation. In consequence, they set off cheerfully. The moderate speed of the vehicle followed the gentle slope of the icy surface. Obviously, he voyagers were nearing the foot of the mountain

Toward eleven o'clock, however, one last stretch of rapids presented itself. They engaged upon it fearlessly. As far as the eyes could see, the broadening river presented a smooth surface. The raft, like a warmed-up horse, glided faster and faster, without a shock or a jolt. The passengers were only aware of the rapidity of their course by virtue of the wind that was whipping them violently and the hectic gallop of the banks, fleeing in an inverse direction.

Suddenly, Lavarède uttered a hoarse exclamation. All eyes went toward him. His hand extended toward the horizon. His friends looked, and their hearts skipped a beat.

A neat line cut across the entire width of the river, and in the distance, much lower down, they received the road of ice continuing.

"A waterfall!" murmured Murlyton.

Crouching down on the planks, Armand and the guide dragged the directive poles in order to try to steer toward the bank, but scarcely had they seized them than there was a cracking sound. Under the formidable pressure of the slope, they had snapped.

The sled experienced a shock, oscillated briefly, and then pursued its rapid course, like a train under full steam.

The catastrophe was about to occur; nothing could prevent it. The frail raft and its crew would be precipitate into space and smashed to smithereens. Eyes dilated with fear, they all watched the line barring the river, which, by virtue of an optical illusion, seemed to be rushing toward them at top speed.

The distance diminished. As if intoxicated by the crazy velocity, carried away by the dream that was leading them to the abyss, the voyagers were no longer speaking, or even thinking.

Armand's voice rose up once more: "Hang on to the raft!"

Two hundred meters remained to cross. It took two seconds. The sled reached the waterfall, overshot it, and, describing a long curve, fell into the void. Their hands clinging to the poplar trunks, they all closed their eyes, expecting death.

Instead of the terrible impact they feared, however, they felt a relatively sight shock, while a warm rain fell upon them.

They looked around with fearful eyes.

The raft was floating on a small lake of open water.

"What does this mean?" asked the gentleman, recovering the use of his voice.

It was Lavarède who replied. "A warm spring maintains a basin here, which doesn't freeze.

Indeed, a jet of water as broad as a human torso sprang forth from the rock in the midst of dense vapors.

As the Frenchman's friends pulled themselves together, cries rang out from the bank. Two men who had emerged from a hut crudely built from unstripped tree-trunks were hailing the voyagers. They were hunters, brave men who spent the greater part of the year in this remote country. The hut was their general headquarters.

They had chosen that location because of the vicinity of the hot spring, which maintained a mild warmth within a radius of fifty meters. In the heart of winter, those cenobites could harvest vegetables! They celebrated the arrival of the voyagers, who, through the intermediary of Rachmed, learned that they were in the land of Wakan, or Oakand, and that "their" river was the Oxus of the ancients, now the Amu Darya.

Lavarède summoned his erudition—quite forgotten during recent weeks—to his aid. "The Oxus," he said, once traversed Lake Aral and emptied into the Caspian; since then its bed has filled in between those two expanses of water, and it ends at the lake.

Murlyton declared, like a good Englishman, that he liked the river a lot. "It's a pity that it flows through Russian territory," he affirmed.

After an excellent night sent in the wooden house, the passengers on the raft aid goodbye to their hosts.

"We know where we are," said Aurett, "but do we know where we're going?"

"To Chardzhou," replied the journalist, with a smile.

"Do you know the way there?"

"The road will carry us there of its own accord; it's the river. It appears that it's about thirty leagues away; the Amu Darya ought to be free of ice. Fortunately, we have an amphibious craft that can take us to the Sarte town of Chardzhou."

"What sort of a town is it?"

"It's a station on the Transcaspian railway, established by the Russian general Annenkov[54] between the Caspian and Samarkand. Thank me—I'm taking you back to civilized countries; it will be more comfortable for you than for

---

[54] Mikhail Annenkov (1835-1899).

me…civilization doesn't approve of people traveling gratis, as in barbaric countries!"

"Pooh!" murmured the young woman. "After what you've done, reaching Paris is a trivial matter."

"I don't share your opinion. Back there the voyage was more dangerous; in future, it will become more difficult."

Meanwhile, the raft had been drawn on to the ice, and they were leaving the hospitable hunters behind. The country was populated; from time to time, a cabin appeared. In the evening, they arrived at the extremity of the ice-sheet. Beyond that point, the muddy river, already two kilometers wide, ran between low banks.

After a few days of rather monotonous navigation, Armand drew the attention of his friends to a dark band running over the surface of the water. "The Transcaspian," he said—and there, on the left bank, the town of Chardzhou." When the gentleman expressed a doubt, he added: "I recognize Annenkov's wooden bridge, which carries the Samarkand trains for four kilometers."

"You've been here before," said Aurett.

"Yes, in an armchair."

"What do you mean?"

"That I've read the book illustrated by my friend Napoléon Ney, *De Paris à Samarcande*,[55] and I'm discovering here the 'original' of his drawings."

An hour later, the raft landed a little upriver of the wooden bridge, a masterpiece of audacity and patience, completed in six years by the first battalion of the Russian Railways.

"We'll go to the station," said Armand.

"Do you know the way?"

"Nothing easier." Accosting a passing Sarte he said to him, in an interrogative tone: "*Vodza?*"

The man replied in incomprehensible words, but his gestures were clear. It was necessary to turn left, and then right.

"You haven't mentioned that you can speak Russian," said the young woman, smiling.

"I only know that one word, *Vodza*, again from my friend's book. I remembered it at the right time, didn't I?"

Rachmed intervened. "I'm definitely going to leave you here, since you're heading toward the Occident, all the way to the lands that touch the sea; your land, my valiant master…but in Chardzhou, I can still be of service to you. I understand and speak the language of our Slav brothers. As they not a little Asiatic, like us?

---

[55] Napoléon Paul Ney (1849-1900) published an account of his journey to Samarkand in 1888 as *En Asie centrale à la vapeur*.

"Thank you, my brave Rachmed, son of Iskander. I'm beginning to believe that the legend is true, and that you have the blood of Alexander the Great in your veins, for you have been, in these days of peril, as courageous as skillful. Thank you for your offer to continue to be useful to us, but I'm quite tranquil now—the stationmaster is bound to speak French."

"What makes you so sure?" asked Murlyton.

"He's certain to be a Russian officer, belonging to the Railway battalion..."

XXV. The Transcaspian

Lavarède was not mistaken. Lieutenant Mikhail Karine, the stationmaster of Chardzhou, spoke French. Brought up to date with the adventures of the voyagers he said: "I thank you for the pleasant hour you've helped me pass. Can I be agreeable or useful to you in my turn?"

"Oh, yes," replied the journalist, frankly, "and I'll even confess that I'm very much hoping for your collaboration."

"Speak."

"You know now that I need to get back to Europe, still without opening my purse."

"Understood. As far as Uzun-Ada, the terminus of the line on the Caspian, nothing is easier. My brother is rejoining his regiment in the Caucasus, and if it wouldn't displease you to travel with a Russian officer...?"

"I'm a reserve officer in the French army, which is equivalent."

The lieutenant bowed. "In addition, I can give you a letter for Monsieur Djevol, the director of the Caucasus Mercury Navigation Company, who will be able to furnish you with the means to reach Baku on the other side of 'our sea.' There my influence ceases."

The two men shook hands.

"And now," said Karine, "since you're not leaving until tomorrow, do me the honor of having lunch and dinner with me, and we'll drink to France."

"And to Russia."

Murlyton declined the invitation. It was repugnant to him, as a British subject, to profit from the Franco-Russian entente. Until seven o'clock the following morning, when the train departed for Uzun-Ada, he would take lodgings in the town for himself and his daughter.

"Oh, by the way," asked the Parisian, "I lost track of time weeks ago—what's the date?"

"The twenty-seventh of January on the Russian calendar—which is to say, the eighth of February on yours."

"So I still have nearly two months to get back to Paris."

"More than enough time."

Lavarède shook his head. "Crossing Europe might be more difficult than all the rest."

As he got up to take his leave, the gentleman knocked a few papers placed on the stationmaster's desk on to the floor. Armand picked them up and started in surprise.

"Why, you have German correspondence!" He indicated a sheet of paper covered in Gothic characters.

The lieutenant shrugged. "A note from the Austrian police."

"Ah! Some malefactor on the run."

"I don't know. Like all good Slavs I have a horror of everything German and I don't speak that language." Laughing, he added: "It's what you would call chauvinism."

"In France, we learn it now—also for reasons of chauvinism. Permit me to translate the document for you."

In response to an acquiescent nod, Armand read aloud:

"Rosenstein, Fritz, born in Berlin, Prussia, manager in Trieste of the branch of the Cisleithanische Bank of Vienna. Absconded with five hundred thousand florins of his clients' money. Height, medium; eyes, hair and eyebrows brown; forehead, high; nose, straight; mouth, average; chin, round. Lived for a long time in Paris and Rome. Speaks French and Italian correctly. Will doubtless profit from that advantage to dissimulate his nationality. Last seen in Odessa."

The Parisian finished with a vague smile on his lips. He replaced the piece of paper on the table. "At Odessa on the Black Sea," he said, pensively. "This Rosenstein is capable of following the route to the Caucasus and falling into your hands some day."

"We'll receive him as he merits," Karine replied. "Let's go have lunch."

While Murlyton dew away with Aurett, the stationmaster took his guest to his apartment. The national caviar was celebrated. Amicable toasts were exchanged, and then the lieutenant had to resume his duties. He asked the journalist to be on time for dinner and left him free to visit the town.

It was not a long visit: no monuments, and very simple habitations. The only curiosities are Annenkov's wooden bridge and the little settlement of Amu Darya, founded by the Russians a few kilometers from Chardzhou. The bazaar of that embryonic town already has twenty-four shops in which objects manufactured in Europe can be bought.

In the evening, Lavarède was introduced to his traveling companion, Captain Constantin Karine. The latter was serving in the regiment of dragoons of Ninji-Novgorod, garrisoned at Tiflis, the lieutenant-colonel of which was a French prince, Louis-Napoléon Bonaparte, now a colonel in Warsaw. By the time dinner was over, Lavarède and the captain were the best of friends.

The station-master put a room at the Frenchman's disposition, and the latter, for the first time, lay down on a bed, primitive, to be sure, but far superior to the rocks of the high plateaux.

At six o'clock in the morning, Armand was on the quay. A violent wind was blowing from the north, and the Frenchman was huddled in a warm vicuna-pelt that he owed to the liberality of the Tibetans.[56]

"I'll complete my voyage," he said to the Russian, but it's annoying to return to Paris in this Buddhist uniform. I'll be accused of wanting to make a sen-

---

[56] Given that the vicuna is native to South America, it is not obvious how the Tibetans were able to make the gift in question.

sational entrance." He changed his tone. "In any case, we're not there yet. For the moment, Lieutenant Karine, I only want to express my gratitude to you. Please accept this souvenir of a guest who will be very happy if he can entertain you in Paris."

He handed the stationmaster his Tibetan knife, with a hilt made of horn, ornamented with curious silver incrustations. Mikhail sketched a gesture of refusal.

"I understand," said the Frenchman. "You think, as we do, that the gift of a knife severs friendship. Well, adopt our custom—give me a sou in exchange, and the bad luck will be averted." As his companions laughed, though, he slapped his forehead. "No, in fact, for you it will be dearer. The Chinese took my twenty-five centimes; you can return them to me. Give me seven kopecks, twenty-eight centimes. I'll augment my fortune."

The exchange was effected cordially. At the same moment, Murlyton and his daughter appeared on the platform.

They were, of course, unrecognizable. Aurett was wearing an elegant traveling costume over which a pelisse was thrown; she was wearing a delightful little hat in velvet and sable. As for the gentleman, his ample overcoat opened over a maroon suit in the most English fashion. He was holding a voluminous package in his hand.

Armand uttered an exclamation: "Ah! So, there are fashion shops in Chardzhou?"

"No," Aurett replied. "All this comes from the bazaar in Amu Darya. And in an impudent tone, she added: "We're very tired, Monsieur Lavarède—relieve my father of the parcel he's carrying for a moment."

The young man obeyed. Then the young Englishwoman laughed joyously. "You can keep it. Oh, Monsieur offers a demoiselle a yak-skin in the desert. A correct father can't tolerate that. He's returning it to you."

A slight blush rose to Armand's cheeks. "That's the second time you've renewed my wardrobe, Mr. Murlyton," he began.

"You've saved my life more often than that," Aurett interjected, "and I'm not complaining. Look, we still have ten minutes before the train arrives—you have time to resume a European appearance."

Mikhail Karine immediately took the journalist to his office, and when the train, puffing, steaming and whistling, made its entrance into the station, the Parisian, in his gray suit and his quilted overcoat, looked nothing like the dethroned god of Lhasa.

One last handshake for his Russian friend, and the Frenchman leapt into the compartment where his friends had already taken their seats. The train set off.

Merv, in the middle of its oasis irrigated by the Mourgah, the Tejenk River and Douchak passed before the voyagers' eyes.

Then the country became severe. Everywhere, on both sides of the track, there was the tawny sand of the desert. Sometimes imposing ruins extended over several kilometers, traces of the passage of the ancient Mongol conquerors: Tamerlane, Timur, Nadir.[57]

"One understands, on seeing that," said Captain Constantin, "How those mean acquired the title of the Scourge of Heaven. After them, nothing remained. Towns of three thousand inhabitants stood here, in the midst of a fertile land. They came, took the inhabitants away in captivity, and eviscerated the dykes containing the waters. Now, it's desert. Carnivores rest from their hunting in the ruins. The Mongols have killed life."

A few versts from Askabad, the train had to stop. A tempest had blocked the track with sand. Men of the second railway battalion, aided by Turkmen, were busy clearing it.

"Once," the Russian explained, "the service was provided by the first battalion, but as soon as the Transcaspian was finished, Annenkov took them with him to Siberia. He's working on the great line that will unite the Urals with Kamchatka."

The traffic was to be interrupted for more than two hours. Constantin Karine proposed to Lavarède that they get off.

The two officers who were supervising the work were delighted to learn that a Frenchman was there. The captain had some excellent cognac in his valise, and the opportunity to toast France and Russia was too good to miss. There were toasts.

One of the officers gave a rapid order to one of his Cossacks, who went out joyfully, dancing a national jig reminiscent of am Auvergnat *bourrée*, but heavier.

"What's happening?" asked Lavarède.

"A surprise, my dear Monsieur. You certainly know that exercises in equitation are in great honor among us, among our Kazakhs in particular; we're putting on a *djighitoffka*, to show you both sympathy and respect."[58]

Shortly thereafter, the twenty Cossacks of the *stanitza*, or military village, launched themselves from the depths of the train, standing on their mounts, leaning forwards. One threw his saber into the air and caught it in mid-air by the hilt, another whirled his rifle vertiginously and then, without taking aim, fired and hit his target. Several leapt to the ground and, without slowing down, leapt back

---

[57] Tamerlane and Timur are the same person, the former name being an adaptation of Timur the Lame. Nadir Shah, the ruler of Iran from 1736-47, idolized Genghis Khan and Timur, and saw himself as following in their footsteps as a military leader.

[58] There is an engraving of "Djighitoffka Cossacks" dating from the 1870s, used as an illustration in several travel books and nowadays available as a poster, which depicts a rider standing on his horse.

into the saddle; the most agile picked up their whip or their poniard, always at a triple gallop. The spectacle was as curious as it was satisfying, and Lavarède, enthused, clapped his hands at the exploits of the bold cavaliers.

When the performance had finished, a sergeant of the battalion came to announce that the track was passable again, and the train pulled away again. At nightfall they reached Askabad. For a moment the voyagers considered its animated streets, and the large camels with sleepy eyes circulating cautiously in the midst of the variegated crowd.

Then the landscape was drowned in darkness. At Heok-Tepe, Armand could not make out the Turcoman citadel whose walls were pierced by the two breaches crossed by Skobelev's French soldiers.

When daybreak came, the locomotive was once again speeding though the desert.

At one time, the train stopped. The Frenchman put his head out of the window and was astonished to find nothing before his eyes but an isba[59] painted bright blue and a sheet metal cistern.

"There's no station," Karine explained. It's a replenishment stop—the machine is taking on water, that's all.

"Where does the water come from?"

"From Uzun-Ada. There are trains that transport mobile cisterns to the points in the desert where it would otherwise be impossible to aliment the locomotives. The guardians of the posts also drink it."

"Poor fellows—how sad their existence must be in these solitudes," Aurett murmured.

Night had fallen again when, after having passed through the station at Makiailowsk, the voyagers reacted Uzun-Ada. The captain knew the town. He left the English duo at a hotel near the port, and then took the journalist to see Monsieur Djevoi, to whom the stationmaster had recommended him.

The director of the Caucasus-Mercury line gave the voyager the most cordial welcome. Brought up to date with the situation by Karine, he declared that the Frenchman would take passage on one of the ships due to depart the next day, and gave him a ticket giving him the right to travel and nourishment. Armand thanked him lavishly.

"Wait—you can thank me this evening," said Monsieur Djevoi.

"This evening?"

"Yes, after dinner, for I'm taking you out. I could keep you here, at my home, but that wouldn't give you the same pleasure."

"Long live Russia, in truth!" exclaimed Lavarède. "This hospitable country where everyone seems to be happy for me to travel without paying my fare!"

"We're doing what we can, but from Baku onwards, it probably won't be the same. Military in origin, the Caucasus line now has shareholders. The disci-

---

[59] A Russian log cabin.

265

pline there is very severe, and an agent convicted of a tolerance like the one from which you have benefited thus far would be running a great risk."

"Damn it!"

Darkened momentarily, Armand's expression was brightened by a smile. He shook his head as if to say: *We'll see.* Then he followed his new host.

The director of the Caucasus-Mercury was not wrong to affirm that the journalist would be obliged to him for dining in town. He took him to an establishment run by a Frenchman, who surpassed himself for his compatriot. After the international soup, a dinner in the French style was a feast to which the voyager did full honor.

Accommodated and fed by his amiable host, Armand waited patiently for the moment to embark. On the eleventh, he went aboard the *Feodorowna-Pablewna,* a steamer bound for Baku, where Murlyton and Aurett had already preceded him. Monsieur Djevoi supervised his installation personally, and only left him when the ship was ready to depart.

Although the season was advanced, the sky was clement and the crossing was exempt from unfortunate incidents. The Caspian, the Hyrkanian Sea that the alluvions of the Volga and the Ural will one day fill in, was as smooth as a mirror, and toward midday on the thirteenth of February, the *Feodorowna-Pablewna* entered Baku harbor.

Captain Constantin was obliged to say farewell to his friend. An order from his colonel had summoned him to Tiflis and he could not linger. Lavarède went with him to the station, hoping to encounter a stationmaster as amiable as Karine, but he perceived very quickly that what Monsieur Djevoi had told him was true. On the Caucasus line, no one traveled without paying his fare.

As the stationmaster, a civilian functionary, was making that painful confession, albeit courteously, the journalist noticed two men standing on the platform whose appearance struck him. Both were blond, with red faces framed by side-whiskers, and they seemed embarrassed by their Russian uniforms. They were not used to wearing them; that was evident in a certain stiffness of their movements.

The stationmaster followed the direction of the Frenchman's gaze.

"Do those individuals interest you?"

Armand was silent for a moment, but then said: "Yes; they're foreigners, doubtless German in origin."

"You've guessed correctly—they're Austrian policemen."

"Ah!" the journalist sat up straight. His eyes were shining with malice. Then his face contracted and he lowered his voice. "What are they doing here?"

The stationmaster had not missed a single one of his reactions, and his features expressed a vague suspicion. "They're on the lookout," he said, measuring his words carefully, his eyes riveted on Armand's, "for a certain Rosenstein, seen recently in Tiflis. A fellow who speaks French without an accent."

"Ah," murmured the voyager, with a perfectly-simulated shudder. "Thank you for the information. The railway is closed to me; I'll try to find another means of leaving the city." And he left rapidly.

On turning his head, however, he saw the stationmaster run to the policeman and speak to them animatedly while pointing at him.

Good, he thought. *For want of any other means, let's go with the Austrian police. The other day I was honored with a djighitoffka; perhaps today I'll be honored with handcuffs.*

A second glance assured him that the little impromptu comedy he had played for the stationmaster had borne fruit. The agents followed him, affecting indifference.

While carefully avoiding losing the Austrian sleuths he put on an appearance of trying to do so. He went around a block of houses, dodged into a side-street, doubled back—in a word, behaved like a criminal tracked by the bloodhounds of the authority.

The trick had the desired effect. The policemen, suspicious by nature, passed from suspicion to conviction. The man that had interrogated the stationmaster about them, who seemed embarrassed by their presence, must be the banker Rosenstein. And their faces broadened. They were thinking about the reward they would collect.

The shorter of the two, Herr Schultze, represented intelligence in the association. The taller one, Herr Muller, incarnated brute force.

They were still hesitant however. The fear of an error prevented them from taking hold of Armand. The later understood their scruples.

They need to acquire certainty, he thought.

He went to the hotel where the English duo were staying and proposed an excursion about the town. While his friends were getting ready, however, he took a piece of paper on which he traced a few rapid words. Then he folded it up carefully and slipped it into his pocket.

As he left the hotel he observed that the two detectives were stationed on either side of the street.

"My dear friends," he said to the English duo, "I'm going to take you to visit the oil wells of Baku, which, together with the wells of Pittsburgh in Pennsylvania, furnish two-thirds of the naphtha oil consumed on the globe. I'm in a hurry, because I might be leaving the city in a matter of hours."

Interrupting the question that was on his friends lips, he said: "By the way, a request: whatever happens, you don't know me; you met me in the harbor, and that's all. I have an opportunity you wouldn't want me to miss."

"Certainly not," said Murlyton, with the most entire good faith, "but aren't you going to tell us what it is?"

"There's no need—the drama will unfold before your eyes."

Passing close to the Zoroastrian temple of Balakani, a celebrated place of pilgrimage for the Persian fire-worshipers, the voyagers reached the oilfield. The vast sand plain, from which an acrid odor emerges, is dotted with wooden scaffolds twenty-five meters high, similar to those that stand above our mine-shafts in coalfields. The *vishas* support the drilling apparatus above the reservoirs where naphtha accumulates by infiltration.

As Lavarède was talking, without losing sight of the policemen who were still following him, he suddenly stopped. Twenty paces away a man was making a speech, with grand gestures, while a group of individuals whose costume revealed them to be minor functionaries were listening respectfully.

The orator turned round at the same moment and, quitting his audience abruptly, came toward the Parisian.

"I've caught up with you at last, Monsieur Lavarède."

The journalist remained silent. Bouvreuil, glimpsed for the last time on the flaming roof of the pagoda of Lhasa, was standing before him in the flesh and bone.

Taking advantage of his interlocutor's amazement, the landlord struck an arrogant pose, and continued: "You're surprised to find me here. It's quite simple. While you were drawing away from Lhasa to the north, I fled southwards, in the costume of a lama snatched from the flames. Custom was my salvation. It gave me the right to the veneration and the table of the natives who crossed my path. Through the passes of the Himalaya, I reached the plains of India. I couldn't speak, since I don't know the first elements of Parsi or Hindustani. The worthy people assumed that it was a vow. I became a saint to whomever invited me to his table. In brief, I reached Calcutta."

At this point Lavarède rediscovered his voice. "Believe that I regret it, Monsieur Bouvreuil."

The usurer's face cleaved from ear to ear in a broad smile. "Wait, Monsieur Lavarède. At Calcutta, the chancellor of the French consulate, an amiable Provençal from Carnoules, declared that I was a great explorer. To come from Tibet as a lama was genius. I hadn't thought of it that way—the cares of the journey—but I recognized that the means was, indeed, far from ordinary."

"And hazard put that disguise under your hand."

"No, Monsieur, it was reasoning."

"During the fire? My compliments, Monsieur Bouvreuil—you too have become a southerner."

Pénélope's father assumed a disdainful expression: "Joke, Monsieur, joke. In Calcutta, people are no less intelligent than you. I was fêted, pampered. Banquets were given in my honor. The press was excited, and I could show you more than one newspaper that displayed the caption in large print: *Lecture by the celebrated explorer Bouvreuil.*

"Is there a colony of money-lenders in that English city, then?"

"In sum," the usurer continued, without deigning to notice the interruption, saturated with glory, "I thought about finding you again. I had money cabled from France. But toward which point on the globe should I go? 'Well,' the consul said to me, 'your companions departed northwards. There's only one available route: the Transcaspian. They'll surely pass through Baku.'"

"The pestiferous Provençal took it into his head to speak the truth for once," grumbled the Parisian.

"Now," Bouvreuil concluded, "don't hope to indulge in any more practical jokes at my expense. Preceded by my reputation as a voyager, I have the ear of the authorities, and I'll prevent you from cheating the transport enterprises. You'll only get back to Paris if I permit it, and if Pénélope..."

"I'm leaving for Vienna this evening," sniggered Lavarède.

"You?"

"Me."

"I defy you to do it."

"Would you care to bet, Monsieur Bouvreuil?"

"My word, yes. A hundred francs."

"Agreed."

While talking, the journalist was walking. A visha masked him from the Austrians' eyes. Rapidly, he crumpled the piece of paper on which he had scribbled at the hotel and dropped it, and then drew away without affectation, mocking the landlord.

The policeman, faithful to their duty, arrived at the scaffold in their turn. Lavarède, who was watching them out of the corner of his eye, rubbed his hands. They had both come to a halt before the crumpled piece of paper. One of them bent down, picked it up and, having unfolded it, nudged his companion.

The sheet of paper bore these words:

My dear Rosenstein,
Everything is arranged. Patience. A few weeks in the Caucasus will soon pass, and they won't be searching for you there.

Yours, Florent.

The blond agents consulted one another with their gaze and marched as one toward the group surrounding Lavarède. They stopped at the same time, leaned toward the journalist, and in the same voice, in the same tone and with the same measure, said: "Bonjour, Monsieur Rosenstein, how are you?"

Armand looked them up and down, and very calmly, emphasized his words, he said: "You've been misled by a resemblance, Messieurs. I am Lavarède, a Parisian journalist."

The Austrians shook their heads, and Schultze said, in a sly tone: "You doubtless have papers?"

"Alas, no, I've come from China, where they were stolen from me."

"China," repeated the agents, in a mocking tone, shaking their heads knowingly. They had placed their hands on the Frenchman's shoulders. He did not put up any resistance, but he objected: "You're mistaken, I repeat. Ask the people who are accompanying me."

"The Monsieur, whom we met in the harbor, did indeed tell us that his name is Lavarède," Aurett was quick to respond.

"Ah! You don't know him otherwise?"

"No, Monsieur."

The policemen smiled. "In that case, Monsieur Rosenstein, will you please come with us."

"Where?"

"To Trieste, where the law requires your presence."

Bouvreuil started. "Trieste—two paces from the French frontier—not on your life!" He raised his voice: "Messieurs, you're making an error. This is indeed Monsieur Lavarède whom you're arresting. He's my friend."

"Your friend?"

"Yes."

With a rare dexterity, the Austrians had imprisoned the journalist's wrists and ankles with cords. That operation terminated, Schultze, the custodian of the letter, placed it before the usurer's eyes.

"Your friend, you say? Then you're Florent, his accomplice?"

"His accomplice, indeed, since I affirm to you..."

Bouvreuil did not finish. Muller tied him up like Armand and searched him. His portfolio contained twenty-five thousand francs."

"A part of the stolen money," proclaimed the agents.

"Stolen money!" howled the landlord, foaming at the mouth with rage. "Oh, I'll make you repent your stupidity!"

Schultze leaned toward him and whispered in his ear paternally: "Believe me, don't aggravate your offence by insulting the public authorities. You're pinched, behave yourself."

Muller had disappeared. After half an hour he came back with a carriage, into which Lavarède and Bouvreuil were put. The policemen sat down facing them."

At Baku station, the vehicle stopped. The prisoners were extracted and locked in a small room.

Soon, the Austrian agents reappeared, in the company of a functionary in the Russian police, on the other side of the glazed door.

The latter examined the accused rapidly, observed that he matched the description given—one of those general descriptions that fit nine people out of ten—and then added his signature to a piece of paper headed with a double K, for *Kaiserliche* and *Koeniglische*, like everything official in Austria-Hungary. It was an order of summary extradition, such as the police of the two empires sometimes exchange in order to proceed more rapidly, the reciprocal consuls having signed it in advance. After which, the Russian saluted stiffly. Schultze and Muller did likewise.

It was finished. The prisoners now belonged to the Austrian police. The journalist burst out laughing.

"Monsieur Bouvreuil," he said "we're about to leave for Trieste."

"Damn these imbeciles!" roared the exasperated usurer.

"Does it annoy you, then, to go there?"

A groan was is only response to that question.

"Personally," said the Frenchman, "I'm delighted. I'm traveling at the expense of the Austro-Hungarian government, and I'm earning a hundred francs."

"You're earning…"

"Of course, my dear Monsieur Bouvreuil. You've lost your bet."

XXVI. German Philosophy

Two hours went by like that, Lavarède smiling and Bouvreuil cursing. The usurer could not keep still. He kept going to the door. Mechanically, he tried to open it—and the Parisian brought his exasperation to a peak by telling him to calm down.

"Don't worry, my dear Monsieur Bouvreuil. After all, what do these policemen want? To take us to Trieste. Well, that's almost a direct route to get back to Paris."

The effect can be imagined.

Gradually, the room became dark.

"Damn!" murmured the journalist. "I hope they're going to give us something to eat."

Scarcely had he said it than a key turned in the lock. Schultze and his companion Muller came in, followed by a restaurant waiter carrying a basket in which bottles, glasses and crockery were clinking.

Armand bowed. "The requested meal," he said. "It's magic."

"I thought," Herr Schultze replied, modestly, "that these Messieurs are accustomed to good food. Not wanting to inflict the detestable Muscovite cuisine on them, I've taken the liberty of removing a few florins from the sum seized at the moment of arrest in order to alleviate the regime."

Lavarède burst out laughing. Again, it was the usurer who was paying the expenses of the adventure. But the latter lost his temper, as was only natural. He roared, bellowed and lamented, threatened the impassive Austrian, and finally shouted: "We'll see how you'll justify this abuse of authority!"

Schultze looked at Muller. Muller looked at Schultze. Then, in perfect unison, the syllables flowing simultaneously with military precision, they said: "The expenses of the journey will be placed on account as expenses of the investigation, with the justificatory receipts." And as the landlord continued his imprecations like a simple hero of the *Iliad*, he added: "I thought I was doing you a favor. I was mistaken. I apologize. I won't do it again."

The Parisian, who was sniffing the dishes with evident satisfaction, immediately interrupted. "Not at all, not at all, Monsieur Schultze. I'm infinitely grateful to you for your kindness. Continue, I beg you, continue." Without paying any heed to his enemy's fury, he added: "By the way, Monsieur Schultze, have you eaten?"

"No, Monsieur Rosenstein."

"Pardon me—Monsieur Lavarède; I'm correcting you without insisting, and I repeat the question: have you eaten?"

"We were just about to."

"The frightful Muscovite cuisine…pooh! Dine with us, then. You've been very generous, in terms of quality and quantity."

The Austrian's nostrils dilated. The uncovered dishes were spreading the most tempting odors through the room. But to accept an invitation from a prisoner…might that not be an attempt at corruption?

The journalist understood their scruples. "Messieurs, we have two bottles of wine. Split four ways, no one is at risk of getting drunk. And since we have to travel together, let it be as amiably as possible."

Muller was already sitting at the table. As for Schultze, won over by Armand's good grace, he did not hesitate any longer.

"I accept, Monsieur, and am very grateful to you. Trust that I shall ameliorate as for as possible the rigors that my duty imposes on me.

With that, he sat down. Bouvreuil did the same, murmuring despairingly: "I'm the one who's paying for the meal, and he's issuing polite invitations!"

Everything was excellent, having come from the ultra-modern hotel that a Saint-Petersburgian had recently opened in Baku: delicious Caspian eels cooked in wine and onions, fresh caviar and a succulent leg of salted Petresk lamb; nothing was lacking.

Good humor spread over the diners' faces, except for that of Pénélope's father, who ate angrily, snorting—which appeared to aggravate Herr Schultze. But Armand was cheerful enough for four. He laughed, and joked. The policeman were greatly amused by the boulevardian anecdotes that the journalist pulled out of his stock. In response to his request, Muller went in search of two more bottles of Crimean wine.

"Oh, you know," exclaimed Schultze, suddenly, "I regret that I'm only going to Trieste with you. I'd like the journey to last for a month."

"You're really too kind."

"No, I say what I think. You have that which attracts and attaches: philosophy."

Lavarède could not suppress a start of surprise.

"It astonishes you," the Austrian went on, his tongue having been loosened by good cheer, "to hear a policeman talking about philosophy? I've made use of my leisure time. Hegel, Schelling, Kant, Darwin and Schopenhauer have no secrets for me."

"My congratulations."

"That's how one learns logic, the reason of things, and one is able to judge men. Thus, you, who are in a situation that I would qualify as awkward if I dared…"

"Dare, Monsieur Schultze."

"Well, you're demonstrating a superiority there. You're imposing silence on your Self. It's becoming a kind of Non-Self, rising above vicissitudes and maintaining the smile on your lips and in your eyes."

"Pardon me," the Parisian put in, "but it's something other than philosophy that explains my complacency."

"What's that?"

"My innocence."

The policeman made a superb gesture of negation and pity. "Not that, I beg you—all guilty parties play that game. With me, it's futile. You won't lead me to confuse the Objective and the Subjective."

"But my guilt," Armand continued, adopting in his turn a philosophical tone, "is merely hypothetical."

"Wrong! In Hypothesis, the concept is double. You are either at fault or not. Here, there is unity: you are guilty."

"I don't admit your postulate."

Schultze patted the pocket of his overcoat, and continued, in a triumphant tone: "Because, in synthetic reasoning, you're forgetting the revelatory letter that permitted me to arrest you." And, with a hint of consideration: "About which I'm very glad, for I have the acquaintance of a man distinguished in every respect; the thief of a million is not an inferior individual."

The Parisian shook his head. "You'll see in Trieste, since that's where you're taking me. Let's not talk about it anymore. When are we leaving?"

"This evening, by the ten-twelve train…unless you have some objection?"

"Not at all, not at all! We have a special compartment, no doubt."

"The Russian authorities did not put one at our disposal, but I thought that you'd prefer isolation."

"And our surveillance will be easier."

"In fact, that's true—to you one can say everything. You understand…that I've paid for it with the money seized…"

The usurer started at those words. "Again!" he groaned, bringing his fist down on the table with a blow that made the crockery shake.

"Expenses of the investigation," Schultze replied. "An account of the price paid is appended to an official Company tariff." He turned to Lavarède, who was holding his sides. "How difficult relationships are with people who have not acquired your philosophy and the faculty of reason."

At quarter to ten the policeman asked his prisoners to allow themselves to be handcuffed. "Only until we're in the carriage," he said, by way of consolation. "Once the doors are closed I'll hasten to rid you of that uncomfortable adornment." He seemed genuinely sorry to be taking that precaution with regard to a man with whom he had dined so well.

Armand lent himself to the operation with a good grace, but for Bouvreuil, the placid Muller, whose strength was Herculean, was required to employ violence.

The journalist had one slight anxiety: that Murlyton and his daughter would not have been informed of their departure. He was mistaken. He perceived them on the station platform. The methodical Englishman had sought information. He had learned that there was only one train per day leaving Baku for Batoum, on the Black Sea, and that the departure of that train was fixed for ten-twelve in the evening. He had come to make sure that the Frenchman would not leave the shores of the Caspian without him.

The young man had time to exchange a rapid glance with Aurett; then the young woman, giving her arm to her father, headed for a carriage, into which she climbed.

A few moments later the bell rang. In Russia, the bell replaces the whistle. The train drew away. Armand settled down in a corner and went peacefully to sleep.

It was daylight when he woke up. Sprawling on the banquette, the usurer was snoring, shaken by abrupt nervous starts. His agitation contrasted with the immobility of Muller, placed facing him, who maintained a military attitude even in his sleep.

Schultze was on watch, revolver in hand.

"*Bonjour*, Monsieur Schultze," said Lavarède. "What time is it?"

"A few minutes to six. We'll arrive shortly at Udshany station." His tone changed abruptly. "That's admirable philosophy," he said.

"Again?"

"Still, Monsieur Rosenstein."

"Lavarède, I beg you."

"I was watching you sleep—as calmly as if you were traveling for your pleasure."

"Ah! That's because the concept is double, whatever you might think."

Smiling, he leaned out of the window. After passing through Udshany station the train traversed a flat, marshy, monotonous plain. At intervals, the isbas of the track guards appeared; they were raised on stilts in order to be isolated from the feverish miasmas of the ground.

The prisoner had lowered the glass.

"Close it," the Austrian advised him. "Otherwise we'll be devoured by mosquitoes. They're so dangerous and so numerous that the agents, in order to be able to sleep at night, are obliged to perch on those platforms you can see, supported by poles six meters long."

At two o'clock the train stopped at Elisawotopol station for ten minutes. Muller ran to the buffet, and fetched back some rather meager provisions."

"Russian buffets are poorly supplied," he said, "but we'll dine well this evening, since you've authorized my colleague not to skimp on the nourishment."

Bouvreuil, half-awake, exhaled a sigh. "Where will we be?"

"In Tiflis."

He policeman was telling the truth. At ten to five, they reached the great city, formerly Persian. Muller immediately disappeared. For a second, Lavarède perceived Aurett, and she saluted him with her hand. It was doubtless hazard that brought her gloved hands so close to her lips that she seemed to be blowing the captive a kiss. Then, once she had passed by, the young man looked round.

Some distance from the station the low, or European, city extended, connected to the indigenous city by a bridge spanning the river Kama. Half-hidden in the mist, the blurred silhouette of the ruined citadel was visible.

With the aid of his prodigious memory, the journalist imagined wandering through the opulent city. In thought he visited the Jardin d'Europe, where French operettas were performed, and then the museum, the steep, narrow and tortuous streets of the Persian quarter, bordered by houses surmounted by terraces with curiously-wrought balconies.

Muller's return brought him back to reality. The agent had surpassed himself. He had taken a cab to the Caucasus Hotel, celebrated by all travelers, and had sacked he larger, the cellar and he kitchens. Cost: thirty-five roubles.

Bouvreuil dared not strangle the Austrian. He had learned the strength of his fists at Baku station. But at every new dish complacently displayed on the banquette the unfortunate man raised his eyes to the heavens with the mute desolation of a voiceless Harpagon.

"My purse, my dear purse!" the Parisian murmured, at the moment when, like a man sure of his effect, the agent exhibited a bottle of champagne.

At six o'clock the train moved off again. Everyone ate. The usurer stuffed himself. He seemed to want to eat as much as all the others put together. That was one way of getting value for his money.

And he wasn't on the high plateaux, sniggered Lavarède, privately. *If he'd have had to tighten his belt like us, what would he have done?*

Suffocated and congested, however, the landlord was obliged to stop. He went to sleep heavily in a corner, while the Parisian, stimulated by the foaming white wine of the Champenois plains, sang the praises of the Caucasus, which they were traversing almost without seeing it.

To Schultze, stupefied by his erudition, he related the philosophical fable of Prometheus, chained and lacerated by a vulture. He brought back to reality the legend of the ship *Argo*, which had landed in Colchis, he present Imereti, at the spot where the town of Poti stands. Then he related the heroic history of the Lesghien Schamyl, the Abd-el-Kader of the Caucasus, and talked about the inexhaustible mines and the limitless forests.

Finally, civilization arrived. The railway cut through the mountains, throwing its bridges over the gulfs, taming nature and linking Batoum to Baku with a ribbon of steel nine hundred kilometers long.

It was nearly eleven o'clock when the lecturer decided to go to sleep. He did not see the stations of Kvirily, Riou and Sautredi pass by, nor the prodigious Sourham tunnel, whose piercing required for years of hard labor.

He opened his eyes again when they reached Kourais, where the temple of the enchantress Medea once stood. The track was bordered by rose-bushes, sheltered from the cold by straw muffs. Soon, the sea appeared.

"We're approaching Batoum," Schultze declared.

"Good."

"And I'll make you a proposal, Monsieur Rosenstein."

"Lavarède."

"Yes, that's understood. Rosenstein-Lavarède. Will you permit me to offer you my arm to traverse the city?"

"Your arm?"

"Instead of handcuffs."

"Gladly, my dear Monsieur Schultze. Would you also like me to give you my word that I won't try to escape?"

"No, no..."

"I give it to you. It's my pleasure to allow myself to be taken to Trieste by you. Truly, that's quite sincere—more so than you can believe."

The train pulled into Batoum station. Briskly, Muller enclosed Bouvreuil's wrists in handcuffs. The usurer complained. Since his "accomplice" had his hands free, why was he being treated differently?

Herr Schultze shrugged his shoulders, and said, quietly, in a tone in which one sensed an unshakable conviction: "To protest against fate, as Kant says, is folly. You always protest; I tie you up. One more word, and I'll be reduced to gagging you in order to avoid attracting a crowd."

The usurer shut up, but if, in accordance with the popular saying, his eyes had been pistols, the policeman's career would have ended there and then.

The other passengers were allowed to descend first. Then, arm in arm, the agents and the accused went to the Europa Hotel. There, they learned that the *Volga*, a steamer of the Imperial Black Sea Navigation Company, was leaving the following day, the sixteenth of February, for Odessa.

"We'll take passage aboard that ship, if that's all right with you?" the Austrian told the journalist.

"Perfectly," the later replied. To himself, he added: *February sixteenth; I have to be in Paris by the twenty-fifth of March, before Maître Panabert's office closes. I'll be there.*

Perhaps Pénélope's father read the thought in his eyes, for he riposted with a frightful grimace, and did not say another word.

After a substantial lunch, Armand permitted himself the luxury of an excellent cigar. He blew the odorous smoke maliciously into the face of the increasingly somber landlord.

"Are you annoyed, my dear Monsieur," he said, finally.

"I'm not talking to you," replied Bouvreuil, dryly.

"That's what I thought," the Parisian went on. "Ennui, the terrible ennui that even renders disagreeable the people who are always there." He addressed

Schultze, whose searching eyes were going back and forth between them. "We're leaving tomorrow. What if we were to take a stroll instead of remaining shut up in his room?"

"It's just that…"

"I know. But you can hold on to me as you did this morning…and in any case, I don't want to escape."

"Even if you had an opportunity?"

"I wouldn't take advantage of it."

The policeman smiled. "Diabolical man," he said. "You're convincing enough…"

"To disconcert Razil-Mograb?"

"Who's that?"

"The Persian philosopher who was the first to say: *let destiny take its course.*"

Involuntarily, the Austrian nodded. His prisoner knew Persian philosophy of which even he was unaware! Encouraged by his attitude, Armand completed his persuasion by adding gravely: "Razil-Mograb was also the precursor of Sidi-Moufmouf, the philosopher of Montmartre."

"I don't know that one either."

"On the basis," the young man went on, imperturbably, "that nothingness is anterior to creation, he was able to say: everything is in nothing. Now, there is nothing in my pocket. I therefore possess everything, in the form of nothing. That is the situation to which you have reduced me."

The agent was on the brink of shaking his prisoner's hand. He respected him. What could one refuse such an individual?

"The stroll," he said, "would be all right with me…but it's your friend…"

"Him, my friend? Oh, don't insist on that. *Errare humanum, sed perseverare diabolicum.*[60] I also have a little theology, as you see. Let's leave him here in Monsieur Muller's custody."

Paying no heed to the rage of Pénélope's father, they both went out.

As they went downstairs Lavarède noticed a young woman who was chatting in the lobby with a man with gray side-whiskers. He recognized Aurett, and she recognized him.

In her hand she was holding a small bunch of violets, the early flowers of the region. She dropped them, and, without affectation, moved a few steps away from Murlyton.

---

[60] The actual quote from Seneca is *Errare humanum est, perserverare autem diabolicum* [to err is human, to persist therein is diabolical]. The saying was paraphrased by St. Augustine of Hippo, lending further support to Lavarède's reference to theology.

Armand had followed all her movements. He picked up the flowers, and detached two of them, which he slipped into his pocket. Then, going to the Englishwoman, he held the bouquet out to her.

"You dropped this, Mademoiselle." He stopped, started in surprise, and added, with perfectly feigned hesitation: "But if I'm not mistaken, Mademoiselle, is it really you that I met in Baku?"

"With my father." Aurett indicated the gentleman. The hazarded a bow, not knowing exactly what the young man was trying to do."

"Didn't you tell me that you were going to Trieste?" asked Armand.

"Indeed."

"I'm going there myself—or rather, I'm being taken there on a charge of theft, fraudulent bankruptcy, or something or other. It will be easy for me to establish that I'm the victim of an error, but I beg you, for the moment, to reserve your opinion of a voyager whose hand you have shaken."

He addressed a profound bow to the bewildered English duo, and, without appearing to notice the amazement of the policeman, he took his arm. "Let's be on our way, my dear Monsieur Schultze."

He was delighted. Thanks to that little scene he would be able to exchange a few words with the young woman aboard the *Volga* without the Austrian raising any objection to it.

The latter interrogated a cab-driver whose vehicle was stationed nearby. What was there to visit in Batoum?

"In the city, nothing," replied the Automedon. "It's a military port surrounded by redoubtable defenses, but no monuments." In an insinuating tone, he added: "If you wish, though, I can take you to Adjari-Tszali. It's not yet the season, but it doesn't matter—going up the River Tcholok it's a pleasant excursion."

He was not lying. Indeed, one cannot dream of anything more picturesque than the Tcholok valley. Sometimes hemmed in and sometimes extending at its ease between low-lying plains, the river changes its aspect continually.

Ten versts from Batoum, at a marvelous location, at the confluence of the river and a torrent stands a *Gostinitza*, where one can eat and drink. The inn has replaced a post of Zaporogues, Cossacks of the military line, who were once resident there, like our spahis on the Algerian frontier or the ancient Hungarian honveds.

In the summer, merchants from Batoum have the habit of spending Sundays with their families at Adjari-Tszali.

In order not to violate custom, Armand and his companion went into the isba. Schultze paid, and invited the cab-driver to refresh himself. The latter, as chatty as one of ours, started recounting stories about the region, among others the legend of the Armenians who conquered all of the Caucasus commercially.

"One day, God said to Satan: 'How have you managed to unite so many sins in one human being?' The Devil sniggered. 'It's easy: I take a little Greek, add in a strong dose of Persian and a lot of Jew. That's an Armenian.'"

Distracted by the muzjik's verbiage, the policeman ceased to keep watch on Lavarède. In a trice, the latter was outside, and, leaping on to the seat of the carriage, roused the horse, which departed at a gallop.

In response to the noise, Schultze came running. "Too late! The fugitive was already a hundred meters away, and the rig was drawing away at a vertiginous speed.

The Austrian grabbed hold of his hair with the evident intention of tearing it out...but he suspended his movement. After having described a smooth curve, the carriage came back toward Gostinitza. On the seat, the journalist burst out laughing. When he arrived alongside the policeman, he leapt to the ground and said, cheerfully: "I had an opportunity to escape, didn't I?"

"I have to admit it."

"You can see that I didn't take advantage of it. Henceforth, when I assure you of something, believe me. Now, let's go back to Batoum. We'll be there in time for dinner."

On the way back, Schultze became pensive. Evidently, the actions of his prisoner had shaken his certainly and the philosophical formulae with which he had stuffed his German skull were further augmenting his disturbance.

If my premise was false, he said to himself, *my logical reasoning is false, not to mention that there's doubt. A man ought not to say "I'm certain," but "I believe that I'm certain"...from which it follows that I'm no longer certain at all of the verity of his culpability. And isn't there error even in verity itself? Two and two only make four by convention; in absolute reality they make nothing, for number employs the hypothesis of a measure, and measure does not accord with the immeasurable...one cannot measure infinity...so number is devoid of meaning. Therefore, the man cannot be guilty!*

The result of these divagations was that the following morning, Herr Schultze announced, as they embarked on the *Volga*, to the great wrath of Bouvreuil and the keen satisfaction of Lavarède, that the former would remain locked his cabin, kept in sight by Muller, while he latter would enjoy the liberty accorded to the other passengers, under his surveillance.

The signal for departure soon resounded. The steam, crowned with a plume of smoke, emerged from the harbor and then steered northwards, following the coast.

At about midday, the ship stopped within sight of Poti in order to drop dispatches into the mail-boat, and continued on her way.

Leaning on one of the uprights of the footbridge, Armand gazed into the distance at the snowy summits of the Caucasus. Ten paces away, the policeman was reading a newspaper, only interrupting his reading to cast an occasional glance at his prisoner. A soft voice became audible next to the journalist.

"Don't turn round," it said. "I'm behind you with my father, I wanted to say *bonjour* to you."

In spite of the instruction, the young man turned to face his friends. "There's no need for precautions," he replied. "I spoke to you yesterday at the hotel purely to prepare for our meeting on the boat. To shake your hand might appear excessive to my guardian, but mentally I'm doing so, and as a cordially as possible."

In a few words, he told them about Bouvreuil's tribulations, which amused them enormously; then they separated, promising to meet again the following day.

The policeman had seen everything from where he was sitting. "The gentleman is less reserved than he was yesterday," he observed, when the Parisian came toward him.

"Quite natural."

"I don't think so...in your situation..."

"It no longer exists for him; he's understood that I'm telling the truth."

With that, Armand turned on his heel and moved away, whistling. The Austrian went to lean on the bulwark and plunged into laborious reflections. His perplexity was still increasing.

"They eyes are the mirror of the soul," he muttered. "All thinkers are in accord on that. I've never seen a clearer, franker gaze than this Rosenstein's..." After a brief hesitation, he added: "Lavarède's...but in that case, what about this damned letter that I have in my pocket?"

And he pressed it to his forehead—which, as everyone knows, is a means of getting light into the brain. Vain pressure! His ideas became increasingly confused.

On the seventeenth and eighteenth the *Volga* stopped successively at Otchemtchini, Soukoum, New Mount Athos. Goudaou. Adler, Sotchi, Thouaspse, Djoudga, Novorossisk, Anapa and Kertsch.

The halt in the large town commanding the strait of Ienikaleh and the entrance to the Sea of Azov lasted two hours. Lavarède, escorted by Schultze, made a rapid excursion into the town and found time to climb the interminable stone staircase that departs from the old market place to end at the summit of Mount Milthridates. He affirmed that he was recompensed for his climb by the view of the neo-Greek monument erected n the site where, according to tradition, the king of Pont had himself struck in the heart by the sword of a Gaulish soldier in order not to fall into the hands of his Roman enemies.

From the plateau, in any case, one discovers a marvelous panorama. The town lies around the harbor. To the west is a plain studded with little eminences, strewn with the white patches of towns and villages. To the south is the rocky massif of Skati-Kourgan, in which the cave known as the tomb of Mithridates is located, and further away, the sea. In the evening, one can see Theodosia, with the ruins of its ancient Genoese towers.

When the Parisian was locked in his cabin, Herr Schultze summoned Muller and he two policemen went up on deck.

The night was clear, and permitted them to divine the coast of Crimea, which, in summer, is simultaneously reminiscent of the Algerian coast and the landscapes of Switzerland.

The agent made his colleague party to his doubts regarding Rosenstein/Lavarède.

"I've already thought that," replied Muller, who did not know any philosophy, having only common sense. "Either he's not guilty, or he's very clever."

"That's your opinion?"

"Look at him, no matter when. Nothing about him betrays anxiety, whereas the other one never stops raging. If he could, he'd demolish the ship. I repeat, the young man's either very clever or innocent."

"And which way do you lean?"

"Toward innocence."

Schultze appeared to reflect. "Then he's a Frenchman and an artist, as he claims?"

"Probably, and I think we should let him go."

"Oh, not that! Philosophical certainty is only obtained point by point, mathematically. We can only be sure after experiment. All the same, if you're right, it's a terrible error."

"No."

"Why no?"

"He's amiable, and a good fellow. He'll forgive us."

"For having taken him away from Baku?"

"You can see that he's enjoying himself. He laughs, so he won't bear a grudge."

Then the conversationalists lowered their voices, and after a quarter of an hour of whispering they went to bed.

The next day, the *Volga* went past Yalta and reached Sebastopol, sixty-five minutes ahead of schedule. There was a great deal of cargo to unload, however, and the captain assured everyone that the stopover would be at least four hours instead of the two anticipated by the itinerary. Schultze rubbed his hands, and went over to Armand, who was chatting with Murlyton and Aurett.

"We have four hours to ourselves; would you like to go ashore?"

"In truth, my dear policeman, I was counting on your good will, and I was proposing to Monsieur and Mademoiselle that they visit the valiant city with us."

A launch took the voyagers across the bay of Streletskaia, the commercial port of Sebastopol, entirely separate from the southern bay, which has become the property of the navy.

Schultz guided his companions through the brand new city. He showed them the factories; the barracks; the church of Saint Vladimir, raised to the memory of the Russians who died in 1854-56 during the siege of Sebastopol; and the administrative headquarters of the "patriotic Russia fleet," the navigation Company between the Black Sea and the Far East, founded in 1878 "by means of collections made throughout the empire."

"Now let's go to the French cemetery," said the agent, in an enigmatic tone.

"The French cemetery?" repeated Aurett.

It was the journalist who replied. "Yes, Mademoiselle, the resting-place of our compatriots killed in battle during the terrible Crimean campaign. They're numerous, for in the two years of that war, four hundred thousand men perished, half belonging to the Russian army and the rest to the allied French, English, Turkish and Sarte forces."

It was necessary to take a cab, the field of rest being six kilometers from the city.

On perceiving the rectangle, twenty-five meters by fifteen, enclosed by walls worn away by storms, an intense emotion took hold of the Parisian. How many were sleeping eternally there beneath the cubes of stone lined up on either side of the central pathway?

He bared his head, thoughtful and grave.

Schultze's voice suddenly made him shudder. "The Franco-Russian alliance justified, eh?"

Armand turned round as if he had been bitten by a snake. His brow furrowed, and in a slightly tremulous voice, he said: "Monsieur Schultze, in France, after an honest combat, the adversaries shake hands. In Crimea, the Russians and the French learned to hold one another in esteem, for, in the very true words of General Saussier, so much heroism was deployed on either side that there were truly no victors and no vanquished. You were right just now: it's the blood of these dead men that caused the seed of amity to germinate between the two peoples."

The policeman shook his head. "For what reason, then, is everyone in your country hostile to a Franco-German alliance?"

"For as many reasons, Monsieur Schultze, as there are inhabitants in Alsace-Lorraine."

And the young man went back to the carriage with the English duo. The agent followed them, murmuring: "First point acquired. He's French, thoroughly French."

They went back aboard. The captain's anticipations were exceeded. They had dinner before the steamer resumed its route.

Ni la zalouska—hors-d'oeuvres—and *ni l'ikra*, or fresh caviar, washed down with Chersonese wine and *piro*, an excellent Slav beer, did not succeed in unfurrowing Monsieur Schultze's brow. His philosophy had been subjected to its first check, and he remembered sadly that his wife and nine children were waiting in Trieste for the reward of five thousand florins promised for the arrest of the German banker Rosenstein.

On the twentieth of February, they made the acquaintance of Eupatoria, the Russian Nice, and at about three o'clock, the steamer drew up alongside the quay at Odessa.

While the prisoners and Schultze dined in a restaurant in which everyone was speaking French, Muller ran to the railway station and bought tickets for the Jassy-Bucharest-Szegedin-Trieste train that was due to depart that same evening at five past eleven.

Lavarède was glad to hear the vocables of his own language. His jailer had authorized him to take his meal in the common room, and he explained to Aurett, sitting facing him, that the French colony in Odessa is numerous and flourishing.

"What's astonishing about that?" he said. "The city baptized the city of Ulysses, Odysseus—hence Odessa—by the Empress Catherine, who was smitten with Hellenism, was, in reality, founded by the Duc de Richelieu, named as governor in 1803.

"Oh, you're a fount of knowledge," Murlyton put in.

"I've read a great deal, seen a great deal and remembered a great deal. Soon, if my good Austrian consents, I'll show you over the city. Four things to see: a superb boulevard, running along the crest of the eighty-meter cliff on which Odessa is perched; a beautiful bronze statue of Richelieu; a stairway of five hundred steps leading down to the harbor; and beneath the boulevard, a tunnel followed by the carts transporting cargoes to the ships at anchor. There."

Schultze raised no objection to that program. Muller went directly to the railway with Bouvreuil, submitted to an increasingly tight surveillance. The others took the educational route.

Thus, the Parisian and his friends were able to enjoy an admirable view of the port lit by electricity, where the basins formed black patches and which the positional beacons on the ships strewed with red and green dots.

At ten to eleven, they all went into the immense glass-roofed hall of the passenger station. The English duo went to their own carriage. Lavarède's place was reserved in the special compartment retained by Muller. The worthy agent, accompanied by Bouvreuil, foaming with rage—he was handcuffed—was already installed therein.

At exactly five past eleven, the train moved off under the benevolent eye of the gendarme wearing a green uniform with red trimmings, with a revolver in a holster attached to a shoulder-strap, that one encounters in every Russian railway station.

The next day, after a rapid journey across the steppe, they reached Ungheni, the station on the Rumanian frontier.

They were obliged to change trains. The tracks in the Tsar's empire are, in fact, twelve centimeters wider than those of other European railways, so that

Russian equipment cannot emerge from its own territory, nor foreign equipment enter it. That is a fact of considerable military importance, because it renders an invasion of the powerful Slav state almost impossible.

At five-thirty they had dinner in Jassy.

At eight o'clock thy glimpsed Paskany.

The train went through Marasesti during the night and reached Bucharest on the twenty-second of February, at nine o'clock in the morning, two hours late. The connection for Szegedin had been missed, and the voyagers were forced to wait for the four p.m. departure

To have lunch first and then visit the city was sufficient to occupy them until then. The banks of the Dumbowina, which traverses Bucharest, the churches, the convents, the Russian and Austrian residences received successive visits from Lavarède and he English duo, escorted by the policeman, who had fallen completely silent.

The Austrian remained in the rear, mingling with groups of idlers, listening to conversations. At one moment, a smile distended his lips.

"Right," he muttered, "We'll see whether he's a financier."

He was the prisoner.

As they returned to the station the agent bought a newspaper, which he slipped no his pocket. In the train, he absorbed himself in reading it. Suddenly, he interrupted himself, and addressed the journalist, who was looking distractedly at the Rumanian countryside.

"Is this comprehensible?"

"What, Monsieur Schultze."

"A banker has just been arrested on the strength of a complaint from one of his clients."

"It seems understandable to me."

"Wait. The client deposited fifty thousand florins in bonds from the city of Vienna."

"All right."

"Two months later he reclaimed them."

"Didn't the banker give them to him?"

"Yes, except that the bonds didn't have the same serial numbers. For that he was arrested. Why? I give you a sum, you reimburse me. Whether it's in gold or bills, I have no complaint."

"Well," murmured the Parisian, "that seems evident to me..."

A burst of laughter from Bouvreuil cut short his speech. The usurer had been listening to the conversation, which evidently amused him greatly.

"What's the matter with you?" asked Lavarède.

"I find you admirable. You don't see why the banker was arrested? It's as clear as crystal. He speculated with a deposit."

"Speculated? Where do you get that?"

Schultze had become very attentive, at least in appearance.

285

"Of course," the landlord continued, blowing into his cheeks. "Every city loan gives rise to print runs, sets of bonds, you follow? For Vienna there are two per year. A few days before the issue, the chance of making a profit driving the public, the obligations rise in value. Afterwards, they fall. Hence a difference that sometimes extends to four or five francs. That's why the bonds didn't have the client's numbers, His banker had sold them before the issue and bought them back afterwards, pocketing the profit of the operation, and exposing the depositor to the risks of the issue."

He laughed while talking, crushing his interlocutor, the ignorant artist, with his disdain as a practical man.

His joy was of short duration, however. Schultze bowed profoundly to the Parisian, and with an embarrassed expression, began: "Monsieur Lavarède..."

"What?" the latter interrupted. "You're no longer calling me Rosenstein?"

"At the cemetery in Sebastopol, I recognized that you're French; a moment ago, I acquired the certainty that you're not a financier. I believe, as you have affirmed, that you really are Monsieur Lavarède, a Parisian journalist, and I beg you not to cause a poor fellow who believed that he was doing his duty in arresting you to lose his job."

"My dear Monsieur Schultze, I don't blame you at all; on the contrary, I'm so pleased with your company that I shall continue the journey as far as Trieste."

"No, no—I don't want to inflict the annoyance of my company upon you any longer." In response to a protest from Armand the policeman went on: "Please: at Szegedin, a large city from which communications are easy, we'll settle our account. Please."

"So be it," said Armand, with a sigh of regret.

And the two men shook hands.

"Now," cried Bouvreuil, "the two of us, Monsieur Policeman. I can assure you that I'm not so generously inclined."

The Austrian looked him up and down. "But I'm not letting you go."

"What?" stammered the landlord. "You think...?"

"That you're the thief—exactly."

"A thief, me?" He stood up, menacingly, but a simple push from Muller set him down on the banquette.

"I'll appeal to the tribunals!" he protested.

"And they'll convict you," replied Herr Schultze, placidly. "I was blind. I should have realized at the first glance that you're Rosenstein."

"I'm Rosenstein?"

"Yes. In Baku, your friend had no papers. You did."

"You admit it!"

"That alone should have put me on your track."

"What do you mean?"

The agent raised a finger doctorally. "That criminals are always well-organized."

Bouvreuil opened his mouth in amazement.

"And since then," the Austrian continued, stubborn in his new conviction, "your increasing rage as we come closer to the city where you'll be punished for your crimes..."

"The rage of being handcuffed."

"Among others...and the fashion in which you explained your colleague's speculation."

"What colleague?"

"The banker in Trieste. Everything points to you, including the letter from your friend Florent."

Pénélope's father raised his arms to the heavens. "Florent, now! Who's that?"

"The judge will inform you."

Devastated, at finding himself more a prisoner than ever after having thought himself liberated, Bouvreuil lapsed into silence. That damned Lavarède definitely brought him bad luck. His voyage round the world had been nothing but a long series of disasters. And the latest one appeared even harsher than the others.

The journalist, once free, would finish his voyage without encumbrance, while he, the delegate of the shareholders of Panama, would be moldering on the damp straw of a dungeon. Lavarède would marry the little Englishwoman. And what would become of Pénélope then?

At the idea of his daughter's wrath alone, the usurer felt a chill run along his spine.

He peeped at Lavarède surreptitiously: that devil of a man, who passed effortlessly over all obstacles, as if it were child's play. An idea formed in his mind.

If he wanted to, he could get me out of this. But how can I persuade him to do it?

The train had crossed the Austrian frontier at Vercioreva. It was the middle of the night. The policemen, having only one prisoner to guard, had decided that instead of taking turns to keep watch, they would both go to sleep. The locked doors and a steel chain wound around Bouvreuil's ankles were sufficient to prevent his escape.

The landlord made sure that the Austrians, somewhat wearied by the previous days, were profoundly asleep, and then tugged at the sleeve of the sleeping journalist.

The latter opened his eyes.

"Damn you," muttered the young man. "I was having a pleasant dream. It was much better than putting such a vile reality before my eyes."

"Don't get carried away—I have a proposition to put to you."

"Futile, Monsieur Bouvreuil. I won't work with you—I have clean hands."

287

The captive bit his lip, but it was necessary to swallow the insult, until he could avenge himself later. He adopted his most amiable expression.

"Always the humorous remark."

"If it amuses you, so much the better."

"One question. If you were a prisoner like me, you'd succeed in escaping your guardians, wouldn't you?"

"Certainly."

"You say that, but it's not as easy as you seem to think."

"One can do what one can do, Monsieur Bouvreuil."

"Really? What would you do, then?"

The young man examined the usurer, and a light dawned in his eyes. "You imagine that I'm going to tell you my means? Don't delude yourself. Three months on remand in prison for the investigation of your case appears to me to be quite just. You wanted a son-in-law, even by violence! The law is protecting your victim."

"Come on, Monsieur Lavarède, be generous."

"Generous? You know how to pronounce that word?"

"You have imagination, I have money; let's trade."

"You want to pay me?" said Armand, in a trenchant one—but he changed his mind. "In fact, why not?"

The landlord uttered an exclamation of joy. "You accept?"

"Not yet. It will cost you excessively dear."

Bouvreuil's eyelids blinked with emotion. "From you, my dear Monsieur, that astonishes me. You're not guided by interest."

"With you, my dear Monsieur, it's quite natural. You've taught me interest…usurious interest."

"What are you asking?"

The journalist remained silent momentarily. "Well, acquit me of my little debt."

Bouvreuil jumped up, but sat down immediately with a cry of pain. The chain imprisoning his ankles had hurt him.

"Twenty thousand francs!" he stammered.

"Let's forget that I said anything. You prefer prison—fine. You'll end up there none day, in any case."

At that moment Muller turned over on the banquette. The two interlocutors fell silent.

The usurer reflected. Sure of being released, he could have tolerated the cell, but Pénélope's anger inspired an insurmountable terror in him. Anything rather than unleash that tempest.

The Austrian had resumed snoring. Suddenly, Bouvreuil thought that he could put one over on his adversary. A receipt for twenty thousand francs given in the course of his voyage would prevent him coming into possession of the coveted inheritance. Between twenty-five centimes and such a sum there was a considerable difference.

"Monsieur Lavarède" appealed Bouvreuil.

"What now?"

"It's agreed. The quittance for the means."

"The quittance first."

"You won't trust my word?"

"Oh, I barely trust your signature."

Without responding to that last gibe, the landlord rummaged in his pocket. He took out a sheet of paper and a portable inkwell. Installing himself as best he could he prepared to write.

"By the way," said Lavarède, you're discharging me from my debt and all the charges?"

"The charges too?"

"Liberty is the greatest good of all."

"So be it."

"Good. Only, permit me to dictate the terms of the document to you. I absolutely insist."

Pénélope's father sensed that his intentions had been divined. He lowered his head. "You're not stupid," he murmured, between his teeth.

"I know."

"Dictate, then."

And, with an angry pen, he wrote the lines as Lavarède pronounced them.

23 February 1891, in a railway carriage near Szegedin. Monsieur Armand Lavarède having rendered me a signal service today, I release him fully and entirely, in all liberty, of the debt of twenty thousand francs that he had contracted toward me, as well as any charges to which it might have given rise.

He handed the paper to the journalist, murmuring: "A receipt in the ordinary form would have sufficed."

"No it wouldn't, Monsieur Bouvreuil. You would have demanded the sum in Paris. Either I would have produced the receipt and thus lost any right to my cousin's inheritance, or, having destroyed it, I would have been constrained to pay you."

While speaking, he examined the quittance. Having done that, he folded it up methodically—but he did not complete the operation, and was shaken by a fit of wild gaiety.

On the other side of the paper, he had just read these lines:

Abroad, go for preference to English hotels... In case of difficulty, go to see the consul.

It was the piece of paper to which the usurer, when departing on his voyage, had consigned a few indispensable items of information.

"And the means?" Bouvreuil demanded, surprised.

"Well, on arrival in Trieste, demand to see the French consul."

"Oh, how stupid!" exclaimed the landlord, administered a mighty thump at his head. "I hadn't thought of that!" And, in a tone of indescribable regret: "That's a distraction that has cost me dear!"

At seven o'clock they pulled into Szegedin station.

Schultze, faithful to his promise, conducted Armand to the buffet, where, in spite of the early hour, they both had a copious meal.

As they finished, twenty musicians carrying their instruments—violins, cellos, double basses, cymbals, etc.—came into the establishment.

"Here's the czarda," said the policeman.

"Oh yes," said Lavarède. "The orchestra one encounters on all Hungarian trains."

"Yes. There must surely have been some trouble on the line, for there are two czardas here: one will leave with us and the other will take tomorrow's train."

"How do you know?"

"The buffet-manager told me."

The moment of the departure arrived.

"Monsieur Schultze," said the journalist, as he took his leave of the agent, "I have a favor to ask you."

"What is it?"

"Do you have my ticket to Trieste?"

"Of course."

"Give it to me; I'll keep it as a souvenir of the adventure."

The Austrian acquiesced to his request. Suddenly, however, he exclaimed: "But it's necessary for me to return to you what I seized from you in Baku!"

Armand was careful not to remind Schultze that he had not seized anything at all. Such a confession could only complicate the situation.

"Let's not talk about that. A few hundred francs. Give them on my behalf to Madame Schultze, in testimony of my esteem for you."

"But what about you?"

"My newspaper has a representative here, so I have a banker in Szgedin."

The whistle of the locomotive and a brilliant assault by the czarda cut short the policeman's hesitation, who remained at the window for some time waving his handkerchief as if bidding farewell to a friend. Armand remained on the platform, with Murlyton and Aurett.

"What are we going to do?" asked the gentleman.

"We could leave at three o'clock, since I have my ticket for Trieste—but the journey lasts a day and a night, so I need to assure myself of nourishment."

"That's true."

Fifty minutes later, Lavarède announced to his friends that, utilizing a petty talent as a violinist, he had been enrolled in the czarda. They would quit Szegedin the following day, the twenty-fourth, and all the way to Trieste, the improvised musician would be accommodated, fed and refreshed with the rest of the orchestra.

XXVIII. *The* Goubet

After leaving Szegedin, Schultze and Muller observed with amazement that Bouvreuil's attitude had been completely modified. No more shouting, no more resistance. The prisoner, so nervous the day before, had suddenly calmed down. He even smiled ironically, in a most aggravating manner, when he was called by the name of Rosenstein.

Szabadka—the Maria-Theresianopel of German Austrians—Baja, perched on the bank of the Danube, Agram and Steinbruck filed past the eyes of the travelers without the usurer saying anything, but a few kilometers from Trieste he said to his guardians: "Messieurs, I'm notifying you that I demand to see the French consul, and that I demand to be taken to him."

"You're going to police headquarters first."

"So be it, but from there to the consulate. It's my right."

Following Bouvreuil's instructions, the chancellor telegraphed Sens, where Pénélope was waiting for Armand's return. The response established the identity of the landlord peremptorily, who was released after a few hours in a "secure room." After that there was a confrontation with the policemen, in the course of which the latter placed before their former prisoner's eyes the letter that the Parisian had fabricated in Baku.

"But that's Lavarède's handwriting!" exclaimed Bouvreuil, recognizing it at the first glance.

The three of them quickly reconstituted the whole adventure. For Schultze and Muller, furious at coming back empty-handed, it was evident that the journalist had deliberately deceived the police and put them on a false trail; that he had engaged in fraudulent and murky maneuvers to the detriment of the Austro-Hungarian police, from which the real guilty party had profited. From there to arresting him it was only a short step.

Bouvreuil affirmed that the trickster would come to Trieste. He recalled the fashion in which he had asked for his ticket. He persuaded his listeners.

That same day, the chief of police, insufficiently informed by the detectives, who were blinded by rage, put his brigade at their disposal, and traps were set up at all the stations—Saint-André, the Arsenal and Trieste Port—in order to seize the delinquent as he left the train.

Meanwhile, the latter, mingled with the czarda, was traveling toward the Adriatic city at full steam, scrapping his violin.

He would inevitably be captured. It would take him weeks to demonstrate to the law, limping in all countries, the inanity of the charges leveled against him, and the inheritance would escape him. That was what cheered Bouvreuil up. For the occasion, he had become a police volunteer.

But Heaven was not on his side.

On the twenty-fifth of February, at ten o'clock in the morning, the train carrying Lavarède and his friends was derailed between Miramar and Trieste. Bouvreuil had anticipated everything...except a derailment. The travelers, constrained to become pedestrians, came into the city via the splendid Giacomo-in-Monte, which the police were not watching.

Leaving the castle and the Cathedral of San-Guisto to the right they reached the Piazza Grande, and then the quay of the port known as "del Mandrocchio," and headed for the Grand Canal that departs from the sea and divides the new city in two.

Murlyton and his daughter spotted the Hotel Garciotti on the riva, or quay of the same name, and stopped there, while Armand, confident in his lucky star, wandered along the quays, seeking a means of continuing his curious world tour.

Luck was absent that day. The voyager walked in vain from the Molo del Sale to the Molo San Carlo, and from there to the Molo Benita. He wandered along the Via Carradori, Antonia, de Viena, le Corso and le Ponte-Rocco, the red bridge over the canal, but no inspiration arrived. Then too, the morning's derailment had prevented the czarda from having lunch, and the young man's stomach was formulating demands that were harming the labor of the brain.

Annoyed but not discouraged, Armand had prolonged his walk as far as the Riva Gramala, from which he could see the artillery arsenal and the canteen on the Molo Santa Teresa, when a group of people shouting and gesticulating attracted his attention.

A sailor was haranguing a dozen of the dock workers, with forceful gestures, sometimes designating the crates placed on the quay and sometimes the sea. His listeners interrupted him by uttering in guttural voices all the onomatopoeias in the Italian language, still spoke in Trieste, to the great despair of Austria.

Finally, the mariner raised a menacing fist, and at that demonstration, the band fled in all directions. Lavarède had drawn closer.

"Thunder and damnation!" howled the furious sailor. "What cowards these Italians are!"

"What's the matter, my friend?" asked the journalist.

The bronzed face of the sea-dog brightened. His anger melted away, as if by enchantment.

"A countryman," he said.

"Yes, attracted by the noise of your quarrel."

"Don't talk to me about that. These Chinamen don't understand a word of French. I've never been able to make them understand that it's necessary to transport the crates you see here to the *François-Joseph*."

"The *François-Joseph?*"

"Yes, the vessel there at the quay."

Lavarède looked. Beside the quay, only surpassing the level of the water by thirty of forty centimeters, a narrow metallic platform emerged. A light balustrade surrounded it; in the middle there was a little circular dome, the upper part of which was formed by a thick glass lens. Its appearance was slightly reminiscent of the deck of a torpedo-boat.

"But I know that," murmured the journalist. "It's the *Goubet*, the French submarine torpedo-boat whose trials I watched at Cherbourg with my colleague Émile Gautier."[61]

The sailor blinked, and seemed embarrassed. "It resembles it, Monsieur. Yes, certainly, it must resemble it...but what you're looking at is the electric submarine of Seigneur José Miraflor."

"José Miraflor? That's curious—I've heard that name before."

"Possibly, if you've traveled a little."

"Quite a lot, in fact. Can I see this noble foreigner?"

"Oh, his portrait is displayed in the boat's saloon."

Armand felt an impulse of keen curiosity. "And what is he doing with this boat?"

"He's trying to sell it to one of the powers of the Triple Alliance. In the meantime, he permits people to visit it at an entrance fee of a florin."

The Parisian reflected. "Tell me," he said, after a moment, "didn't you mention that you had crates to take aboard?"

"Yes—provisions of powder, for we're leaving for Fiume shortly. It appears that to sell it, it's necessary to go to a military port."

"Well, I'll help you."

"You, Monsieur?"

"Well, between compatriots..."

"I don't know if I should..."

"You should—and in return, you can break a crust with me while I cast an eye over the boat."

The slang expression, deliberately employed by the young man, convinced his interlocutor.

"It's a deal!"

---

[61] The *Goubet I*, the first electrically-powered submarine, designed by Claude Goubet (1837-1903), was constructed in 1885, but the trials in Cherbourg did not go well, and the French navy declined to commission the vessel. His second attempt, the *Goubet II*, constructed in 1889 and also tried out at Cherbourg, fared better, but the navy preferred a rival, and Goubet went bankrupt. The second vessel was sold at auction, reputedly to an eccentric, and was not seen again. Paul Deleutre might well have watched the trial in company with Émile Gautier (1853-1937), who worked for several newspapers, including *Le Figaro*, as a science reporter before taking over the editorship of *La Science Française*. He published a story of his own about an electric submarine, "*Le Désiré*" (1893 in *La Science Illustrée*; tr. as "The *Désiré*", included in *The Conqueror of Death*, Black Coat Press, ISBN 978-1-61227-230-6.).

In a trice, the packages were transferred from the quay to the deck. The dome pivoted on a hinge like a lid, unmasking an opening on the edge of which were the supports of an iron latter.

"The stairway of the *François-Joseph*," said the sailor.

"You've introduced everything but yourself," said Lavarède.

"Oh, me—Marie-Anne Langlois, of Saint-Malo."

And I'm Armand Lavarède, of Paris."

One by one, with the aid of ropes, the crates were lowered into the interior. When the last one was embarked the two men went down the ladder.

The first thing that Armand saw in the saloon was the portrait of his old acquaintance in Costa Rica. It was superbly displayed, attached to a panel, bearing the flattering but deceptive caption, in German and Italian: *Don José Miraflor, inventor of the submarine torpedo-boat powered by electricity.*

It's really him, thought Lavarède. *In consequence, there can be no doubt— I smell some villainous coup.*

The sailor offered his new friend bread, goat's cheese, mortadella and a fiaschetto of excellent Chianti, while showing him the vessel.

"You can see, Monsieur, that it's a kind of steel fish divided into three compartments: in the bow, the electric searchlight that illuminates the route and the post of the man responsible for identifying obstacles; at the stern, the chamber of the accumulators and the electric motor; in the middle, a elegant saloon with an oval window to each side. Glass lenses seal those openings hermetically, over which a plate of the boat's metallic carapace can be slid at will, forming a shutter. To pass from one compartment to another there are no doors, but a double niche pivoting on its axis in a thousandth of a second, its points of contact with the walls being fitted with rubber stoppers. Two crewmen: my eldest son Yan, whom I'll introduce to you, at the prow, me at the poop, and Don José Miraflor in the saloon, at the control-panel." As he pronounced the final words he pointed to a set of levers and handles, each of which bore an inscription.

Curiously, Lavarède read: *Forward; Reverse Engine; Rise; Dive; Dead Stop; Pumps*; etc. etc.

One last label attracted his particular attention. "Safety weight," he read aloud.

"Yes," the sailor hastened to reply. "Under the keel there's a block of cast iron and lead weighting three thousand kilograms. If there's an accident on the sea-bed, one turn of the handle and bang—the weight is released...and the unballasted torpedo-boat pops up to be surface like a cork."

"And it's Don José who invented all that?"

The sailor hesitated. "Of course," he said, with the air of a man who fears that he might be compromising himself.

"It's not true!" declared the journalist. "I know this Don José. He's capable of setting up an ambush, but not an apparatus of this kind. And this, except for the accumulators, which my comrade Goubet, judging them to be too dangerous, replaced with piles, is exactly the same submarine boat that that technologist of genius proposed to the French government."

"Which refused it."

"So—you're up to date, Master Langlois."

"Well, yes," said the mariner, coming to an abrupt decision. "After all, it's not my fault if the inventor, ruined by his trials, let himself be taken for a ride by the foreigner. For ten thousand, and a cut of any sale, he let the torpedo-boat go."

"And Goubet consented to selling it abroad?"

"No—not that. He even stipulated the contrary, but as Monsieur Miraflor keeps saying, his money-box is empty—he won't sue."

The Parisian's visage had become severe. He drew nearer to the sailor and looked him in the face. "Do you know that your Don José is a thief?"

"I don't say any different," stammered the poor devil, troubled by Armand's tone.

"And one thing astonishes me—which is that the clown has found two French sailors to serve him, two Malouins."

Marie-Anne Langlois' sun-tanned skin took on a brick-like hue. His eyes had a wild gleam; then, suddenly calming down, he extended his arm in a gesture of resignation and abandon.

"What do you expect? One has to live." And in a dull voice, almost veiled by tears, he went on: "I was the owner of a fishing-boat. It had cost me twenty thousand francs—all that the old man had left me. The *Margaret* flew like a seagull, playing with the waves. One day, a big wave capsized her and she sank. What could I do? The wife, four boys and a little girl. They all have to eat. The youngster—who has a good brain, it seems—is at the naval school. Since he can be an officer, and not lead the same hard existence as the rest of us, he needs to stay there…but the fees have to be paid. Then Miraflor came along. He was offering high pay. I accepted, with Yan, so that the little ones don't choke on the north wind and so that the youngster can wear a uniform. That's why I'm here."

Two tears ran slowly down the Malouin's bronzed cheeks.

Moved by the story, Lavarède shook the sailor's hand. "There's one thing you haven't thought of, comrade." He addressed him as *tu*—the familiar and affectionate custom of the people—which caused Langlois to shiver. "Which is," Armand continued, "that the boat, delivered to the Triplice, will launch torpedoes against our own in wartime. You might perhaps be preparing the death of your son, at the very moment that you're trampling your dignity in order to ensure him a rank in the navy."

"Damn it!" groaned the man. "That's true!" And, after a perplexed silence, he asked: "Tell me, then, what I ought to do."

"Call your son."

Yan immediately appeared. Brought up to date, he declared without hesitation that the Monsieur was right.

"Then we're in agreement my lads," said Lavarède. "I too have Breton blood in my veins, and I don't want countrymen to do anything inadmissible. I'm going to fetch two friends who are staying close by, I'll bring them aboard, and we'll take the boat back to France."

"Agreed!"

"We're not robbing Don José?"

"No fear. In the month that we've been going from port to port, the visitors have brought him more than fifty thousand francs."

"In that case, to your posts, and at the signal from the control panel, forward ho!"

The mariners went back to their respective compartments, while the journalist climbed the ladder of the *François-Joseph*, murmuring: "I'm thumbing my nose at the Triplice, and returning to Marseilles without opening my purse. José is decidedly my Providence."

On reaching the deck he uttered an exclamation of joy. He had just perceived Murlyton and his daughter strolling on the Rive Gramala. He waved his handkerchief and signaled to the English duo to join him—but his mime attracted the attention of two men who were coming out of the Via Salita.

They were Bouvreuil and Don José.

When the news of the derailment of the Szegedin-Trieste train had reached him, the usurer, enlightened by a presentiment, had not hesitated to declare that his enemy must have been on that train. He convinced Schultze and Muller, and, escorted by them, had started searching the city. During his comings and goings he had found himself face to face with Miraflor.

It was not a time for arguments. In any case, between honest men of that stripe, there is always an understanding. José swiftly declared that his situation was prosperous and that he intended to reimburse the landlord the sum of which he had relieved him in America. If Bouvreuil forgave him, he knew the city and could assist him in his search.

At the sight of Lavarède, Pénélope's father shivered with pleasure. He ran to the policemen who were following him a few steps behind, spoke to them in a low voice, and came back to his "friend." Then they both headed for the *François-Joseph*.

In the meantime, Armand had undone the mooring-rope attaching the torpedo-boat to the quay. Having terminated that operation he straightened up, and nearly burst out laughing. On the gangway leading to the deck he saw the usurer and the ex-governor of Cambo marching behind the English duo.

"Go down," was all he said to the gentleman, who questioned him with his gaze. "You too, Mademoiselle."

"You're doing the honors of my boat marvelously," Miraflor remarked.

"Indeed, Señor. Would you like me to be your cicerone too?"

The proposal provoked a mild hilarity in Bouvreuil. "Go on ahead, my dear Monsieur Lavarède."

"As you wish."

Soon, they were all assembled in the saloon. Before starting down the ladder, the landlord had looked at the quay. The agents were there.

"My dear Monsieur Lavarède," he said, with a sneer, "you have a little receipt from me for a few thousand francs, the price at which you set my liberty."

"Yes, my dear Monsieur Bouvreuil."

"Well, your liberty is worth a great deal more to you than that."

"Three million, exactly."

"It will be dolorous for you to lose such a sum."

The ironic tone caused Armand to prick up his ears. "What are you insinuating?" he asked.

"Only this: the police are waiting for you on the quay when you go up again."

The journalist smiled. "When I go up again?"

"Yes, my excellent Monsieur Lavarède."

"In that case, I'll go down. Thank you for warning me."

A dry click was heard. The Parisian had turned the handle that closed the dome sealing the hole at the top of the ladder. Standing next to the control panel, he had seized another lever.

"What are you doing?" howled Bouvreuil and José, stupefied.

"As you can see, Messieurs, I'm going down."

Indeed, a singular noise, the sound of water sliding over the flanks of the vessel, reached the audience.

The acolytes made as if to hurl themselves upon the young man, but the latter extended his hand to a black button placed on the center of the control panel and said, coldly: "One move, and I open the *Goubet* to the sea."

"The *Goubet*!" roared the adventurer—who stepped back nevertheless.

"Yes, the *Goubet*. That's the true name of the boat that you were going to deliver to Austria, when the inventor, ruined by his practical trials, had confided it to you uniquely in order that his idea might triumph in his own country."

"Oh!" murmured Aurett. "This gentleman is still a thief, then."

An electric bell rang, and a green light suddenly filled the saloon. The panels were open. The torpedo-boat was resting on the bed of the harbor, in the midst of the green spectrum of the waters. Fish, frightened by the presence of that unaccustomed guest, were fleeing, black shadows in an emerald fog.

The young woman made no attempt to retain her cries of admiration, and her father's lips opened under the pressure of a prolonged: "Oh!"

"I'm going to return this stolen boat to France," Lavarède continued, after having given them time to look, "if you have no objection."

"I think that's fair," Murlyton replied, simply.

"But I protest!" said Miraflor.

Profiting from the general inattention, the wretch had drawn his revolver, and now he aimed it at the Parisian.

"Good," said the latter, in a mocking tone. "I know you as a shooter—you aim poorly and your hand trembles."

Foaming with rage, the Colombian leveled his arm, about to fire. Suddenly, there was a swoosh in the air, and José was lifted up, knocked down and imprisoned in a tangle of cords that had reduced him to immobility.

The niches communicating with the other compartments had rotated, bringing Langlois and Yan into the saloon, summoned by the bell. At a signal from the new captain, the Malouins had accommodated the former captain in the fashion described.

Lavarède approached Miraflor, leaned over him and took a wallet from his pocket.

"You're robbing me!" howled the defeated man.

Making no reply, the journalist took a wad of banknotes from the wallet, which he counted methodically.

"Seventy-six thousand francs. The produce of the visits that the Italians and the Austrians made to the vessel, for I know that you don't have an honest sou. That's thirty-eight thousand francs for you and thirty-eight thousand for Goubet." Having become cheerful again, he continued: "Speaking and acting on his behalf, I'll deduct ten thousand francs from his share, in order to annul the bargain that need constrained him to make, and which you've abused. That's forty-eight thousand that I'm putting back into your wallet and into your pocket." He carried out the action as he spoke. "As for the remaining twenty-eight thousand, I'm giving them to the Langlois in order for them to purchase a boat. Goubet won't think that's too much, for having saved his work from dishonor."

As the Malouin protested, he went on: "Take it. You can be sure that the inventor would approve. In any case, I hope to indemnify him. With Gautier's aid, we'll mount a serious press campaign, and the Ministry will end up listening to us." Then, assuming the tone of a commandant, he said: "Yan, to the searchlight! Langlois to the engine! If we stay here, the police will send divers down."

Instinctively, as men habituated to passive obedience, the sailors had launched themselves to the indicated posts. Bouvreuil sketched a movement in the direction of the control panel but Murlyton stopped him, saying: "No, you can't. No point in killing us all." And he backed up the advice with a solid shove.

The boat set off, gliding slowly at a depth of two meters. It veered to the right in order to go along the Molo Santa Teresa, went around the platform of the Lanterna, and headed due south, into the Adriatic. Through the panels the passengers could see green bands of water flowing past, slightly rippled by the friction of the *Goubet*, to which we shall henceforth apply that French appellation. The ground was no longer visible beneath the torpedo-boat.

"At what depth are we?" asked Aurett.

Armand consulted the manometer. "Twenty-two brasses."

"And what's a brass?"

"One meter sixty. The agitations of the surface are no longer transmitted here. You'll notice that none of us is suffering any sea-sickness. Now, as the average depth of the Adriatic is two hundred meters, I can give the vessel its maximum speed without any danger."

"Which is?"

"We're going to find out."

A turn of the handle, and the susurrus of the water accentuated, becoming strident. The young man's eyes were fixed on a dial on which a needle was spinning rapidly. The pointer finally settled down.

"Fifty miles an hour," said the young man. "That's phenomenal—and frightening."

They all looked at one another, the same thought crossing all their minds: at that speed a collision would be catastrophic. If a rock happened to be in the way and the submarine hit it, it would burst like an empty nutshell under the impulsion of its propeller.

A large chart of the Mediterranean, indicating the depths from Gibraltar to Candia, was hanging on the wall opposite the control panel. With the aid of a compass, the Parisian calculated the route.

That evening, at nine o'clock, after a dinner take from the on-board provisions, they were off Ancona. Everyone settled down to spend the night on the divans circling the saloon. As a precaution, Don José was not untied.

Armand remained at his post, alone. Keeping watch, he passed Civita-Nova, Benedetta, Cuillanova, Pescara and Vasto. As he had no fear of being seen by night he took the boat to the surface and opened the cupola in order to renew the respirable air without having recourse to the machines. Toward midnight, he skirted the island of Tremiti.

Piesti, at the extremity of the cape of the same name, Manfredonia, in the depths of a picturesque bay in which particular alga gives the waters a saffron tint, Barletta, Trani, Bari and Brindisi, the port of attachment of the steamers carrying mail to and from India and Australia, were passed by the submarine in its hectic course.

When Aurett opened her eyes at six o'clock in the morning, the *Goubert* was emerging from the Otranto channel and was within sight of the city, couched at the extremity of the heel of the Italian boot. Leaving the Ionian archipelago to the left and the Gulf of Tarente to the right, the torpedo-boat headed for Sicily.

From time to time, Lavarède made the apparatus dive. They went down into submarine valleys carpeted with algae, fucus, coral and sponges. In the luminous circle of the searchlight, the voyagers, glued to the glass, contemplated a strange spectacle of which no terrestrial landscape can give any idea.

By virtue of the density of the environment, the wrack and the long sea-grass rose toward the surface with a rigid verticality, and in the fissures in the ricks, amid the coralliferous vegetation, unsuspected monsters were swarming:

cephalopods, ea-spiders with glaucous eyes and giant lobsters, surprised by the electric radiation, raced from the depths of the shadow, bustling urgently toward the luminous source, like moths to the flame of a candle. Here, though, instead of graceful insects, there was a legion of horrible creatures that seemed to have been vomited by a nightmare.

Bouvreuil was bewildered. Perhaps all that reminded him of the bad dreams of a corrupt businessman. He had also learned that among the packages that had been taken aboard was a barrel of gunpowder, with the result that, like Buridan's ass, he did not know whether his fear of the explosive mixture was greater than his dread of the crustaceans.

A more fearful vision awaited the passengers. In one of the descents into the depths, they found themselves in the presence of the hull of a ship lying to starboard. It was a large vessel. Its masts, severed a meter above the deck, and its flank, ripped open by a tear three brasses long, testified to the catastrophe it has suffered. The boat had sunk after hitting a reef.

The *Goubet* suspended her march and approached the wreck. A cry rang out.

"There! There on the deck, look!" said Aurett, putting her hand over her eyes.

Among the marine lianas growing from the rotten wood and the stony concretions of polyps, they recognized human skeletons. One of them, half-emerged from the aft hatchway, entirely devoid of flesh, washed away by the salty waters, had even conserved an attitude of agony. The zone where they were was not reached by any agitation at the surface, and the skeleton remained with its arms in the air, its heads tilted backwards, seemingly continuing a supreme appeal, making a final effort to flee asphyxia.

Slowly, the torpedo-boat made a tour of the wreck. At the rear, half eaten away, the voyagers were able to read the name *Sémillante*, and Lavarède's grave voice broke the silence, emotionally: "The *Sémillante* was transporting troops to the army of the Crimea. She hit a reef not marked on the charts and sank, taking down three hundred and fifty crewmen and nine hundred and seventy-five soldiers. Let's salute them, my friends: they were French!"[62]

The *Goubet* drew away at top speed, as if she had understood the desire of those manning her.

For a long time she flew like that, without anyone thinking of speaking.

Suddenly, the apparatus suffered a slight shock. The sound of the friction of the water stopped. The boat became still in the green immobility. Almost immediately, Langlois appeared.

"The motor's no longer working."

---

[62] The wreck of the *Sémillante* in the Lavezzi islands on 15 February 1855 was one of the most famous disasters of the era.

"Ha ha!" sniggered Don José. "The accumulators have run dry. I was waiting for others before leaving. Now we can neither rise nor descend."

Lavarède consulted his chart. "We're almost opposite Messina…scarcely a kilometer away."

"In that case," said Langlois, "the collapsible boat can get there."

"The collapsible boat?"

"Yes—it's in a box. It's a fabric canoe that can be stretched over a wooden frame. Once on the surface, we can assemble the apparatus and row to the shore.

"Good," said Bouvreuil. "But we need to get up to the surface."

Armand shrugged. "What about the safety-weight? Goubet didn't attach it to his keel for nothing." In a loud voice he added: "Pay attention—everyone hold on tight." He turned to Aurett, who was very pale. "Having on to a divan, Miss. They're fixed to the wall. Good…are you ready?"

She nodded her head.

"Let's go, then!"

A handle grated twice under the captain's hand.

"Go with God!"

A violent shock was produced. The passengers were shaken like leaves in a tempest. They had a vertiginous sensation of falling from a height, and then a further shock that sent them tumbling pell-mell to the floor—and the torpedo-boat stopped.

Soon, they are all on deck. Armand is right; they have a marvelous landscape before their eyes, the unique spectacle offered by the Strait of Messina, with the high mountains of Calabria to one side, whose dried-up torrents are roads leading to Reggio, where King Murat was shot, and the Sicilian coast on the other side, with Etna dominating the high mountains, while at the foot, gently bathed by blue waves, the town of Messina, inundated with sunlight, is displayed in stages around its pot.

Without wasting a moment, Langlois and Yan set the collapsible afloat.

Don José laughs malevolently. "We'll see whether the Italian authorities will permit Monsieur Lavarède to take my torpedo-boat back to France!" he says to Bouvreuil.

The journalist shivers. The foreigner will lodge a complaint. The boat will be confiscated until an investigation is mounted. Plans will be drawn up and the French invention will become a weapon for Italy.

No, it shall not be. The young man's gaze is irradiated by a saintly exaltation.

All the travelers take their places in the canoe, with provisions carefully packed up by the Parisian. The oars are shipped. Then Armand makes a wild gesture.

"In my place, Goubet would do it," he murmurs.

He is seen disappearing into the submarine. Two minutes go by. The young man returns, a trifle pale. He jumps into the canoe and says to the sailors: "Row with all your might, lads!"

The Malouins do not understand, but they obey. The distance separating them from the submarine increases rapidly. A hundred meters, two hundred, three hundred...

Suddenly, a frightful explosion rips the air. A column of fire and smoke rises up above the torpedo-boat, which is lost in a frightful whirlpool.

"There was powder on board," says Lavarède, his eyes shining with enthusiasm. "I've blown up the *Goubet!*" And, with an ironic smile, he adds: "You ought to be satisfied, Señor Miraflor. The debris of the vessel will remain in Italian waters."

XXVIII. The Mafia

"The two Italian associations of brigandage have no connection, Messieurs. The Camorra, or Caldaia, is mainland-based. It was synthesized by Fra Diavolo, sometimes perfumed and pomaded, more often a highwayman, a cruel looter, simultaneously a condottiere and a bravo, mingled with political ambitions. The Cauldron—the English translation of our Caldaia—can lead anywhere, as witness Antonelli Abruzzais, appointed a colonel by Murat, Gasparoni, the former chief of the mountains, selling his wares in Naples, and numerous *galantuomi* who extend their hands to the winners in gambling dens, never refused thanks to the magic formula: 'For the Camorra, Signor!' But the Mafia, Messieurs…oh, the Mafia is another thing entirely."

The man who was speaking, a short fat man, dark-skinned, with circumflex eyebrows, expressing himself with the volubility and abundant gestures of Sicilians, crossed the room, opened the door, made sure that no one was listening, and returned to his interlocutors, Messieurs Bouvreuil and José Miraflor.

On disembarking, the two rogues had held a conference. The submarine boat was destroyed, reduced to smithereens. If they lodged a complaint against Lavarède, the authorities would intervene weakly, not wanting to provoke a Franco-Italian incident that the disappearance of the torpedo boat rendered pointless.

In any case, the journalist was not a man to allow himself to be convicted without protest. Then again, José's past forbidding him the assiduous frequentation of men of law, the Colombian had opted for…clemency—a triumphant euphemism that even drew a smile from Bouvreuil. Both of them, therefore, confirmed the story concocted by Armand in the presence of the port officer, which the latter recorded in his register of new arrivals.

Seven foreign passengers, names following, manning the Espérance, *an electric boat, lost within sight of Messina in consequence of an explosion. Cause of accident unknown.*

That done, the usurer and the adventurer made their decision, and went to see Signor Giovanni Eserrato, of Eserrato, Lifanti & Co.

Bouvreuil had been an investor in the company in question or a long time. He wanted to take advantage of his arrival in Sicily to inform himself regarding a mention that had been made in the printed report of the last shareholders' meeting. Several losses suffered by the bank had been justified by means of the single word *Mafia*.

That was what had motivated Signor Giovanni's speech in the office in which the present scene was taking place.

When the door closed again, the petulant banker came back to his visitors and lowered his voice.

"The Mafia," he went on, "is not an association, it's a people: it's Sicily entire, and nothing but Sicily. All of us in this country are, if not affiliates, accomplices of the Mafia."

"All?" exclaimed the landlord. "Not you, I imagine?"

Eserrato placed his hand on the shareholder's arm, and said, with a hint of dread: "Don't talk like that. I'm a Mafioso, and proud of it."

"You?"

"Me. I would never assist the pursuits of the police or the bersaglieri against the Bravos of the Mountain." And in a whisper: "I intend to preserve myself from the two Ss."

"The two Ss?"

"Yes," whispered the banker. "*Stilettata* and *Scoppiettata*: the thrust of the stiletto or the blast of the rifle, iron or lead. The bravos who stop travelers in order to claim a ransom never show any mercy to informers."

"A fine country," muttered Pénélope's father. "Bandits who hold you to ransom and poltroons who sustain them."

Signor Eserrato laughed loudly. "One can mind one's own business and live for a long time. If you lived here, you'd do the same."

Bouvreuil sat up straight. "Me…," he began. But he remembered the prudent fashion in which his interlocutor had opened the door a little while before. Perhaps an invisible listener was eavesdropping on the conversation. In consequence, he terminated his response, by saying: "Well, obviously"—in a tone so convincing that the banker exclaimed:

"You see. You're a Mafioso already!"

The usurer addressed a strange gaze to the Sicilian, which turned slowly to fix itself upon Miraflor. "After all," he said, moderately. "It's a resource."

"What?"

"Nothing—I was joking.

Shaking the banker's hand, Bouvreuil left the office with José.

"My dear Miraflor," he said. "Don't you find Signor Giovanni's explanations very suggestive?"

"Yes, yes," sniggered the American. "It seems to me that there's something to be done on this island, where no one will enounce us to the carabiniers."

"Isn't there? And when one wants to avenge oneself on a man who revolutionizes Costa Rica, who destroys torpedo-boats…"

José's eyes were shining. "You have an idea, my dear Bouvreuil?"

"Of course!"

"And it is…?"

"A little Mafia…"

"For our…"

"Personal usage. Exactly!"

Arm in arm, the worthy acolytes drew away, beaming.

While they were plotting against his repose, Lavarède received the emotional farewells of Langlois and Yan and then set off in quest of shelter. He was carrying under his arm the package containing the provisions taken from the boat.

"I have the food," he said, cheerfully. "I only lack a table. That's superfluous in this fortunate country where the February sun is a match for our Phoebus in June, but I'm becoming a sybarite."

Aurett laughed, infected by his good humor. Perhaps, too, the gracious child was thinking, deep down, that Paris was close at hand, for a globetrotter like herself: a mere two thousand kilometers away; a day's flight for a swallow, a mere stroll for the love that borrows its wings.

The Palazzo—meaning hotel, the Italian accent metamorphosing the word in that fashion—della Gloriosa Italia, on which Murlyton had designs, was owned by Signora Gabriela Toronti, a sturdy matron on whom forty years had weighed heavily. She flattered herself that she was able to repair the baneful ravages of time with the aid of false hair and polychromatic make-up, but alas, her decorative endeavors only served to emphasize the inanity of her pretentions.

When the voyagers arrived she hurried forward to meet them. In a blue silk dress tailored in the French fashion, a white mantilla on her head and her forehead striped by an enormous kiss-curl describing an inverted question mark, she rolled her eyes as she launched into her patter.

"Would your lordships care to honor the palazzo with their presence? Beppo, Andrei, Petrucchio, show these Excellencies to their apartments."

Beppo, Andrei and Petrucchio refrained from putting in an appearance; no such personnel existed within the hotel.

Signora Gabriela went on: "Undoubtedly these noble persons have need of a *collacione*. They could not have chosen better. The Archangel Gabrielo himself, my benevolent patron, has guided them by the hand. Here, one finds *polenta* unique in all the world, and the *vino* of Zucco, so *buono*, so *amoroso* that the omnipotent Lord..." She signed herself, while continuing: "If he tasted it, would establish his paradise in Sicily."

At this point there was a pause, motivated by the necessity of drawing breath. Armand took advantage of it to bow profoundly to the hostess and say a few words to her of a very Italian complexion, in pure Tuscan:

"Those titles, lordship and excellency, are appropriate to this galantuomo and the signorina, his daughter, rich people: very rich, colossally rich..."

The gentleman tugged Lavarède's sleeve and said to him, in a contained voice: "Don't say another word—she's going to ask me for a nabob's price."

"No, don't worry—a colossal fortune, in Italian, signifies an annual income of ten thousand francs."

And, smiling broadly, more amiable and more seductive than ever, he went on: "I, on the contrary, am only a poet. Povero! Fleeing the mercantilism of my homeland, I have come to ask Italy, the mother of the arts, for her protection. Of you, *cara signora*, as beautiful as the evening star, faithful follower of Phoebe, I solicit a bed to relax my weary limbs, a roof to shelter my head."

Tenderly moved by the journalist's amphigoric compliments, Gabriela nevertheless hesitated. It was necessary to administer the final stroke. Adopting his most insinuating voice, the Frenchman continued: "Parisienne as you seem..."

The hotelier struck an advantageous pose. Throughout Europe, the term "Parisienne" represents an ideal, criticized on high and envied from beneath.

"...You surely have intelligence. You evidently possess an album. I shall put verses therein. Like a bird, the disciple of Apollo pays in song."

"You'll do that?" said the stout woman, breathlessly.

"Right away."

And, with an inspired expression, his arms extended in an attitude of adoration, Armand, abandoning the language of Dante for that of a street-arab, crooned this bizarre quatrain, to which the English contrived to listen without laughing.

"To the charming eyes of the scintillating Signora Gabriela:

Your eyes are the loveliest in Sicily's isle
Possessed of more than six lashes the while,
Each is jealous, neither can be met nor
Outshone in its gaze, even by Etna!

For Italian poetry, Gabriela did not care much, but those French lines, with their ludicrous redundancies, of which she did not understand a word, subjugated her. She offered the young man the best room in the hotel. He was to regret that she had consented to give him as much as a mansard. That evening, she gathered all her best friends, ladies of high Messinan commerce. Very happy to play the patroness of the arts, she exhibited her versifier as the "resident poet of the Palace of Glorious Italy."

The next day, Lavarède, rested by a night's sleep and comforted by a breakfast drawn from his provisions, examined his situation.

Trapped on an island, it's only by boat that I have any chance of getting off it. In consequence, I'll make a tour of the strand where the sailors are.

As in all merchant ports, there is a place in Messina where all the unemployed seamen congregate. The captains go to recruit their crews there. For an hour he waited, studied curiously by all those present. Suddenly, he pricked up his ears. A tall man was walking through the crowd, repeating in a loud voice: "A qualified mechanic? Any mechanics?"

When he arrived beside Lavarède, the latter stopped him.

"A mechanic to go where?"

"Livorno, with stops at Lipari, Naples, Civita-Vecchia and Piombino."

"How long?"

"Five or six days."

"I'm your man—a former student of the school of maritime engineering at Brest."

"You have you diploma?"

"No, for the simple reason that I was shipwrecked here, within sight of the port, and all my papers were lost."

"Shipwrecked! You were on the electric boat, then?"

The previous day's accident had naturally been a topic of conversation for the mariners, and they all knew about it.

"Yes."

"What position did you occupy."

"Captain mechanic."

"Do you have proof?"

"A passenger, Mr. Murlyton was aboard. He's staying at the Glorious Italy hotel.

"Good."

At that moment, Lavarède perceived Langlois and Yan crossing the square. He stopped his interlocutor, who was about to draw away. "Wait—ask those men."

"Why?"

"They made up the crew of the boat."

The Malouins confirmed what he had said, and without further ado, Armand was engaged by Captain Pietro Antonell, commandant of the three-masted steamer *Santa-Lucca*, which was to set sail the following day, the twenty-ninth of February, at three o'clock.

The sailors accompanied the young man to the Piazza del Senatorio, the town hall square, where they said their farewells.

"But we'll see you again in France, won't we, Monsieur? We'll thank you for all you've done for us."

"My friends, it's only mountains that never meet again."

"We're leaving Sicily on the second of March aboard a steamer from Gallipoli, destination Marseilles," said Yan. "Until then we're staying on the outskirts of Messina, in the Via Capranica."

"Almost the countryside," added Langlois.

On arriving at the hotel, the voyager found the door cluttered by beggars. Aurett had made a few large donations that morning; the rumor had spread and all and sundry had come running. On their return, the English duo had had difficulty getting through the ragged crows in quest of a *piecetta* from Their Excellencies. They seemed delighted to discover that their friend had found a means of continuing his voyage. The young woman, in particular, applauded wholeheartedly.

"It's curious," she explained, blushing a little under Armand's gaze. "I've seen you in a crate, as Bouvreuil; you've shown yourself as a sailor, an engineer, the President of a Republic, a warrior, a newsvendor, a ghost, a man condemned to death, an aeronaut, a Buddha, a diplomat, a physician, a sled-conductor, a banker, an electrician and a poet. I'm in haste to see you as a Parisian."

"Me too!" murmured Lavarède, in a tone so tender that the Englishwoman lowered her gaze, understanding that when one is in love, even the simplest words are amorous in their expression.

On the twenty-eighth the voyager went to visit the *Santa-Lucca* to assure himself that everything in the engine room was in good condition, Captain Antonell accompanied his improvised mechanic, and was impressed by his knowledge. In a rapid inspection, the former pupil of the school of maritime engineers identified two defects, slight and easily reparable, which were impeding the transmission of movement to the axle of the propeller.

"Have those small repairs carried out today, he said to the master of the vessel, and your ship will gain a knot and a half in speed."

In the meantime, Murlyton being slightly indisposed. Aurett hired a *corricolo* and undertook an excursion around the town. The archepiscopal palace, ornamented with curious frescoes, and the cathedral, whose flamboyant Gothic fantasy was reminiscent of the audacious lightness of Moorish edifices, interested her greatly. She went along the promenade of Corso, and went to the top of the lighthouse, from which one enjoys an incomparable panorama.

The sun was going down, setting the horizon ablaze, gilding the roofs and coating the facades of the houses crimson. The young woman forgot herself in the contemplation of the magical spectacle. When she climbed back into the vehicle, it was getting dark.

A thin woman with sun-tanned skin and dark eyes was talking to the driver. The latter indicated the voyager. Immediately, the woman came to Aurett and, extending her hand with a supplicant expression, pronounced a few rapid sentences. Although she only understood Italian imperfectly, the young woman understood.

"I'm a poor woman, but proud. I don't want to be confused with the professional beggars who swarm hereabouts, but I've been ill for a long time, there's no work and my children are hungry. Come and see them, and, if you have pity, help a mother."

"Is it far?" asked Aurett, moved.

"Only ten minutes."

"Well, my poor woman, climb into the carriage and tell the coachman where he has to take us."

The Sicilian woman obeyed, after some ceremony. She gave the address to the driver, and the carriage moved off, heading westwards.

To the Englishwoman's questions, the woman replied that she had three children of six, four and two. Poverty had made her ill. For three months she had disputed with death in the big hospital. On coming out she had found the children weeping beside the bed where her husband was already cold. He was a roofer and had broken his neck in a fall. For weeks she had struggled, and that day, desperate and defeated, she had decided to hold out her hand. She had confidence in the generosity of the blonde foreigner with the gentle expression, and had come to her.

The corricolo had left the prosperous quarters and was rolling through a maze of narrow, sinuous streets.

On the doorsteps and at the windows men and women in rags could be seen. They darted bitter looks at the passers-by; then, on perceiving the Italian woman in the carriage, they laughed silently, showing their white teeth.

"We're arrived," said the beggar, replying to a question that her companion had not formulated.

In fact, they stopped almost immediately outside a house of sad appearance, with decrepit walls and a warped roof.

"It's here," she said. "Come and save them."

Aurett leapt to the ground and followed her guide inside. At the end of a somber corridor, the other opened a door and two women went into a narrow room, in which the stale air gripped the throat.

There was a rumbling sound in the street. Aurett sketched a movement toward the entrance, but the beggar-woman was already barring her way.

"It's nothing, Signorina. I sent the carriage away."

"Away? Why?"

"There's no need to indicate your retreat to the bersaglieri."

Light dawned in the young woman's mind. "Ah! Do you intend to keep me here?"

A snigger from the Italian woman replied, and the room was suddenly illuminated. The beggar-woman had lit a lamp. With terror, the Englishwoman saw six motionless men. Considering them attentively, she saw that two of them were familiar.

"Monsieur Bouvreuil," she murmured. "And that José!"

Smiling, the usurer approached her.

"You have no need to tremble, Mademoiselle. A sojourn of twenty-four hours in this hovel won't be an agreeable matter, but we'll make sure that you don't lack anything." "As she looked at him in amazement, with a mixture of scorn and dread, he added: "In return for a hundred louis, your father will see you again."

"What?" stammered Aurett. "You also follow that métier?"

"No, Mademoiselle, but these for brave fellows"—he pointed to the men lined up against the wall, "Would only consent to work for us for five hundred francs each." Smiling, he continued: "I'm bringing Mr. Murlyton an excellent business deal. He'll have Lavarède's millions, and I don't even want to be paid a commission."

With those words, the usurer bowed to the Englishwoman and left, with the adventurer.

This is what had happened. On quitting the banker Eserrato, the rogues had set out in quest of individuals capable of helping them in a scheme they had just hatched.

Lavarède's affection for Aurett had not escaped the usurer's attention, and he had said: "The gentleman is treating him kindly. If the journalist wins the bet, he'll grant him his daughter. It will be a means of recovering possession of the deceased's inheritance—but if the worthy Armand hasn't a sou, the practical Englishman will change his attitude. It's more necessary than ever to ruin Lavarède." And, remembering that from Eve all the way to his Pénélope, all the tribulations of men have been caused by women, he had concluded: "It's therefore by way of the lovely Aurett that it's necessary to reach him."

With the aid of the adventurer, the landlord had easily recruited four villains, one of whom was the legitimate husband of the thin woman who had drawn the victim into the trap. Now, delighted, savoring his vengeance in advance, the usurer went back to dine at the *Sicilia e Roma* hotel, where he was staying.

After visiting the ship, Lavarède had returned to the Palazzo de la Gloriosa Italia, he had found the gentleman alone, occupied in tidying up his travel notes.

"Do you know," the latter said to him, on perceiving him, "that our excursion hasn't been banal? Thanks to you and your ingenuity, it's completely picturesque.. What a man you are! When I think that without spending a centime you've traveled from Paris to Sicily, via America, China and Tibet, and that furthermore—I was counting up just now—you've made more than sixty thousand francs, which you've distributed generously along the route, I'm truly delighted to have made your acquaintance."

"I've simply profited from circumstances," said Lavarède, modestly.

"When you haven't created them, as in Bordeaux, Cambo, San Francisco, Lhasa, Chardzhou and Baku."

Commenced in that amicable tone, the conversation went on until dinnertime.

"What can Aurett be doing?" said the Englishman, as the bell summoned the voyagers to table. "She isn't back yet."

Armand got to his feet. "Where did she go?"

"I'll ask."

Anxiety had paled the young man's face. In the lobby they learned that the signorina had departed in Sieur Fierone's corricolo, and that the latter lived across the street from the hotel. That affirmation reassured Lavarède, but an instant later he was told that Fierone had returned a long time ago. This time, he could not help murmuring: "As long as nothing bad had happened to her!"

In Armand's mouth, always cheerful, such a supposition became frightful.

"What do you fear, then?" said the gentleman.

"What do I fear? How do I know? But we're in the classic territory of brigandage and the Mafia..."

"That exists, then? I've read terrible stories in the newspapers, but I assumed that the imagination of the reporters..."

"Nothing of the sort, unfortunately. No longer ago than last year, a poor devil who couldn't pay the ransom demanded by the Mafiosi was reduced to a pulp."

"But then...my daughter?"

"Come to the coachman's house. We'll interrogate him."

Following the directions given by Signora Gabriela, they found Fierone's lodgings easily. The latter was eating dinner tranquilly. His wife was singing as she served him. Both looked satisfied, which would not have astonished the voyagers had they known that the Sicilian had just received a hundred lira for taking the young Englishwoman to the place where Bouvreuil and his accomplices were waiting.

"How can I be of service, Signori?" he exclaimed on seeing the visitors come in. "An excursion, no doubt? No one knows the city and its surroundings better."

Lavarède interrupted him brusquely.

"It's not that. You took out a young woman resident at the Gloriosa Italia a little while ago."

Fierone exchanged a knowing look with his wife, and then assumed a more open expression. "That's true, Signor."

"Where did you take her?"

"To the archbishopric, the cathedral, the Corso and the lighthouse."

"And afterwards?"

"We were coming back when, in the Place du Senatorio, a man signaled to me to stop."

"A man?"

"Yes, Excellency: tall, slim, dark and very richly dressed. He talked to my client, and she paid me, saying that she would return on foot."

"And then?"

"I came back here, where you've found me. But these questions? The young lady has not returned, then?"

"No."

"Jesus! Madona!" the coachman groaned, taking on a grave expression.

"What do these exclamations signify?"

"I'm afraid that this will cost you dearly."

"Dearly? Why?"

"The Bravi della Montana," murmured the Sicilian, shaking his head.

In their turn, the visitors looked at one another anxiously. They left without noticing the ironic expressions of the worthy Italian household. Murlyton had lost his phlegm.

"My child," he said, in the hands of those wretches! And no power can help her!"

"Perhaps," said Lavarède, pensively.

"Oh, my friend, you have an idea?"

"Wait for me here."

The journalist raced into the brightly-lit vestibule of Signora Toronti's palace. A minute later he reappeared.

"Come," he said.

"Where?"

"To see the captain of the bersaglieri."

On the way he told the Englishman that in consequence of a serious investigation the Italian government had acquired a strange certainty some time ago: the majority of Sicilian gendarmes were affiliated to the Mafia; so crimes multiplied from day to day while arrests diminished.

Radical measures were taken. The Sicilian gendarmerie had been transported en masse to the continent and replaced by carabinieri from the north, to which bersaglieri had been added, hunters whose recruitment was primarily made among the Piedmontese. The latter, at least, were waging a merciless war against the bandits.

The gentleman listened carefully, imposing silence on his paternal anguish in order to comprehend. It was necessary to learn about this bizarre country. Aurett's life was at stake. A rapid journey took the two men to the residence of bersaglieri Captain Margaritora.

The officer was about to leave, but at the first words he introduced the visitors into the small room that served as his study, as the files stacked up in one corner testified. With great attention he listened to Armand's story.

"There's one important piece of evidence," concluded the journalist.

"And that is?"

"That of the coachman Fierone. He saw one of the actors in the probable drama. The man who stopped him in the Plaza del Senatorio is young, elegant..."

The captain shrugged his shoulders. "And dark, no doubt?"

"You know him?" cried the visitors, hopefully.

"Alas, no, because he doesn't exist."

"But..."

"You're not local. You have no suspicion of the cowardice and ill will of the Sicilians. The dark man features in every judiciary investigation. One or several witnesses have always seen the dark man at the scene of the crime. The dark man indicates that the witness is a Mafioso; the man who knows nothing is also a Mafioso; and the victim herself, for fear of future vengeance, becomes mute. All Mafiosi! Among the hundred and twenty thousand inhabitants of Messina, I dare say that if one encounters only a hundred and fifty who are hostile to the Mafia, those one hundred and fifty are men of my company, and myself."

As his listeners looked at him with desolate expressions, he went on: "I'll send out patrols, but we have little chance of running across the abductors." With a hint of disappointment, he added: "And in the interests of the prisoner, since you're able to pay, and these brigands don't desire anything else, it's to be hoped that we don't discover their lair, for that would be the end of the young lady."

The officer made an energetic gesture. "Bitch of a country!" he growled. "Oh, I prefer my Lombardy. I'm from Milan—it's civilized there."

"But then," said Murlyton, bewildered, "Italian law is impotent to protect the subjects of Her Britannic Majesty?"

"Very nearly. Be certain, however, that my soldiers will do their best."

"And me—what can I do?"

"You? Wait. Don't leave your residence. Tomorrow, no doubt, you'll receive a note telling you the figure at which the Bravi of the mountain evaluate your daughter. Above all, don't worry. She will only be in real danger if you refuse to pay the ransom."

Although his heart was beating as if to burst his breast, and although his mental suffering was at least equal to that of the poor father, Lavarède was conscious that the captain was telling the truth.

Guiding his unsteady friend, he returned to the hotel. The two men sat up together. It would have been impossible for them to sleep, and they experienced a dolorous satisfaction in talking about the person they both loved, differently but with an equal tenderness.

Day replaced night; the hours succeeded one another. The city clocks chimed eight, then nine, and then ten. The Parisian could no longer keep still. At noon precisely he was due to embark—and at the idea that, bound by his engagement, it would be necessary for him to leave without knowing his beloved's fate, he felt a sharp and profound pain, like a laceration of his entire being.

Eleven o'clock and still nothing!

Suddenly, hurried paces sounded in the corridor, and Gabriela Toronti opened the door.

"For the English signor," she said. "This envelope has just been found on the table in the lobby."

Murlyton had seized the missive. With an impatient gesture he opened it, but scarcely had he cast his eyes over it than he uttered a cry of despair.

"In Heaven's name, what is it?" stammered the Parisian, distressed.

The Englishman handed him the piece of paper. "Read it, my friend."

Armand deciphered the following lines, traced by a maladroit hand.

Illustrissimo Signor,

A treasure has gone astray; it is your figlia carissima that is concerned. We have been fortunate enough to encounter her and are ready to return her to your hands. Separated from her, you would wish death; we are returning you to life, and beg you humbly in exchange to ensure the existence of poor folk who will bless Your Excellency. A signora Inglese, belonging to the foremost people in the world and one of the foremost families of that people, has an immense value.

We believe that we are being moderate in asking Your Grace to remit, in exchange for the giovinetta, forty thousand pounds sterling. You do not carry such a sum on you, but your word supported by a legally binding promissory note will be sufficient to full us with joy. Your handkerchief attached to the sill of your window will signify acceptance. If between now and this evening you have not thought it your duty to make that signal, we shall bear the expense of a shroud to confide to the ground the incomparable jewel that the blessed Santa Maria has placed in our hands.

"The wretches," groaned the young man, dully. Then, shrugging his shoulders with his artistic insouciance for the golden calf, he said: "It's no use crying. They're asking for a million. It's necessary to pay."

"To pay...," said the Englishman, in a hoarse voice.

Lavarède considered him with astonishment. He thought it a revolt on the part of a possessor, and said, not without a certain dryness: "They'll kill her otherwise. Do you prefer your money or your daughter?" But he regretted his words immediately. The gentleman had paled under the insult, and, wringing his hands, he moaned: "My money! If I had the sum I would pay it, and return to work in order to remake my fortune, but even by liquidating everything I have, I could scarcely find thirty thousand pounds. And they won't believe me, the bandits— since even you have no suspicion!"

The young man seized his interlocutor's hands, squeezed them vigorously and, running to the window, fixed his handkerchief to the sill.

"What are you doing?" cried Murlyton. "Since I affirm that I don't have...."

He stopped. Lavarède was looking at him, smiling.

"My dear friend," he said. "Lend me ten louis."

"What! Have you gone mad?"

"No—you'll understand. As far as Livorno, I have to serve on the *Santa-Lucca*; I've given my word. Once there, though, there's nothing to prevent me from paying for a rail ticket to Paris. My cousin's inheritance will thus belong to you, since I shall have violated the testamentary clause, and the prisoner is saved!"

He said that simply. Without hesitation and without regret, he renounced the colossal fortune.

"No," the Englishman replied. "I can't accept..."

But the journalist cut him off. "Then I have nothing more to do than put a bullet in my head, in order to force you to inherit the money and extract the treasure, as they call her, from the Mafiosi..."

And, flicking away a tear that was pearling in the corner of his eyes, he said: "Hurry up. I ought to be aboard already. My ten louis, my friend?"

The gentleman did not put up any more resistance. He handed over the money. Then he opened his arms. "My friend," he stammered, weeping. "My son..."

For a moment, the two men embraced. Then Lavarède headed for the port with a light step. At five past three, the *Santa-Lucca* left Messina, carrying its new mechanic.

On the jetty, Bouvreuil was walking with his inseparable associate Miraflor. When the ship was a certain distance away, he started to laugh.

"Now," he said, we can go to reassure the worthy Englishman."

"You're certain that everything has gone to plan?"

"The handkerchief was attached to the window-sill by the damned journalist himself. Hidden in Fierone's house I could see into the room and I followed the scene. The Englishman admitted that he doesn't have a million. Without that, of course, we would have demanded more! Then he gave money to the young man. From which I conclude that, as stupid as a fiancé, Armand has sacrificed his fortune to save his beauty."

"The information you received was absolutely exact?"

"I was sure of it. The Calcutta banker who gave it to me when I was passing for a great explorer possessed a list of English fortunes. I have a few properties there, and they figure on it to the penny—that's why I believed the others. But let's leave it there. Go back to the little one—I'll take care of the Papa."

The two rogues shook hands. Bouvreuil took the road to the Gloriosa Italia.

Don José Miraflor plunged into the popular quarter where Aurett was detained. While walking, he talked to himself. "Why not? It's a good idea. The old Englishman will be furious, obviously, but he'll have to get used to it." And a sinister smile parted his lips.

Soon he reached a street where a broken sign bore the name Via Capranica. He stopped at one of the last houses, went along a dark corridor and penetrated into the room where the young woman, under the guard of the four blackguards, had been imprisoned since the previous day.

José spoke to the Sicilians in a low voice. They went out, leaving him alone with the captive. Then he went to her and said, slyly and menacingly: "Mademoiselle, in Cambo our conversation was interrupted; here, I hope, it won't be."

"What do you mean?" murmured the young woman.

"This. Summoned by a letter, your father is coming here. He will fall in the corridor, stabbed by knives, if you don't marry me."

And as Aurett kept silent, terrified, he continued: "A good monk lives nearby. It's necessary to inform him. He'll bless us before Mr. Murlyton arrives."

The Englishwoman bowed her head. It was necessary for her to yield, renounce the fiancé she had chosen, or her father would be murdered. And, in a low voice, she said: "Inform the monk, but spare my father."

José uttered a cry of triumph, but a tempestuous din suddenly broke out in the corridor.

The door opened, banging against the wall, and three men rushed into the room. Before the wretch could take account of what was happening, a blow from a club laid him out on the ground, and Aurett, lifted from the ground like a feather, was in her father's arms.

When she had recovered from her surprise, he told her what had happened. Langlois and Yan, while waiting for the second of March, had taken lodgings in the Via Capranica, as they had told Lavarède. Learning that a foreigner had been sequestered in a nearby house, they had investigated, and had acquired the certainty that the unfortunate woman was the passenger on the electric boat. They, who were not Mafiosi, had immediately run to Signora Toronti's hotel. At the same moment that the *Santa-Lucca* was leaving port, the gentleman had received the brave mariners, and, at the first words, had got up and left with them to liberate his daughter. Without difficulty, boxing like an Englishman and thumping like Bretons, they had knocked down the scoundrels gathered in the corridor. They had arrived just in time.

Aurett's only desire was to get away from the place where she had suffered so much anguish. They went back to the hotel.

On the way, Murlyton told Aurett about Armand's generous resolution. She shivered from head to toe, gripped by an infinite joy.

"How he loves me!" she said, falling into her father's arms. And suddenly, she asked: "But he won't lose his inheritance until after Livorno?"

"Indeed."

"Well, Father, it's necessary that the man who so deserves to triumph should not be vanquished."

"How can we prevent it?"

"A dispatch."

"But to what address?"

"To the *Santa-Lucca*, as soon as she enters Livorno, marked urgent."

Very happy, she accompanied her father to the telegraph office, and only consented to leave after the telegram had been transmitted.

At the hotel, a fuss was made of the Englishwoman who had escaped from the hands of the bandits. They were told that someone had come to speak to Signor Murlyton after his departure. From the description, Aurett recognized Bouvreuil.

"All right!" growled the gentleman. "If I ever encounter that individual again, I swear that I shall give him an important lesson."

XXIX. France

On the morning of the fifth of March, the *Santa-Lucca* moored in the harbor of Livorno. A squall off the island of Elba had been the only incident of the voyage. The boat was scarcely at the quay before a telegraphist leapt aboard, asking: "Signor Lavarède?"

Alerted, the latter presented himself, and the messenger handed him a dispatch.

"A telegram? For me? Here? Who the devil can...?"

Very intrigued, he looked at the signature first. "From Murlyton...oh, good, he's letting me know that the miss has been returned."

That was the case, but it was not all. The dispatch read:

Abduction of Aurett simulated. Maneuver by Bouvreuil to dupe you. Not honest to profit from situation. Correct to warn you. My daughter beside me. Says continue voyage. Meet in Paris 25, chez notary. Since no longer able to monitor, furnish certificates indicating means of transport employed. Truly Murlyton.

For an instant, the young man remained motionless. An intense joy was singing within him. Aurett was no longer in danger. And it was her, the dear girl, who was saying, in the laconic dryness of the telegram: "Continue your voyage. My heart is with you, I want you to arrive victorious."

A few seconds accorded to sentiment, and then the Parisian found himself full of ardor again.

He needed certificates: first of all, that of the captain of the *Santa-Lucca*. The latter did not raise any difficulty to attesting that during the journey from Messina to Livorno, from the twenty-ninth of February 1892 to the fifth of March, Armand had zealously and skillfully fulfilled the duties of a ship's mechanic, and had received no retribution other than nourishment.

No less graciously, he accorded that model mariner a few sheets of letter paper, and Lavarède immediately placed in an envelope the two hundred francs he had borrowed from Mr. Murlyton, converted into a check by Captain Antonell. In his finest handwriting he added the subscription: *To Maître Panabert, notary, Rue de Châteaudun, Paris. To be remitted to Mr. Murlyton, esq.*

Once ashore, humor got the upper hand again.

"I have twenty-five centimes to spend. That's the price of a postage stamp in all the countries of the postal union. Nothing, therefore, prevents me from attaching one to my letter to Maître Panabert."

Once the epistle had been put in the post, the voyager occupied himself with obeying the injunction of his two friends.

The master of a tartan completing his crew hired him, and from Livorno to Spezzia, and then Genoa, he learned to maneuver a lateen sail by day and to fish with a net by night. At Genoa he passed on to another boat to Vintimiglia, successively making war on tuna, the common sponge and roseate coral.

A day's march on foot along the marvelous upper corniche brought the journalist to Monaco, where, in order to reach Nice, he followed the lower corniche along the edge of the sea.

There, a sailor having been grievously injured in a brawl, Lavarède replaced him on a coaster laden with oranges and pomegranates. Disembarked at Toulon, the voyager had the good fortune to encounter the yacht of a Parisian friend, the son of a chocolate manufacturer known throughout the five continents of the world.

Very interested by the story of his adventures, the later offered to take Armand to Marseilles on his pleasure-yacht, which was wandering the Mediterranean aimlessly, and might as well go to Marseilles as anywhere else.

In brief, on the sixteenth of March, at eight o'clock in the morning, the journalist set foot on the Quai de la Joliette. His first exclamation was one of joy.

"Native soil, soil of France, I finally see you again and salute you! Oh, it's good to breathe the air of one's homeland."

He took a deep breath.

"Sapristi!" he said, gaily. "It's not as pure as Nice, and reeks terribly of garlic and soap…but anyway, here or there, it's still the fatherland."

He arranged what he called his papers—which is to say, the attestations of his chance patrons, from the master of the tartan to the yachtsman.

"That way, I won't pass for a vagabond—the greatest danger I'm running now. I don't want to be pinched by the gendarmerie, who, with the placid slowness of our administration, would wait three months for proof of my identity. With these papers, I'm tranquil."

His satisfaction soon gave way to painful reflections, however.

"I'm eight hundred and sixty-five kilometers from Paris. No point in thinking of covering them on foot—I don't have the time. So I have to find a vehicle. But what? What? That's the question. Here, it's no longer a matter of employing heroic means…I'm in the heart of the prosaic now. It's necessary to find a ploy, as they say on the boulevard."

The railway was attractive, of course. If he had known a stationmaster, he would have been able to return to Paris as he had left. Any crate would have done—but he did not know anyone in Marseilles.

While thinking, Lavarède wandered along the Canebière. The wide street bordered with shops, cafes and commercial or maritime agencies, was crowded with vehicles. Bales of coffee and cotton were crossing the path of boxes of soap. Carts were rumbling heavily, the drivers abusing one another. On the sidewalks men laden with burdens were moving in all directions, warning strollers to get out of the way with shrill cries and sonorous exclamations. The familiar terms of the local dialect mingled in a deafening racket.

Calm in the midst of the chaos, young boot-polishers were circulating in uniform smocks, leaping at the feet of any pedestrian who paused, and removing the white dust tarnishing the footwear with nimble brush-strokes.

Avoiding collisions, Lavarède arrived on the Cours Belzunce. The stroller noticed two men who were coming out of a café on the corner of the Rue Pavé-d'Amour. They were talking in loud voices, like the true Marseillais that they were from head to toe.

"Well, then" said one of them, "come to lunch, Bodran."

The other resisted. "No, I have to go..."

"To the mechanics and stokers' depot—fine! The trains will roll without you. As you're the depot chief, they can do everything perfectly well without you..."

"Except that if my absence is observed, I'll be reprimanded. No, you'll take the kid, that's all. Come with me—he must be playing over there."

Lavarède had pricked up his ears. This time he had his idea. A former steamer mechanic, he knew how to drive a locomotive. And he had the depot chief to hand! How could he interest him in his fate?

He followed the two men, who went up toward the Allées de Meilhan, leading to the Gare Saint-Charles. They stopped, and the railway employee pointed at a group of small boys on the opposite sidewalk.

"Look, there's Victor. Take him with you. Hey, Victor—come here."

At that appeal, launched in a stentorian voice, one of the children raised his head.

"It's my father!" he exclaimed—and bounded into the road in order to re-join the author of his days.

In his haste, the child had not noticed a cart that was arriving at top speed.

The speeding vehicle was about to run over the child. The pedestrians say the danger and uttered cries of fright...but abruptly fell silent, amazed. Lavarède had not cried out but had launched himself forward. With the back of his hand he had thrust the child out of the path of the horses, and when the vehicle had passed by he lifted him in his arms and carried him, quite bewildered, to his father.

The latter was literally mad. He embraced the child, shook his savior's hand, made grand gestures, gesticulating and weeping, beginning sentences he did not finish, and finally restored sufficient order to his thoughts for Armand to hear him say: "You've saved Victor's life; remember Père Bodran—he is devoted to you until death."

The Parisian smiled and placed his hand on the Marseillais' shoulder. "As it happens," he said, "I have need of you."

"Of me?"

"Precisely. Without intending to, I overheard your conversation. Monsieur will take charge of your little Victor. A walk and a good lunch with dispel the memory of his fright. While we head for the station I'll explain my plight to you."

With exaggerated manifestations and gesticulations, the friends separated, and the depot chief remained alone with the Parisian. The latter had already prepared his story. He had been living in Messina, getting by from day to day, when he had learned of the death of a relative with a heritage. The decease had been some time ago, and the twenty-fifth of March was the legal limit for claims. His letters to the notary had received no reply, so he had embarked as a mechanic; he had proofs in his pocket. Having arrived that morning in Marseilles, he had no money.

Bodran frowned. The speech seemed to him to be bound to end in a request for a loan. But Lavarède concluded negligently: "To ask for charity or solicit a loan are usual among people who have the habit of idleness, but they're not my way. I'm a worker, and what I'm asking for is a job to do that will enable me to get to Paris."

"Very good," said the depot chief, visibly relieved. After a moment's reflection, though, he added: "But that doesn't tell me what you expect from me."

"But yes."

"You think so?"

"It's obvious. An ex-mechanic, I know how to handle a machine, and you have every facility to offer me one."

Bodran scratched his nose. "Damn! That's not easy."

"Really?"

"Of course—the Company has its mechanics and stokers, qualified by examination. The rotas are fixed, and unless there's an accident..."

"Cause one."

"Cause an accident!" exclaimed the employee, shocked.

"Or rather," Armand continued, "An incident, a gap in the schedule. Look, you're devoted to me for life and death—at least, you said so just now."

"I don't deny it."

"Well, take me to the depot. Invite me to lunch and dinner."

"Good!"

"And make me the gift of a liter of eau-de-vie. With that, I'll take charge of putting a stoker in no condition to depart. That's the incident required. I replace the man on the footplate, and I head for Paris."

The proposition amused Bodran greatly. "Well," he said, "you're a sly one. Come on then. The crews at the depot only go as far as Tarascon, but I'll give you a note to my colleague—he'll send you further."

While talking they had arrived at the Gare Saint-Charles. The journalist went on to the platform with his guide, crossed the tracks and reached the depot.

Ten minutes later, with the aid of his memories of the school at Brest, he had given proof of a knowledge of machines sufficient for Bodran not to have any scruple or anxiety. The section chief gave him lunch.

At two o'clock, as a locomotive pulled in with its crew, he gave him the liter of cognac he had asked for, and Armand scrutinized the face of the incoming stoker. Under the coal dust with which he was masked, his nose was rutilant. What a clue! Lavarède leaned toward Bodran's ear.

"One thing—when is that fellow scheduled to leave?"

"Here's the rota. Goods train 3014, fifty-two minutes after midnight."

"Understood! That's the train I chose."

And, leaving the depot chief, he approached the crewman that he hoped to replace. The stoker was cleaning the locomotive. The Parisian questioned him, representing himself as a company engineer passing through the depot for twenty-four hours.

When the work was finished, he knew that his interlocutor's name was Dalmuche, that he was not satisfied with his lot—a state of mind common to all employees—and that he wanted to be promoted to driver.

Armand pretended to be interested in what he had to say, which flattered the stoker. He promised to recommend him to the administration, which charmed him, and, to finish up, offered him a glass of cognac. The man was conquered at a stroke. His rubescent nose had not deceived the observer; it belonged to a drunkard. As soon as he perceived the liter of alcohol, the crewman conceived a keen affection for the so-called engineer. Instead of devoting the hours of rest granted to him by the schedule to sleep, he wanted to accompany his new friend, take him to Tarascon and show him the Pont du Rhône. But Lavarède calmed him down.

"Get some rest. We'll finish the bottle after dinner. That clears the head."

As promised, things transpired. At eight o'clock the two men were at table, facing one another, the bottle of cognac between them. At eleven o'clock, Dalmuche was snoring on the table after having emptied the bottle.

"He'll take at least twelve hours to sleep off his drink," muttered the depot chief, who had followed Lavarède's maneuver with interest. "I have no alternative but to make a note of the incident. There being no other stoker available, I engage you—my responsibility is covered."

"But you won't report that the reason is drunkenness," objected the young man.

"Why not?"

"I don't want to cause trouble for the poor devil. Put *sudden indisposition*."

"I'll do that." Slapping his forehead, Bodran added: "Better than that: *choleriform indisposition*."

The journalist looked at him in surprise. "There's talk of cholera in France?"

"Yes—don't you read the papers?"

"I've only just arrived."

"That's true. Know, then, that the papers are reporting a lot of stories of microbes, with the result that no one has the disease, but everyone's afraid of it. If you have a cold, the doctors immediately call it 'choleriform,' a fluxion becomes 'nostral,' a corn on the big toe 'asiatic.' In consequence..."

"*Choleriform* will look good in the report."

With that, Lavarède shook the worthy fellow's hand, slipped into his pocket his letter of recommendation to Monsieur Berlurée, the depot chief at Tarascon, and leapt on to the machine. At his request, Bodran also gave him a certificate establishing the employment of his day.

At 12:52 the 'fire-horse,' as the Arabs say, moved off, drawing the twenty-four wagons of goods train 3014. Because of a broken axle they lost more than two hours at Rognac and arrived in Tarascon at eight o'clock.

Monsieur Berlurée, off duty, was not at the depot. The furnished rooms where he lodged were indicated to Lavarède. The house was near the station. The ground floor was occupied by a wine-shop, whose proprietor was contemplating the shop-front with an expression of despair.

"Monsieur Berlurée?" he replied, to the journalist's question. "He takes his meals here, like almost all the railway employees, but he's gone to the fête at Lunel and won't be back until tomorrow." Without noticing his interlocutor's expression of disappointment, he added: "Damn these votive feasts!"

Armand was struck by his bitter tone, and said, with hypocritical commiseration: "The competition deprives you of clients."

"Oh, I'm above all that. I'm upset about the façade of my house."

"Ah!"

"Yes—I got a painter to come to renew it. He scraped off the old paint, scorched the wood—and bang! Off to Lunel. And I know him! When he's on the spree it lasts a week. In the meantime, my establishment remains in this condition."

In fact, the shop was in a pitiful state. The voyager's face cleared. "He'd be astonished," he said to the wine-merchant, "if he came back and found the shop repainted."

"He'd deserve it...except that I'd end up paying twice over."

"No."

"What do you mean, no?"

"Look," declared Lavarède, "I'll be frank. Monsieur Berlurée's absence inconveniences me a great deal. One service for another. Assure me food and shelter for twenty-four hours and I'll repaint your façade."

The bargain was advantageous. The merchant was soon convinced. His wife, a cheerful matron with a turned-up nose, ran to a paint-shop and brought back the necessary utensils and ingredients, plus a varnish designated by the voyager, who mixed it adroitly with the colors.

An hour after his arrival, the Parisian, clad in a blouse obligingly provided by Madame Félicité Croullaigue, the proprietress, was daubing away with enthusiasm.

Madame Félicité came out frequently to make sure that it was going well. In reality, she was seduced by the fine physiognomy of the painter, his laughing eyes and a certain *je ne sais quoi* that had not encountered in any of her usual clients.

Then again, never had a worker so expeditious been seen in the neighborhood. Thanks to the varnish that Lavarède had requested, the colors dried almost instantaneously, with the result that by dusk the shop had received two coats of sky blue, on which the name of the proprietor, Aristide Croullaigue, stood out in yellow outlined in black. It was superb.

The merchant was exultant. He proclaimed his guest a great artist, and although his wife did not say a word, her gaze was eloquent. Like Signora Toronti in Messina, she was perhaps dreaming of attaching the painter to her establishment. Lavarède was a true Don Juan: no woman escaped his fascination.

The next morning, word arrived from Monsieur Berlurée, brought by a comrade. The depot chief told Croullaigue that, having met some old comrades from the École des Arts et Métiers in Lunel, he was taking five days' leave, with the authorization of his superiors.

At that news, Armand felt a shock. He could not stay in Tarascon until the twenty-second or the twenty-third of March. Oh, he would certainly not have lacked anything in the meantime. Delighted to keep him, Madame Félicité offered to find him work. If necessary, she would have had him paint her broomhandles in the national colors. Her husband had never suspected that there were so many things in the house in need of painting. And Armand covered various objects in various hues, while searching for an idea that did not come.

To reach Paris in good time, the railway alone was a sufficiently rapid means. A visit to the station proved to him that he would not obtain any help from the personnel, trembling under the command of a severe chief.

The eighteenth of March had gone by and the nineteenth was advancing. Desperately, Lavarède plied his brush. He had sworn to leave town the following day no matter what, not to reach Paris but to change location, to escape the nervous excitement that was taking hold of him.

Of a whitewood cupboard he had just made a mahogany one, and was having a vermouth at the counter offered by the proprietor when a crewman came in.

"By the way, Croullaigue" he said, "Tomorrow morning you're expecting two more for lunch."

The merchant nodded his head. "You're expecting friends?"

"No, ambulant employees of the postal service."

"From mail-train 4, Marseilles-Lyon? Why?"

"Because the Perpignan-Cette mail will be late."

"You know that in advance?"

"Yes. A landslide near Narbonne. Provisional service on a single track—hence, delays to trains. But you won't have any cause to complain. There's a certain Poirier, an ambulant, who doesn't engender melancholy. He eats and drinks—there's a man who isn't afraid of the cholera."

Madame Félicité was listening at the door. She uttered a fearful gasp. "Don't pronounce the name of that horrible disease!" Her voice was tremulous.

"All right," said the employee. "What's up with you?"

"What's up? Go to the corner of the street and read the Maire's decree, and then tell me what's up: *In case of observed indisposition, have the invalid transported to hospital immediately, in order to avoid contaminating private houses*."

Lavarède started. Train 4 would have to wait here. The station personnel were therefore expecting ambulant auxiliaries who could be sent with the dispatches from the Midi by another train. A gleam came into his eyes, while his lips parted under the effort of an involuntary smile. Tarascon was no longer annoying Armand, the Croullaigues had become tolerable. For two pins, he would have embraced them.

The next day, early in the morning, the shop filled up with customers. It was Sunday, and everyone knows that on that day, one drinks for the rest of the week. Carafes were emptied, glasses clinked. An alcoholic odor floated in the air.

There was talk of the town, markets, building work, crops and politics, especially local politics. How did the conversations get around to the cholera epidemic? No one could say, but it happened, and the poor proprietress, who was going from table to table in her Sunday dress and bonnet, felt her legs becoming unsteady beneath her on hearing the name of the terrible enemy sent by conquered Asia to assault victorious Europe resonating in her ears.

First her features had been cover by a poppy hue, and then the unfortunate woman had gradually gone pale. Her turned-up nose was palpitating in the middle of a wan face when, at half past midday, the employees of the ambulant post office of train 4 arrived for lunch. Their train was waiting in the station for the mail from the Midi.

Immediately, Lavarède ran to Madame Croullaigue. "Sit down," he said, in a tone that the matron thought anxious. "These gossips have frightened you. I'll serve those messieurs."

The roses returned to the lady's cheeks. She accepted with the gesture of a queen handing over the cares of government to a favorite.

And, light and gracious, Parisian to his fingertips, napkin over his arm, Armand took the postal workers' order. Then he disappeared and came back with a snap that made the compatriots of Tarascon assembled in the room start in surprise. Dexterously, he served the food. Except that, without anyone being able to see, he dusted the portions of one of the agents with a white powder contained in a bottle hidden on Félicité's mantelpiece: a little bottle with four faces, on one of which could be read the eloquent words: *English magnesia*.[63]

The agent, who was none other than the famous Poirier, announced the day before, ate gluttonously, only interrupting himself to declare that Tarasconian cuisine had a slightly peculiar taste…not fundamentally disagreeable, if one ate quickly.

Imperturbably, the journalist listened to the postman's appreciations.

Suddenly, the latter stopped eating. He looked to the right and left with a surprised expression, and ran an anxious hand over his epigastrum and abdomen.

"What's the matter, Poirier?" asked his companion.

"I've…I don't know what I've…it's odd. I beg your pardon, Tolinon—I'll be back directly."

At a run, Poirier accosted Lavarède, whispered something to him, received a response and flew like an arrow into an uncultivated area behind the shop. At the back of it, a small stone shed was distinguishable, the yellow door of which displayed the number 1000. In the North, people are content to identify the place in question with the number 100, but that was insufficient for the Tarasconian fluency of Croullaigue, who had added a zero.

There was a large rusty key in the door. Poirier disappeared into the tiny building, the discreet confidant of more than one suffering, and, after a few moments of meditation, thought about going to rejoin his friend. But no matter how hard he pushed the oak batten, it refused to turn on its hinges. He exhausted himself in vain efforts, shouting and howling. He could not be heard at such a distance. The unfortunate fellow roared in his prison for half an hour.

Finally, he heard a noise. He uttered a sigh of satisfaction. His appeals had been heard. He was about to be liberated.

The door opened. He hurtled out, with thanks on his lips, but a sheet of cloth came down over his head. Before he could protest against this new misadventure, he was knocked down, tied up, placed on a stretcher and carried away by two men toward an unknown destination.

In the middle of a group of worried people gathered on the uncultivated ground, Lavarède was speaking. He forced himself to remain serious, although it was difficult because he had such a strong desire to laugh. He had left the common room of the shop behind Poirier, imprisoned the poor ambulant mailman with a turn of the key, and when his colleague Tolinon had become anxious about his long absence, he had exclaimed: "I'll go look for him, Monsieur."

Five or six times he had pretended to enquire about the postman. At each trip his expression became darker. The third time, he had murmured in a low voice as he passed close to Madame Félicité: "What if it's cholera…?"

The fourth time, he had added: "What if he dies in there…?"

---

[63] Magnesium sulfate, known in England as Epsom salt, a common laxative.

The proprietress had lost her head, sent her husband to the Commissaire at the station, and that functionary, accompanied by two porters and a stretcher, had taken possession of Poirier in order to transfer him to the hospital, as prescribed by the Maire's edict.

Now the other postman, Tolinon, was lamenting. He had been left alone to ensure the service between Tarascon and Lyon. No auxiliary again! He was certain to make errors that would impede his promotion, for although the administration can absolve itself from all responsibility to the public by means of invoking *force majeure*, employees are not permitted to make use of the same excuse.

"It's all right," said a voice beside him. "During the Turko-Russian war, I was a mailman in the Balkans. If you like, I'll help you."

Tolinon turned round. Lavarède was smiling at him. He was telling the truth...almost. As a correspondent of his newspaper, circumstances had led him, in Turkey, to accompany a courier to make sure that his dispatch was sent, which did not always happen in those days in the Ottoman Empire.

In the ambulant mailman's situation, a man who had some knowledge of what he was doing was salvation. After a few rapid questions, he shook the Parisian's hand.

"Come on, then; it's nearly time to go."

"Just a minute."

To run to Madame Félicité, address an emotional adieu to her, and obtain a certificate as a good painter was the work of a moment. Soon, triumphantly, the voyager climbed into the mail van with Tolinon and the train moved off, transporting him toward Lyon, instead of Monsieur Poirier, for whom the orderlies at Tarascon hospital were caring with such devotion that the patient thought that he was going mad.

Montelimar, Valence, Vienne and Givors filed past the eyes of the journalist, charged by Tolinon with throwing out the sacks of dispatches at the stations through which they passed without stopping—and he threw those sacks with such enthusiasm that for a week, the postal service in the départements of the Ardèche, the Drôme, the Isère and the Rhône suffered a sudden perturbation that the inhabitants remembered for a long time...

"Lyon-Perrache!"

At that cry from an employee, Lavarède had to resign his functions. Tolinon introduced him to the stationmaster, who congratulated him warmly. The whimsicality of his distribution was as yet unknown. The deputies, inspectors and overseers insisted on having the honor of shaking his hand.

All that glory did not prevent him from finding himself back on the street. But he put on a brave face, confided to Tolinon that he intended to join the postal service, and obtained a certificate from him to serve "whatever purposes might be necessary" and went his own way, muttering: "Thanks to that imbecile's gratitude, all the personnel at Perrache know me. Nothing to be done here. Let's go elsewhere."

Lengthening his stride, he went through the town and into the countryside.

This way, he said to himself, *at least I can spend a night under the stars without the risk of being arrested by the police.*

While walking, he soliloquized.

"Let's see, let's recapitulate what I've already done in a matter of days: from Livorno to Marseilles, a fisherman, coaster and tourist; from Marseilles to Lyon, a stoker, painter and postman. What does the future have in store for me, and what will I be tomorrow?"

After a sight, he concluded, cheerfully: "Bah! I'm almost half way to Paris already, and something always turns up. *Avanti! Adelante! Worwaert! Forward ho!* I've said it already in so many languages…and now in French: *En avant!*

XXX. Racing

It was late in the evening, and Lavarède was still marching.

Where am I? he wondered, for he had already passed through several villages.

Through the shutters of the ground floor of a rustic building, light was filtering, illuminating a signpost.

"Saint-Germain-au-Mont-d'Or. Good. This is definitely the road to Paris. It's a matter of finding shelter for the night. This looks like a big farm. Let's knock!"

The noise of an animated conversation immediately ceased. In the country, people are suspicious, and have a particular dislike of beggars, tramps and vagabonds. He was reminded of that by the rude fashion in which someone replied to him: "Who is it?"

He represented himself as a famous walker, a record-breaker, since records are in vogue.

"The celebrated Lavarède, who went from Dunkerque to Perpignan in ten days—well, that's me! Now I'm coming back from Perpignan to Dunkerque...you know, all the newspapers have mentioned the race."

"Oh, that's true...I read about that, said one of the farm-hands."

Victor Hugo was right: one always finds someone who has seen more and knows better than everyone else. Then again, there have been so many records and races in recent times that one can easily become confused, and Armand was counting on that.

"I've simply come to ask for a bale of straw for the night, in the corner of a barn."

"That can never be refused."

"Oh, I always pay my expenses—but today, I'm obliged to make an exception. Taking advantage of the crowd that was waiting for me as I passed through Lyon, a pickpocket slipped into the crowd and made off with my purse. I can't pick up any more subsidies until Villefranche, at the control-point of the foot-race, but I'd be glad of a crust of bread and a glass of water."

Requested in that fashion, the crust of bread was transformed into a slice of bacon and a plate of cabbage, and even a delicious morsel of local goat's cheese, all washed down with an honest claret.

The farmer and his son had resumed their discussion. They were talking about the market at Tonnerre, in the Yonne. Jean, the farmer's son, had to take fourteen horses there—two full wagons.

"I'll embark them in the railway at three forty-two in the morning, and get aboard one of the wagons."

Seven horses and one man; that would be fine—but he was claiming that a farm-hand was indispensable in order to take the animals to the station, while the father was arguing that he had no need of one.

"Would you like me to bring you into accord?" said Lavarède, between two mouthfuls.

"Go on."

"I'll accompany Monsieur Jean. It will enable me to start my stage early, and give me the pleasure of rendering you a small service in exchange for your hospitality."

The proposal was accepted immediately, to the great joy of the Parisian, whose fertile mind was imagining a new expedient.

At three o'clock on the twenty-third of March, the young man left the farm, guiding a group of seven horses. Jean was leading the other seven.

The peasant was astonished to observe that his companion had turned his jacket inside out, so that the lining was outside. He asked him the reason for that disguise.

The journalist replied, gravely: "I don't like attracting attention. I'm fulfilling the functions of a groom, so I ought to look like one. Now, the checkered flannel lining gives me the appearance of a coachman on duty. Nothing more natural, then, than to see me embarking horses."

Jean was surprised by that scrupulous scene-setting; his ruddy face took on a bewildered expression, but he said no more.

Lavarède played his role marvelously. He supervised the embarkation of the animals, installed the farmer's son in his wagon with a solicitude for which the boy was grateful, and closed the door carefully.

Having done that, he looked around. The railway employees were paying no heed to him. Jean was local and well-known; no one had any reason to keep watch on his movements. The moment was propitious for the voyager, who leapt into the second wagon and hid behind the bales of hay piled up in one corner to nourish the animals on the way."

He was putting into execution the plan made the previous evening.

The whistle-blast signaling the departure resounded, and a sigh of satisfaction responded to it. The train moved off slowly, heading for Tonnerre. It was a long day, however. Fortunately, Armand had equipped himself with a solid hunk of bread, which prevented hunger from gnawing at him.

Villefranche, Macon, Chalon-sur-Saône and Chagny were passed without any difficulty, but at Perrigny, near Dijon, the undeclared passenger was nearly caught. Taking advantage of a two-hour halt, Jean came to renew the horses' nourishment. Fortunately, it was already dark, otherwise he would inevitably have discovered the journalist crouched in a corner of the wagon.

They set off again. Fatigued, Lavarède lay down on the floor and went to sleep. While he was asleep the train went through Dijon, and then Nuits-sous-Ravières.

At eleven o'clock in the morning on the twenty-second of March, it pulled into Tonnerre station.

There, it was necessary to make himself scarce quickly. The young man opened the door of the wagon and looked outside. Nothing disquieting was in view. He leapt on to the platform—but he as unlucky. Just as his feet touched the ground, Jean emerged from the wagon that had served as his lodgings for thirty-one hours.

Recognizing his father's guest, and convincing himself that the individual in question could not be emerging from a vehicle hired by him without some dark design, was the work of an instant for his suspicious rustic mind. Without hesitation, in a resounding voice that attracted the attention of all the employees, he howled: "Stop, thief!"

Lavarède made a gesture of rage. The idiot was about to set a mob of employees on his heels. He would be arrested, and then...

Well, no; it would not be said that he had run aground in sight of port, without having done everything possible to avoid the disaster.

Spring-heeled, and with the hectic pace of a hunted beast, he ran through the station and the goods yard, and found himself in the town. A hundred meters behind, Jean was running after him, with the crewmen and the porters, shouting: "Stop, thief! Stop, thief!"

There was a side-street facing the fugitive. The open gate of a small garden continuous with the first house caused him to stop in his flight.

Putting an enemy off the track is the surest means of gaining ground, the young man thought.

He went into the garden, closed the gate behind him and waited. Hobnailed footsteps rang on the cobles of the street. He breathed deeply. His adversaries went past his hiding-place.

"I saw him turn the corner over there," shouted an employee.

And the whole band, howling "Stop, thief!" ran in the direction indicated. Armand thought he was safe—but then a slight noise made him shiver. A young woman had come out of the house.

Seeing a stranger in her garden, she could not suppress a cry of alarm. The Parisian looked at her. She was a pretty brunette with a rosy complexion. Her white camisole, short skirt, and, especially, the smoothing iron she was holding in her hand testified to her profession: laundress.

His decision was made. He bowed respectfully, took off his hat, and said, in the most amiable fashion: "Mademoiselle, this garden is marvelous; it's as if the flowers were animate."

She lowered her eyes, a vague smile floating over her red lips. The compliment had reassured her.

"It's a supplicant who is addressing you," Lavarède continued, without taking a step forward. "Charming, you must be good, and will take pity on a poor fellow whom the fatalities of politics have driven into your home."

331

"Politics?" she said, with genuine amazement.

"Yes, Mademoiselle," he said, with formidable aplomb. Privately, he thought: *My God! As long as the child doesn't understand anything about the workings of our parliamentary institutions!*

He told her an improbable story. Compromised in a conspiracy whose aim was to overturn the Ministry, they wanted to arrest him for having dangerous papers. Fortunately, he had remembered a gracious face glimpsed on day at the town's annual fête and had come to ask her for shelter until nightfall

Fortunately, the girl was as naïve as her soul as poetic; to save a conspirator of such attractive appearance seemed heroic to her. Deep down, she was delighted to play the role of Providence, and it was not until nightfall that she permitted him to leave, wishing him *bon voyage*—after having certified in writing the time of his departure, without really understanding why.

Lavarède passed the last houses of the town without any inconvenience and found himself in a bare countryside. To his left, the luminous signals of the railway line guided his march. He felt certain that he would not go astray if he regulated his itinerary in accordance with the disks.

That reasoning, however, so logical in appearance, caused him to deviate from his route. He did not perceive that he had left the line to Paris for that from Saint-Florentin to Troyes—with the result that in the morning, a peasant that he interrogated told him that the twenty kilometers he had covered had been a complete waste of time.

That was devastating. The day of the twenty-third had begun. By virtue of the incident that had occurred at Tonnerre, the journalist took account of the danger of presenting himself at a railway station. His description, furnished by Monsieur Jan, must have been circulated by telegraph throughout the region, and was probably in the hands of the gendarmes. It was necessary to rely primarily on his legs.

The leagues that he had covered uselessly during the night had, alas, provoked a certain heaviness in his ambulatory limbs. Despair was, however, not in Lavarède's nature. Courageously, he set forth again. A farmer to whom he repeated the story of setting a walking record without money gave him a meal and certified the fact. Another gave him a lift in his cart for more than four leagues. That night, the exhausted pedestrian slept in a barn, after having eaten a hunk of bread. Joigny station was not far away.

At daybreak he went into the town and prowled around the station, but an employee looked at him suspiciously. "That looks like the man from Tonnerre," he muttered.

Before the agent's suspicion could be transformed into certainly, Armand thought it prudent to decamp. He was beginning to doubt his success. He had to be in the Rue de Châteaubrun in Paris the following day before six o'clock in the evening, under penalty of losing any right to his cousin's inheritance, and he still had sixty kilometers to travel.

All day long he marched, desperately, but the previous day's forced march was weighing heavily upon him. The necessity of avoiding towns by means of long detours slowed him down. And with that, his only nourishment was a bowl of milk and a crust given to him by a peasant woman.

By nightfall, he was within sight of Sens, but his knees were buckling under him. At the corner of a little wood, two men in smocks had lit a fire. From their satchels, set down beside them, they took slices of bread, the charity of cottages.

The young man approached them, hardly able to support himself. "I have no money," he told them, "and I'm tired and hungry."

"Sit down and eat," said one of them, in a hoarse voice. "We're nomads; we go from town to town in search of work, and we know what it is to have an empty stomach. Here's bread, and in a little while, you can share the potatoes that are baking under the ashes, and the half-liter of wine I have in my bag."

The paupers shared what they had. With them, Armand had no need to make up a story. It had been sufficient to say that he was hungry.

While he indulged in those philosophical reflections, breaking a crust, the two men resumed their interrupted conversation.

"You said just now that you were betting on Chapurzat?"

"Yes, that's what I said—twenty sous that he gets there first."

"Agreed—I'm on Serront."

"Twenty sous?"

"Twenty sous."

"What are you betting on?" asked the journalist.

"The big bicycle race organized by the *Petit Journal*, between Lyon and Paris.[64] The riders are leaving this evening from the Place Bellecoeur." After a pause, the man added, with a knowing air: "There are serious champions. Serront won the Brest race and Chapurzat beat the record at Hoelurs. They'll fight it out."

Lavarède admired the "nomad" who was so knowledgeable about the velocipedal sport. But the potatoes were cooked. He received his share, drank a gulp of wine and lay down alongside his companions.

He woke up fresh and ready. The workers were bewildered when he asked them to certify that they had granted him hospitality beneath the stars, but he shook their hands in such a vigorous fashion that they watched him draw away along the road to Sense, saying: "I don't know what he is, but he's a character."

---

[64] The *Petit Journal*'s editor, Pierre Giffard, was an enthusiastic sponsor of long-distance races of every kind, including the pioneering Paris-Brest bicycle race of 1891, which was caused an enormous sensation, and the world's first car race, from Paris to Rouen, in 1894. He later became the editor of the sporting paper *Le Vélo*. The Paris-Brest race was won by Charles Terront, using a prototype of a new kind of pneumatic tire invented by Michelin.

Armand strode toward the Sénonaise town at a lively pace. He was about to play his last card. That same evening, at six o'clock, he was awaited at Maître Panabert's, whose office was some thirty leagues distant from Sens. At all costs, he had to procure a vehicle more rapid than human legs. There could be no more shilly-shallying. At the risk of being arrested, he had to use the railway.

At nine o'clock in the morning, he reached Sens, and asked for directions to the station. Having obtained the information, he launched himself into the streets of the town.

Suddenly, an exclamation nailed him to the spot. "Monsieur Lavarède!"

He raised his eyes and stood there, stupefied. Mademoiselle Pénélope Bouvreuil was standing in front of him. Starchier and more angular than ever, the usurer's daughter smiled at him. "Ah!" she said. "To think that I've been waiting here for a year for you to come back."

"Really?" said Lavarède, in order to say something. He wondered how he could get rid of that tenacious admirer.

"If you knew how happy I was when Papa telegraphed me from Messina: *Am coming home. Lavarède has renounced his inheritance.* I thought immediately: I shall marry him…to secure his happiness."

"You're very kind," said the young man, mechanically.

"My father repeated in vain: *That Monsieur Lavarède is no match for you.* I sensed that he was mistaken. I was right, since you're here…you've finally come!"

The journalist clenched his fists as he listened to that speech. "And Monsieur Bouvreuil?" he asked.

"You're unlucky—he left for Paris just now. I came with him to the station. He told me that he's going to the notary's—but that doesn't matter. Come to the house. He'll be very glad to see you when he comes back this evening."

Affectionately, she slipped her arm through that of the young voyager, who had begun to rage when he heard the word "notary."

"You've led poor Papa quite a dance," added the tender Pénélope. "Can you imagine that the physician threatened him with a congestion if he resumed his old sedentary habits without transition. He prescribed vigorous daily exercise—with the result that he's bought a bicycle and pedals for three hours every day."

"Sapristi!" exclaimed the voyager.

"What's that?"

He swiftly changed his tone and his attitude. "How unpardonable I am! I'm keeping you standing in the middle of the street. Accept my arm, I beg you, and lead me to the house where you've been dreaming about securing my happiness."

Pénélope did not need the invitation to be repeated. Her wiry hand gripped Armand's arm and she drew her chosen future away at a rapid pace. The young woman's feet hardly touched the ground—she had wings!

In a matter of minutes they reached the Bouvreuil residence, an elegant house preceded by a courtyard closed by a wrought-iron gate. To the right and left were the stable and the garage. Mademoiselle Bouvreuil pointed to the former: "That's where we keep Papa's horse…his bicycle!" She laughed at the joke.

"Let's have a look at the horse," riposted Lavarède, gaily.

"Oh, it's very pretty: nickel-plated, fitted with pneumatic tires, with all the latest improvements. It's superb."

Armand opened the door, and, in order to examine the velocipede, took it out into the courtyard.

"And he can ride this?" he said, after a moment.

"Very well."

"It must be horribly difficult."

"It appears not."

While speaking, the Parisian had sat astride the bicycle, but the apparatus leaned to the right or the left as soon as he tried to put his feet on the pedals. Pénélope laughed.

Her inamorata adopted an offended expression. "Here in this cobbled courtyard," he said, "it's impossible. On a road I could do it."

"Try. The road outside is flat."

Armand went out and recommenced his attempts. Zigzagging, almost falling at every step, he gradually drew away. Standing on the sidewalk, Pénélope was clutching her sides.

Suddenly, it was as if she were petrified, open-mouthed. Having traveled thirty of forty meters, her fiancé had abruptly and solidly sat up straight in the saddle, and the machine maintained its equilibrium.

"Monsieur Lavarède!" shouted the landlord's daughter.

The other turned round. "I'm going to join your father. I'll send the velo back this evening, by train."

With those words he started pedaling so furiously that he had disappeared before the abandoned woman had recovered from her surprise.

Then Armand began a mad race. Leaning over his handlebars, he went with his head down, sensing with a kind of intoxication the road gliding under his wheels. He went through hamlets and villages without a pause, without glancing at the housewives on the doorsteps, astonished by the impetuosity of the cyclist.

At Chapigny, he came upon a group of velocipedists. Exclamations were uttered, cries of surprise, in bewildered tones. He paid no attention. Overwhelmed by the intoxication of speed, he left the group behind without seeing the animated gestures of pedestrian.

When he came close to Montereau, however, Lavarède went past a young man mounted on a bicycle whose shorts, leotard and small round helmet testified clearly enough to his passion for the velocipedic sport. The latter also ut-

335

tered an "Oh!" of surprise, but unlike the previous ones, he launched himself in pursuit of the journalist, whom he caught up in the town. "What!" he said, maintaining a parallel course. "It's you, already?"

Without lifting his head, Armand said: "Yes, it's me."

"Bravo! Keep going. They'll never catch you. I'll go telegraph. It's quite astonishing."

"What is he telegraphing?" the Parisian muttered, still pedaling.

The kilometers succeeded one another. Eventually, the young man experienced cramp in his legs. He slowed down then, and paid some attention to the forested landscape. In one of the "rest stops" a signpost set up beside the road furnished him the indication: *Fontainebleau, 1km 200m.*

In front of him, the road extended through woods to the first houses of the town. A bizarre movement was astir there. People were coming and going. As he came closer, Armand observed that a table had been set up on the sidewalk.

Messieurs with buttonholes ornamented by a flood of multicolored ribbons were standing motionless, but as the voyager arrived they hastened toward him.

"Stop for a moment."

"I don't have time."

"Will you have a glass of champagne?"

"That, gladly."

A flute of the foamy liquid restored his initial vigor. He resumed his course.

I don't understand what just happened...but what does it matter? The champagne was good.

At Melun, it was something else. With strenuous politeness, he was urged to accept some chocolate. Again, he accepted, still unable to explain such generosity.

And thus, all along the route, there was tea, cognac and cordials.

These people are very kind, but I'm damned if I understand why they're so interested in me.

From time to time, cyclists accompanied him, cleaving the air ahead of him. All of France seemed to understand his desire to reach Paris.

At four o'clock he made a triumphant entry into Charenton, and there drank an excellent consommé augmented by pellets of chicken breast.

"Don't lose your way in Paris," a cyclist cried out to him—and handed him an itinerary of streets leading to the *Petit Journal.*

Just at the entrance to the Rue de Châteaudun, thought Armand. *Who told that young man that I was going to the notary's then?*

Almost at the same moment, Mr. Murlyton and Aurett were following the Rue Lafayette in Paris, on their way to see Maître Panabert for the fifth time that day.

Their preceding visits had filled them with anxiety. No news had reached the notary since the letter postmarked Livorno. In consequence, the gentleman was grave and his daughter slightly sad.

They were walking side by side, without exchanging a word. What could they have said, except that the absence of their friend seemed inexplicable? How was it that he, so adroit, had not yet arrived, or given any sign of life?"

Level with the offices of the *Petit Journal* the English duo were stopped by the crowd. The sidewalks were crowded, and people were engaged in discussion. The windows of the building were crowded with spectators

Monsieur Figard, the organizer of the velocipede race from Lyon to Paris, was showing up everywhere, sometimes at a widow, sometimes in the street, speaking with the accompaniment of grand gestures. Everything about him testified to alarm.

"No, it's not possible," he replied to nervous interrogations. "They only left Lyon yesterday evening; none of them can be so close to Paris. It's an error, or a false alarm."

As if to mock his accurate appreciation, one of the paper's newsboys pasted a poster to a billboard mounted on the first floor, which aroused cheers from the audience. It bore the words: *First rider signaled at Charenton. His name not known.*

Murlyton and Aurett drew away, shrugging their shoulders. They had no suspicion that all the fuss was being provoked by their friend, mounted on Bouvreuil's machine.

In Maître Panabert's office, they did not find Armand, merely the radiant landlord.

"I wanted to witness my son-in-law's defeat with my own eyes," he said, with a victorious smile. Since Messina, he had been applying that title to him again.

On quitting the hotel of Glorious Italy, where he had gone while the gentleman was rescuing his daughter with the collaboration of the Malouins, the usurer had gone back to the Rue Capranica. He had found his accomplice there, gasping, his skull fractured, and had rapidly guessed what had happened. Not caring either to find himself in the presence of the Englishman or to have to reckon with the police, he had abandoned José and had returned to France.

In Sens, he had declared to Pénélope that the journalist would never enter into possession of his inheritance, having convinced himself of the fact—but on the twenty-fifth of March an ill-defined anxiety had gripped him.

The journey to Paris by railway—a trivial affair for a man arrived from China—was no deterrent. He had made it. So, in the notary's office, Bouvreuil was manifesting his joy loudly.

"When I get involved in something," he said, puffed up with vanity, "it always succeeds. I've never made a bad deal in my life."

Without saluting him, the father and daughter sat down, waiting.

Five o'clock chimed.

And suddenly, there was a hubbub in the street. Ten seconds had not gone by when the doorbell rang. Rapid footsteps sounded on the floor of the outer office. The door of the study opened, and Lavarède appeared on the threshold, covered in dust.

Three cries greeted his appearance.

"Lavarède!"

"Him!"

"Ah!"

The young man addressed a tender gaze to Aurett. Then he approached Maître Panabert.

"Today, the twenty-fifth of March, at five o'clock—which is to say, an hour in advance of the deadline fixed by my cousin Richard, I've completed a journey around the world, spending only twenty-five centimes. Until Messina, Mr. Murlyton, here present, monitored me; from that point on, here are the certificates establishing the employment of my time. Please verify them, Maître Panabert. One word, however. At Sens, this morning, I took a velocipede. I have no paper proving it, but tomorrow's newspapers will bear witness to it. That is, I believe, sufficient."

Then, while the notary was riffling through the evidence in question, he turned to the usurer and said, slightly sarcastically, but very politely: "Mademoiselle Pénélope lent me your bicycle. They're keeping it for me outside; you can take it back. Please thank your daughter on my behalf."

"Everything is perfectly in order," declared the notary. "My compliments, Monsieur: the inheritance is yours. One detail only; in your absence, creditors have pursued you. Your concierge, remembering my address, came to consult me. Certain that you would wish me to maintain your clientele, I took the liberty of having all the legal documents, protests judgments, seizure orders, etc. sent here, in order to proceed with their settlement on your return."

The journalist began to laugh. "I have only one creditor, and that is Monsieur Bouvreuil. He bought out all the others and put the debts in the hands of various bailiffs, as I see."

"Well, twenty stacks of stamped paper comes to a total of at least twelve thousand francs in expenses."

"You can put them to the account of this Monsieur. He will settle them, in accordance with this written obligation here.

He presented the complete and definitive quittance given to him by the usurer near Szegedin. Pénélope's father uttered a dull moan.

"Everything is liquidated," the young man went on, joyfully. "After satisfactions of self-respect, let me turn to one of pure love." And, bowing to the gentleman, he said, in an emotional voice: "My dear adversary, I have the honor of asking for the hand of Mademoiselle your daughter."

"And I, my dear friend," cried the Englishman, hugging him, "have great pleasure in granting it to you."

Aurett had risen to her feet, blushing. Armand kissed the young daughter of Albion.

"All right!" said Murlyton. "Now that the conjugal question is settled with Monsieur Lavarède, I have another to regulate with Monsieur Bouvreuil here."

"With me?" murmured the landlord, in an amiable one.

"With you, Monsieur. When you sequestered my daughter in Messina, I swore to teach you a lesson the next time I encountered you."

"A lesson?"

"Yes. I keep my word."

And the Englishman's fist, launched violently forward, struck the usurer face with a dull thud.

That day Bouvreuil, had definitely not made a good deal.

It was Lavarède who had, in finding both his fortune and his happiness at the same time.

FERNANDEL *dans*

LES 5 SOUS DE LAVAREDE

DE 5 STUIVERS VAN LAVAREDE

Bibliography of "*Les Voyages Excentriques*"

1. Les Cinq Sous de Lavarède (co-written with Henri Chabrillat)
* First publication in *Le Petit Journal*, 24 August-27 December 1893.
* Furne, Jouvet et Cie., 1894.
* Furne, Jouvet et Cie., 1895.
* Combet et Cie. (formerly Furne), Bibliothèque pour tous, 1902, as two volumes : (1) Les Cinq sous de Lavarède ; (2) Les Compagnons du Lotus blanc.
* Ditto, 1903, as three volumes: (1) Les Cinq sous de Lavarède ; (2) Les Compagnons du Lotus blanc ; (3) Miss Aurett.
* Éditions Georges Fayard, Librairie Universelle Illustrée, then Librairie des Publications Illustrées, 1903, as six volumes as part of a 60-volume Paul d'Ivoi imprint : (1) Les Cinq sous de Lavarède ; (2) Président de république malgré lui ; (3) Un mort qui se porte bien ; (4) Protégé des Boxers ; (5) Aux frais de la police ; (6) Le Triomphe de la bécane.
* Combet et Cie., 1905.
* Tallandier, Œuvres choisies de Paul D'Ivoi, c1910.
* Boivin et Cie, 1914-17
* Tallandier, Le Livre national, Bibliothèque des Grandes Aventures et Voyages Excentriques Nos. 25 & 26, 1924.as two volumes :(1) Les Cinq sous de Lavarède ; (2) Les Compagnons du Lotus blanc.
* Boivin et Cie., 1927.
* Boivin et Cie., 1932, as two volumes : (1) Les Cinq sous de Lavarède ; (2) Les Compagnons du Lotus blanc.
* Tallandier, Œuvres de Paul d'Ivoi, 1934
* Boivin et Cie., 1937, as three volumes.
* Boivin et Cie., 1948, as two volumes.
* Tallandier, 1953 (abridged edition).
* Hachette, Bibliothèque Verte No.144, 1959 (abridged edition).
* Livre de poche, 1976.
* Gallimard, Collection 1000 soleils or, 1980.
* Slatkine, 1982 (facsimilé of the first edition).
* Éditions J'ai Lu, No. 1512, 1983 (abridged edition).
* Casterman, 1993, as two volumes.

2. Le Sergent Simplet à travers les colonies françaises [*Sgt. Simpleton Across the French Colonies*]
* Furne, Jouvet et Cie, 1895.
* Éditions Georges Fayard, Librairie Universelle Illustrée, then Librairie des Publications Illustrées, 1903, as six volumes as part of a 60-volume Paul d'Ivoi

imprint : Les Petits Cousins de Lavarède : (49) Le Sergent Simplet ; (50) La Petite Reine de Madagascar ; (51) Volcans, Pingouins, Brahmes ; (52) La Conquête de Bangkok ; (53) La Mariée par surprise ; (54) La Photographie vengeresse
* Combet et Cie., c.1905.
* Boivin et Cie., c.1907-1908.
* Boivin et Cie., 1914-17
* Tallandier, Le Livre national, Bibliothèque des Grandes Aventures et Voyages Excentriques Nos. 281, 282, 1929, as two volumes : (1) Le Sergent Simplet ; (2) Miss Diana.
* Tallandier, Œuvres de Paul d'Ivoi, 1935.
* Tallandier, 1949 (abridged edition).

3. Cousin de Lavarède / Lew Bolide de Lavarède [*Lavarede's Cousin / Lavarède's Bolide*]
* Furne, Jouvet et Cie., 1897.
* Éditions Georges Fayard, Librairie Universelle Illustrée, then Librairie des Publications Illustrées, 1903, as six volumes as part of a 60-volume Paul d'Ivoi imprint : (7) Cousin de Lavarède ! (8) Un Roi esclave ; (9) Les Geôliers pianistes ; (10) Un fou de génie ; (11) Dix mille lieues dans les nuages ; (12) Patrie et nom perdus.
* Boivin et Cie., 1908, as two volumes.
* Tallandier, Œuvres choisies de Paul D'Ivoi, c.1910.
* Boivin et Cie., 1914-17.
* Tallandier, Le Livre national, Bibliothèque des Grandes Aventures et Voyages Excentriques Nos. 34, 35, 1924, as two volumes : (1) Le Diamant d'Osiris ; (2) Le Bolide.
* Boivin et Cie., 1927.
* Tallandier, Œuvres de Paul d'Ivoi, 1934 under the titlle : Le Diamant d'Osiris.
* Boivin et Cie., 1938, as two volumes.
* Boivin et Cie., 1947, as two volumes (abridged edition).
* Tallandier, 1953, under the title : Le Diamant d'Osiris (abridged edition).
* Hachette, Bibliothèque Verte No.203, 1962, under the tirle : Le Bolide de Lavarède(abridged edition).
* Slatkine, 1984 (facsimilé of the first edition).

4. Jean Fanfare.
* Société d'Édition et de Librairie Ancienne librairie Furne, 1897.
* Éditions Georges Fayard, Librairie Universelle Illustrée, then Librairie des Publications Illustrées, Bibliothèque choisie de Paul d'Ivoi, 1903, as six volumes as part of a 60-volume Paul d'Ivoi imprint : Les Petits Cousins de Lavarède : (55) Jean Fanfare ; (56) La Fiancée en aluminium ; (57) L'Automobile chariot-barque ; (58) Le Clown rit et pleure ; (59) Le Siège de Litzaris ; (60) Les Armures parlent.
* Combet et Cie., c1905.
* Boivin et Cie., 1914-17.
* Tallandier, Le Livre national, Bibliothèque des Grandes Aventures et Voyages Excentriques Nos. 295, 296, 1930, as two volumes : (1) Diane de l'archipel ; (2) La Forteresse roulante
* Tallandier, Œuvres de Paul d'Ivoi, 1935 under the title : La Diane de l'archipel.
* Éditions J'ai Lu, No. 1404, 1982, under the title : La Diane de l'archipel (abridged edition).
* Slatkine, 1984 (facsimilé of the first edition).

5. Corsaire Triplex
* Société d'Édition et de Librairie Ancienne librairie Furne, 1898.
* Combet et Cie., 1901, as two volumes : (1) Le Corsaire invisible ; (2) : Triplex.
* Éditions Georges Fayard, Librairie Universelle Illustrée, then Librairie des Publications Illustrées, Bibliothèque choisie de Paul d'Ivoi, 1903, as six volumes as part of a 60-volume Paul d'Ivoi imprint : Les Lavarède : (13) Le Corsaire Triplex ; (14) La Revanche de Toby ; (15) Entre la corde et le poison ; (16) Les Touristes sous-marins ; (17) Sous la dent des anthropophages ; (18) La Justice du cinématographe.
* Boivin et Cie., 1914-17.
* Tallandier, Le Livre national, Bibliothèque des Grandes Aventures et Voyages Excentriques, Nos. 40, 41, 1925, as two volumes : (1) L'Ennemi invisible ; (2) L'Île d'or.
* Boivin et Cie., 1931.
* Tallandier, Œuvres de Paul d'Ivoi, 1934.

* Boivin et Cie., 1936-39 , as threevolumes : (1) Corsaire Triplex ; (2) L'Ennemi invisible ; (3) L'Île d'or.
* Tallandier, 1953, under the title : Le Corsaire Triplex (abridged edition).
* Hachette, Bibliothèque Verte No. 219, 1962, sous le titre : Lavarède et le Corsaire Triplex (abridged edition)
* Slatkine, 1982 (facsimilé of the first edition).
* Éditions J'ai Lu, No. 1444, 1983 (abridged edition).

6. La Capitaine Nilia
* Société d'Édition et de Librairie Ancienne librairie Furne, 1898.
*Éditions Georges Fayard, Librairie Universelle Illustrée, then Librairie des Publications Illustrées, Bibliothèque choisie de Paul d'Ivoi, 1903, as six volumes as part of a 60-volume Paul d'Ivoi imprint : Les Lavarède : (19) La Capitaine Nilia. (20) L'Éclosion du patriotisme ; (21) Vers la liberté ; (22) L'Âme noire ; (23) Un valeureux orang-outang ; (24) La Pluie de roses.
* Boivin et Cie., 1911, astwo volumes.
* Boivin et Cie., 1914-17.
* Tallandier, Le Livre national, Bibliothèque des Grandes Aventures et Voyages Excentriques Nos. 48, 49, 1925, as two volumes : (1) La Capitaine Nilia ; (2) Secret de Nilia.
* Tallandier, Le Livre national, Bibliothèque des Grandes Aventures et Voyages Excentriques,Nos. 450, 451 1932, as two volumes : (1) La Capitaine Nilia ; (2) Secret de Nilia.
* Tallandier, Œuvres de Paul d'Ivoi, 1935.

* Boivin et Cie., 1947, as two volumes.
* Tallandier, 1954 (abridged edition).
* Éditions J'ai Lu, No. 1405, 1982 (abridged edition).
* Slatkine, 1982 (facsimilé of the first edition).

7. Le Docteur Mystère
* Combet et Cie., 1900.
* Éditions Georges Fayard, Librairie Universelle Illustrée, then Librairie des Publications Illustrées, Bibliothèque choisie de Paul d'Ivoi, 1903, as six volumes as part of a 60-volume Paul d'Ivoi imprint : Cigale, émule de Lavarède : (25) Le Docteur Mystère ; (26) Les Cinq rubis de Siva ; (27) L'Ours Ludovic ; (28) La Folle du temple d'or ; (29) Les Ruses du Brahme ; (30) Le Secret des 7 tombes.

* Boivin et Cie., 1914-17.
* Tallandier, Le Livre national, Bibliothèque des Grandes Aventures et Voyages Excentriques Nos. 126, 127, 1926, as two volumes : (1) L'Ours de Siva ; (2) Le Brahme d'Ellora
* Boivin et Vie., 1933.
* Tallandier, Œuvres de Paul d'Ivoi, 1934.
* Boivin et Cie., 1934, as two volumes.
* Tallandier, Grandes aventures, 1951 as two volumes : (1) Le Docteur Mystère. ; (2) Le Brahme d'Ellora.
* Slatkine, 1982 (facsimilé of the first edition).
* Éditions J'ai Lu, No. 1458, 1983 (abridged version).

8. Cigale en Chine [*Cigale in China*]
* First publication in *Le Français*, from 3 December 1900 to 8 March 1901.
* Combet et Cie., 1901.
* Éditions Georges Fayard, Librairie Universelle Illustrée, then Librairie des Publications Illustrées, Bibliothèque choisie de Paul d'Ivoi, 1903, as six volumes as part of a 60-volume Paul d'Ivoi imprint : Cigale, émule de Lavarède : (31) Cigale en Chine ; (32) La Ville interdite ; (33) Le Fleuve de sang ; (34) Les Captifs de Tsou-Hsi ; (35) Le Colisée chinois ; (36 L'Assaut de Pékin.
* Boivin et Cie., 1914-17.
* Tallandier, Le Livre national, Bibliothèque des Grandes Aventures et Voyages Excentriques Nos. 143, 144, 1927, as two volumes : (1) Cigale en Chine ; (2) La Princesse Roseau-Fleuri.
* Boivin et Cie., 1928.
* Tallandier, Œuvres de Paul d'Ivoi, 1934.
* Boivin et Cie., collection Les Voyages excentriques, 1936, as two volumes.
* Boivin et Cie., collection des Voyages excentriques, 1949, as two volumes.
* Tallandier, Grandes aventures, 1952 as two volumes :(1) Cigale en Chine ; (2) La Princesse Roseau-Fleuri.
* Éditions J'ai Lu No. 1471, 1983 (abridged edition).

9. Massiliague de Marseille
* Combet et Cie., 1902.
* Éditions Georges Fayard, Librairie Universelle Illustrée, then Librairie des Publications Illustrées, Bibliothèque choisie de Paul d'Ivoi, 1903, as six volumes as part of a 60-volume Paul d'Ivoi imprint : Cigale, émule de Lavarède : (37) Massiliague de Marseille ; (38) Le Captif de Chicago ; (39) Les Pionniers du désert ; (40) Peaux Blanches et Peaux Rouges ; (41) Un traître dévoué ; (42) Le Gorgerin des Incas
* Boivin et Cie., 1914, as two volumes.
* Boivin et Cie., 1914-17.

* Tallandier, Le Livre national, Bibliothèque des Grandes Aventures et Voyages Excentriques Nos.93, 94, 1926, as two volumes : (1) Massiliague de Marseille ; (2) Le Voeu des Incas.
* Boivin et Cie., 1931.
* Tallandier, Œuvres de Paul d'Ivoi, 1934.
* Boivin et Cie., 1936-1937, as two volumes.
* Tallandier, 1949abridged edition)..
* Slatkine, 1982 (facsimilé of the first edition).

10. Les Semeurs de glace [*The Sowers of Ice*]
* First publication in L*e Journal des Voyages*, 1902-1903.
* Combet et Cie., 1903.
* Éditions Georges Fayard, Librairie Universelle Illustrée, then Librairie des Publications Illustrées, Bibliothèque choisie de Paul d'Ivoi, 1903, as six volumes as part of a 60-volume Paul d'Ivoi imprint : Cigale, émule de Lavarède : (43) Les Semeurs de glace ; (44) Deux anglaises dans l'embarras ; (45) Sur le fleuve Amazone ; (46) L'Azur qui tue ; (47) L'Échafaud vaincu ; (48) La Source du soleil.
* Boivin et Cie., 1914-17.
* Tallandier, Le Livre national, Bibliothèque des Grandes Aventures et Voyages Excentriques Nos. 103, 104, 1926, as two volumes : (1) Les Semeurs de glace ; (2) Le Poison bleu.
* Boivin et Cie., 1927.
* Tallandier, Œuvres de Paul d'Ivoi, 1935.
* Tallandier, 1948 (abridged edition).
* Slatkine, 1982 (facsimilé of the first edition).
* Éditions J'ai Lu No. 1418, 1983 (abridged edition).

11. Le Serment de Daalia [Daalia's Oath]
* First publication in *Le Journal des Voyages*, 1903-04.
* Combet et Cie., 1904.
* Boivin et Cie., 1914-17.
* Tallandier, Le Livre national, Bibliothèque des Grandes Aventures et Voyages Excentriques Nos. 84, 85, 1925, as two volumes :(1) Le Serment de Daalia ; (2) La Chasse au Mystère.

* Boivin et Cie., 1932.
* Tallandier, Œuvres de Paul d'Ivoi, 1934.
* Tallandier, 1954 (abridged edition)

12. Millionnaire malgré lui / Le Prince Virgule [*Millionaire In Spite of Himself*]
* First publication in *Le Journal des Voyages*, from 6 November 1904 to 25 June 1905 under the title : Le Prince Virgule.
* Combet et Cie., 1905, under the title : Millionnaire malgré lui (Prince Vigule)..
* Boivin et Cie., 1910, as two volumes.
* Boivin et Cie., 1914-17.
* Tallandier, Le Livre national, Bibliothèque des Grandes Aventures et Voyages Excentriques Nos. 229, 230, 1928, as two volumes : (1) Millionnaire malgré lui ; (2) Le Prince Virgule.
* Tallandier, Œuvres de Paul d'Ivoi, 1935.
* Boivin et Cie., collection Les Voyages excentriques, 1937, as two volumes.
* Tallandier, 1953 (abridged edition).
* Slatkine, 1982 (facsimilé of the first edition).

13. Le Maître du Drapeau Bleu [*The Master of the Blue Flag*]
* First publication in *Le Matin*, from 25 July to 2 November 1906.
* Société d'Édition Contemporaine Ancienne librairie Furne, 1907.
* Boivin et Cie., 1914-17.
* Tallandier, Le Livre national, Bibliothèque des Grandes Aventures et Voyages Excentriques Nos. 174, 175, 1927, as two volumes : (1) Les Masques d'ambre ; (2) Le Maître du drapeau bleu.
* Boivin et Cie., 1933.
* Tallandier, Œuvres de Paul d'Ivoi, 1935.
* Tallandier, 1953, under the title : Les Masques d'ambre (abridged edition).
* Slatkine, 1982 (facsimilé of the first edition).

14. Miss Mousqueterr
* First publication in *Le Journal des Voyages*, from 7 October 1906 to 21 July 1907.
* Boivin et Cie., 1907.
* Boivin et Cie., 1914-17
* Tallandier, Le Livre national, Bibliothèque des Grandes Aventures et

Voyages Excentriques Nos. 195, 196, 1928, as two volumes :(1) Miss Mouqueterr ; (2) Vers la lumière.
* Boivin et Cie., 1928.
* Tallandier, Œuvres de Paul d'Ivoi, 1935.
* Tallandier, 1953 (abridged edition).
* Slatkine, 1982 (facsimilé of the first edition).

15. Jud Allan, roi des « lads » / La Fiancée du Diable [*Jud Allan. King of the Lads/ The Devil's Fiancée*].
* First publication in *Le Matin*, from 21 July to 19 November 1908, under the title : La Fiancée du diable.
* Boivin et Cie., 1909, under the title : Judd Allan (Roi des Lads).
* Boivin et Cie., 1914-17.
* Tallandier, Le Livre national, Bibliothèque des Grandes Aventures et Voyages ExcentriquesNos. 240, 241, 1928,as two volumes : (1) Jud Allan ; (2) Le Roi des gamins .
* Boivin et Cie., 1932.
* Tallandier, Œuvres de Paul d'Ivoi, 1935.
* Tallandier, 1954 under the title : Jud Allan, roi des gamin. (abridged edition).

16. Le Roi du Radium / La Course au radium [*The King of Radium / The Radium Rush*]
* First publication in *Le Journal des Voyages*, from 18 October 1908 to 11 July 1909, under the title: Le Roi du radium.
* Boivin et Cie., 1909, sous le titre : La Course au Radium.
* Boivin et Cie., 1914-17.
* Tallandier, Le Livre national, Bibliothèque des Grandes Aventures et Voyages Excentriques Nos. 154, 155, 1927, as two volumes : (1) La Course au radium ; (2) Le Radium qui tue.
* Tallandier, Œuvres de Paul d'Ivoi, 1935.
* Tallandier, 1948, Under the title : Le Radium qui tue (abridged version).
* Éditions J'ai Lu No. 1544, 1983 (abridged version).
* Slatkine, 1984 (facsimilé of the first edition).

17. L'Aéroplane fantôme [*The Phantom Airplane*]
* First publication in *Le Petit Journal*, from 24 February to 21 June 1910.

* Boivin et Cie., 1910.
* Boivin et Cie., 1914-17.
* Tallandier, Le Livre national, Bibliothèque des Grandes Aventures et Voyages Excentriques Nos. 256, 257, 1929, as two volumes :(1) Le Voleur de pensée ; (2) Le Lit de diamants.
* Boivin et Cie., 1931.
* Tallandier, Œuvres de Paul d'Ivoi, 1935.
* Tallandier, 1954, sous le titre Le Voleur de pensée (abridged edition).
* Éditions J'ai Lu No. 1527, 1983(abridged version).
* Slatkine, 1984 (facsimilé of the first edition).

18. Les Voleurs de foudre [*The Thieves of Lightning*]
* First publication in *Le Journal des Voyages*, from 17 October 1909 to 15 May 1910, under the title : Les Trois demoiselles Pickpocket ; then from 20 October 1907 to 21 Lune 1908, under the title : L'Automobile de verre.
* Boivin et Cie., 1912.
* Boivin et Cie., 1914-17.
* Tallandier, Le Livre national, Bibliothèque des Grandes Aventures et Voyages Excentriques Nos. 74, 75, 1925, as two volumes : (1) Les Voleurs de foudre ; (2) Les Bonzes bleus d'Angkhor.
* Tallandier, Œuvres de Paul d'Ivoi, 1935.
* Tallandier, 1948 (abridged edition).

19. Message du Mikado [*Message from the Mikado*]
* First publication in *Le Journal des Voyages*, from 5 November 1911 to 12 May 1912, under the title: L'Ambassadeur extraordinaire.
* Boivin et Cie., 1912
* Boivin et Cie., 1914-17.
* Tallandier, Le Livre national, Bibliothèque des Grandes Aventures et Voyages Excentriques Nos. 55, 56, 1925, as two volumes : (1) Message du Mikado ; (2) Une fillette contre un empire.
* Tallandier, Le Livre national, Bibliothèque des Grandes Aventures et Voyages Excentriques Nos. 481, 482, 1933, as two volumes : (1) Message du Mikado ; (2) Une fillette contre un empire.
* Tallandier, Œuvres de Paul d'Ivoi, 1935.
* Tallandier, 1948, under the title :: Le Message du Mikado (abridged edition).

20. Les Dompteurs de l'or / Le Chevalier Illusion [*The Gold Tamers / The Illusion Knight*]
* First publication in *Le Journal des Voyages*, from 15 December 1912 to 8 June 1913, under the title : Le Chevalier Illusion.
* Boivin et Cie., 1914, under the title : Les Dompteurs d'Or.
* Boivin et Cie., 1914-17.
* Tallandier, Le Livre national, Bibliothèque des Grandes Aventures et Voyages Excentriques Nos. 116, 117, 1926, as two volumes :(1) Les Dompteurs de l'or ; (2) L'Épreuve de l'irréel.
* Tallandier, Œuvres de Paul d'Ivoi, 1935.
* Tallandier, 1949 (abridged edition).
* Éditions J'ai Lu No. 1596, 1984 (abridged edition).

21. Match de milliardaire [*Billionaires' Match*]
* First publication in *Le Journal des Voyages*, from 9 November 1913 to 31 May 1914, under the title : L'Évadé malgré lui.
* Boivin et Cie., 1914, under th title : Match de milliardaire.
* Éditions J'ai Lu No. 1559, 1983.
* Slatkine, 1984 (facsimilé of the first edition).

Acknowledgments :
Coolmicro of the site booksgratuits.com ; Dr Mabuse, Pfinge, Ignatz Mouse, M. L., from litteraturepopulaire.winnerbb.net;

SF & FANTASY

Adolphe Alhaiza. *Cybele*
Alphonse Allais. *The Adventures of Captain Cap*
Henri Allorge. *The Great Cataclysm*
Guy d'Armen. *Doc Ardan: The City of Gold and Lepers*
G.-J. Arnaud. *The Ice Company*
Charles Asselineau. *The Double Life*
Henri Austruy. *The Eupantophone; The Olotelepan; The Petitpaon Era*
Barillet-Lagargousse. *The Final War*
Cyprien Bérard. *The Vampire Lord Ruthwen*
S. Henry Berthoud. *Martyrs of Science*
Aloysius Bertrand. *Gaspard de la Nuit*
Richard Bessière. *The Gardens of the Apocalypse; The Masters of Silence*
Albert Bleunard. *Ever SMalher*
Félix Bodin. *The Novel of the Future*
Louis Boussenard. *Monsieur Synthesis*
Alphonse Brown. *City of Glass; The Conquest of the Air*
Emile Calvet. *In a Thousand Years*
André Caroff. *The Terror of Madame Atomos; Miss Atomos; The Return of Madame Atomos; The Mistake of Madame Atomos; The Monsters of Madame Atomos; The Revenge of Madame Atomos; The Resurrection of Madame Atomos; The Mark of Madame Atomos; The Spheres of Madame Atomos; The Wrath of Madame Atomos* (w/M. & Sylvie Stéphan)
Félicien Champsaur. *The Human Arrow; Ouha, King of the Apes; Pharaoh's Wife; Homo-Deus*
Didier de Chousy. *Ignis*
Jules Clarétie. *Obsession*
Michel Corday. *The Eternal Flame*
André Couvreur. *The Necessary Evil*; *Caresco, Superman; The Exploits of Professor Tornada* (3 vols.)
Captain Danrit. *Undersea Odyssey*
C. I. Defontenay. *Star (Psi Cassiopeia)*
Charles Derennes. *The People of the Pole*
Georges Dodds (anthologist). *The Missing Link*
Charles Dodeman. *The Silent Bomb*
Harry Dickson. *The Heir of Dracula; Harry Dickson vs. The Spider*
Jules Dornay. *Lord Ruthven Begins*
Alfred Driou. *The Adventures of a Parisian Aeronaut*
Sâr Dubnotal *vs. Jack the Ripper*
Alexandre Dumas. *The Return of Lord Ruthven*
Renée Dunan. *Baal*
J.-C. Dunyach. *The Night Orchid; The Thieves of Silence*
Henri Duvernois. *The Man Who Found Himself*
Achille Eyraud. *Voyage to Venus*
Henri Falk. *The Age of Lead*

Paul Féval. *Anne of the Isles; Knightshade; Revenants; Vampire City; The Vampire Countess; The Wandering Jew's Daughter*

Paul Féval, *fils. Felifax, the Tiger-Man*

Charles de Fieux. *Lamékis*

Louis Forest. *Someone is Stealing Children in Paris*

Arnould Galopin. *Doctor Omega; Doctor Omega and the Shadowmen* (anthology)

Judith Gautier. *Isoline and the Serpent-Flower*

H. Gayar. *The Marvelous Adventures of Serge Myrandhal on Mars*

G.L. Gick. *Harry Dickson and the Werewolf of Rutherford Grange*

Delphine de Girardin. *Balzac's Cane*

Léon Gozlan. *The Vampire of the Val-de-Grâce*

Edmond Haraucourt. *Illusions of Immortality; Daah, the First Human*

Nathalie Henneberg. *The Green Gods*

Eugène Hennebert. *The Enchanted City*

V. Hugo, P. Foucher & P. Meurice. *The Hunchback of Notre-Dame*

Romain d'Huissier. *Hexagon: Dark Matter*

Jules Janin. *The Magnetized Corpse*

Michel Jeury. *Chronolysis*

Gustave Kahn. *The Tale of Gold and Silence*

Gérard Klein. *The Mote in Time's Eye*

Fernand Kolney. *Love in 5000 Years*

Paul Lacroix. *Danse Macabre*

Louis-Guillaume de La Follie. *The Unpretentious Philosopher*

Jean de La Hire. *Enter the Nyctalope; The Nyctalope on Mars; The Nyctalope vs. Lucifer; The Nyctalope Steps In; Night of the Nyctalope; Return of the Nyctalope; The Fiery Wheel*

Etienne-Léon de Lamothe-Langon. *The Virgin Vampire*

André Laurie. *Spiridon*

Gabriel de Lautrec. *The Vengeance of the Oval Portrait*

Alain le Drimeur. *The Future City*

Georges Le Faure & Henri de Graffigny. *The Extraordinary Adventures of a Russian Scientist Across the Solar System* (2 vols.)

Gustave Le Rouge. *The Mysterious Doctor Cornelius* (3 vols.); *The Vampires of Mars; The Dominion of the World* (w/Gustave Guitton) (4 vols.)

Jules Lermina. *Mysteryville; Panic in Paris; To-Ho and the Gold Destroyers; The Secret of Zippeliu; The Battle of Strasbourg*

André Lichtenberger. *The Centaurs; The Children of the Crab*

Listonai. *The Philosophical Voyager*

Jean-Marc & Randy Lofficier. *Edgar Allan Poe on Mars; The Katrina Protocol; Pacifica; Robonocchio; Return of the Nyctalope;* (anthologists) *Tales of the Shadowmen 1-11; The Vampire Almanac*

Xavier Mauméjean. *The League of Heroes*

Joseph Méry. *The Tower of Destiny*

Hippolyte Mettais. *The Year 5865; Paris Before the Deluge*

Louise Michel. *The Human Microbes; The New World*

Tony Moilin. *Paris in the Year 2000*

José Moselli. *Illa's End*

John-Antoine Nau. *Enemy Force*

Marie Nizet. *Captain Vampire*
C. Nodier, A. Beraud & Toussaint-Merle. *Frankenstein*
Henri de Parville. *An Inhabitant of the Planet Mars*
Gaston de Pawlowski. *Journey to the Land of the 4th Dimension*
Georges Pellerin. *The World in 2000 Years*
Ernest Pérochon. *The Frenetic People*
Pierre Pelot. *The Child Who Walked on the Sky*
J. Polidori, C. Nodier, E. Scribe. *Lord Ruthven the Vampire*
P.-A. Ponson du Terrail. *The Vampire and the Devil's Son; The Immortal Woman*
Edgar Quinet. *Ahasuerus; The Enchanter Merlin*
Henri de Régnier. *A Surfeit of Mirrors*
Maurice Renard. *The Blue Peril; Doctor Lerne; The Doctored Man; A Man Among the Microbes; The Master of Light*
Jean Richepin. *The Wing; The Crazy Corner*
Albert Robida. *The Adventures of Saturnin Farandoul; The Clock of the Centuries; Chalet in the Sky; The Electric Life*
J.-H. Rosny Aîné. *Helgvor of the Blue River; The Givreuse Enigma; The Mysterious Force; The Navigators of Space; Vamireh; The World of the Variants; The Young Vampire*
Marcel Rouff. *Journey to the Inverted World*
Léonie Rouzade. *The World Turned Upside Down*
Han Ryner. *The Superhumans; The Human Ant*
Pierre de Selenes: *An Unknown World*
Angelo de Sorr. *The Vampires of London*
Brian Stableford. *The New Faust at the Tragicomique;The Empire of the Necromancers (The Shadow of Frankenstein; Frankenstein and the Vampire Countess; Frankenstein in London); Sherlock Holmes & The Vampires of Eternity; The Stones of Camelot; The Wayward Muse.* (anthologist) *News from the Moon; The Germans on Venus; The Supreme Progress; The World Above the World; Nemoville; Investigations of the Future; The Conqueror of Death; The Revolt of the Machines*
Jacques Spitz. *The Eye of Purgatory*
Kurt Steiner. *Ortog*
Eugène Thébault. *Radio-Terror*
C.-F. Tiphaigne de La Roche. *Amilec*
Simon Tyssot de Patot. *The Strange Voyages of Jacques Massé and Pierre de Mésange*
Louis Ulbach. *Prince Bonifacio*
Théo Varlet. *The Golden Rock. The Xenobiotic Invasion; The Castaways of Eros; Timeslip Troopers* (w/André Blandin); *The Martian Epic* (w/Octave Joncquel)
Pierre Véron. *The Merchants of Health*
Paul Vibert. *The Mysterious Fluid*
Villiers de l'Isle-Adam. *The Scaffold; The Vampire Soul*
Philippe Ward. *Artahe ; The Song of Montségur* (w/Sylvie Miller) *Manhattan Ghost* (w/Mickael Laguerre)

MYSTERIES & THRILLERS

M. Allain & P. Souvestre. *The Daughter of Fantômas*
A. Anicet-Bourgeois, Lucien Dabril. *Rocambole*

A. Bernède. *Belphegor*; *Judex* (w/Louis Feuillade); *The Return of Judex* (w/Louis Feuillade); *The Shadow of Judex*
A. Bisson & G. Livet. *Nick Carter vs. Fantômas*
V. Darlay & H. de Gorsse. *Arsène Lupin vs. Sherlock Holmes: The Stage Play*
Séamas Duffy. *Sherlock Holmes in Paris*
Paul Féval. *Gentlemen of the Night; John Devil; The Black Coats ('Salem Street; The Invisible Weapon; The Parisian Jungle; The Companions of the Treasure; Heart of Steel; The Cadet Gang; The Sword-Swallower)*
Emile Gaboriau. *Monsieur Lecoq*
Goron & Emile Gautier. *Spawn of the Penitentiary*
Paul d'Ivoi. *Around the World on Five Sous* (w/Henri Chabrillat)
Rick Lai. *Shadows of the Opera: Retribution in Blood; Sisters of the Shadows: The Curse of Cagliostro*
Steve Leadley. *Sherlock Holmes: The Circle of Blood*
Maurice Leblanc. *Arsène Lupin vs. Countess Cagliostro; Arsène Lupin vs. Sherlock Holmes (The Blonde Phantom; The Hollow Needle); The Many Faces of Arsène Lupin; The Island of the Thirty Coffins*
Gaston Leroux. *Chéri-Bibi; The Phantom of the Opera; Rouletabille & the Mystery of the Yellow Room; Rouletabille at Krupp's*
Richard Marsh. *The Complete Adventures of Judith Lee*
William Patrick Maynard. *The Terror of Fu Manchu; The Destiny of Fu Manchu*
Frank J. Morlock. *Sherlock Holmes: The Grand Horizontals; Sherlock Holmes vs Jack the Ripper*
Jean Petithuguenin. *The Adventures of Ethel King*
Antonin Reschal. *The Adventures of Miss Boston*
P. de Wattyne & Y. Walter. *Sherlock Holmes vs. Fantômas*
David White. *Fantômas in America*
Pierre Yrondy. *The Adventures of Thérèse Arnaud*

Victor Margueritte. *The Bacheloress; The Companion; The Couple*

SCREENPLAYS

Mike Baron. *The Iron Triangle*
Emma Bull & Will Shetterly. *Nightspeeder; War for the Oaks*
Gerry Conway & Roy Thomas. *Doc Dynamo*
Steve Englehart. *Majorca*
James Hudnall. *The Devastator*
Jean-Marc & Randy Lofficier. *Royal Flush*
J.-M. & R. Lofficier & Marc Agapit. *Despair*
J.-M. & R. Lofficier & Joël Houssin. *City*
Andrew Paquette. *Peripheral Vision*
Robert L. Robinson, Jr. *Judex*
R. Thomas, J. Hendler & L. Sprague de Camp. *Rivers of Time*

NON-FICTION

Stephen R. Bissette. *Blur 1-5. Green Mountain Cinema 1; Teen Angels*

Win Scott Eckert. *Crossovers* (2 vols.)
Jean-Marc & Randy Lofficier. *Shadowmen* (2 vols.)
Randy Lofficier. *Over Here*

ART BOOKS

Jean-Pierre Normand. *Science Fiction Illustrations*
Raven Okeefe. *Raven's L'il Critters; Rave's Faves*
Randy Lofficier & Raven Okeefe. *If Your Possum Go Daylight...*
Daniele Serra. *Illusions*
Randy Lofficier. *Over Here*

HEXAGON COMICS

Franco Frescura & Luciano Bernasconi. *Wampus*
Franco Frescura & Giorgio Trevisan. *CLASH*
L. Bernasconi, J.-M. Lofficier & Juan Roncagliolo. *Phenix*
Claude Legrand, J.-M. Lofficier & L. Bernasconi. *Kabur*
Franco Oneta. *Zembla*
L. Buffolente, Lofficier & J.-J. Dzialowski. *Strangers: Homicron*
Danilo Grossi. *Strangers: Jaydee*
Claude Legrand & Luciano Bernasconi. *Strangers: Starlock*
Thierry Mornet & Juan Roncagliolo. *Guardian of the Republic*
J.-M. Lofficier, M. Garcia, F. Blanco & J. Pima. *Strangers in a Strange Land*